The Heretic

CHRIS SCOTT

The Heretic

Quartet Books

London Melbourne New York

The author would like to thank The Canada Council, from
whom he received an Arts Bursary during the writing of
this book.

First published in Great Britain by Quartet Books Limited 1985
A member of the Namara Group
27/29 Goodge Street, London W1P 1FD

British Library Cataloguing in Publication Data

Scott, Chris, *1945–*
    The heretic.
    I. Title
    813'.54[F]   PR6069.C584

    ISBN 0-7043-2549-7

Printed in Great Britain
by Mackays of Chatham Ltd, Kent

For Heather Sherratt
And also for Jonathan Williams, with gratitude

Those two hemispheres were then as two worlds ... this opposite earth being called Antichthon and its inhabitants Antichthones.
Thomas Burnet, **The Theory of the Earth,** 1684-90.

The tenth is Antichthon, an Earth above, or opposite to ours.
Thomas Stanley, **The History of Philosophy,** 1687.

I

*Agree with thine adversary quickly, whiles thou
art in the way with him, lest at any time the
adversary deliver thee to the judge, and the judge
deliver thee to the officer, and thou be cast into
prison.*

— Jesus of Nazareth

Rome, February 1600

This eight year's dying is almost done. Tomorrow, the day after
— no matter — the last act will have its elegant consummation,
non effusio sanguinis, without the shedding of blood. Often, I
have imagined the final dawn, hoping perhaps to gain some im-
munity. But no, I am bound and gagged — the customary usage
— and led from my cell to the beat of a drum, its tawdry imperative muted by the guttering rain, a persistent February rain
greening the radial walls of the Castello Sant'Angello. A cry of
command echoes from the courtyard where the guard and the
Brothers of Death are assembled. The fortress gates are opened
now and this pilgrimage begins, a weary procession of penitents
following the Cross. A company of statuary angels keeps watch
over the bridge, brown Tiber stippled by the still falling rain, the
drum still beating its muffled time to our tread, down, down
through the huddled dwellings of the bank of the Campo de'
Fiori, once the field of flowers, now the place of death.

It is always raining in my rehearsal for death, and there is something overly solemn about that drum, its funeral tread heralding the entrance of despised and damnable opinions, something which confounds my worst expectancy. What a fine day this is for a burning and what a fine throng has assembled, and has been assembling these past few hours: the eager and the curious, miracle seekers and miracle workers, my lords temporal and my lords ecclesiastical, every man's neighbour his own equal in the mob. What democracy there is in death; what a riotous concurrence inaugurating this carnival of ashes.

Eternal Rome, ragged imperial Rome, how you crowd the colours of the mind! The guard rings the square, a line of rain-washed steel and tinctured plumes, their faces indistinguishable through the veil. I watch and wait for the trumpet's call. The tenements' yellow façade, the red rooftops, the square and the day itself — these fade in my mind. An absurd thought strikes me: I, who have so often lived out this day, could weep for the pity and shame of it but no one would notice. Should I hope then for a change of imagined weather, trust in God's apostolic descent? The sky's wind-blown arpeggios descant a mythic harmony. Oblivious to the Lord's careless orchestration, the Brothers of Death close round me. There is one I recognize, one whose serpentine gaze I must carry to the flames. I know you, my old familiar, my accuser — myself. Death is our earthly measure: a trumpet, a banner and a drum. You watch as Christ's golden oriflammes are unfurled, snarling and snapping before high heaven. No majestic host triumphs there but a transport of clouds, enigmatic and indecipherable, a celestial mockery not our own. How could it be otherwise? You smile now, though it is too late. . . .

Magnum miraculum! What a great miracle is man, a being worthy of reverence and honour. For he assumes the nature of a god as if he were himself a god, has familiarity with the race of demons, knowing that he is of the same origin, and despises that part of his nature which is only human, having put his faith in the divinity of the other part. *Magnum miraculum!* Greedy for hell, the mob shouts and roars, one with the fire that blinds

10

and burns.

Later, the guard will kindle new fires, the guts and heart of my present self, satellites to the old central sun. Later, they will dismantle the *palchetti* constructed for my lords' infinite elevation. And later — who knows? — the day will give some sign, a hint or a breath as yet unannounced, of a bounteous and boisterous spring.

So many times have I visited the still uncreated scene that I can hardly believe this future, this death, is my own; another's maybe: *yours*, my friend, you who force me to stand outside of myself. Such detachment is surely pardonable — in the circumstances — and you are right to smile. An abstraction compounded of others people's abstractions, I know that past and future are both equally uncertain. We are not what we see, nor even what we imagine we see, and I have never been able to read the future, the awful predatory future, quite clearly enough.

I am not one who can claim a powerful family, though my father was related to the patrician Bruni of Asti, a house that has seen better days. I was baptized Philip, after the lord of the soil, but since the age of ten, when I was taken to the Dominican monastery in Naples, I have acquired other names, other characters. You, my distant yet close auditor, will know me as Giordano, after Saint Dominic's successor, the second Superior General of the Order; the name I have used in my writings is Filoteo, lover of God, after Fra Teofilo da Veranno, who was responsible for my earliest instruction; and I am also known to the world as the Nolan — this after the town of my birth, Nola of the kindly skies, the white courtyard of my father's house, the hill Cicala, and, on the horizon, Vesuvius.

A man who cannot remember his childhood usually has every reason to forget it. In my case, the years of earliest memory are best described by the word 'conventional.' My father was a soldier, an officer and a friend of the poet Tansillo, a minor functionary in the service of the Neapolitan Viceroy. "Heaven," quoth this venerable bard, "scorns giving a second good to one who has not held the first dear" — a fit sentiment for the ears of His Demi-majesty. This sort of thing used to make me laugh even as a child. So pompous and severe it seemed, so demeaning of heaven's bounty. As if God were a niggardly fellow to be thus chary of his goodness! But then, conventional though my early life was, I have never been able to understand what the mass of mankind means when they speak of God.

There is one other circumstance I remember (apart from these visits of Luigi Tansillo and his didactic pronouncements), a circumstance that is not so well served by the adjective conventional. When I was an infant still in the cradle, a serpent of hideous aspect appeared to me. Herculean augury! Do I remember the scene exactly as it was, or have I reconstructed the dappled play of light and illusion, the timeless imagery of childhood and the garden into which the snake made his easeful way? My mother often referred to this episode, and perhaps that is how it came to be fixed in my mind. To her at least, it was certainly portentous — a sure sign that her son was destined to make his way in the world.

It is well over forty years since I played in the streets of Nola. As a child, I was Marcellus, the Roman General who defeated Hannibal, trapping his armies between Vesuvius and the mountains to the east. Later, when my father took me to Lake Avernus, which the Romans regarded as the entrance to hell, I became Aeneas — Aeneas seeking old Anchises' shade. And later still, when I had fallen under Fra Teofilo's spell, I became Actaeon, the hunter transformed into the prey, Actaeon who was pursued by thoughts of divine things and vanquished by the dogs of Diana. Soon, it will be time to turn and face the pack....

Eight years ago in the summer of 1592, my defence against the Venetian Inquisition was simple enough. I spoke for truth and science against ignorance and superstition, with — it is true — an eye on posterity. And if I eventually abjured my errors, throwing myself all too theatrically at the feet of the Tribunal, I did so to gain time, nothing more. Magus, I would shake the planets from their accustomed course; call down the stars and infuse their powers into the divine statues, animating so much

12

dead clay with the breath of life, and hence, in the universal light of a new age, proclaim everlasting peace and brotherhood among the nations of men.

But that was eight year ago, and since then I have retracted the retraction. Was it pride that made me speak out, pride and a certain stubbornness of character? My lord Cardinal Bellarmine, my present interlocutor, thinks so, but my lord is nothing if not cautious, a pre-eminently safe prince. "Are you more than the wisdom of the ages," he enquires, "more than the Church's magisterium? For God's sake, brother, remember who you are." Truly, I answer, I cannot forget; neither the last eight years nor the last twenty, years of constant flight, first from one town to the next and then from one country to another. I cannot forget, how could I?

My lord is most anxious to know — as was the Inquisition — why I returned to Italy. He believes it was the desire to prove myself a martyr, a temptation easily gratified, God knows. There were one hundred and thirty articles of heresy against me when I left, the work of the Neapolitan Provincial, Fra Domenico Vito. They were trivial enough, compared with what followed, and the Cardinal is surprised that I should laugh at his question. "My lord, I returned when I did," so I tell him, "because young martyrs are undignified. In any case, I shall not burn all by myself. If I am to be a martyr, then you are responsible, and so is the Tribunal, and Mocenigo — especially Mocenigo and all the generations of that house. . . ." A most excellent, mysterious and Catholic argument.

Giovanni Mocenigo (Zuan to his friends, especially to his friends), was ever there a host like you? And was I too compliant a guest?

"A heretic, my lords! A heretic! I knew it from the start. . . ."

You must have seen the humour in it, Zuan, with your guest imprisoned in your warehouse, waiting the arrival of the guard and drinking your wine. How importunate you were; how flattering with your *magister,* your *magis elaborata Theologia*; how anxious for his health, fortune and worldly being.

Oh, Zuan, I knew you for what you were: a Venetian boy, angel-faced and delicate of your kind. But vicious, Zuan, and skilled in certain things. It was the bookseller, Ciotto, whom I'd met in Frankfort, who gave me your letters. "I have heard much of your fame," you wrote, "and desire only instruction in the speculative arts. You will find our Venetian winters milder than in the north, and our language — our common language — so much more conducive to those labours you have made uniquely your own. It is said that the new Pope is himself well disposed towards the new learning. Has he not summoned Patrizi to Rome and given him a chair at the university? But as for yourself, the journey is not far for one who is so greatly travelled. You will find our Republic liberal in its laws, and will perhaps secure a place here or in Padua. The costs of your removal I will gladly bear at my own expense, and I think you would be well served to accept this modest invitation...."

Well served, Zuan? Was it for the love of philosophy that you acted so? But how you played the part, getting up before my judges and feigning such outraged honesty and innocent stupidity that it was all I could do to keep from laughing. And how they peered down at you as you grovelled like a performing ape, my lords' creature, trained in the art of self-abasement.

"And he spoke many times, my lords, setting on foot the opinion of Copernicus that the world goes round the sun, which is the centre of all things; and he said that apart from this, our world, there was a great infinity of worlds, peopled with folk just like ourselves. I listened, my lords, I listened and I remembered. For I longed, you see, to have such knowledge as was his, but when he talked like this, I heard only heresy and vile heresy at that, such as I have witnessed here on other occasions, because, my lords, I have served both the Court and the Council and the name Mocenigo is respected in Venice, and has been since the time of Doge Tommaso, which is why — it is written in my delation — I acted as I did. What else could I do?"

What else indeed, princeling Judas!

"And he said, my lords — this I could not understand — that life came from putrefaction. The human soul, my lords, he likened to a broken mirror, and heaven itself he called a river of broken mirrors. There was treason, too, in what he said, treason as well as heresy. Many times, my lords, he spoke of the heretic Prince of Navarre and of the English Queen whom he called divine — *la diva Elizabetta* —it is true, my lords. But mostly he spoke of Prince Henri, saying he hoped this Prince would come to Rome and that therefore he must hurry to publish his works to gain credit with the Prince so that when the time came, my lords, he would not always be poor, as he now was, but would enjoy the treasures of others and be capitano as well. And he said he was surprised, my lords, that the Republic, so wise in other things, should leave the monks to enjoy their revenues, and not confiscate them as had been done in France...."

It took wit, Zuan, and presence of mind. You should have been a board treader. For though it was an act, my lords of the Tribunal believed you, investing their own convictions in the performance like playgoers who have paid too dearly for the meanest of plays. A farce of worms: opulent Venice grown verminous.

I cannot say what moved him. Fear, security, honour even, something of each; requittal of some imagined wound festering to the bone; malice intended, or worse, motiveless — the effect's the same. Or was it chance, nothing determined or planned? I do not know. Yet I trusted him. Then what if we had never met, would things still stand this way? Another would have been found, or failing that, invented; witnesses bought, the truth sold. I know this and have no cause to complain. Here now lies the germ of a different idea: that my trust in him was absolute assurance of betrayal. There's security in betrayal, certainty of the type. I said that I recognized him for what he was, but he was more, much more than the petulant darling of all his peers. Zuan Mocenigo, a frequenter of trials, my lords' punctilio — I saw the danger in him. It was no accident that he sought me out, nor that I should have complied with their designs. Who then was the less deceived: my judges or myself?

The Cardinal would love to hear this. Confess! Confess! Some thoughts are best left buried....

I am changeable, I contradict myself. Free, I am shackled; bound I am liberated. Infigurable, I am time's geometrician. Perspective is all. Trusting you, Zuan, was one error in a lifetime of errors, abjured or not. Another was writing to my brother in Christ, Gryphius Simplicius, he with the heart of a lion and the mind of an oyster.

Suspicion is universal. Even this simple brother of mine they dragged into the trial; because of a letter, they made him my co-conspirator against God and the Republic of Venice, threatening him with everlasting hell and more immediate punishments. It was his soul that concerned them — his soul and mine —, the soul to be squeezed out of a man, drop by drop. What was it the Inquisitor said? The soul of man begins at his fingertips. Or even before, he claimed. "All living things, Giordano, are surrounded by an aura which the Blessed Saints have seen. That is the soul, and I know it is there. Confess, Giordano. You will find it the easiest way. We are merciful men, not given to inflicting unnecessary pain. You will confess, Giordano. You know that you will...."

Mother Church has the straightest way with heretics, will damn them in body and soul, burning them on earth in preparation for the greater fire. Francesco Pucci was the last to die here. He was a philosopher who confessed his sins before man and God. They were merciful with Francesco. It is three years since they came for him in the middle of night to reprieve him — of his life.

He was beheaded in his cell and burned the next day on the Campo. It was done very quickly.

Sometimes I awake, crying like a child in the night. A passing dream, that's all, or footsteps outside in the corridor. Only the dream is always the same, and when I wake I can hear them coming for Francesco again, hear but not see. The axe dropped once, a muddy sound, and then again, sharper on the stone.

They call this place Hadrian's tomb, though his sepulchre is shared by many. We are all dead men here, all mortally immortal as good Christians should be. They will not dare kill me, I tell myself; I am too alive to die. I listen to my pulse, a dead man's heartbeat. What confirmation! I taste my breath, blood warm, and I am afraid, possessed by the terror of death — no, not that, *completion*.

My death, like any other, is a fiction: the only way to keep on living.

In the house of dead, the Jews proscribe mirrors and water, for they multiply the number of demons. My keepers' reasons for denying me both are less metaphysical. Dry, I shall make better tinder. Meanwhile, my vanity suffers.

T

Rome, 18 February 1600

And so he perished miserably in the flames, and in those other worlds which he imagined he can narrate how Romans are wont to treat such blasphemous and profligate folk as himself. . . .
Kasper Schopp, eyewitness to the burning
— fragment from a letter.

Kaspar Schopp is my name, Knight of Saint Peter and Count of Claravelle, titles I owe to His Holiness Clement VIII — for services rendered to the Inquisition, though not in this case, this one did not concern me. The case of my friend Campanella did, however. But that's another story.

Schopp, Kaspar, an unprepossessing name and one to which a certain odium has been attached. It's true I gave evidence at Campanella's trial, a case as different from this as night from day. Tommaso's designs were on this world, not the next. He's safe — from the stake at least, though how it profits a man to spend his life in a dungeon I do not know.

Schopp, then... Scioppius sounds better, the German Latinized. Gaspare Scioppius, it has a Roman ring, befitting one who has cast aside his native heresy for the True Faith.

Scioppius, Schopp, Claravelle, does it matter what a man is called, providing he is true to himself?

Yesterday, a Sunday, they made a rogus, a pyre, as they used to in Florence at Carnival time. Bruno, the condemned man himself, was brought into the square and made to stand while the sentence was read. An ancient heretic, he looked older than his fifty-two years, and smaller than I'd expected. From tip to toe he could not have been more than five and a half feet, his size making the verdict seem greater thereby. What heresies were his! They say he believed the stars to be visible messengers of grace, and that there are, besides this earth, many others. He taught, they say, that magic is a good and licit thing, that Moses worked his miracles by magic, at which he was cleverer than the Egyptians, and — *o haereticus!* — that Christ himself was a magician.

I'm no theologian but a grammarian and historian. Still, you don't have to have read the Church fathers to see that Giordano was a heretic. So there he was, bound with his hands behind his back, alone in the square. The Brothers of Death laid hands on him then, cropped his hair and beard, put the conical cap on his head and a placard around his neck with the word 'philosopher' on it, and in this manner led him to the stake. When the fire was lit he did not cry out but died bravely enough, turning aside at the last from the Cross. That made the crowd gasp, but people are easily bored. A band of flagellants took to scourging themselves, and were applauded. So too were some of Giordano's brethren, who threw a whole library of books on to the fire (I did not approve of this, being a scholar myself), and some of the women in the crowd began to dance around the stake. One old dame hurled a mirror into the flames, another a pack of playing cards, and then they all found something to part with: false hair, cosmetics, veils, trinkets, the little vanities of this world. A Roman custom, so I'm told.

My part in all this? None, except as a faithful witness to God's truth, the end of a miserable sinner. Oh yes, and to quash certain rumours already rife in Rome, rumours not uncommon in such cases. I saw the man once in Germany. There's no doubt in my mind it was Bruno they burned and not someone else. Why should they do that, why now?

No, the man is dead and will soon be forgotten. Catullus is apt: *Sed hæc prius fuere* — but these things are past and gone.

Fama volat! This afternoon, a Dominican approached me on the Campo de' Fiori. "Is it true?" he asked, his eyes full of hope. "Is what true?" I asked him. "Why, that Brother Jordanus still lives," he replied. "No, no," said I, "I watched him die." "So you knew him then, did you?" This reckless friar grabbed me by the sleeve and gave me a fearful look. "I saw him once," said I, "ten years ago." "But you were a child then," the other scoffed. "I knew him as a child and as a young man, and I tell you it was not him they burned," he said, giving me another wild look.

Not long after this a Cardinal of my acquaintance, the Cardinal di San Severina, asked if I had heard the news. "They say that Bruno is alive," he said. "They say the Pope spirited him away and burned another in his place."

"But this is murder," I protested.

"If true. The Forum, Kaspar — at dusk." So saying, he bade me farewell.

Is it possible? No! Yet stranger things have happened in Rome, and though he looked like the man I had seen, I was a child then, as the friar said. Bruno had changed, of course. I made allowances for that. Was I too hasty? I'm willing to admit fault, where the fault is mine. But this! No, it is past all belief.

At our assignation the Cardinal says that Bruno was burned but that His Holiness wished to create the contrary impression. A trick, but why? San Severina does not know, or will not say. I was amazed to see His Eminence dressed in ordinary clerical garb. "It is occasionally necessary to go about incognito," he said, and asked if I would go to Venice for him.

"To Venice? At this time of year?"

"The Patriarch there, who sat on the tribunal which tried Giordano, is dying. I want you to see him. Perhaps he will confess to you what he would to no priest. You should also see the

Inquisitor, a Fra Giovanni. And the Papal Nuncio, Monsignor Taberna, you should see him as well. Mention my name, but discreetly.... Are you familiar,'' said the Cardinal, suddenly breaking aside, ''with van Heemskerck's engravings? He has captured the line of these columns exactly.''

A beggar eyed us from the ruins. ''Alms!'' he cried, and the Cardinal gave him a copper coin.

''Rome is full of spies,'' he said. ''Hurry, Kaspar, or it will be too late.''

Tonight his servant Bastiano came to my lodgings with a purse of gold and a note. ''A galley leaves from Ancona in five days,'' San Severina had written. ''At your age you should have no difficulty in making the journey.''

At my age, what is wrong with my age? I was born the same year the Emperor Rudolf came to the throne, 1576. They say this Nolan was with him at Prague, making gold out of base metals, an alchemist.

T

Venice, February 1600

Letter of Giovanni Mocenigo, former Venetian Ambassador to France, to Kaspar Schopp, Count of Claravelle, etc.

Sir, I beg to inform you that His Excellency Bishop Priuli, who, as patriarch of all Venetia, presided over the process against Giordano Bruno in our republic, departed this life some three days ago. In the hour of his death, having heard of the late auto-da-fé in Rome, His Excellency expressed his satisfaction that justice had — at last — been seen to be done.

I wonder if you have had the curiosity to read the *Spaccio della Bestia trionfante (Bestiae triumphantis expulsio* to give the Latin; you will not find it in German or English.) We all know in

Venice that by the triumphant beast the Nolan meant the Church. The greatest danger in the man was not heresy but the truths he spoke, and there were some truths in his work, sugaring the poison that murders insidiously.

The truth itself is the subtlest corrosive. The Nolan's one undoubted talent was that he could show men what they wanted to see, enticing them on with their reflections until they were captivated. He was oblique and evasive like a mirror, a dealer in illusions, not false so much as superficial. And yet the surfaces were innumerable, glittering, brilliant.

It is true then that I invited him to stay at my house, an invitation he did not immediately accept, perhaps because he did not trust me. Instead, he preferred to pass the time of day in Ciotto's bookshop, staying initially for three months in Padua, where he was well received by the professors of the new learning, or those of them who saw him as the Messiah, so high was his ambition. There, he struck up a friendship with Gian Vincenzo Pinelli, one of our modish Venetian liberals, a man of some wit and rarefied designs. This Pinelli had made his library into a kind of fashion house of learning, frequented by those tangential doctors of arcane lore too fantastic for any school who congregated here like crows at roost. Here too I was sent under orders from the Council, for a sizeable body of opinion thought these colloquies treasonable, and if only they could be understood the treason would be manifest to all. Another thought it healthy to debate certain mysteries, no matter how impenetrable or above the common understanding. This second faction looked to Valois for salvation, and then, after his assassination, to Navarre. The first looked to Rome and, when politic, to Spain.

At Pinelli's the Nolan held forth to as ardent a circle of admirers as he could possibly have wished for, that little galaxy of cosmographers who considered the universe too small a place to hang their hats in and too large to call home. When I first came across him, he was discoursing frantically on the subject of Fabrizio Mordente, whom he'd met in his Parisian days and subsequently in Prague. Another Italian, Mordente, was also another wandering Magus, whose travels, like Giordano's, had taken him across all Europe. They're a familiar breed, and will talk to anyone who listens — especially if they have money or a position to offer. Mordente had invented some new kind of compass, a marvellous achievement, according to the Nolan, but for the fact that the poor inventor had utterly failed to appreciate the significance of his discovery. To use a compass for something as base as mere geometry, said Giordano, was like suggesting that a cobbler employ philosophy in his shoe mending. Granted, cobblers were often philosophic, but Mordente was neither a cobbler nor a philosopher. His invention, Giordano claimed, mimicked nature, and should therefore be used to chart the course of the comets, those fiery exhalations which had struck portentous fear into the hearts of the old Romans but which in our day and age were readily comprehensible to anyone with the slightest degree of intuition. For the same reason, if that is the right word, Copernicus, whom the Nolan called more a student of mathematics than nature, was to be praised for his art but condemned for his lack of intuition — intuition, the only true form of knowledge.

He was perched at a high desk when I entered the library. His complexion was light and his hair reddish, not the usual type of southern Italian, though his gestures were certainly animated. There was something inconceivably alien about him, something which his complexion alone could not explain. He was quite small and his head disproportionately large, but my immediate impression was not of his physical appearance. The spirit of the man was the thing, even in that crowded room: brittle, nervous — unbalanced, I would say. Afterwards, I would learn that he was capable of enormous rages, a volatility that did credit to his origins.

"Triumphant idiot!" he was declaiming — this in reference to the unfortunate Mordente. "And is it not typical of our age that here is a man who has discovered what was unknown to grandiloquent Greece, operative Persia and subtle Arabia, and yet speaks from inspired ignorance like Balaam's ass!"

He spoke with incredible rapidity, so that it was impossible to follow the logic of his argument. Once in a while he would pause significantly, dropping some key phrase that it might be imprinted on the minds of his audience. And then he would take up the thread again, weaving a crazy fabric of ancient and modern learning, all the time jabbing his hands in the air, his voice high-pitched and cracking with the strain of his performance.

It was his aim, he said, to restore the world to its original condition, reaffirming the gospel of love which had been preached by the Apostles but which had been corrupted by the Church's temporal ambitions. In his travels throughout Catholic and heretical lands, he had found some three or four men of a like mind (he did not mention their names), and although the learned professors had everywhere received him with hostility and suspicion (everywhere, that is, except Wittenberg), the ordinary people had rejoiced to hear him. He did not expect, he told us, that the moral pollution and wickedness of the world would detract from the eventual success of his mission, for in many ways he noted great similarities between our present age and the time of Christ. The world itself, he believed, had reached a crucial phase in its cyclical existence — why else these new worlds discovered? No common understanding might penetrate these discoveries, whose true nature went unheeded, these new worlds heralding the advent of a new age. His whole life, he said, had been spent looking for a prince to lead mankind towards its true destiny. He was not speaking of the Second Coming; it was not Christ he referred to but *one greater than Him*. The earth, the heavens above, and all the elements around us, were animated by living spirits, who would be at the command of this new man, this world leader. Lest we doubted this, or thought it fantastic, we should remember that the Greeks had taught that the visible leads to the invisible. Such indeed had been Christ's intuition. To call Him the Son of God was to acknowledge his divinity, but Christ had also been a man, a Magus, like Moses before Him. Christ Himself was of the same lineage as Prometheus, Zoroaster, and Hermes Trisgemistus, the thrice-blessed master of ancient lore, known to

23

antiquity as the messenger of the gods. It simply was not good enough, he said, to look upon these ancient magicians as mythical figures, for they had been the first men of science in the world, the first *humanists*. Hence, it was to these children of the world's innocence that we were to look in order to unlock the secrets of nature. After all, the Egyptians had mastered the secrets of life, and with the use of incantations and astral magic had animated the statues of their divinities. Not, of course, that there was anything miraculous in this. It was all very natural — as indeed were the supposed miracles of Christ....

He finished on an inspired note with a cry of, "Take up thy letters and laws, O Egyptians!"

His address completed, he bowed to the plaudits of his flock. No more were they crows at roost but birds of paradise, parroting the master's gaudy phrases as if they would take wing to the outermost bounds of the universe.

Gian Vincenzo, enjoying his part as the host, came across with the Nolan and said one or two words of introduction. I remember Giordano's first remark, and that for a singular reason.

"My saviour," he said. "And my destiny."

He reminded me of a scarab. When I was a boy, an uncle of mine had owned one and told me of its magical powers. I would wait for it to move or rattle or give any sign of life, but the amulet merely regarded me with that cold self-possession of agelessness.

Looking back — such are the deceptions of memory — it is conceivable that the scarab marked the first time Giordano crossed my path. At the very least it was an augury of sorts, or so I would come to look on it in later years.

Not until March of 1592 — several months after the meeting at Pinelli's — did he take up my offer of hospitality. It was, and he must have known this, dangerous to us both; to him because of his all too numerous heresies, and to me because of my associations with the Council and the Court of the Holy Office. Yet, however it must have seemed to Giordano, no trap was intended.

The original understanding that I was to be his pupil was superseded by the course of events. Navarre had triumphed in France and there was talk of the King abjuring the reformed religion. Our domestic *politiques*, of whom Pinelli was one, saw in this the wondrous workings of providence and looked to the new King for the resolution of all earthly miseries. Henri's arrival in Italy was imminently expected. *He* was the Prince for whom Giordano had been so long searching. Navarre was to inaugurate the era of universal reform in Church and state, all Europe flocking to his banner as the stars descended from heaven and peace and light prevailed in the general harmony. The principalities would be converted to Empire; the pulpit into a throne, the keys into swords, and the King would die Emperor of all Christians. To speak French in the Republic was angelic; to be a Frenchman, divine.

Majesty gained through force lacked papal solemnization. King Henri waited, that cynical smile tipped on his face while he promised chickens to the populace and religious toleration to the nobles.

I know the French. Henri's intentions were ambiguous. Did the Pope wish for a conversion? Why then, it was easily done. Twice a Huguenot, twice a Catholic, the King ordered his tailor to cut new robes for a second coronation. All he needed was time.

All? Time and a prophet of the new order, a little cosmic engineering, new constellations for old.

As for Giordano, he was full of praise for the new King. If only he would come to Italy!

Ensouled by our resident luminary, an influx of astrologizing virtuosi made my house their locus. Twice I warned him. He should not mistake our liberal laws for justification. The High Council was alarmed at his presence here. Venice must preserve her independence against any foreign threat, Spanish or French. Besides, and I made this very plain, there were rumours of magic and sorcery.

He would go to Rome, he said. No man, devil or god would deter him from submitting his case to the highest spiritual authorities. These stellar doctors with whom he was presently surrounded were as timorous as the rest. Idle pedants, their eyes befogged with stardust! He could see now that Venice did not deserve its reputation as a liberal state. Its doctors were gulls, imbeciles! They were men of no learning and less wit. But Giordano! Nature beckoned him on; there could be no turning back. He had plundered the secrets of the charnel house, had crossed the seal of Hermes on a waxen corpse and seen it stir and tremble; had summoned demons from the ethereal regions and could name them familiarly, Rhamanoor and Rheianoor, knowing that they healed the sick in body and mind. Was I, his friend, to turn against him? What was this talk of sorcery? The Church, not he, had instilled the fear of spirits into the people; it was the Church, not the Nolan, that had elevated the worship of dead things into a religion.

He raved and stormed, swearing he was afraid of no man or thing. Throughout the month of April, there were several tempestuous scenes between us. He was at work, he said, on his final creation. When he had finished the book he would dedicate it to the Pope; and the Pope, he was sure, would accept. And then, his studies over, it would be possible at last to live and think freely in Italy, for that was all that he had ever desired. Therefore he would go to Rome, before the English doctors Dee and Kelley, whom he'd met in London; before Francesco Pucci, for whom Kelley had conjured the angel Michael (seen only by the wizard himself), to Rome, always to Rome, *where else but Rome?*

Where else indeed? Early in May I found out that his true destination was Frankfort. Morosini, another of our Venetian liberals, told me. "The Nolan," he said, "plans to visit Germany."

The Nolan, who was afraid of nothing, was running away.

I decided then that if he would not go to Rome, Rome must come to him. In the second week of May, I gave my delation to the Papal Nuncio. After supper on the night of the 25th, I mentioned that I had some talismans arrived from Egypt. "Tomorrow," I said, "it might be worth a visit to my warehouse."

That night, I made sure his door was locked.

In the morning, we went without servants — something he noticed.

"The cargo," I said, "is too valuable."

And still he seemed to suspect nothing, although he did notice that we were followed along the Giudecca.

It was surprisingly easy. At the quayside I began a conversation with my steward and told Giordano to go on ahead. Meanwhile, the officers of the Inquisition, who had been following, had landed at another quay and kept themselves hidden. Giordano could not have seen them, or if he did, he failed to recognize them. He gave a cheerful wave, I remember, turned and walked towards the warehouse. When he was safely inside I locked the door on him.

The guard arrived later in the day.

Four times my house has occupied the highest office of state. I have seen much go down, authority breeding insolence and splendour decay. I seek no vindication. Honour, justice, truth are abstract virtues too often invoked after some purposeless act or else in justification of treachery.

There is a story of a certain *condottiere* who liberated the state of Siena from foreign tyranny. So great was this man's service that the citizens knew of no reward to match the deed. Daily, they met in council until at last one of them rose and said, "Let us kill him and then worship him as our patron saint."

The state needs its heroes; science its martyrs; the Church her saints. I gave Giordano many things, my friendship and hospitality, gifts of money and books, and, if God had willed it, I might even have secured him a certain place in the state. He spurned my friendship, and yet it was my lot to give him what he most desired: surety of immortal fame. In this I proved faithful, for though he was inconstant, I loved him. I did not betray Giordano but myself.

I have eternity on my hands. Do you know what that is like? Neither heaven nor hell but nervelessness, as if the nerves had been extracted one by one. A painless operation. I have

never been able to bear great suffering.
I did not attend the execution.

II

*I am of the earth; but the laws are born of God's
wisdom. God has proclaimed the laws through
His words. But I am relegated by Him to the
realm where accidents in experience cause
constant variations. I am exposed to accidents
and I myself belong to the realm of the
accidental. But the law is based upon eternal and
universal justice.*

— Coluccio Salutati

*Who does not know of the great prudence that
exists in the forms of society of bees and ants
and similar insects? Both justice and compassion
are much more developed among certain animals
than among certain men.*

— Antonio de Ferrariis, 'il Galateo'

Venice, Summer 1592 — Rome, February 1600

"This," Fra Giovanni Gabrielle da Saluzzo, Father Inquisitor
of the Venetian Holy Office, was saying, "this is the Apostolic
Nuncio, Monsignor Ludovico Taberna. And this is your
Patriarch, the Most Reverend Archbishop Lorenzo Priuli,
whose duty it is to superintend the legality of our proceedings. . . ."

Giovanni, Ludovico and Lorenzo — the Trinity.

For the first three days after my arrest I was housed in the prison of the Inquisition and was left alone. Compared with this Roman dungeon, my accommodation was luxurious. I had a bed to sleep on, good food to eat, pen and paper. Twice a day, I was allowed to exercise and also to wash (I have long since abandoned the effort of cleaning myself by dipping the torn end of my sleeve in the water that accumulates on the floor of my present abode); and above all I had light and fresh air which streamed in through the barred window of my cell.

Apart from the physical constraints and inconveniences of imprisonment, my life then was no worse than what it had been earlier — monastic. I had no thoughts of escaping but was content to prepare my defence, which I felt sure was bound to succeed. No formal charges had been laid against me, though accusations there were in abundance. The lack of an indictment is of course perfectly suited to the procedure of the Inquisition, which, as the Inquisitor said, is not a court of law but of dialectic.

On the twenty-ninth and thirtieth of May, I was required to give a written account of my life and submit a list of my writings which I was prepared to defend. On the second of June, the investigation proper began before the Tribunal, and was to last, with various interruptions (including eight weeks for the application of torture) until July thirtieth, 1592.

The courtroom of the Venetian Inquisition is calculated to impress the prisoner with the power of state. He is brought up from an anterior room and emerges into a little maze which screens his view of the judges. The device resembles a slaughter pen, in which the beast being led to the kill is spared the sight of his predecessor's death. This labyrinth, however, is not constructed for any such humane reason, but is intended to inculcate a very real sense of foreboding. Its walls are fashioned from a bland and characterless marble, and into them are set some eight or ten booths where the prisoner, or prisoners, may rest during recess. But the most ingenious feature of the maze is its shape, a triumph of simple design. It is set in the form of an expanding square, so that the prisoner must negotiate four right-angle turns before he gains full view of the court. Even then, no attempt is spared to make him aware of his lowly status. He must stand while his judges sit. His only support is a balustrade against which he may lean from time to time; his judges preside from velvet thrones and are elevated on a dais. In itself, this structure is at once formidable and imposing. It is hung with the gold and crimson flags of state, and is framed on either side by a crocodile and winged-lion carved in ebony.

There are no public trials in Venice. In the proceedings of the Inquisition, the accused cannot hear the evidence against him. He has no right of cross-examination and does not know whether his judges are lying or telling the truth. He has nothing to help him except his wits. And, if he still has them left, he will have learned after a few days that his best defence is silence....

And this was a free and liberal state!

The Inquisitor spoke softly. A master of the *distinguo*, this brother in Holy Orders, a scrupulous examiner.

"We are alone here," he said. "You may speak as freely as you wish."

"No man is alone, father," Archbishop Priuli observed. "We are none of us alone."

This line of Lorenzo's, delivered with episcopal complacency, created then the same feeling as it does now, a feeling of detached inevitability, as if I were a spectator at my own trial. Insignificant details, a slight odour, the smell of camphor filtering down from the Patriarch, or Fra Giovanni's quivering smile, these too have stayed with me over the years and are intensified in the mind's re-enactment. Lorenzo the magnificent resembled an emaciated cherub. He was very pink, and his face was streaked with a cosmetic. His skin seemed as though it were made of wrinkled wax, and I pictured him in the secretive act of polishing his head and combing his eyebrows, those fine, flaxen eyebrows which cascaded over the sockets and caused the reverend gentleman no end of trouble.

"Before God," he said, "we are not alone."

"Just so, my lord," the Inquisitor murmured.

He sat to one side of the Patriarch, his pallor contrasted against Lorenzo's sheen. Fra Giovanni was not merely pale. His complexion was mottled, and the brown patches daubed on his sallow skin combined with his singularly luminous gaze to lend him the appearance of a thrush.

The Papal Nuncio, Ludovico Taberna, sat aloof on the right-hand of my lord. The Monsignor strove to assert his dignity as the representative of the Holy See by gazing heavenwards. His manner was formality itself, and when he was not speaking he cultivated a cadaverous indifference to the proceedings.

I can see the tableau now, the gold, crimson and black dais crowned by my judges: a corpse, a cherub, and, to one side, the thrush softly pecking at the worms of the matter.

The questioning began with a procedural wrangle. Fra Giovanni asked me, as is the custom, if I had any idea why I was before the Tribunal. When I gave the equally customary response and answered in the negative, Lorenzo Priuli indulged the court with a lavish display of irony.

"Of course not! Of course he has no idea why he is here. Because he is innocent, my lords. You only have to look at him to see that. Innocence is written all over his face."

The Patriarch's mouth was extremely small, his speech rasping as if the words had been compressed in their effort to escape. "But, my lords," he continued, "I thought we had agreed to ask him about the letter...."

"The letter?" Ludovico Taberna enquired.

"*The* letter!" Lorenzo's brows convulsed.

"My lord is referring to a letter you wrote," said the Inquisitor, "before you returned to Italy. The letter was written from Frankfort and was addressed to Brother Simplicius in Naples."

"Be advised," said the Patriarch, "that we have examined both the letter and its recipient."

Fra Giovanni sighed. "My lord is most anxious to know," he said wearily, "why you wrote that letter."

Over a quarter of a century has passed since I last saw Gryphius Simplicius, and I do not think that I shall see him again. We grew up together, climbed Vesuvius as children and haunted the shores of Lake Avernus. It was there that I had told him I was leaving Italy, possibly forever.

Another world, alien yet of this world, came to mind as I stood before my judges — Avernus, a weirdly beautiful landscape of rocks frozen in grotesque entablature, primal witnesses to the earth's tortured parturition. A mist hung on the lake's surface; dead trees gestured at the sky, their white boles reflected in the still waters, finality's true mirror.

Filoteo, Teofilo, Magus. So it was in the beginning and shall be in the end...

"Giordano! Giordano! What are you going to do?"

"What is there to do, Brother? Fra Vito is convinced I'm in league with the powers of hell. Tomorrow, I shall go to Rome. And later — who can tell? — Geneva; Paris, maybe...."

How could I answer them?

"My lords," I said something of the sort, "if you have examined the letter, you know that it is harmless and that my Brother is surely blameless. The letter was written to renew an old friendship, for no other reason. You must know that we took Orders together...."

"You were stripped of those Orders!" Lorenzo Priuli darkened, his polished cheeks inflating and deflating. "Excommunicated! Cast out! You sought to make this friar a party to your schemes, a simple man who is now under penance. I can read between the lines. I know what you intended. You longed to be received back into the Church, to work your damnable heresies from within!"

"My lord, my lord," Fra Giovanni sought to anoint the storm, "your vigilance is most commendable. But we must not be over-zealous. The letter shows no evidence of conspiracy, and I really see no point in continuing this line of questioning."

Lorenzo demurred. Simple men, he declared, were easily led into licentiousness. Nothing should be overlooked. Not, of course, that this Brother Gryphius had shown any sign of heresy, though the letter itself was a *potentially* incriminating document — that was the point he wished to make. As for the prisoner's response, he had expected that. Indeed, he had predicted it. Their lordships would do well to remember how, in their preliminary hearings, he, the Patriarch of all Venetia, a man of some experience in life, had expressly stated that the guilty always protest their innocence *in direct proportion to the amount of their guilt.*

It was the first of many such tirades from Lorenzo Priuli.

"You have been in our Republic before, I think," Fra Giovanni took up the questioning again, "as a fugitive from the Spanish Inquisition in Naples. That was in the year 1579. . . ."

The plague year, the year of Titian's death. It passed — unnoticed. The bells tolled night and day: *orrendo! orrore!* — fires burning to ward off the pestilence. Wandsmen appointed to collect the dead patrolled the streets, a red wand their mark of office. Bodies floated in the canals, first rats, then dogs and men. And the children sang, how they sang.

The wandsman! Beware the wandsman!

It was the same in every city across the north that year. From Genoa to Venice, the children sang and the children died.

I spent most of the year teaching in Noli, a small commune outside Genoa. I was attracted to the town for a superficial reason — its similarity, in name at least, to my birthplace. Such are the accidents of life. The greater part of my income was gained from teaching grammar, a tedious occupation. This meagre living I managed to supplement by giving lectures on astronomy to the sons of the wealthier citizens. Finally, when there was nothing left to teach but corpses, I left for Savona. It was the same there.

Beware the wandsman! Beware the wandsman!

From Savona, I made my way to Turin; from there, to Venice. I did not stay long, for I was in perpetual fear of arrest. The last thing I wanted was to be transported to the south.

The next year, I was in Geneva, safe from imprisonment — or so I thought.

Fra Giovanni allowed himself the semblance of a smile. "This court," he said, "has no business with the charges that were brought against you in Naples, related, it seems, to certain books annotated by Erasmus, works of Jerome and Chrysostom."

Those books! What trouble they caused me. I was forced to destroy them. . . .

The Patriarch opened his tiny mouth at this. "Byzantine pursuits," he warbled, lapsing into a reedy silence.

"However," Fra Giovanni ignored him, "there are other books which are of singular interest to us; books, Giordano, of which you are the author."

"*The Expulsion of the Triumphant Beast* is one of them," said Lorenzo, waving a copy in the air. "A keynote of your early work. This book was written in France and dedicated to His late Majesty King Henri III. What do you mean by the 'triumphant beast?' The Pope?"

"Error, my lord. Ignorance."

"Nevertheless, in this book you propose a radical modification of the heavens, a change-about of the constellations so that the malign influences are removed and the beneficent ones enhanced. How was this to be accomplished — by magic?"

"I'm pleased that my lord displays such familiarity with my works," I said — foolishly, I'll admit. "But I was speaking figuratively, and did not mean to be taken literally. . . ."

"No? Well, we shall see. I say that you were not speaking figuratively — as you claim — but that you were in earnest. For example, this passage from the third dialogue of the *Expulsion*. I beg your indulgence, my lords. It will take some time to find the piece. Ah yes," Lorenzo held the book close to his nose, "you have arranged it so that the god Isis is speaking to the god Momus. Or is it the other way round? No, Isis to Momus. So, I quote," and he did: " '*And in truth I see how the wise men by these means had power to make familiar, affable and domestic gods, which, through the voices that came out of the statues, gave counsels, doctrines, divinations and superhuman teachings. Whence with magical and divine rites they ascended to the height of the divinity through the same scale of nature by which the divinity descends to the smallest things.' "*

The patriarch closed the book with a resounding clap. "Vile, pagan, detestable doctrine," he said.

"If the court would allow it," said Ludovico Taberna, "I submit that the accused has not had sufficient time for reflection. With all due respect to my lord Archbishop, I scarcely think that such characterizations as he has used can serve our purpose at this stage in the proceedings. Concerning the nature of Giordano's style, it is so obviously the language of allegory that I think the point is unworthy of discussion. We shall be wasting our time and God's if we bicker like aestheticians in the academy."

A friend — Ludovico!

My judges put their heads together. At length, the Inquisitor spoke. "Monsignor Taberna," he said, "is going to read a passage from Ficino. The Tribunal would be interested in your opinion...."

The passage was from Ficino's *Pimander*, which he had translated for Cosimo de' Medici before the old man died. It was read with some feeling by Ludovico, who had temporarily abandoned his aloofness. Indeed, he descended from the dais into the body of the court, and, after first requesting that I be given a chair, a request which the Tribunal most graciously allowed, began his recital from the philosopher's *magnum opus*.

" *'Unless you make yourself equal to God, you cannot understand God: for the like is not intelligible save by the like. Make yourself grow to a greatness beyond measure, by a bound free yourself from the body; raise yourself above all time, become Eternity; then you will understand God. Believe that nothing is impossible for you, think yourself immortal and capable of understanding all, all arts, all sciences, the nature of every living being. Mount higher than the highest height; descend lower than the lowest depth. Draw into yourself all sensations of everything created, fire and water, dry and moist, imagining that you are everywhere on earth, in the sea, in the sky, that you are not yet born, in the maternal womb, adolescent,* * *old, dead, beyond death. If you embrace in your thought all things at once, times, places, substances, qualities, quantities, you may understand God.' "*

The words of the thrice great Mercury, ageless beyond age, echoed and died in the courtroom. Ludovico Taberna resumed his seat to the right-hand of the Patriarch.

"Well, Giordano?" said the Inquisitor.

"My lords," I replied, "the author of this text is not suggesting that a man can actually become God...."

"Answer the question," Lorenzo snapped. "Do you or do you not agree with what Monsignor Taberna has just read?"

"I was not aware that that was the question, my lord. But yes, I am in substantial agreement...."

"Then you must also be aware that the scribblings of this renegade doctor, which your own so closely resemble, have been condemned as false and pernicious by the Church."

"I speak as a philosopher, my lord, and seek only to present that duality of truth according to which philosophy and theology, science and faith, may coexist."

"You speak as a philosopher!" The Most Reverend Archbishop was on his feet. "In God's name, think of what you say! The doctrine you plead in your defence was rejected as false by the Council of 1512. You must and do know this! What is false is contrary to the truth, and what is true is contrary to falsehood. What is contrary truth? A lie! How can a lie coexist with the truth?"

"My lord," Fra Giovanni intervened, "please do not distress yourself. Giordano is well aware that the ruling to which you refer has several times been rescinded. In the case of Pomponazzi by the Roman Censor four years after it was introduced; and in the prisoner's own case by the University of Paris. There is no error in holding one thing philosophically and another theologically. The light of reason has led many doubters to the truth...."

"On the other hand," Ludovico gave the Inquisitor a deathly smile, "and seeing that we are on the subject, though why I do not know, it was Pomponazzi who declared — was it not? — that the Church is based neither on the stupidity of the philosophers nor on human reason, which is altogether lost in fog, but on the Holy Ghost and the indisputable evidence of miracles.''

And on this note, with Lorenzo Priuli fervidly asking for my opinion on miracles (which opinion I gladly gave him, the Nuncio making no attempt to conceal his boredom), the first day's examination concluded.

It was not until the second day, June third, that I discerned the trend behind the investigation. It was a day of angry threats, a day in which Lorenzo Priuli expounded his theory of the universe to the detriment of my own. It was also a day in which the possibility of torture was hinted at for the first time.

The session began with a rambling address from the Patriarch. He was pleased, he said, that I had not disagreed with him on the miracles of Christ. They were indisputable proof of the divinity of Jesus. Therefore Lorenzo, a Christian, the shepherd of his flock, was pleased that I had not questioned this foundation of his religion. However, there were other matters of equal importance to him, which, although his understanding was not as perfect as that of his learned peers, interested him deeply. These new developments in astronomy, for example. He could see how men of science must proceed dispassionately, but there was the question of appearances. The sun seemed to him to rise in the east and set in the west, for so it was expressed in *Ecclesiastes: Terra autem in aeternum stat — Sol oritur et occidit.* The earth abideth forever, the sun rising in the east and setting in the west. If, on the other hand, the sun was stationary, how could it move and *be seen to move?* Therefore it was reasonable to say that the sun moved and the earth stood still. Reasonable and in accordance with Holy Writ.

The Patriarch did not believe it was given to man to enquire too deeply into celestial mysteries. He for one was prepared to accept the evidence of his eyes. Although he was willing to concede that there were other things which he believed to be true but could not see (this applied equally to matters of faith *and* science), such arguments did not concern him *per se*. No, the new ideas, all well and good in themselves, were not *in themselves* at issue. Nor was he competent to speak on them. That much was crystal clear, pellucid, by which he did not mean his competence, or lack of it, but the *challenge to authority*. The fact that heretics had taken up the new cosmology was extremely significant. Where would it stop? Question one thing, and all is soon called into doubt. Was the teaching of generations to be dismissed in a night of star-gazing? Men and women, persons of simple understanding — children, really — appealed to the Church for guidance. Now their necks were so craned towards the heavens that they could hardly see their way about the streets. We all remembered the new star of 1572 and the comet five years later. What a hubbub they had caused! Obviously, these extraordinary events in the sky had been caused by the devil, who was very subtle and knew how to turn men's eyes away from the conduct of their lives. What next? They would be claiming irresistible grace like the Calvinists and would forget the doctrine of works. Anarchy would be the inevitable result, for everyone knows that social chaos follows fast on the heel of heresy — just as everyone knows that chaos is a favourite tool of the devil.

"The sun," concluded the eloquent Lorenzo, his eyes concealed behind their gossamer lashes, bejewelled now with the most rhetorical tears, "the sun is unruly, the earth a wandering star, the great sphere of the firmament cracked open, and all, all is ruinously called into doubt."

Silence greeted my lord's remarks. The Nuncio coughed, a little too politely.

"Ah," the Inquisitor sighed. "Ah, yes...."

"I had not finished, father," said the Patriarch, and then, magnanimously: "But do proceed. Please, you were going to ask the prisoner a question...."

"You are too polite, my lord," said Fra Giovanni, allowing the Court to reflect on Lorenzo's unprecedented civility, "but your, ah — address — did put me in mind of a question. I would like to ask the accused how he reconciles his teaching on the position of the sun with the example of Holy Writ, wherein it is manifestly stated that the earth, and not the sun, is at the centre of the solar system."

"My lords," said I, "it is my opinion that the language of the Scriptures is not addressed to learned men as such, but only to the faithful. And they, as my lord Archbishop has observed, have only the understanding of children to work with. Therefore, it would have been unwise if God, in His revealed Word to His children, had confused the evidence of the senses by stating that things were not what they appeared to be. But to answer your question scientifically, there are mathematical and observational proofs for the rotation of the earth — proofs which also help explain the retrograde motion of the planets, a phenomenon that has puzzled learned men for countless generations. And it is only in our day and age, through the heroic labours of Copernicus and his disciple, Rheticus, that we have begun to penetrate these mysteries of nature."

"But what do you *believe*, Giordano," the Inquisitor insisted, "the Holy Ghost or a man?"

"My lord, you yourself have stated that there is no error in holding one thing theologically and another philosophically...."

"That is a reasonable reply," Ludovico Taberna bestirred himself. "In my opinion, a very reasonable reply...."

"*Reasonable?*" The Patriarch frowned. "Sophistry, Monsignor, often appears reasonable. The devil is a rational fellow, do not forget that, and he works where his presence is least suspected. Even," Lorenzo raised an admonitory finger, "here."

"Oh indeed," said Fra Giovanni, "and we are fortunate to be reminded of that, my lord. With your permission, however, there is another question I would like to ask the accused...."

"Of course, of course," Lorenzo sulked. "Ask what you will. The answers are all the same...."

"Ah yes, my lord," Fra Giovanni bowed with his eyes. "With your leave, my lords, I would like to turn from the question of the earth's place in the solar system to the stated contention of the accused, namely, the existence of other plants like our own and the supposed infinity of the universe. If, Brother Jordanus, if as you say — in your philosopher's role — there are innumerable stars and infinite worlds which orbit these stars, as you claim our earth orbits the sun, then how can it be that around the lights which are the stars of heaven we do not see other lights which would be these other worlds? And how can it be that we do not detect any motion in this infinity of stars, and why are they always in the same disposition in the fixed and immovable sphere of the heavens?''

"The reason is very simple," I answered. "If you were to place yourself at a great distance from the world, then it would appear as motionless as the stars. Likewise, the inhabitants of another planet, looking to the heavens, would see a different disposition of the constellations, but they would detect no more motion in them than we do."

"Anathema! Heresy!" The voice of the Church Militant sang out. "These planets are populated now! These inhabitants of other worlds," Lorenzo blinked heavily, "no doubt they sprang from Adam too, no doubt Our Lord was crucified to save them as well, no doubt the prisoner has spoken with them and finds them personable, very personable, very human. Oh, my lords, there is devilry in this, and there is more, much more...." The Patriarch paused for breath, then turned his florid countenance on me. "Is it not written that God created man to enjoy the fruits of this world? *This world, heretic, no others!*"

"Even so learned a Patriarch as yourself," Ludovico Taberna observed, "has implied that the question of appearances may be open to dispute. My lords, I must make an appeal to reason. It is evident that we are getting nowhere. I propose that we adjourn...."

"I see no point in adjourning when our business is nearly complete," said Lorenzo. "The prisoner is obviously guilty and unwilling to retract anything he has ever said or done. We should remind him that we have the means to force his confession...."

"It is too premature for that," said the Nuncio icily. "You know my views on the subject."

"Mine also," Fra Giovanni declared. "I must say that I agree with Monsignor Taberna...."

My judges conferred, and, to Lorenzo Priuli's obvious displeasure, an adjournment of two hours was agreed upon. "We shall reconvene this afternoon," said Fra Giovanni. "As for you, Giordano, I suggest that you occupy the recess by seeking the counsel of Almighty God."

Lorenzo's outbursts, I decided, were not as impulsive as they seemed, and the reactions of the Inquisitor and the Nuncio to his veiled suggestion that I be shown the instruments, struck me as contrived. I began to suspect that the questioning was prearranged, and this suspicion was confirmed in the afternoon by an abrupt change of tactics on the part of my judges. Accordingly (and still with the threat of torture in mind), I resolved to play a more conciliatory role. For, despite what Lorenzo had said, there was a great deal that I was prepared to admit.

Fra Giovanni opened the questioning. He was interested, he said, in my travels, and would like to thank me for giving the Court a full account of them in my written delation.

"You're quite a traveller, Giordano," he said, smiling and asking if that was not so.

I answered that it was.

"The fact that you have spent many years abroad," he continued, "is highly suggestive to the Court. Far be it from me to dwell on the time you spent in Geneva or in the Protestant states of Germany. Your association with adherents of the Reformed religion was entirely innocent, no doubt. But I shall let that pass," he smiled again, "for the moment."

"The Tribunal is interested in the period of your first stay in Paris," said Ludovico Taberna. "I refer to the years of 1581 to 1583, immediately before you went into England in the service of His Majesty King Henri III."

"It is true, is it not," Lorenzo smirked, "that the late King, a man who was much traduced by magicians, took you into his ourt at the insistence of his mother?''

"My lord, Queen Catherine had nothing to do with the favours I enjoyed from her son.''

"But it is true, isn't it, that she liked you? After all, you spoke the same language — in more senses than one.''

"My lord, there were many Italians in the service of Queen Catherine. She had never learned to speak French very well, and t was only natural that she should prefer her own countrymen to those of her adopted land.''

"Again, my lords,'' said Ludovico Taberna, "I think the accused's explanation is not unreasonable.''

"Not unreasonable! *Not!*'' Lorenzo Priuli exploded. "It is well known that the mother of that unhappy King consorted with all manner of black magicians and was a witch herself. Giordano Bruno,'' the Patriarch was shouting now, "I say that the late King Henri, who was murdered in the camp of your friend Navarre, summoned you to Paris because he longed for instruction in the diabolical arts. This instruction you gave him as you would have given it to Mocenigo. Then because of the embroiled state of France, the King sent you into England where it is well known they are all diabolical practitioners. There he sent you because he wanted an English alliance against the Catholic party in France. There you made yourself familiar at the court of the apostate bitch, calling her divine and likening her to Venus — to *Venus,* my lords! There you pursued your abominable schemes until Mauvissière, that lick-spittle ambassador, was withdrawn by the King, taking you in train with him back to Paris. In Paris again, you took up your old ways, astrologizing and prophesying until it seemed that the Catholic party would triumph, whereupon you fled into Germany. Oh, my lords, there is no end to this vile taint of heresy. I tell you the devil is in this!''

"You dream, my lord. The late King summoned me to Paris because he was eager for instruction in the art of memory. It is true, my lord, that he did ask me whether this art was to be mastered by magical or natural means, but I was able to demonstrate that it was entirely natural in both cause and effect.

As for the King of Navarre, you said that he was my friend. Yet I do not know the King of Navarre, nor have I ever seen him...."

"As the representative of the Holy See," Ludovico Taberna declared loftily, "I must insist that my lord Archbishop cease badgering the accused. There is not the slightest shred of evidence that Brother Jordanus was ever acquainted with the King of Navarre. And I would also like to remind the Court that Henri, King of Navarre, was recognized by his predecessor as the sovereign monarch of all France. We may not like his religion, my lords, but we cannot contest his title — a title, I might add, which has been victoriously defended in battle. Success in the passage of arms *must* indicate something of God's judgement."

"The King is a heretic!" Lorenzo Priuli cried. "The prisoner is a heretic! Are you agreeing with heretics now?"

"My lords, my lords," Fra Giovanni murmured, "in this Court we are all Christians. It is our business to investigate error, not to accuse one another of error...."

The Inquisitor waited for a few moments before he spoke again. "There is one question I must put to the accused," he said, "and then I shall adjourn this Tribunal for the day. Surely, Brother Jordanus, you would not deny that you have praised many heretics, both princes and commoners? The truth, now, Giordano, I want the truth."

Here was my chance. I presented myself as the most abject of penitents. Not that this was difficult. The heat was stifling in the courtroom; I had been standing for most of the day, and I was weary, weary of Priuli's hectoring, weary of their asinine questions, weary and perhaps a little afraid.

"My lords," I hung my head, "it is true that I have praised many heretics and also heretic princes. I did not do so because they were heretics, but solely for the moral virtues which they had; neither have I praised them as religious and pious, nor used any such religious epithets. And in particular, in my book *On Cause, Principle, and Unity* I praise the English Queen and call her 'diva', not as a religious attribute, but as that kind of description that the ancients used to give to princes, for in England where I then was and where I composed this book, the title of 'diva' used to be given to the Queen. And I was more induced to name her thus because she knew me, for I was continually going with the ambassador to court. My lords, I know that I have erred in praising this lady, she being a heretic, and above all in attributing to her the name of 'diva.' "

"And the King of Navarre," said Fra Giovanni, "what *did* you expect from him?"

"My lord, only that he would confirm the orders of the late King, and that I would have from him the favours I had from His Majesty King Henri III concerning my public lectures...."

"But Mocenigo has sworn that you praised the King many times, and that you expected great things from him, some kind of reform — a religious reform...."

"My lord, I did not say any such thing. In speaking of him, I...."

"Liar! Heretic! A thousand times cursed! Priest, I *know* you lie!"

Lorenzo Priuli leapt to his feet. With a grace that was almost dainty in one of his bulk, he brushed past the Nuncio and descended the stairs at the side of the dais, pirouetting as he reached the floor of the court, turning nimbly to glare at the two remaining judges. "I shall prove it!" he cried, and then advanced on me.

There was no restraining him now. The Patriarch was sweating profusely, and his flaxen brows glistened. For the first time, his eyes became clearly visible to me. In that face, at once wizened and polished, the face of an angry and malevolent cherub, I saw their colour. The irises were yellow and ringed with black, the whites blood-flecked.

"Liar!" screamed Lorenzo Priuli, the Patriarch of all Venetia, whose duty it was to superintend the legality of the proceedings.

"I have witnesses!"

He paraded them the next day. One was a fellow prisoner

who testified fearfully that I had danced in circles, muttering incantations known to the meanest operator, *nomino Sancto Saday*, etc. There were several witnesses like this, each bearing the marks of forceful persuasion. There was even one, God help him, who told the truth.

"And he said, my lords, that the procedure which the Church uses today is not that which the Apostles used; for they converted men with preaching and the example of good life, but now whoever does not wish to be a Catholic must endure punishment and pain. For force is used and not love...."

When the *examen rigorosum* began, it was not so terrible — at first.

"Filoteo," I remember Fra Giovanni using that name, whispering as always, "I wish that I could spare you the pain. I wish ..."

I remember his face, pale in the darkness. And his voice, softly whispering: *"I will tell you our secret. We will become one, you and I. We will become one, and you will cry out not because of the pain but for lack of it...."*

After eight weeks, I confessed.

Perhaps in that other order of time reserved for storytellers and fabulists, I would not have confessed. Perhaps there is still another dimension of time in which I did in fact defy my judges. If there is, I have yet to find it.

Why did I retract the retraction? It would be a truism, useful but imprecise, to say that I knew they were going to kill me anyway. For my life, as my lord Cardinal Bellarmine never ceases to remind me, is entirely in my own hands. Or, as Fra Giovanni would have it, I am the Inquisitor and the accused.

No, it was because of you, Lorenzo Priuli, you who first insisted that I be shown the instruments and then tortured. I can hear your whining lisp now, Lorenzo. Small tears of malice glittered on your cheeks, and around your mouth, pursed and venomous, there formed droplets of a grey effluvia — spittle that had dried in the mouth.

T

The voyage was uneventful. Neither brigands nor sea-monsters interrupted my journey. But, sweet Jesus, my first experience in Venice! I have started to keep a record, for my own convenience — or should I say sanity? I keep this journal close about my person, for I live in constant danger. And nor is it anything natural I fear. No, no, it is too hellish for words: the fiend himself.

But it will pass, it will pass....

I went to the Patriarch's palace where they were all in mourning. Too late, Kaspar, I said to myself. *Requiescat in pace!* A relative of the Archbishop's, a merchant prince, conducted me to his lordship's tomb. He was in some trepidation and fidgeted as we entered the white sarcophagus. "Forgive me, sir," said he, pressing his hand to his brow, "I am ill at ease with myself. My mind..."

"A very natural expression of grief, sir," said I.

"No. I..." he hesitated, and his eyes lingered on the funerary image of his uncle. "It is not grief I feel. Come, sir, let us leave this place, and, since you are a stranger, I will show you what troubles me. You will see with your own eyes," he said, "you will see with your own eyes *and you will hear....*"

This merchant knew an old woman, he said, who had no commerce except with the departed, and he had been in the habit of consulting her upon the success of his own transactions. She lived alone, out on one of the islands in the lagoon, and it would be well worth my while to visit her.

"I will of course accompany you," he said, "and then you will see, sir, then you will see."

I could get no more out of him, but an hour or so later we stood at the entrance of the witch's hovel. Dear God, she was hideous: her body shrouded in yellow silks, her face mummified, her lips painted scarlet, her eyes fish-dead. Emilia was her name, and she knew us by ours, knew what we wanted. Ah Christ, she cracked open her lips and spoke a few words and I almost fainted from the shock.

"Master Schopp, do come in...."

"Perhaps you will find your answer now," said the merchant.

"*Come in, Kaspar,*" the hag spoke again, "*the Archbishop is expecting you.*"

And then, then she began to speak in a man's voice....

"My uncle," said Prince Priuli.

But I have it here, written down exactly as it happened.

T

No, no, *no*! I did not use a cosmetic. It was a natural condition, a disease of the heart... Articulate Lorenzo, sweet-tongued, mellifluous Lorenzo, damned for a certain term to hag speech. But lithping? *Never!* Lies! Damnable, putrid lies! I was born with honey in my mouth, was golden-eyed not yellow. I was not schooled in rhetoric. Eloquence flowed from my mouth like Hippocrene on Helicon. *Heretic! Perjured priest! Liar!* Pity is not dumb. I wept for him. Weep, weep... But lip splitting? That hurts. *False! False!* Lionlike, I roared and raged. *Psicologia*, a touch too many, maybe, but that's all. Believe me, I swear, I swear it was only artifice. There was nothing personal in what I did, no animus. *Anathema!* What, Lorenzo biased? A grievous charge, my lords....*Guilty! Guilty!* A thousand thousand times no! Listen, my lords, tell them how I sympathized with him. I sought to draw him out, that was all; to make him expand his views in free, impartial debate. Yes, yes that's it. Was it my fault he was sent to Rome? Of course it wasn't! My lords, Lorenzo's not to blame. Listen, my lords, listen to me! I even thought there was something to what he said. You believe me, don't you? Yes, my lords, it's true. My faith is firm, but — *Christ's teeth!* — for fifty years and more I was racked by a doubt, one doubt, an awful little tiny doubt, niggling, my lords, nibbling, that's the word, *nibbling*, eating away my soul, nibble nibble nibble. *His* teeth, my lords. His *little* teeth, what became of them, eh? Those little pearls of Our Lord's innocence, His

48

milk teeth, my lords. Nibble nibble. What happened to them? They fell out, yes, and then? When He rose on the third day, did they rise with Him, those little teeth? If so, how so? If not, why not? Nibble. That's where the rot set in, my lords. With little things. I've searched and searched. *What became of the Saviour's milk teeth, heretic?* But I was forgetting. The Scriptures are addressed to simple folk. *Subtle fox! Heretic! . . .* Now there's a thought. Not heretic. *Saint.* How does it sound — *Saint* Giordano? Ever-blessed. A pity there are no relics. But Santo Giordano — there's *psicologia* for you! Make him one of the heavenly party, my lords, that's what we should do. Ah, Lorenzo, divine, witty, peerless Lorenzo, the first to condemn a heretic and the first to proclaim a saint. But we have to make sure, my lords, we have to make certain he's dead. Then let him burn, my lords, let him burn like Lorenzo!

T

"Lorenzo!" My lord's nephew cried. "Where are you?"

"Ah," the hag wheezed through the painted fissure that was her mouth, "in hell, coz, in hell. . . ."

I was going to ask the question that was uppermost in my mind (although it does not do to gossip with demons) when the husk before me stuck out its tongue and gave a shrivelled laugh. "It burns," she croaked, a noxious vapour coming from within.

Ah God, the stench curdled my bowels. . . .

I am sure it is not the first time a saint has been proclaimed in hell. Such testimony, however, is dubious.

T

Monsignor Ludovico Taberna gave me a civil reception. But his lips were sealed on the subject of Giordano's death, a subject, it was plain to see, that caused him some embarrassment. Otherwise, he was most informative. His manner was precise and scholarly, and I have tried to render it as accurately as I could. A useful exercise in historical method. And it helped me to forget the events of yesterday. I was pleased that I told him nothing of what I had seen or heard. It gave me an advantage somehow, a secret advantage.

T

Ah Venice! Was ever a city so blessed, cursed with such inhabitants? Giovanni Mocenigo, for example, scion of a powerful and illustrious family, ambassador to Paris at the age of thirty (he was recalled, by the way, just two years before Bruno came to the Republic — a Navarrist agent had succeeded in breaking our codes. And not just ours! But that's another story); *allora*, here is a man with all the advantages of birth and position, acting like a common informer. You asked me about the trial ... In my opinion, it was irregular and extremely improper. Mocenigo's evidence was not, I think, in strictest accordance with the truth. And yet the principal evidence against Brother Jordanus came from him. My lord Archbishop, God rest his soul, was prepared to give him the benefit of the doubt. Lorenzo Priuli, however, was not the most scrupulous of examiners. I shouldn't malign him — he had his good points, you know. He was a kindly man at heart, which is why he blustered all the time. A combative man but generous. The family, which is very wealthy, gave more than their share to the poor. And Lorenzo saw to that. I would not like you to return with the wrong impression, Kaspar.

To continue. Fra Giovanni and I agreed that Mocenigo's evidence was provoked by something other than a regard for doctrinal probity. And not just his testimony! Mocenigo had broken all the known laws of hospitality and friendship. Inevitably, the question became one of motive. Why had he acted in this way? The suggestion has been made — I'm not permitted to say by whom — that he was misled by his spiritual director. Another theory was that he was anxious to re-establish himself with the Holy Office. He had served once as *savio al'eresia*, a go-between from the Council of Ten to the Inquisition. It was possible that he wanted his old position back. But such an action for such a reason was — to my way of thinking — unconscionable. Even so, it was to be kept in mind and weighed carefully when we came to consider the evidence.

I remember Fra Giovanni asking me for my thoughts on the subject. I told him that I was at a loss to understand Mocenigo.

"Zuan Mocenigo," he said, "is a man in love with what he fears."

"And what is that?" I said, for I thought his remark enigmatic.

"Fear," he said. "I do not envy him."

You will find that Fra Giovanni is very fond of enigmas.

It was soon evident that we could neither acquit nor convict Brother Jordanus. In such a case, it is customary to allow the accused a degree of liberty until the charges against him are more precisely formulated. Failing agreement, the case is often adjourned *sine die* and is only reconvened if and when some new evidence comes to light. This is neither to the advantage nor to the disadvantage of the accused, for evidence of one kind or another is always turning up. In Giordano's case, however, an indefinite postponement was out of the question. For one reason, there was ample information to suggest that he intended leaving Venice. For another, there were political factors to be reckoned with.

You're probably aware of the rumours that were flying around at the time. A great deal of scandalous talk abounded in the Republic, talk which involved Henri of Navarre in a revolution against Church and state. Everybody who had something to say whispered it in the lion's mouth, and I can tell you, Kaspar, that the power of suggestion had never been so strong. . . .

As far as was humanly possible, I determined to ignore this and I thought it best to remove political considerations from the religious sphere. This may sound like a remarkable innovation to you. Had anyone taken the rumours seriously, then things would have been otherwise. But as they were, it was a prime article of the Curia's foreign policy to return Henri of Navarre to the True Faith, and I wished for nothing that might have imperilled the rather delicate negotations. After all, the soul of a King is of no small value to the Church.

Picking over Mocenigo's testimony and the records of the trial, I came across several items of a somewhat contentious nature. The question of the innumerable worlds, for example, which so intrigued Lorenzo Priuli, seemed to me more a matter for philosophy than theology, and Brother Jordanus was technically correct at least in claiming the duality of truths in his defence. More difficult, though scarcely heretical, was his belief that creative nature is God in all things: *Natura est Deus in rebus*. For this he claimed the support of the Ancients, by whom he meant Virgil, Lucretius, Pythagoras, Solomon, as well as many another more distant and obscure authority. God, he said, was to be found in the unalterable laws of nature as easily as in Holy Writ — and indeed this natural God was easier to understand than the God of the Scriptures. Asked *as a Catholic* how he regarded the First Person, he answered that he thought of God as the supreme first sustainer, prime principle and cause — an expression which corresponds to the strictest orthodoxy. In his writings, I must admit, that formula is severely qualified, particularly in regard to the creation of the world.

But I am getting ahead of myself. Concerning the Person of Our Saviour, he admitted to some doubt, but was always careful to speak philosophically when he said that he did not fully understand how the Word became flesh. I should say, while I'm on this point, that Fra Giovanni thought his response was ironical — and there may be something to be said for that. The Third Person of the Trinity he regarded as the *anima mundi* or world spirit from which all life flows — an heterodox, if widely held, opinion. Here, he asserted that he spoke figuratively. He did not mean to impute spirit to inanimate matter, but referred to that principle in nature by which all natural forms, whether sentient or inert, may be said to resemble one another. The appearance of things, he said, is represented superficially to the senses, no more that the vestige of God as first mover. Hence, through meditation on things visible we are led to things invisible. It was one of his favourite figures, as was the image of ascent and descent to and from God. His views on death and the intellectual soul were interesting, but in my opinion they were neither novel nor heretical. He disagreed with the commonly held view in arguing that the soul is not the form of the human body but its captive.

If you want to understand the man, you really must come to terms with the paradoxes in his thinking, especially where the notion of the soul is concerned. The soul, he said, is *forma assistens* not *forma formans*, the pilot of the ship rather than the ship itself. It is an Averroistic view, opposed to the Thomist. Yet Thomas Aquinas was worshipped by Giordano, and the Nolan himself was forever anxious to refute Aristotelian views of nature. But here you have an example of Giordano using just such a view against his beloved Aquinas. I have often wondered whether he was aware of the contradiction, but the mood of the Court prevented any exploration of the point.

Death he held to be a congregation and a division: a division in that the soul is liberated from the body after death; a congregation in that the soul, thus liberated, merges with the world soul whence it came. In these and other arguments, his attitude was consistently, even perversely, eclectic. There was, it has to be admitted, a good deal of magical baggage to his philosophy, expressed, for example, in his insistence that the stars are messengers and interpreters of the divine voice, the sensible and visible angels. It is my heartfelt belief that greater precision and clarity of language on the part of his judges would have convinced Brother Jordanus of the foolishness of such views.

This — and again I concede a point — was rendered difficult by the prisoner's own behaviour, which was far from exemplary. Ordinary caution he despised, lecturing his judges as if they were students at the university. Asked how he justified his teachings on the natural creation, he swore that he did not hold it worthy of God's infinite grace and goodness to have created only this world when He was capable of creating other worlds. "Whoever denies an infinite effect," he said, as if he had been granted a private revelation, "denies an infinite power." The result of this utterance was to place his judges in the position of seeming to deny God, as if we now were on trial and he was the prosecutor. Worse yet. In several of his books, he had written that the symbol of the Cross was much more ancient than the time of the Incarnation of Our Lord (an opinion he had culled from Ficino and the Hermetic books), and that it had been used as an astrological device, "the gift of the stars," affixed by the Ancient Egyptians to the breast of their god Serapis. This proposition he defended, stubbornly at first, guardedly later on. Nor did he help himself (as you can imagine) when he asserted that the Cross was efficacious in natural magic, and could be used with certain of the planets for conjuration, a purpose for which it was especially suited at the times of Birth, Death, or Incarnation of Our Saviour. These and similar outbursts, to say nothing of the rumours of sorcery and his political connections, were sufficient to tip the scales against him in the eyes of Rome, if not of Venice.

The case dragged on interminably, no verdict being reached by his judges, although we had secured a complete recantation from him. The manner in which that was done, I prefer to pass over.

In September, the records of the trial were transferred to Rome, and the Curia also demanded that we surrender Brother Jordanus, sending a vessel from Ancona for that purpose. There has never been any great amity between Rome and Venice, and my position as Papal Nuncio was not easy. Finally, however, I was powerless to alter the result one way or the other. The disposition of the case was the Senate's right not mine, a right they exercised in October by refusing to relinquish the prisoner. The galley sailed without him.

The argument was now advanced that because Brother Jordanus was a Dominican, the Republic must yield its rights to the

Curia. Giordano had lived long in heretical lands, and during all this time he had led a wanton and diabolical life. His was heresy of the deepest dye. Here was no ordinary heretic but Antichrist himself. Had he not proclaimed as much in Germany, where he had found his own sect? Oh yes, Kaspar, you look surprised. You shouldn't be. The Nolan was a sectarian in action as well as name. They were called Giordanisti, and like their founder they lived in imminent expectation of world revolution. Would Venice, then, by its inaction, be seen to support the cause of universal apostasy? His Holiness regarded this as an occasion for the greatest concern and let the Venetian ambassador know that he could not deal lightly with such an affair. Besides, there was His Most Catholic Majesty, Philip of Spain, to be considered. . . .

Early in January of 1593, the Senate yielded. Politics, as usual, had triumphed.

I fear that I have bored you with this account. Your interests are historical, not theological. But of one thing I would like you to be certain. I have no doubt that Brother Jordanus, convinced of his errors, would have proved a useful asset to the Church. His was a remarkable mind, a mind of deep knowledge and wide learning, a mind too quick perhaps for its own good.

My influence in the case was to counsel moderation. I think it reasonable to say that my advice went unheeded.

"My friend, the Cardinal of S--S-------, says that there is some doubt of Giordano's fate. . . ."

"Ah, you will have to ask Fra Giovanni about that." Monsignor Taberna regarded me sternly. "The Commissary of the Inquisition will tell you where to find him. He has become something of a recluse, I hear, and does not get about as much as he used to. But then we are none of us any younger, Kaspar. Time and tide wait for no man. Sometimes I think the Archbishop, may he rest in peace, is better off where he is."

"Amen to that," I said, and left in search of the Inquisitor.

T

He was living in seclusion in a villa on the Paduan road. He was well attended by servants, as was only proper for so venerable a servant of the Church in the declining years of his life. Most of his time he spent in prayer and meditation. Age, however, had not dimmed his faculties. He was very succinct and exact, and welcomed the opportunity to discuss the trial, concerning which his point of view differed markedly from Monsignor Taberna's.

Ŧ

So he spoke to you of moderation. What *is* moderation, Kaspar? I have seen men broken on the rack. Believe me, no more horrible a torture exists, if it is done properly. Are you squeamish? You should not be. There are men that faint at the sight of blood who daily endure worse agonies than the rack, who are torn apart spiritually and do not complain. But perhaps you are too young to understand these things.

Every proposition implies its own opposite. Moderation is often an excuse for the extremest form of action, or for no action at all, for abnegation, that paralysis of the self-divided.

I am intrigued that Ludovico did not touch on the essence of this case. I am speaking of morality, a morality that has nothing to do with truth in the judicial sense. All men strive for mastery and in their striving all men cheat and dissemble, cozening their friends and neighbours with pleasant words, comfortable lies. The contagion is endemic; man is fallen and in his corrupt estate cannot hope for grace except through the mediation of Christ and His Apostles, the Church and her community of saints. The Church is only human, of course, but she is guided in her deliberations by the Spirit of God. The Church is not perfect but she does aspire to perfection, and whoever strikes at that edifice must plead divine inspiration or stand in great danger of heresy. And as you well know, Kaspar, divine inspiration, when used as a defence against the charge of heresy, is frequently nothing but an excuse for the most unwarrantable and erroneous innovations.

My greatest sorrow with Brother Jordanus, is that — to put it in its simplest form — we are too late. Where the danger of heresy exists, it is the first duty of the Holy Office to bring a man to an exact understanding of his true nature. For it is only when a man understands why he has acted in a particular way that he can hope to see what he has done. In this, the Inquisition may differ in degree, but never in kind, from the Church as a whole, making use of the same established precepts and revealed truths which constitute the Church's magisterium. It has always been my experience that once a man is brought into this condition of insight he will be more receptive to a higher level of instruction. The Inquisition will not have to threaten him; he will be sincerely contrite and amenable to the truth. Conversely, it is a good general rule that if a man does not understand the source of his actions, then no amount of doctrinal debate will alter his views. Heretics and saints have this one thing in common: they are seldom moved by reason and this was especially the case with Giordano, who had convinced himself that he was not as other men are, that he was unique, that he was set apart from the rest of humanity. In such a case force is not only justified, it is necessary. Yet even where the accused is most obdurate and impenitent, force can bring him to his senses. It can make him see reason where reason itself has failed. And so it was, in my opinion, with Giordano. His confession, when it was eventually extracted, was genuine and sincere. Of course, you will find others to disagree with me. All I can say is that they are entitled to their opinions — as I am to mine.

The Inquisition is pre-eminently an instrument of reason. We are reasonable men. I am sorry to labour the point, but I am well aware that we have inspired a certain historical fear. For once, I am in agreement with Martin Luther, who observed that if it were an art to overcome heresy with fire, the executioners would be the most learned doctors on earth.

The fire is an admission of failure. Yet for every failure there is a cause, and the Inquisition is not uncommonly faced with men bent on self-destruction. For such, the fire constitutes an unnatural passion, alluring and ravishing. I will be frank with you. The kind of attraction which these men have for death is sexual. In the mind's eye, the fire is conceived of as a mistress, to be entered and conquered until the lover is himself conquered, ravaged by the flames' irresistible embrace. And strange it is that this kind of temperament will very often represent itself as acting from the purest of motives, in the name of the common good, or in the name of an even higher morality, the spirit of self-sacrifice — attitudes which the Church has done much to encourage and which she would herself find, in another context, to be at once ennobling and saintly.

Moderation is alien to such a character and is naturally seized on as a sign of weakness in others. All pity, grief's reciprocity, must be extirpated. How easy it would be to deal charitably with the prisoner, only to have the flames triumph, if not on earth then hereafter! Therefore this temptation is to be sternly resisted. Harsh measures become proper and just, for the Inquisitor now, as well as the accused, can see the flames at the end of the long and tortuous path. Yet here, with the Inquisitor already considering the use of torture — yes, even here — the form is clearly prescribed. The Inquisitor must not act with undue haste, but must first threaten the use of the instruments — the *territio verbalis*. If this results in no modification of attitude, he must then be shown the instruments — the *territio realis*. And if this is still unsuccessful, the *examen rigorosum* must begin. Hence, just as a man's conscience is often felt to work unconsciously, without any knowledge of wrongdoing on his part, so it is the Inquisitor's duty to become that conscience, gaining gradual access to the innermost reaches of another's soul. And, just as the dictates of conscience will eventually seem immoderate and even painful, so the Inquisitor is to proceed. Yet in all this he is required to act dispassionately, without prejudice or cruelty.

In the preliminary stages of an investigation, it is best that he confine himself to remarks of a general nature, observing the accused as if from afar. Let the other judges proceed as they will, the Inquisitor should preserve his objectivity. He may find that one judge will play an aggressive role, another that of a sympathizer. In this situation he can mediate between the two, so gaining the prisoner's confidence. If all else should fail, and it is found expedient to show the prisoner the instruments of torture, the judicious Inquisitor will not be deceived by an extreme reaction. It has been my experience that a man who seems openly afraid at the sight of the instruments may prove most obdurate, whereas one who is unmoved may confess readily at the slightest suggestion of their use.

Giordano's behaviour was characterized by a degree of cunning which you may think is only natural in a man who is seeking to avoid the torture. He was prepared to confess, but he was not prepared to confess anything very specific. At the end of the second morning, my lord Archbishop, blessed be his memory, threatened him with the instruments. At the close of that day, events having taken a turn for the worse, I charged him point by point with the articles he must confess. I then warned him that it should come as no surprise if we were to use those judicial measures which it was within our habit and power to employ against offenders who stubbornly refused God's mercy and the Christian love of the Holy Office. For his part, he replied that he rejected and abhorred all errors which he had held until that day contrary to the Catholic faith and his monastic vows, and all heresies of which he *might* have been guilty, adding that he begged the Holy Tribunal, having regard to his weakness, would provide him with fit means to be received again into the Church and would let mercy prevail. Not one of those errors which he pretended to reject and abhor did he so much as mention by name. Therefore, it was my duty to caution him again. In the most solemn language, I told him we would not hesitate to employ measures by virtue of which we were solicitous of returning to the true light all who wandered in darkness and of bringing back to the way of everlasting life those who strayed from the right path. The implications of this warning he understood, yet on the next day we discerned no change in him. Asked again if there was anything he had specifically to confess, he said that his life had not been as perfect as he would have wished, and then proclaimed that skill in the conduct of life is mostly denied to those whose lives are to be lived for all time. We were left with little choice other than to show him the instruments, a course of action which had no more effect on him than our pleas.

And there, Kaspar, in that terrible place, the torture room of the Inquisition, I remember that he turned to me and smiled.

"So this," he said, "is my father's house...."

Few can long endure the *examen rigorosum*. Here, as with everything else, the procedure is well-established. The officer whose duty it is to work the instruments begins slowly, increasing the level of pain until it has reached an intolerable pitch. In Giordano's case, I thought it wise to introduce an innovation. Considerable pressure was applied at the beginning, and then relaxed — a treatment which induces the fallacious belief that after his initial torment the prisoner can withstand anything.

Contrary to the widely held impression, the Inquisitor is seldom present at these sessions, for he has no need to witness the prisoner's sufferings. The interrogation itself takes place during periods of respite and relative calm which the prisoner learns to anticipate joyfully. Hence, what has been tedious and repetitious to him in the courtroom is now looked upon as a welcome relief from the pangs of his torment. The prisoner will talk, and he will talk readily, for he is anxious to prolong the sessions....

Giordano, as I had expected, bore his ordeal with great fortitude. At the end of the second month, however, he broke, and as so often happens with an obdurate sinner, his confession was all the more pathetic. "I humbly beseech God and your lordships," he said, going on his knees, "to forgive all the errors I have committed, and I am here ready to do what your wisdom has determined and ordained for my soul's good. And if God and your lordships show pity on me, and grant me my life, I promise to alter my life in the sight of all men, and to make good all the evil that I have done."

The value of these sentiments, it must be admitted, is now somewhat academic. Nevertheless, Kaspar, I understood his recantation to be genuine, and received it in the same spirit as it

60

was given, honestly and with an open heart.

His agony he regarded as the prelude to martyrdom. His opinion of himself was too high and he was much in love with his several selves. A talented man but not by any means a saint.

The older I become, the more I am disinclined to believe in the possibility of saintliness. Do you know El Greco's portrait of San Sebastian, Kaspar? The Saint is transfixed by five arrows: three on his right side, one in his left arm, and another, almost to the flight, in his left thigh. But it is the face, Kaspar, that compels my attention — a slack-jawed face, and the eyes, Kaspar, the eyes! It is almost as though they express a far greater pain than that which the Saint has cause to endure. Study that face, Kaspar. It is the face of a madman.

"Then he was burned, it was Bruno I saw die?"

"Shall we say he suffered, Kaspar? Surely that is enough?"

Monsignor Taberna was right. Fra Giovanni is a man much given to enigmas.

There is something I forgot to mention. The Inquisitor is going blind. He made no reference to this during our conversation, though it was plain to see. His movements were like those of a sleepwalker.

Something else, too. Fra Giovanni had a question for me: "Why do you think Rome decided to burn him now, after almost eight years?"

It wasn't a question I had thought of before. I had no answer; perhaps there isn't one.

"Ask your friend the Cardinal," Fra Giovanni said. "Everything has to have a reason, otherwise it could not be."

III

Where will you find one of the masculine gender
who is the superior, or the equal, of this divine
Elizabeth who reigns in England and whom
Heaven has so endowed and favoured, so firmly
maintained in her seat, that others strive in vain
to displace her with their words and actions?
None in all her realm is more worthy than this
lady herself; among the nobles, none is more
heroic than she, among doctors, none more
learned, among counsellors, none have a wiser
head.

—Giordano Bruno

The King of France went up the hill
With forty thousand men;
The King of France came down the hill
And ne'er went up again.

—Anon.

Doctor Jordano Bruno Nolano, a professor in
philosophy, whose religion I cannot commend,
intends to pass into England.
    —Henry Cobham, English Ambassador in Paris,
    to Sir Francis Walsingham, March 1583

Henry's getting careless. The despatch is in plain text, not
cipher. Too much easy living. Who is this Nolano? Some

foreigner, Italian by the sound of it. A priest, no doubt connected with my lady of the Scots. God, my guts ache! What does this mean: 'whose religion I cannot commend'? If he is a Catholic, that goes without saying. Priests! Henry becomes long-winded. He's too long abroad. I'll write and ask, using Phelippes's new code. Here's some new ulcer for the body politic, I'll warrant. Nor will I use Capiscum oil and Sassafras coloured red (but that is to no advantage, the colour); no, some stronger medicine ... *Tom, the book!* ... Clever Tom, the customs house boy. How long has he been my spy? Thirty years, nearly that long. Jesus, the pain! I wonder if I am being poisoned sometimes. Oh, but my enemies are numerous and cunning. *Tom, the book. Bring me the book for Paris!* I should get him to look into my food. How I suffer. And the Queen's Majesty is displeased with me. "We know you rejoice, Sir Francis," says she, "at Alençon's defeats in the Low Countries. But he's another Francis too, Sir Secretary, and Francis will triumph." Witty Queen. "Tis a pity, Madam," says I, "that Parma drubbed him." Sooner someone else. "I'll box your ears, sir," says she, and so she could, clip them off if she wished. But she pines for her Frenchman friend; she weeps, he weeps, all weep. *How much longer will it last!* But he's gone, thank God, fifty thousand pounds the richer, gone I hope to die in Flanders mud. *Bring me the damned codebook will you, Thomas Phelippes!* Tom, Tom, the piper's son, stole a pig and away did run. The pig was eat and Tom was beat ... No, they would not dare! Not the pork! And yet ... The cook, is he an Italian? French? Here's Tom, pocky like *le Duc d'Alençon* ...

— *How much longer will what last, Sir Francis?*

— *What's that, Tom?*

— *You said, 'How much longer will it last!' Then you swore, my lord.*

— *Did I, Tom? I was thinking out aloud. How long have you been with me, Tom?*

— *Since 1538, Sir Francis.*

— *Forty-five years, Tom?*

— *Less three months and two days, my lord. A long time, give or take a few hours. Here's the book you asked for.*

I meant life, then. How much longer will that last? The weather is foul. Ah God, how I suffer!

⊤

Your Majesty, there is not a puddle dog to be found in all England. Master John Dee, who sends you his heavenly greetings and is laid up with the rheum, suggests that you send to Germany for the puddle dogs. Doctor Dee has read in the stars that you must avoid the month of August for the next six years, and thereafter the danger will have passed. SHAMSHIEL continues to pester me. Most Excellent King, the Watchers never sleep. HERMES has arrived. He is amusing, and makes himself at home here. I have my instructions from CATO. The weather is atrociously bad; the Queen is wearing the Frog again and begins to look her age. So do I, she says, but still she dances with me. A thousand adorations to the Queen Your Mother.

> *Ever yr faithful and obedient servant, M. de C. de M.*

— Michel de Castelnau Sieur de Mauvissière, French Ambassador in England, to King Henri III of France, March 1583.

⊤

What's this? Tom's put the gallows mark on CATO:
— *Who's CATO, eh? Who is it, Tom?*
— *Francis Throckmorton, my lord. A traitor.*

Good Tom! Clever lad! There he sits, small and hunched, little, blond, pocky Tom. Cipher cipher cipher — all day. But Throckmorton, nephew of Sir Nicholas! Wait till the Queen's Majesty hears of this. I'd love to have her say, "Another

Francis'' again. This one's a Catholic, this Francis — alike the other....

— *No arrests now, Tom. This one sits through the summer.*
— *He is being followed, my lord.*
— *And SHAMSHIEL, Tom, who's that? Cipher cipher like a little gnome. Tom?*
— *I heard you, my lord.*
— *Well,·Tom; who is it?*
— *Yourself, my lord.*
— *Hah! That's good, Tom. Very good. And HERMES?*
— *This Italiano Nolano, my lord. A magician ....*

So that's it! That's what Henry meant. When Catholics fall out with the Church of Rome, no religion's good enough for them. A wizard, eh; friend of Dee's no doubt. Well then, magic must be matched with magic.

— *Have him watched, Tom.*
— *Already done, my lord.*
— *Oh, Tom, what would I do without thee?*
— *You would manage, Sir Francis.*

An occult connection: the Italian and the French. I met this Doctor Jordano Bruno Nolano *etc* at court yesterday, where he was with Sidney, Greville and a host of lesser wits. In appearance, he is meagre; in conversation, skittish — though he would speak not a word of English. "A word with you, sir," says I, and he, in great confusion, turning aside from Sir Philip, with whom he was engaged in some cosmic flippancy: *"Momento."* To me! "He finds your tongue barbarous, Sir Francis," says Sir Philip. *Your* tongue, as if it were not his own too! "Is it some plot you fear, Lord Secretary?" says Greville. "But, God save you, sir, you look as if you are in some pain." The fop! "A mere trifle, sir. It is England that God needs to save." That made him cock his head. "And you, sir," says I to Sidney, "ask this gentleman what brings him to England, and do not flower your speech. Ask him plainly, without ornamentations." Poet he may be, but the Queen dislikes his family: "You are impertinent, Sir Francis, to interrupt our private conversation." Bold!

"Ask him yourself," says he, knowing that my skill in the language is not as perfect as the world would wish, "and we'll listen." Bolder! "Sir," says I, "then I shall be pertinent. Ask him now or the Queen will not love you." "God save Her Majesty!" says he. "I will translate, my lord."

Which, being done, the Nolan declares his mission is diplomatic. Hah! His faith, he says, is Roman, though he is excommunicate. As I thought! On this account therefore he does not prefer the Italian more than the Briton, the male more than the female, the mitred head more than the crowned head, the circumcised more than the uncircumcised, *etc*, but, as an approved and honourably received philosopher (whose genius the noble everywhere applaud), knows only the culture of the mind and of the soul. This copious advertisement over, he continues speaking like a book, saying that his master, the French King, who has ever admired the English for their toleration in questions of religion, that this same Henri, noblest of all the noble Valois (Puff!), is a lover of peace, tranquillity and harmony (Puff! puff! puff!). The civil wars besetting France are not the King's doing, he who trembles at the noisy uproar of martial instruments, but the work of false, traitorous, unchristian men. Blessed are the peacemakers! In vain shall the French rebels despoil the coasts of others. Blessed are the pure in heart! Let these rebels attempt the vacant throne of Portugal and be solicitous over the Dutch Provinces, but they shall not bloody the earth of France. The meek shall inherit the earth! (Agreed: with the same noisy uproar of martial instruments which makes His Majesty tremble in his silk stockings.) *All* that the King desires is peace, peace, eternal peace. That, and English assistance against Henri Duke of Guise and the Catholic League — strange, since he has put himself at the head of the League and is Guise's temporal lord. "Tell him," says I to Sidney, "that the King can put his own house in order. The French can keep their lovers' wars." Then up sidles Mauvissière, the Scots lady's friend, and embraces the Nolan with a fine to-do. "How do you like my guest, Sir Francis?" says he. "As I like my game," says I, "hung." And he, "A word in your ear," wanting to know of these damned puddle dogs with which His mad Majesty is much obsessed of late. "And them too," says I, "let him keep his puddle dogs, I care not for them." Next, Mendoza hoves into view, all streamers and gallants to the wind, a bloated galleon of a man. "Thir Franthith, a pleathant day to you." The devil take them! I left them to discourse unintelligibly in their tongues.

Here's treason and witchcraft, France and Spain, mixed in one man — an Italian! "He is a philosopher," Sidney says. A philosopher! So am I, of men not stars. Astrological doctors were in short supply that night they leached the Huguenots in Paris. What would the Nolan have done then but cry, 'Oh peace! peace! No killing now, the stars forbid it. Tomorrow we murder with Mars in Scorpio. Tonight we dance.' The Queen forgets her friend, forgets the past. Ever since the pocky frog Alençon and his ape Simier came to court, she has looked too kindly on all manner of foreigners. But how soon, how soon he has gained her presence. Not a month has gone by and she is very vain about her Italian, the language and the man. Amphititre, he calls her. Amphititre! I should get me yellow legs and scrape up a flourish or two, beg a million pardons when I fart and kiss the air most courteously. Domestic traitors we have enough of without this foreign wizard; a glut of sorcerers without this importation. Throckmorton visits the French Embassy by night. Mauvissière intends something; Mendoza too. I have the Frenchman's letters from the Scots bitch, and his secretary is mine corrupted. Hah! Soon, soon, I'll tell the Queen. But not yet, not yet. It is Mauvissière's letters to Mary that I must have. He is to write on paper dipped in alum, or between the lines of books, using every fourth page and marking them with green strings; cut the cork from the heels of slippers and place his letters in the hollow, or else he is to write on cloth measured an odd half-yard to distinguish the piece. I see the pattern. Still the Queen dreams of a French marriage and is distracted while Mary plots with France and Spain; still she mopes after her pocky frog and dares nothing to offend his brother Henri, the King who sent the Nolan here as Alençon's pander. Even the other day I heard her ask him, "How is it with my lord Francis?" And the Nolan, artful, concupiscent: "The Duke intends some valiant exploit in Holland." Long may he intend. It will be the death of him. Was it for this that Stubbs lost his hand, the hand most cruelly cut off for writing against the Valois Duke? Is it peace the Nolan wants, peace and a marriage with France that would make Elizabeth and Mary widowed sisters in more than titles? Let him change the stars around first, mine is a more earthly craft. Therefore have I written to this adulteress Mary, assuring her of my undying friendship. Undying? Unto death, God willing hers. I'll soon pluck her feathers, crop her neck at the head's line — a fit exchange for Old Stubbs's hand. A polled chicken dances merrily. Dance one, dance all to the same tune.

Conspiracy! Wars, and rumours of wars! Alarums unto nations! And now a wondrous comet arcs over London, the firmament illumined in its baleful glare. Throckmorton a proven traitor, and with Spain not France. And to think we discovered him by chance.

I was to Richmond today to see the Queen. She commands festivals and banquets in the Nolan's honour, puts on trumpery and dresses fit to kill. She says it's for Alasco, the visiting Polish Prince, but I know better. It's the Italian that charms her. "You are jealous, Sir Francis," she says like a winsome girl; then asks if I will bend a knee with her, well knowing that I am not the dancing kind. Frippery! She is deceived by this Nolan; neglects the danger. "I have come on serious business, Madam," says I. "My mood is light," says she. I tell her of the plot, the list of conspirators, the points of landing. "Then wait, Sir Francis," says she. "Wait, watch, listen." I remind her of the awful portent in the sky. "Have you grown sky struck?" says she. "Giordano says these things are natural." Giordano, Giordano it is now! "Madam," says I, "my lady of the Scots, this—"

"Speak not of her!" cries the Queen's Majesty. "Your black presence here, sir, spoils our festival." Now she walks away as pretty as you please and stands by the great window overlooking the river. Next she turns to face me. "As you wish, Sir Secretary," she says. "*Jacta est alea*. The dice are thrown, Francis." I make a very low bow. "Return to London!" she cries. "You have your work to do...."

And she was smiling, the Queen was. Sometimes I am afraid of her. She is twice as clever as her father, twice as clever as a King.

Here's Tom, and in a hurry....

T

The court hums with the news of the Nolan's brave deeds. All the wits are agog. He publishes books here and dedicates them to the Lord of Mauvissière, citing his protection against our laws of censorship. Fantastic dialogues they are, and would be incomprehensible even if written in English. He writes of a moral topography through which, as he takes his way, he looks about him with the penetrating eyes of Lynceus (he means the lynx), not lingering the while, so he writes, but contemplating the great structures of the universe and seeming to trip over every tiny thing, every stone and stumbling block. What does it mean: a lynx stumbling? He imitates the painter (it is a conceit of Horace, I recognize that) but such a painter, he says, who, not satisfied with confining himself to a *simple* picture, puts in stones, mountains, trees, springs, rivers, hills, in order to fill the canvas and bring his art into conformity with nature. His art! Here he will show you a royal palace, there a wood, there a strip of sky, and from time to time a bird, a boar, a stag, an ass, a horse, of which animals, so he writes, it suffices to show the head only, or a horn, or a part of their hind quarters, or an ear .... I can make neither head nor tail of it! Here he says that men are moles who may not gaze on the lights of heaven but are destined to dwell in the infernal circles of Pluto's dark prison-house. But he himself, so he claims, is destined to lead them into the light of day, the moles.

It makes no sense to me, not one jot or tittle. Is he mad? O
is he hiding something: is it a code? The man is an enthusiast
but for what cause? Here's Tom again. Will he enlighten me?

— *Master Phelippes, will you lead me into the light of day*
Enlighten me, Tom. I am a Secretary Mole....

— *Better than a Spanish Worm, my lord. Master Norton has pu*
Throckmorton to the rack.

— *Oh-oh. And?*

— *Chi a perso la fede, a perso l'honore, he said. Faith broken*
honour lost. He complained bitterly, my lord, that he had
betrayed the secrets of her who was the most dearest thing to
him in the world. And he asked to die, my lord.

— *We'll grant him that, Tom. Next year. Or whenever. Do you*
ever think, Tom, that because of the great love we bear the
Queen we go too far?

— *My lord?*

— *Are we cruel, do you think?*

— *He is a traitor, Sir Francis.*

A traitor, why that he is. It is written in the heavens. Wha
makes men act: is it chance or design? Even the Nolan canno
answer that. They say he is to Oxford where he'll make himsel
invisible to entertain the doctors. Well then, I'll have him in
visibly followed there. The mole will match the wizard any day
Whatever his purpose, whatever he wants, I'll find out — and
not by magic.

T

Michel de Castelnau de Mauvissière, the French Ambassador.

Paris, January 1592

Sir Francis neglected the obvious course. He could have asked,
though I do not think he would have believed the answer.

It was at Toulouse in the year of 1580 that King Henri first

70

came across Giordano. The Nolan was then in his thirty-second year, having fled Geneva where he'd been imprisoned briefly — the usual thing. His tactlessness was quite ecumenical in spirit, yet for once Giordano was the accuser rather than the accused, a part not to his liking and one that he played, indeed, with contrary effects. He had brought several charges of heresy against Antoine de la Faye, one of the divines there, and not until he dropped them was he released. He was lucky to escape so lightly, something which doubtless saddened him. In later years, he would often say of himself that he cried where other men laughed and laughed where they cried — his only consistent principle in an otherwise inconsistent life.

He was lecturing at the University when the King arrived in Toulouse. Giordano had published a treatise on the *Sphere* of Sacrobosco, a magical work, and he took care to see that the King received a copy. All the world was aware of Henri's fondness for the arcane, a fondness generally attributed to his mother, who, with her penchant for dwarves and monkeys, also dabbled in magic. It was no emulation of Queen Catherine that drove Henri to employ magicians in the affairs of state. The King hated his mother, yet she dominated him. Being a man — of sorts — he resented this maternal control, which he could only ascribe to witchcraft. Hence the use of sorcerers and the like, for the King was continually casting about for an antidote. More sorcerers.

The King had gone into the provinces to court Henri of Navarre, the Queen Mother having decided that Bartholomew's Eve was a lamentable error and the death of some four or five thousand souls an accident of state. In one of those shuddering alterations of course, France was again put about, tacking before the impending storm of renewed civil war, The new policy Henri inaugurated by dancing. He danced in Paris and he danced in Lyons, once for four days without stopping, His Royal Person dressed in a doublet of mulberry satin, with stockings and a cloak of the same colour, the cloak being very much slashed in the body, its folds set in white and scarlet, and the King himself decked out in ribbons and bracelets of coral.

Wherever he went, Henri danced, accompanied with a new breed of courtiers, the Knights of Sodom the people dubbed them, their hair crimped and curled, and their heads sitting on ruffs like the head of John the Baptist on the platter. There was foolishness in this, but wisdom also. The Knights could claim no lineage except yesterday's and owed their titles to Henri alone. As for the dancing and ribaldry, this led the King's enemies to declare him dissolute, and when, as was his wont, he would occasionally join the bands of flagellants and scourge himself for his sins, this led them to declare him not only dissolute but mad.

He was sane enough to see in Giordano a man of ability and potential use. The Nolan was quickly elevated from the obscure depths of a provincial professorship to the starry heights of a court magician. As Bion says, it was not that he had acquired a fortune; the fortune had acquired him. The King loved his Magus and showered him with favours, in return for which it was said that he would call down the stars against Guise and Navarre, utterly confounding them — as who would not, could they but work such a miracle.

These wonders I heard of distantly, having had charge of those star-crossed and tear-stained negotiations to marry the King's brother to Elizabeth *R*, a lady who could act any part she pleased. I had been in England for about eight years, time enough to gain a fair knowledge of the land and its people, and I was more than surprised when I learned that Henri, as a special mark of his favour, was sending his magician into a country whose natives have long regarded aliens with a mixture of superstitious horror and misplaced pity.

What purpose could this serve, other than to increase the already formidable confusions attending the King's policy? Henri's course had never seemed very certain. On the one hand, religion and familial ties bade him support the Scottish Queen, a policy identical with Spain's. His throne depended on no less. Yet on the other hand, and for precisely the same reason, he needed English help against Spain and the Duke of Guise. The Duke coveted the crown more than anything else in the world, unless it was the Catholic Faith, which had taught him obedience, if not to the King, then to a higher law. Navarre, too, could claim the light of inner justification that the reformed religion gave to rebellion.

Giordano played his part well, so well indeed that I wondered if he knew what he was doing. In the summer of his first year in England, the Queen commanded a series of entertainments to be held in honour of the visiting Polish Prince, Albert Laski. In addition to the usual festivities, which suited the Nolan well enough, he was to engage in debate with the learned doctors of Oxford, who had worked themselves into a furious controversy over the new astronomy. For several months he busied himself in writing and preparation. He was confident of victory; right was on his side, he said, and although he had a low opinion of his opponents, at least they had ears to listen with. They were not stones, he said, but Englishmen. Eloquence and logic would prevail — his eloquence and his logic. His reception at court had proven his influence. The Queen admired him for his wit and learning, and so would the doctors. It was a mistake to underestimate one's own persuasiveness. Not for him the ridiculous error of false modesty. His lamp would never be hidden under a bushel, no, not in a thousand years.

I was content to observe him and listen to his fondest hopes. "It will be so, Michel," he said. "It *will*." And I said that it would.

Giordano loved contradictions — of his own making. If another contradicted him, he liked it not at all. Personally, I feared a debacle.

It was a royal cavalcade that rode out of London that summer of 1583. Laski journeyed with us, and Giordano, who relished the company of princes, entertained him with pithy prognostications on the fate of the Oxonian doctors....

Giordano began his address with a cannonade against the modern university, praising the old school for its metaphysics and damning the new for its Ciceronian eloquence, the language of hypocrites and frauds. The speech of ordinary folk was worth more than all their learned phrases, he declared, lambasting the doctors as an idle set of pedants who lived perniciously off the works of others, parasites, bloodsuckers grown bloated and dull.

Having failed in the first art of an orator, which is to enlist the sympathy of his audience, Giordano turned to the ostensible subject of his address, Nicholas Copernicus. According to the Nolan, this great astronomer represented the divinely ordained appearance of that dawn which was to precede the full sunrise of the ancient and true philosophy, for so long buried in the dark caverns of blind and envious ignorance. Alas, Copernicus was only the false dawn, whereas he (Giordano) was the sun in the fullness of all his glory, arisen to chase the clouds from out the English sky. (Of all impossibilities the most impossible!) What was Copernicus but a mathematician? A calculator? A clerk who knew not the real meaning of his scribblings? While we should not misjudge him, because of some omissions in his work, as being on the same level as the vulgar herd, swayed hither and thither by brutal superstition (here Giordano frowned at the doctors, leaving them in no doubt of whom he spoke) these same omissions were serious in scope and consequence and must be overlooked on account of our natural sympathy for natural genius — a genius untutored in the art of thaumaturgical mysteries. "The astronomer," Giordano announced, "did not penetrate deeply enough into the mysteries of nature, did not succeed in disentangling all the difficulties on the way, and hence he failed to free himself and those coming after him from the pursuit of vapid enquiries and groundless pursuits...."

Giordano now paused for breath. Then this brave disentangler astonished the good doctors by stripping up his sleeves like a juggler, and, leaping from the platform, continued his speech by wandering up and down the rows of the audience, his arms windmilling, his legs skipping and capering. "And now," he asked, pressing his arms to the back of his head, "what would I say concerning the Nolan? Perhaps it does not become me to praise him," he averred modestly, "since he is so near to me, as near indeed as I am to myself. Yet no *reasonable* man would reprove me, for it is sometimes not only convenient but ecessary to speak well of oneself."

Proof of this was quickly forthcoming. If in days of old, 'iphys, who invented the first ship and sailed across the seas 'ith the Argonauts, was praised for his deeds; if in our day :olumbus was honoured, then what should be said of the Jolan, who had liberated the spirit of man and had shown him he way to the stars?

What should be said of him would soon become apparent, iut for the moment he was allowed to continue. "The man who ongs to know God," said Giordano, "must first study nature. 'or just as the divinity descends to nature, so there is an ascent nade to the divinity through nature." This scale he ran through irettily enough, diminuendo and crescendo, reminding his isteners of that great chain of being in which all nature is iound. A consideration of scale in the animal and vegetable :ingdoms, he said, would readily illustrate his point: crows, :ocks and crocodiles; onions, daffodils and turnips — *exempli ;ratia*. Everybody knew that owls hoot, horses whinny, wolves iowl; few were acquainted with the undoubted fact that these lifferent creatures represented different spirits and powers. All hings breathed divinity, even turnips. Thus crocodiles, cocks, iunflowers and turnips should never be worshipped for hemselves, but for the gods and divinities in them. One could hink of the sun, for example, as being in a crocus, a cock, or a laffodil. As for Mars, that maleficent planet, it could be found in a scorpion, a viper, or a toad, nay even in an onion or a clove of garlic.

Some of the doctors turned up their noses at this stew, others hooted, and one dignified greybeard was sufficiently moved to raise himself up on his hind legs and squawk, "Marsilius Ficinus!" at the Nolan: "This is from a book of his!" Others now took up the cry, one shouting, "I remember it myself!" another, "Me too!" while the first swore that he would go to his study and fetch the book.

"You see then," said Giordano, much put out, "how one simple divinity, one fecund nature, mother and preserver of the universe, shines forth in diverse subjects...."

"Garlic!" cried one.

"Onions!" another.

"Therefore," it was a very angry Nolan who spoke now "each manifestation of the divinity is propitiated with suitable rites, is honoured and cultivated in so far as we seek favour from it...."

"From a cockerel," cried a third to his fellows' great delight, "he wants eggs from a cockerel. Cock-a-doodle-do!"

"Which art," said Giordano, frowning horribly, "is known as Magia...."

There came a shout of "Copernicus is an ass!" and it was all over for the Nolan. Reason, if nothing else, dictated his immediate retirement from the field of honour, and with a cry of "Pedants!" and further scowls, he took his leave to a chorus of crows and whinnies, boos and jeers.

Oddly enough, he thought he had scored a singular triumph. And in one sense he had. If Sir Francis Walsingham's spies were in that audience, as doubtless they were, their honest reports could not have failed to convince him that Giordano was a man to be reckoned with. Hatred distracts, and Sir Francis hated anything smacking of sorcery. I welcomed any opportunity at that time to divert the Secretary from my dealings with the Scottish Queen. A forlorn hope, of course, for *Shamshiel* was single-minded to the point of mania.

On our return to London, we had agreed to stop in Mortlake at the house of Doctor John Dee. Prince Albert was anxious to meet the Magus who was then fresh from his triumphant invention of an aerial crab. The doctor, who was a tall, rosy-faced, white-bearded man (being in his fifty-sixth year), was already something of a legendary figure. He was the Queen's astrologer, physician, dentist, and sometime buyer of horse; he was a mathematician and geographer, whose studies had recently led England to adopt the Gregorian calendar. Anything old and everything new was of interest to him, and his house had several times been wrecked by the mob, who supposed him to be the Fiend's confederate.

Giordano affected some diffidence towards the meeting, his mood having changed for the worse after his triumph in Oxford; and I could easily have given the visit a miss (the magician was no stranger at court), except for the reputation of Sir John's newly acquired assistant, the incorrigibly crooked wizard, Edward Kelley.

Sir John's apartments were littered with skulls and bones like a graveyard after an earthquake. He welcomed us profusely, especially the Prince, whom he had met on his travels in the east, and with his customary good humour apologized for the absence of his assistant. Kelley at length arrived, an intriguing specimen of his kind. This was partly owing to the novelty of his appearance (he had come straight from some combustible disaster which coincided with our arrival, so that the house reeked of sulphur and the assistant's robes were in tatters, his face coloured green and black, matching the skull cap he wore to conceal the stubs of his ears — they had been removed as a punishment for digging up the dead); and partly it was because I was charmed by the facility of his conversation. Through the use of *ars sigillorum*, various signs and numbers, the major and minor arts, practical and speculative Cabala, he was, he explained, very conversant with demons and nightly shades, phenomena that led him into a fluent discourse concerning the vanity of human life and the worthlessness of earthly things. Life was all suffering, he said, and gave his latest experiment as an example of this stoic precept. It was in aid of a rejected suitor, for whom the assistant had made a necklace of human teeth and fingernails, as well as a jacket from the skin of a corpse. Thus attired, the suitor had departed even as we arrived, again to pledge his troth, though with what effect — in view of the operation's explosive termination — the assistant wisely declined to say.

"But why," Prince Albert enquired, "this extraordinary dress?"

"Ah," said Kelley, fixing himself limpet-like on the Prince's attention, "to inhibit the deathly influence in his love...."

Laski also expressed an interest in the angel Michael, for he had heard that Kelley was on equitable terms with the Prince of Light as well as the lesser angels. "Sabathiel!" exclaimed the assistant, hurling up his hands. "Deliverer of the faithful Prince of the Presence and Ruler of the Fourth Heaven, whose wings are the colour of green emerald and who is covered with saffron hairs, each of them containing a million faces and mouths and as many tongues, every one of them imploring the mercy of God."

"So they should," said Giordano sourly.

He was in a vile temper and begged to be excused, making some reference to the evil smell in the house. Sir John suggested a walk by the river, and Giordano left. He did not reappear for the rest of the afternoon. Afterwards, when I asked him where he'd been, his reply was quite mischievous. "To see the angel Michael," he said, "who is not what you think." That was all I heard of the matter until many months later.

Meanwhile, Edward Kelley, having proven his familiarity with the destroyer of Babylon and the conquerer of Satan, announced that the angel, who was also the slayer of the dragon, was exceedingly difficult to conjure, and required, besides great skill on the part of the operator, and at no small risk to his person, copious sums of gold.

"In return for which," he assured us, "this angel brings the gift of patience."

At his best, Giordano could tell a story as well as any man. On Ash Wednesday night in the year 1584, Sir Fulke Greville and Sir Philip Sidney dined in our company at the embassy. The conversation was rare and ingenious and turned to many things on the far side of paradise.

Greville it was who raised the subject of angels. What sex were they, he wanted to know.

Giordano delighted the company by pretending that, when he was a child on the slopes of Mount Vesuvius, he had encountered vast numbers of angels, swarming like bees.

"But as to their sex," he said, "they are neuter, though being spiritual creatures they can appear in whatever form they please. For example, when I was at Mortlake I saw the angel Michael. She was very pretty...."

"She?" said Sir Philip.

"As delectable a Thames nymph as could be imagined," said Giordano. "And quite naked."

"How divine!" said Greville.

"Ah yes, an angel needs no clothes," said Giordano. "She showed me her wings," he added, describing them with a sweep of both hands. "They were — transcendental."

"And did you talk?" Sir Philip asked.

Giordano shook his head sadly. "I told her I was Gabriel, but she knew no Latin and did not understand me. Ourselves we made a language," he sighed, "and communed perfectly together."

"They say the angel is greedy," Greville mused.

"Not for gold," said Giordano. "She is too natural. But a little might help — at the beginning of the operation."

Many of the court bloods fell into making the pilgrimage to Mortlake. Kelley's conjurations soon became the talk of the town and the angelic doctor prospered. I do not think he ever knew why.

The troubles the Nolan encountered at Oxford, though not at Mortlake, followed him to the capital. Once, on his way to Greville's house, he was attacked by a mob in the Strand and pelted with mud. Another time, a deputation of citizens besieged the embassy, convinced that it was the source of accursed practices, of which papistry was the very least evil.

In this and other events, the hand of Sir Francis Walsingham was clearly discernible....

The island realm was in an unsettled condition. War seemed probable with Spain over the Netherlands; the Enterprise of England (the Great Armada itself) had been announced, and the Secretary of State found it necessary to redouble his meticulous efforts to bring Mary to the block. In the summer of 1585, he began to sniff out the conspiracy that would prove her final undoing. A group of Catholic gentlemen, led by Sir Anthony Babington and acting under the instigation of the priest,

John Ballard, planned to assassinate the Queen and her principal advisers. The Duke of Parma was to land an army in the north; the Catholic nobles would join him, and Mary would be liberated and set on the throne as a Spanish puppet.

Since the time of the Throckmorton plot, two years previously, I'd been holding certain of Mary's letters from her Paris representative, a man called Morgan. The letters, which I'd had copied and deciphered, were dangerously compromising. An ingenious system, however, was contrived to convey Mary's correspondence to Chartley, whither she had been transferred in December of that year, under the vigilant eye of Sir Amys Paulet.

Another priest, one Gilbert Gifford, contacted the embassy, was given the letters, and in turn gave them to a brewer from Burton whose job it was to supply Chartley with its ale. . . .

Ingenious though it was, the system was flawed. It is a valuable maxim that a priest who meddles in the business of this world is not to be trusted. Gifford was a traitor, with what consequence the world knows. Babington and his fellows were arrested, racked, broken, disembowelled and quartered. Sir Francis had all the evidence he needed for his final coup against Mary, and for a time there was not a crossroads in London without its crop of gibbet carrion.

Fortunately for my reputation, I was in no way responsible for this bungled matter of the letters in the ale casks. In October of 1585, I was recalled and given instructions to take Giordano with me. The Pope had declared Henri of Navarre a heretic; Paris was crowded with armed Guisards, and King Henri, or rather his mother, had undertaken yet another change of course.

It was a grey and grizzly morning when we stood on the quayside at Dover, watching our vessel being loaded. Giordano threw his cloak about him, shuddered, and declared that he had no stomach for the voyage. "Which means?" I asked, for I did not think it was the crossing he feared. "Which means," he replied cheerfully enough, "that there will be trouble — in Paris, if not before. You and I will have to find new friends, Michel. I do not think the King is so well disposed to us as he used to be.''

I smiled, though as it happened his remarks could not have been more accurate, and the crossing itself presaged what was to come: for France, years of disaster; for Giordano, flight; for myself, a place in the shade — until that most puissant of monarchs, Henri of Navarre, came to mount the throne of war-weary France.

We were about half the seas over when we ran foul of an English privateer, out scavenging from Plymouth. Our master tried outrunning her before the wind, but she was too quick for us and we were boarded. Happily, or so I thought, our visitors did not think my papers worthy of attention and contented themselves with the usual prizes of fortune. "You see," said Giordano, who was much amused by this adventure, "our little ship is France. . . ."

Not until the trial and execution of the Scottish Queen did I discover why my papers were of no interest to those English privateers. *Shamshiel* had been reading them for the last ten years, and the incident of the crossing was his last farewell, a reminder of sorts that he had bested me. But I bear him no ill will, Sir Francis.

The news of Mary's death was pleasurably received by both the Protestant and Catholic factions in France — the Huguenots because they welcomed the end of a wicked woman; the Guisards because they had a spotless martyr. Guise's sister said the execution had done more for the True Faith that all her brother's armies, which was true enough. She had a priest put up a poster (in the Cemetery of the Innocents) depicting Mary's final moments and the deaths of all unfortunates from time immemorial. A gruesome thing it was too, full of stranglings, roastings, eviscerations, and suchlike. The canaille loved it, so much so that Henri feared to act. For two weeks he let it stand, then had it ripped down, arresting some of the priestly party. Too late, of course. The mob howled desecration and sounded the tocsin, flocking to the cemetery which they made into a shrine of armed might.

I could see then that the dagger was not far off. There were three kings for France that year, three Henris, and only one to call the crown his own.

Giordano busied himself at the university, calling the doctors together to hear him expound some one hundred and twenty articles against Aristotle and the Peripatetics. I did not attend these lectures, for I expected a repetition of the Oxford scandal, and it was Jacopo Corbinelli, another Italian in Paris and a man very close to the King, who told me of them. The Nolan argued his case with accustomed vigour, daring the doctors to attack him and defend the Greek. When none replied he called on them in an even louder voice. Finally, a young scholar got up to join the debate, saying that his elders had not bothered to refute Giordano because they did not deem him worthy of a reply. The Nolan listened to this from a door leading to the garden — evidently he had learned the value of discretion — and the next day, when he was himself to speak again, he did not reappear.

He had gone to Germany. "The Nolan fears the tumults," said Corbinelli, "and thinks that he has offended Guise."

The King heard of Giordano's flight and sent for me at the Louvre. His Majesty was sprawled in the throne, surrounded by a worshipful company of puddle dogs, which he had adorned with all manner of silks and ribbons. One of the dogs, grey and pink about the muzzle, wore a little crown and had its jowls trimmed to resemble Navarre's whiskers. Another, a darker sort, was caparisoned with a small cassock and answered to the name of Guise. It was very curious to see these creatures totter on their back legs while their peers yapped encouragement. Curious and instructive. For the canine dance was an apt representation of the state of France, *un masque animal*, so to speak, which afforded some diversion from the cares of the merely human world. Yet here also was morality — and something of mortality. With what strutting similitude the dogs mimicked the lords of the earth, each step serving to emphasize their condition of fawning dependency.

But who was I to deny Henri so harmless a pleasure or to

moralize in the face of such witty frivolity? None but the King's creature myself, as ready for the dance as any of the four-legged kind.

"Guise dances well, your Majesty," said I.

"Navarre better," he replied.

Henri was playing with a yo-yo, a toy he'd introduced to court as an innovation, so that it was dangerous to be seen without one, for a time at least, and then after Guise's murder (the man, not the dog) it was dangerous to be seen with one. In his other hand, the King was holding a book. "I sent to Spain for this," he said, smiling. "Strange, but I do not understand it. My mother tells me it is rare...."

There was a certain malign delicacy to Henri's speech. The mention of the Spanish book was his way of referring to Guise, but it was impossible to say what he had in mind. Henri's intentions were, I thought, hidden even from himself. In a lesser man, this lack of self-knowledge might have stemmed from a failure of the intellect; in Henri's case, it was the result of too much intellect. His understanding of power, the power that was his by right, combined with his knowledge of his own peculiar dependence on his mother, produced in him a morbid degree of self-consciousness. An air of ineffable menace clung to him, and behind the brilliant show and panoply of state, there was a man more dangerous to himself than any of his rivals.

He was a sad and sorry King, too intelligent for the crown he wore.

Suddenly he spoke up. "Where's Bruno?" he said, and then: "I am a man with many enemies, a king. You, Michel, will stay with me, won't you?"

My compliance was unhesitating. Such, after all, is the prerogative of a King: to dismiss present friends and complain when they are gone.

During this time, Henri was preoccupied with thoughts of death — his own and others. At his instigation there came a renowned preacher to court, who preached mightily on the subject, enquiring whether there were any of the assembled lords and ladies who might remain unmoved at the spectacle of a man's destruction, or fail to tremble when confronted with the cold sweat and foam of death. If there were any here, let them step forward. "Oh, no," said Henri, attired resplendently in a costume of the darkest crimson, yo-yo to match, "there are none."

The King had obviously designed to steal the preacher's thunder. A tight smile was engraved on Henri's lips, and, except for the sinuous motion of his hand, which controlled the yo-yo as if he had the world on a string, he kept himself very still and attentive, the incessant whir of the toy accompanying the preacher's dolorous tones.

Discomforted by this reception, the preacher asked uneasily that we get down into the grave ourselves and become spectators of what takes place there. "Even," as he put it, "to the most beautiful person in the world. What a prodigious quantity of worms we would see there! Some eating the eyes, others twisting in the mouth or issuing from the nostrils, still others coming and going out of the opened chest, while the hair drops from the head, and the nose, lips and cheeks fall piecemeal away, leaving no more than a dunghill, a cesspool, a noxious heap of decay and corruption!"

"Very pretty," said Henri, a titter running round the court, and the words, "pretty, ah pretty!" falling from everybody's lips like the preacher's worms. "And is it so," said the King coldly, "is it so even with one, who, *in life*, is a dunghill and a cesspool?"

I do not know if Guise heard of this. Evidently not, for in May of 1588, forbidden to come to Paris, the Duke arrived with a mere nine of his followers and paraded himself through the streets. In no time at all he had thirty thousand at his heels and forced himself on the King at the Louvre, where, mocking and bowing, he claimed that he had disobeyed the royal command for the greater good of France.

Henri took himself off in a rage to Blois, and the Duke occupied the capital, making himself King of Paris. The Pope said he was a reckless fool for putting himself in the hands of a king he had insulted, and that Henri was a coward for letting him go.

But then His Holiness could afford the luxury of idle comment.

At Blois the King kept aloof from the court and planned his revenge. Once or twice he sent for me, asking if I'd heard from Giordano. Henri missed the Nolan and was sorry he had seen fit to leave France.

"Poor France," he said. "Poor King."

His mother, whose only solace now was in her dwarves who infested the palace like cockroaches, was dying and feared for the realm. "Witchcraft cannot help her now," said the King. "All physic is impotent against death."

Queen Catherine had dreamed a strange dream of a city in the sun ruled by a wise and powerful king. No priest, doctor or wizard would say what it meant, and I would do the King and his mother a great favour if I could persuade the Nolan to return.

"He was our friend," said Henri, "as you are, Michel. For all the world loves a King."

Two days before Christmas, Henri summoned Guise and his Cardinal brother to Blois for a Council meeting. As the Duke climbed the stairs to the chamber, the guard closed ranks behind him, blocking his line of retreat.

Henri's personal bodyguard was waiting for him. The Duke reached the door of the King's bedchamber, and finding it locked, turned to meet his assassins. The old Queen, who was dying in the room above, heard the noise of the brief struggle, and, it is said, cried out in her anguish. Her son had finally broken the maternal spell. . . .

When he saw Guise's murdered body, Henri bit his thumb and laughed. "How tall he is," he said, making a circle of the thumb and forefinger, "much taller than in life." Then he fell to lecturing the corpse, explaining why the murder was both just and necessary.

"For the greater good of France," he said.

The next day, he had the Cardinal murdered. With his usual sense of timing, the King said he thought it was fit that one so close to God should die on the Eve of Christ's Nativity.

With martyrs in such a plentiful supply, the Guisards needed no excuse to avenge old bones with fresh blood. The city rose again, following the example of the little children, who, led on by their curés, marched in torchlight procession, halting every now and then to throw down their torches with cries of, "So may God quench the House of Valois!" — and similar professions of Christian zeal.

Threatened with excommunication for the Cardinal's murder, Henri decided he might as well be hanged for a dog as for a knave and hurried to join Navarre. I followed him, faithful after my fashion to the end. It came one fine August evening in the year of 1589. A Dominican friar arrived in the camp, claiming that he had a message for the King — from God. Why Henri agreed to see him I do not know. Perhaps it was because he belonged to the same Order as Giordano: perhaps in his own way the King thought that this was Giordano, returned at the thirteenth hour. Nor do I know if he ever understood the friar's message. The knife flashed once, twice, and Henri fell, mortally wounded.

He lived to see the dawn, and before he died recognized Navarre as his successor.

Le Roi est mort! Vive le Roi! The ritual cry sounded, closing one reign and inaugurating another. I joined in, my voice suitably hesitant on account of its late service to the late King. I need not have worried. His new Majesty was a very accommodating man.

The scene was not lacking in sentiment. As the King stepped forth to receive our sincere expressions of loyalty, a lark and its mate rose from the hedgerow and spiralled heavenwards, the earth of France seeming to turn under their most melodious flight. "Michel de Castelnau," I said to myself, "you are alive." A redundant thought, even a little incautious. . . .

Later that day, the King very courteously requested my presence. He was, he declared, anxious to secure the services of a certain Italian.

"You know the man I mean," he said.

It was the one favour I could not grant him. Giordano and

Henri never met, although they both expected the world of each other. Perhaps that is why.

I am growing old and a little tired. Today there was dancing in the streets instead of killing. New Year's Day, the beginning of my seventy-third year under God's constantly inconstant heaven. Has it really been so long? It seems only yesterday since we were riding hard to Oxford, and yesterday itself years away.

My heart gives me some trouble. Now and then, a little pain. It has been a good life, and I have lived it as if there were no other.

Who knows?

IV

*With a goose quill and a few sheets of paper I
mock the universe.*

— Aretino

Rome, April 1600

In the city of the wolf, Kaspar Schopp, leaving the Church of
San Andrea, emerges from hallowed gloom into the light of day.
Beneath him a broad expanse of steps sweeps down into the
piazza. A stage set for heroes, it is in fact a fishmarket, God's
cupola soaring over the huddled dwellings of the bankside, its
bulk laying claim to a heaven built on earth. He shudders, the
newly confessed Kaspar, oppressed by the redundancy of the
magnificent, turning and hurrying down the steps with the air of
one who has much to do, a man who will not be submerged in
the crowd below, nor lost in the flurry of the day.

Kaspar, en route to see his Cardinal friend, listens to the
buzz of the crowd. The Second Coming is imminently expected
in this year of grace, a century year; the price of vegetables has
unexpectedly declined; a two-headed calf has been born in
Ostia. The fishwives of Rome are talking of the Nolan; they,
who danced at his burning, now say he is alive. They say the
Pope has given him a red hat and made him apostolic secretary;
the Nolan *is* the Pope, and Clement has been thrown into the
dungeons of Sant'Angelo. Giordano, a new Saint John — how
else could he have escaped the baptism of fire? Giordano,
Christ, Antichrist — the Nolan.

In the fishmarket of the Piazza San Andrea, Kaspar bought a perch for the Cardinal of San Severina. Its dead fish-eye filmy, scales viridescent in the April sun, it looked none too appetizing on the slab, but Kaspar bought it all the same, watched, hands-on-hips by the *peschivendola,* who, vast, sleek, brown and smiling, stank like a beached whale too long out of the water.

"Good eating," she said, her smile seasoned with lechery, that yellow Roman light, filtering down from pagan hills, reverberating around the square.

His Eminence, overcome by the gift of the fish, called upon his secretary to remove it: "And, Bastiano, bring the Count of Claravelle my letter of introduction to Fra Ippolita Maria, will you?" His Eminence dispelled fish and secretary with a wave of his hand. "A perch, you say?" his nostrils quivered. "A very ripe fish."

"And a very ripe Archbishop too."

"Ah?"

"I visited the tomb, saw his effigy, and heard Lorenzo in hell. I think I was bewitched."

"All this in Venice, Kaspar?"

"In Rome they say the Nolan is still alive. These rumours. Not a day passes without—"

"Some new and even more incredible story," the Cardinal sighed. "And you, my friend, are doubtless anxious to find out who is responsible. So am I, Kaspar, so am I."

"Then you have no theory—?"

The Cardinal hinted at a shrug, a spare movement as if he begrudged the expenditure of energy on such a poor thing as a theory. "The other day in consistory," he began, "I spoke with Cardinal Bellarmine, who gave me to understand ... Ah, Bastiano...." The secretary returned with the letter, the envelope scabbed with the Cardinal's seal. "Fra Ippolita Maria, *magister generalis* of the Dominicans, or, failing him, Paul of Mirandola, Giordano's Vicar, who is still in Rome — worthy gentlemen both — may be of some assistance," San Severina continued. "I took the liberty of penning this letter in the hope that you might visit the Minerva. After all, it is not every day that the brethren prosecute one of their own, though after such a delay between the trial and execution of sentence you might find their memories of the case somewhat impaired. . . ."

"Fra Giovanni thought there was a reason for that delay," said Kaspar.

"Undoubtedly. There is a reason for everything."

"Fra Giovanni said that too."

"You would hardly expect anything else from a functionary of the Holy Office."

"Though it was Rome who burnt Giordano, not Venice. Fra Giovanni wondered at the timing," Kaspar lowered his voice; the secretary still lingered. "Did His Eminence Cardinal Bellarmine perhaps give a reason?"

"His Eminence said only that there were those in the Church who wished to keep the spirit of this Nolan alive."

"In the Church?"

The Cardinal's hand fluttered, Bastiano retreating with a flourish. "In the Holy See," rejoined the Cardinal of San Severina *sotto voce*: "In the *appartamento Vaticani*."

T

At the della Minerva Monastery, Kaspar, seated uncomfortably in an alcove, contemplated a fresco secco of hell, seven plutonic zones labelled for deadly sinners, Lucifer presiding, horned, satyrical, gleeful. Hypocrites, idolaters and infidels grovelled at his cloven feet while the fiery flames — *fumus igni* — devoured the *heretici*, who were tormented also by *demones puteus*, the demons of the pit. On the wall of the cloister facing, Paradise reserved the most sumptuous quarters for martyrs.

Which was Giordano? Kaspar wondered.

T

Am I to be kept here till I rot? Like the Cardinal's fish. By God I hope I do not stink so. What's a Cardinal but a fishwife in red robes, a gossipmonger? So the Pontiff's agents now are behind these rumours, it is the Pope who would keep the Nolan's spirit alive. Why? Because the Congregation made a mistake? Oh, pardon us, Holiness, we have fallibly burnt the wrong man.... No, no, it must be deeper. The Church, like Janus, looks both ways in time. How can a historian judge future effects of a present cause? For that needs divine wisdom. I do not know what to think. So many times — not once but a hundred, nay a thousand times a day — I affirm the undying truth of such and such, only to find it the next day as corrupt as my lord of San Severina's fish, growing the more putrid the longer it is held. Hence we must spice our stew with the herbs and condiments of dogma to make this rotten fish palatable, for, as Mocenigo writes, the truth itself is often the subtlest corrosive. But, with the Cardinal turned fishwife, I do not know what to think. What can *his* interest be? To cross Bellarmine and the Jesuits? The family Aldobrandini? Would San Severina be *Pontifex maximus*, using this fire to light the consistory's ballots? Who could imagine anything more ridiculous than man, this puny creature that would rend the cosmos from its true frame, calling himself lord and master of all he surveys; who gave him title, the letters-patent and deeds to the universe? None but himself. God, how my haunches ache! I wonder if the Nolan burns in hell?

T

"I see you're admiring the frescoes...." A young Friar, about Kaspar's own age, materialized from the courtyard. "They're after a figure of the Florentine, Cosmas Rossellias, from his *Thesaurus Artificiosae Memoriae*. The brethren have made the art of memory their own special study. Brother Jordanus was much taken with it."

"That's good," Kaspar rose like a ghost from his niche;

"I'd almost forgotten why I was here."

"I'm sorry," the Friar said, his eyes downcast. "Fra Ippolita sends you his regrets. The man you should see is Brother Gryphius."

"And where is he?"

"In Naples."

"Are you sure?" Kaspar injected a note of sarcasm into this question.

"As sure as I am of most things. And he is very willing to see you." Smiling broadly, as if he had played a huge joke at Kaspar's expense, the Dominican dipped into the folds of his robe and produced a small purse, which he gave to Kaspar. "Take this," he said, "and Brother Gryphius will know you by it."

Sorry, and not a little ashamed at his sarcasm, Kaspar opened the purse and found himself looking at a pearl. It was the same hue throughout, flawless, a vinous shade, the colour of deepest arterial blood.

"But it must be very valuable," said Kaspar.

"More than that, priceless," the other replied. "Take it and go to him now. You have a long journey ahead, and will need to rest first. The pearl will protect you, for it is the way and the truth. Take this, and may you go in peace, Master Schopp," said the Friar. Turning, he did not look back, and was soon lost, a shadow gliding among shadows in the cloisters.

In the evening when he had returned to his lodgings, Kaspar drew down an old volume of Isidore's. "Ostrea, Auster," he read the cryptic entry, "the oyster. Ostrinus — purple. Gryphius Simplicius."

That night Kaspar dreamed he saw a human heart on the Campo de'Fiori. It was still beating, pumping forth seemingly inexhaustible amounts of blood, blood guttering down the narrow streets of the bank to the Tiber, as Kaspar's dream filled to the vibrant rhythm of diastole and systole, the heart's measured lapses propounding the ageless imperative of life.

Thunder clouds gathered over Rome.

T

Of all natural creatures, the oyster doth think himself the most secure, the most comfortable, the most secret. The darkness of the living sea is his dwelling place. But for the pearl, his chancre, he is prized by men, and for the meat, his flesh, he is eaten by them. Yet God has endowed even this the humblest of His creatures with the longing for immortality. Often I have seen the oyster ripped open, his heart torn out and discarded for the pearl, the heart still beating many hours after death.

— Isidorus Hispalensis. De natura rerum.

An unfamiliar image: a fisherman with a blood red pearl in his hand — a sign of immortality.

— Corpus Hermeticum.

T

North of Naples we encountered a fearful storm and were almost driven on to the rocky shores off the Island of Ischia. The sky blackened, the waves white with foam, the whole world rent by lightning in which dreadful shapes appeared to beguile us. But when at last the tempest subsided, and the open sweep of the Bay and the Castle lay before us, we, who had lately stood in peril of our lives, rejoiced at our great good fortune. Nothing endures but change, as Heraclitus says. How soon we forget past tribulations in our present joy — Kaspar Schopp, to the Cardinal of San Severina, April 1600.

T

I found this Gryphius Simplicius living in a hovel above Pozzuoli — no Roman would have called it a pigsty, though a few swine were rooting around outside. We had met before, in the

Campo the day after the burning. It was this simple brother who had assured me that the Nolan was not the man they burnt; now he says he meant only that the Nolan was a changed man, as who wouldn't be after eight years in the dungeons. Brother Gryphius wanted to give me the pearl, but I would have none of it, for it had almost brought us to the bottom of the sea. Some sort of attractive influence; I have read of such things, but never until yesterday's storm believed them.

T

"He gave me the pearl at Lake Avernus," Brother Gryphius told Kaspar. "It had belonged to his mother. She was called Fraulissa, a very beautiful woman. The family name was Savolina. Fraulissa Savolina, a type more Greek than Italian — that's common around here. I tried to return the pearl," Brother Gryphius continued, "but they would not let me. Fra Ippolita went to see him towards the end — to offer him a less painful death. He refused, of course. On the day of the burning I couldn't get close enough to see him. The crowds ... " Fra Gryphius paused. "There were so many people. He always had a sense of theatre, you know," the brother added, almost apologetically. "I remember him as he was, that was all I meant to tell you. The man they burnt wasn't the man I remembered. After all, the last time I had seen him was after he had made up his mind to leave Italy. That was twenty-four years ago — your lifetime.... In Venice they showed me the instruments of torture. They said he'd confessed everything, but still they wanted to know more."

Kaspar detected a slightly sour taste in his mouth. His tongue probed at a back tooth and detached a sliver of mussel flesh. His gullet burned with a spasm of bile. Mussels, he decided, did not agree with him. No more than oysters.

"And you told them?" he prompted, knowing the answer.

The Friar was silent. After a while he asked if Kaspar had

read Raymond Lull. Kaspar shook his head, and managed to look shocked.

"A magician? Certainly not," he said.

"Giordano read the doctor *illuminatus* as a young man," Brother Gryphius continued complacently. "Also Agrippa, Ficino, Pico, and Albertus Magnus — as well as the Greeks, Anaximander, Anaxagoras, Pythagoras, and Heraclitus. Fragments, really. Aristotle he never liked because he thought him too literal-minded — a man who saw but did not believe what he saw."

"You call that literal-minded?" asked Kaspar.

"To a degree," Gryphius answered. "Giordano always wanted to look beyond appearances. Of course some things are entirely superficial. Once, I remember, he found me reading some devotional poem. 'The Seven Joys of Mary,' it was called. Giordano flew into a rage. Vulgar trash, he said it was. Another time he turned the images of the saints to the wall and was brought before the Father Provincial. Disciplining him was a complete waste of time. People always said that he lacked discipline, self-discipline, and he would reply that this was a euphemism for discipline of the self by others. The next day he threw out the saints in a heap and said that he would have only a crucifix in his cell. That was Giordano — his mother's blood. They both had the same temper, yet you could never tell when they were serious. He was serious about one thing, though."

"What was that?"

"The art of memory. Magic, some people would call it. Before he was forced to leave Naples, he was taken by coach to Rome where he recited the psalm *Fundamenta* in Hebrew for His Holiness Pius V and Cardinal Rebiba. Mocenigo wanted to learn this art, and it was for this that Giordano returned to Italy. A trivial thing, in my opinion, he did not suffer for this."

"Then for what?" Kaspar asked sharply, fearing that the old Friar would wax garrulous.

But Gryphius did not seem to have heard the question. "I remember the first time we climbed Vesuvius together," he said, and Kaspar, on the point of interrupting, restrained himself.

"There was the hill Cicala and his house in the distance. 'When I was a child,' Giordano said — he must have been all of twelve — 'my father was a soldier, a big man who would fight and conquer the Turks. Cicala, though it is only a hill, seemed like the end of the world to me. But now that I must soon be a man myself, all that has changed. My father will no longer conquer the Turks. The hill is not so large as I thought it was, nor is Vesuvius so far away. But when I come here, I am closer to God — closer than you in all your idiotic devotions.' "

"Well, what else would you expect?" said Kaspar Schopp. "That is the way he was."

"Yes, Kaspar. That is the way he was."

T

"You are closer to God because you are higher."

"Indocta! Imbecile! Do you think God is a cloud? There! There! Look! Look! A miracle! A cloud! The Tabernacle of the Lord! I was speaking of distance, *buffone* — distance and perspective!"

"Then why do you say you are closer to God if you mean you are further away?"

"Idiota! I am speaking figuratively. Vesuvius, it lives, it breathes, it gives life to other things. . . ."

"And everything changes — is that what you mean?"

"No, Brother. Nothing changes, only appearances."

"But your opinion of Cicala, *that* has changed."

"Sciocco! Assino! What is my opinion worth? What is the opinion of a child worth? *Nostri antichi padri*, the Greeks, learned to look beyond opinions. What Cicala is from here and Vesuvius from there, these are illusions and contradictions. And so it is with all nature. Everything contradicts itself, especially the Catholic religion. Man is fallen; now he is saved. Christ is a man; now he is a god. All men are born and all must die; but none, not one single man that has ever lived knows why he was

born and why he must die. Do you not find that fascinating, my little brother in Christ? Are we not taught that man was created to serve God? I affirm the contrary: that God was created to serve man. Do not look so horrified, my friend. As a philosopher, I shall resolve contradictions; as a man I shall delight in them, and as a Catholic I already worship them. For they are most excellent mysteries — to speak philosophically.''

T

"I have known several practitioners of magic," Fra Giovanni told his timid brother. "The line between their supposed science and heresy is a slender one. But surely I do not have to tell you this."

A wooden block lay at the centre of the interrogation chamber, with manacles, a halter, and restraining bands attached. Two pairs of boards, linked to a turning mechanism that enabled the operator to narrow the gap between them, occupied the lower half of the block.

"The boards," Fra Giovanni said. "They will crush a man's legs to pulp." Although the room was ill-lit by the light of flickering tapers, Gryphius could see that both block and boards were darkly stained. "We seldom have to use this machine," Fra Giovanni said, passing on to the Iron Maiden.

T

"If he was what he said he was," Kaspar observed dryly, "why didn't he save himself?"

"People can never see the future," Brother Gryphius remarked inconsequentially.

T

"And now, my good brother," Lorenzo Priuli was beaming, "now that you have seen the instruments, perhaps you would care to tell us what happened when Brother Jordanus left for Rome. Tell us everything now, everything we want to know...."

A vision of wax effigy came into Brother Gryphius's mind, a broken doll, arms and legs akimbo, with Lorenzo's head crushed and bleeding, his polished face still recognizable in the fragments.

T

Lasciate ogni speranza, voi ch'entrate, Gryphius was thinking. "Ah!" he stumbled. The slime sucked at his feet. Tendrils reached out to grasp him. And the stench! Fetid, overripe. A dismal place. Dead, dead....

"The Lake is not far away," his brother said. "We shall soon be there."

Damn you, Giordano! If only you knew what I was thinking....

"*Attenzione!*" Giordano steered him past the lip of a small crater. "Be careful, else the devil will swallow you up. Look, brother, look!"

Repelled yet intrigued, Gryphius watched as a viscid bubble emerged from the crater and grew like a living eye, veined and reptilian. Some horrible malignancy, it seemed to Gryphius, lurked within its sulphurous depths.

"The devil himself!" Giordano cried, giving vent to an awesome incantation: *Beydelus, Demeynes, Adulex; Metucgayne, Atine, Uquizuz, Gadix, Sol, Veni, cito cum tuis spiritibus* — I call you with your spirits...."

The bubble contracted, pulsated, and burst in an evil-smelling shower: cyclopean wink of the world's vision.

"Farewell, malodorous spirit!" Giordano laughed.

"This is a vile place," said Gryphius; "why else is it called Hell?"

"Vile?" Giordano humoured his brother. "Why that it is. Here there be snakes and serpents. Over there lives an old witch who summons spirits from the depths of hell. Circe is her name, she who whispers barbarous and secret hymns to the sun." Giordano threw up his arms: "*Susurrat soli barbara et arcana carmina* ..."

"Giordano," Gryphius wailed, "can you not be serious?"

"Oh but I am," said Giordano, "very serious, *brother* ... Sometimes I think you are worse that the rest of the brothers. Worse than Serafino: 'He's a heretic, father'; worse than Bonifacio: 'He's definitely a heretic, father'; worse than Hortensio: 'Most definitely he's a heretic, father.' Worse! worse! *worse!*"

" 'Of course he is a heretic, father,' " said Brother Gryphius good-naturedly. " 'A serious heretic, father; a despicable, damnable, serious heretic!' "

The lake opened before them, its surface wreathed in dank whiteness, the funereal pall of forgotten gods. It had been a long time, Giordano thought, since his father had first brought him here. As a child he had stood entranced for hours in the ruins of an overgrown temple, its outline scarcely distinguishable from its surroundings. As a man he understood the spell the place had cast over the child, and his understanding saddened him. Nature, which had inspired the temple builders to celebration and worship, was calling back their creation, as if nature herself could not long tolerate artifice. The very fact that the temple had been built had imperilled the reasons for its existence.

The attempt to constrain mystery had ended in ruins. And yet if the architect could see his design now, would men learn to build like this? The thought suddenly revolted Giordano. Artificial ruins for artificial gods! A gesture of contempt was called for, he decided, and turned to spit on the ground.

Nearby lay a faded garland, a votive offering of dead flowers. The gods were not entirely forgotten.

To Gryphius, it seemed that an unnatural calm had invaded

the forest. Depression weighed heavily on him and his thoughts turned to the charges against his brother. God, what an abysmal setting. Giordano was crazy, he had to be crazy....

"Nothing can live here," said Brother Gryphius miserably. "Nothing."

"None but ghosts in the airless gloom!" Giordano regarded the friend with mock astonishment, and then began to lecture him as he had so often in the past. "But surely you cannot believe in a literal hell? The lake is perfectly natural and owes its existence to the central fire, not the sun as Philolaus conceived it, though I think they are of the same origin, but the fire which burns within the earth. So, as there is a sun within the world, like the soul of a man which gives him light and warmth, I think the heavenly sun must be at the centre of our planetary system and believe that there are certainly other suns and planets on which this lake would likewise exist as a natural formation, on the moon, or Mars, or any of the planets. It is very simple and makes perfect sense."

"To you no doubt. Why not turn the world upside down and have done with it!" Brother Gryphius exclaimed. "We are not supposed to be here," he added, "we shall get into trouble."

"Trouble!" Giordano was laughing again. "You're a fine one to talk of trouble! You know, you have the makings of a philosopher. What you said just now — that's not such a bad idea of yours, to turn the world upside down. It might even improve things, especially since the Church insists that the world is downside up. Come, brother, if you talk no more of trouble, and do not tread on the demons or fall into their fiery furnaces, I will show you the way to hell, with which," he raised his hand, "I am entirely familiar. Shall we see old Anchises or walk with Virgil's shade? Come, brother Orfeo, to hell. Eurydice is waiting. Orfeo! Orfeo! Where are you? But I see that you are only a poor chaste friar and not Orfeo at all. Come, brother. *Facilis descensus Averni....*"

"And the way back?" said Gryphius. "That is not so easy."

"No, my friend," said Giordano. "The way back is difficult."

T

History is a kind of memory, Patrizi says, and so I left the friar with his. I asked but one question more.

— *The burning: much bears on the timing, yet I know nothing about this. Why did it take place when it did?*

He could not say.

V

I see clearly that we are all born ignorant and willing to acknowledge our ignorance; then, as we grow, we are brought up in the disciplines and habits of our house, and hear disapproval of the laws, rites, faith and manners of our adversaries and of those who are different from ourselves, while they hear the same about us and our affairs. Hence, just as there are planted in us by the natural forces of breeding — per forza di certa naturale nutritura — *the roots of zeal for our own ways, so in others an enthusiasm for their own different customs is instilled. So it becomes easily axiomatic that we should esteem the oppression and slaughter of the enemies of our faith as a pleasing sacrifice to the gods; as they do also when they have done the like by us. And they render thanks to God for having vouchsafed to them the light which leads to eternal life with no less fervour and conviction than we feel in rejoicing that our hearts are not as blind and dark as theirs.... Do you not know how much force the habit of believing, of being nourished from childhood in certain persuasions, has in obstructing our understanding of the most basic things? It is none other than what usually happens to those who are accustomed to eating*

venom or poison; their constitutions not only do
not feel the harm, but will even convert it into
wholesome food, so that the very antidote of the
poison becomes poisonous to them.

  — Giordano Bruno, *La cena de le ceneri,*
The Ash Wednesday Supper, 1584.

Rome, December 1599 — Prague, February 1588

*Robert Bellarmine, S.J. Confessor and rector of the Collegio
Romano of the Society of Jesus, papal theologian, and
counsellor for the Holy Office.*

' 'Not to be mocked, Holiness,' I said. 'I will not be mocked.'
An answer, I demanded an answer....''

  ''No, no, there is no answer because you do not think he is
guilty.''

  I was at the new Villa Aldobrandini yesterday. Ippolito,
dubbed Clement, dined on fatted swan and sea-robins. ''Go to
him, now,'' His bibbed Holiness commanded. ''Make him confess. And, Roberto — be careful.''

  Careful! I am tired of being careful, tired of the case. No,
Clement. I am not of his party, not the Nolan's. What would
you hear? That the examination is arduous? We lack no examiners. That there are too many propositions? Reduce the
number. So: God, the Son, Holy Ghost and Angels, the Creation, the Afterlife, World and Time — a round figure eight. And
if he should ask me to enumerate, saying I have forgotten this,
omitted that? The matter of vegetable souls, for example, or
creation from worms in the grave? Vermiculate conception!
Well, death and vegetables make ten, the planets eleven, flies
and oysters collectively twelve, thirteen this incessant metem-
psychosis and transmigration of all souls, fourteen and fifteen
the world soul and the soul of man, seventeen the advocation
and practice of magic, real, natural or artificial — I do not care
which — eighteen the occult memory, nineteen the stars, twenty

this infinitude of worlds. There's no end to it! And every poin
in conflict with Holy Writ and the teachings of the Holy
Catholic and Apostolic Church. Should I tell the Pontiff there
are flies in heaven, maggots too? 'Beatitude, the prisoner assert:
there is no difference between the soul of man and that of a fly
Asked if a fly, so considered, is immortal, he answers
affirmatively. . . . '

"Why, yes, Cardinal, the type, like an oyster or a fly."

"And are flies and oysters capable of sin, Giordano; and
are they damned or saved?"

"As natural creatures they are neither damned nor saved."

"But being both natural and — as you say — immortal,
where and what is their heaven and hell? Is the oyster's hell some
arid shore, the fly's heaven a feast of corruption?"

"You are too literal, Eminence."

"Then why is man created man?"

"Have you never stopped to think, Robert, why you were
created Cardinal?"

No, the Pope would laugh in my face as soon as listen. "He
has the advantage of you, Robert; and you know it. . . ."

That's true, and it is a shame that he has. I do not like to see
Giordano. The man's suffering moves some notion of pity in
me, and I must be careful lest reason be confounded with
sentiment.

Old Whittaker's portrait stares down at me, a reminder that
we are not alone in claiming the truth. My puritan adversary
smiles. "Another quarrel, Robert?" he seems to say. "It will not
be the first time you have angered God's Vicar on earth. The
Church is not perfect. Clement may hold the keys, but he is appointed by men."

That is so, doctor; you are right. He is appointed by men,
though freely and with God's help, something you do not
acknowledge. The state of Rome is not tyrannical. We are all
free men in Rome — free in the eyes of God. What must be done
shall be done willingly and with full knowledge of the
consequences.

Obedience is the first law; mine the freedom to obey. I have eard the voice of doubt that comes in scarcely more than a whisper, after prayer or before sleeping, in muted orisons or at the celebration of the Mass, always when it is least expected, when the ritual of the years has suddenly lost its meaning. 'You are alone,' the voice insists; 'there is no God. You are alone and afraid, a child who worships fear.' Reason, the Church's loyal servant, becomes a rebellious slave at such times, desperately struggling to throw off the bonds of its imagined thralldom. Often have I listened and often replied, countering one argument with another until nothing seems too absurd or impossible for this fanatic reason that now has it within its power to make all hell a sweet and reasonable place. I have no illusions. Without faith, the intellect will destroy itself or turn to the destruction of others. Man, *capax rationis*, created a little lower than the angels, will murder most rationally — even and especially in the name of Christ.

We have pushed this man Bruno too far and can expect no retraction. If he is condemned, he will be given to the secular arm, his blood annealed in the fire of martyrdom. If not, my own security is threatened. Either way, conscience must rule. I cannot wash my hands of the case. Pilate had his doubts; Rome no Roman solution.

What keeps him alive? He does not dine on fatted swan — nor on angels' food. . . .

"We have appointed a period of grace," says Clement. "Forty days. In that time you can advise the Congregation of the prisoner's guilt or innocence. If you think him innocent, all well and good. If guilty and uncontrite, then we shall reserve the disposition of the case to ourselves. Ours alone shall be the final verdict."

Time was when Clement smiled on the new learning and would have made Rome a haven for philosophers. Now he does not know what to think, whom to trust. Is it Spain he longs to please? The new Philip, like the old, prefers the shortest way with heretics. Kings come and kings go, the Church alone endures. Therefore Clement temporizes with this temporal power and can say, 'We have reopened the case of the heretic Bruno

105

and shall bring him to trial again. In this we shall proceed a
gently as may be, without haste or malice. Our kingdom is o
this world — as well as the next. Hence, we shall not bow to
king's rule without reason.'

Perhaps not. But these southern troubles have weakened
Clement's hand. Equanimity gives way before violence. The
Dominicans, who once controlled the Inquisition, now have it
turned against them. 'Here,' says His Most Catholic Majesty, "I
have a few rebellious friars for the hanging. Campanella's
brethren. They are yours — at a price."

A month ago, I was given the power to resolve the case as I
thought best. Now it is: *Make him confess. There is no answer
because you do not think he is guilty. . . .*

I do not understand this new-found zeal that makes
Clement discover heresy even in his newly created Cardinal.
Should I confess myself, abjure another man's errors? Not for
this was I made a Prince of the Church. "You are a musician,
Robert. An astronomer and a theologian. We are fond of music,
Robert, the planetary kind. We shall appoint you Cardinal and
confirm you as Consultor to the Inquisition. This case needs
resolving." A red hat for a fiery touch, there's one way to purchase obedience!

To stand outside of time and judge, that is godlike. In Cam-
pania once, I thought I had looked on eternity. It was nothing, a
dusty track and an old woman cajoling the inevitable mule in the
noonday heat. I was no Cardinal then. Nor did it even matter
that I was what I was. The moment was enough, contingent to
itself this burdensome progress of mule and widow. An ageless
design. I watched until they were gone from my view and as I
watched I became a part of all I saw, the hills and the trees, the
light striking fire from the dust, the sky itself. And then came
something to fracture the perfect symmetry of this day. It might
have been a dog, or just the flies and the heat. I do not
remember. Visions in the sun are deceptive.

And now I must forget myself to judge this man. It is not
possible. . . .

Make him confess. Yes, Clement, *yes.* Obedience is the first w; mine is the freedom to obey.

The same law rules all nature. No man is without guilt or free of our first transgression. Giordano makes no secret of his beliefs. Assume he is innocent, what follows? This infinite God of his, everywhere visible and nowhere to be seen, is beyond the common understanding. Such a God as this would not have stopped to create a poor world like ours, for nothing finite can come of this fractionless Titan. How easy to reverse the proposition and infer from our finite world a finite creator, the doting greybeard of childish fancy! The time will come for men to proclaim the death of this God, to look up at the stars and see the mark of a divine corpse. Then heaven is defiled and all changelessness is shown to be ceaselessly changing. Here is no promise of life everlasting, neither hope of redemption nor faith in the resurrection. Eternity's a faceless dream. No more is paradise our celestial home but a glittering husk, a gilded replica of its once glorious self. How long can men believe in such an empty shell; how long before their belief becomes as decorous as this dainty heaven?

The age of reason, announced by this man, dawns to its own requiem. Human kind cannot live without meaning. Some there may be who will cling to the forms of religion, celebrating only the loss of mystery; some who will chant their ornate devotions, from cynicism and self-interest flaunting their quintessential piety; others despairing who will desecrate the images and tear down the altar of idolatry. And the true and the faithful, shall they ask whether Christ died for this hollow, painted Church? Is this His blood and this His body? Then His sacrifice was in vain; meaningless the agony of Peter, meaningless the agony and the glory of all His Saints and Blessed Martyrs. Let us bow down before new gods, anything but this nailed and broken Christ. Let us worship human reason, for it has vanquished God.

The Nolan himself is his own best disciple. He speaks absolutely, yet with a kind of mockery that comes from self-hatred, as if he had put his own soul to death. This apostle of light claims to have shown men the way to the stars! Yet take

107

him at his word and the earth is a motiveless wanderer, heaven's superscription an infinite maze of paradox and contradiction. Nothing is created and nothing can die. The universe and all beings that have ever lived and are yet to live, these are illusions which exist only in the mind of a God who is Himself unknowable. All is *process*, life and death, the one and the myriad things, all blind and purposeless. Asked if it is so even with him, if his life is but a riddle and a cipher, he answers that he is a philosopher and does not mean to be taken literally. Questioned again, he will say that he is a true Catholic and has always held our faith above controversy or dispute. But when his errors are pointed out to him, when it is shown how inimical they are to that faith, he claims reason in his defence — reason that will not be silenced, reason that defies persecution, punishment and death.

In this struggle, the Church will give no quarter where none is asked. If he does not abjure his errors, he will burn — *and not for what he has done but for what he has yet to do....*

Such is the Nolan's innocence; such his guilt.

T

Cardinal Robert Bellarmine, S.J., to Giordano Bruno, prisoner, in the dungeons of the Castel Sant'Angelo, commonly called Hadrian's tomb, December 1599:

Interrogatus: What is your belief concerning the Incarnation and Birth of Our Lord Jesus?

Respondit: That the Word was conceived by the Holy Ghost and born of the Virgin Mary.

Interrogatus: What things are necessary to salvation?

Respondit: Faith, hope and love.

T

ellarmine is here with his bundle of propositions. He asks what e must, taking the easiest way — the hardest for a Jesuit — and answer him in kind. There is no point in arguing. Were I to say 3od is a worm (which He is), I would be taken seriously.

'A *worm*? With how many heads? A worm segmented or a vorm integral? A worm infinite or a worm temporal? A worm 1 *potentia* or *in essentia*?''

And so it goes. We have established a genuine Christian understanding.

"You are insincere," the Cardinal sighs, warming his hands on a candle supplied by the jailer.

I can never take my eyes from the flame. How it burns, ourns through these hours and days of darkness, the flame and he harsh craterous features of the man behind the flame lingering even after the candle has been extinguished and removed, until, looking back, I wonder which is the greater illusion, the scene itself with its painful iridescence, or the after image, less painful yet more intense — shadowless.

"Sincerely insincere, Eminence."

"It is cold in here," he says.

Cupped and supplicatory, the Cardinal's hands move closer to the flame and are suddenly filled with the translucent glow of reflected blood. He stares at the hands like one who would disinter the meaning beneath the skin. The subcutaneous structure is prominent, the pulse audible. Perhaps we are both thinking the same thing, for our eyes meet and he smiles, an expression exaggerated by the baleful radiancy into which his features are cast, his face appearing strangely disembodied, as if the head and the hands had nothing in common, nothing except this all-pervasive hue, the redness of his robes and another, mysteriously luminous hue, the fragile lading of vein and artery.

"We are below the river," I tell him, although he knows this.

"I could arrange to have you moved...."

"To the Vatican library?"

"Giordano," hand wringing, "will you not be serious? If...."

If! If!

"Yes, Robert?"

"You are very stubborn." An exhalation of sighs. "The Pope has set a period of grace. Giordano, for God's sake admit that you are in error."

"I already have."

"But that was eight years ago. And then under duress... We would like to proceed mercifully — as Christians."

"Is that a threat, Robert? Because if it is, I'll confess anything. I'll confess that day is night and night day....."

"Giordano, be reasonable...."

"That one sleeve and one trouser leg are worth more than a pair of sleeves and a pair of trousers, that a man is not a man and a beast not a beast; that one half a man is not one half a man, nor a half a beast one half a beast, that a half beast together with half a man is not an imperfect beast and imperfect man but *pura mente colendo* — pure mind worship — God himself!..."

"*Giordano!*"

"That your red robes emptied are more than you, that your red hat is your head wherein your brain sits, Prince, but for sweet Jesus' sake do not speak to me of mercy! Nor reason, Eminence."

The Cardinal is silent. Is he my friend or my enemy? I do not know; neither of us do yet.

His face wanes in the half-light, shadows threatening eclipse. The fleshly palimpsest hides a moon-lethal legend. But lethal to whom, Prince?

"We have forty days, Giordano." The Cardinal smiles. "I am going to begin all over again."

"As you wish, Eminence."

"As *you* wish, Giordano." The Cardinal erases his smile. "Remember the poisoned soldier in Plutarch? When he was burned, his belly burst open and extinguished the fire."

I remember.

"Twice, Robert. They relit the fire."

"Yes, Giordano...." The Cardinal rises to take his leave.

"For the damned, there is no resting place."

Three times he strikes the cell door. The turnkey appears, grinning like a gargoyle. "Here I am, excellency," he says. "No sooner called than present, your grace."

"At least," says Cardinal Robert Bellarmine, S.J, absently, "the soldier was dead."

Now there is compassion and mercy most Christain.

T

Interrogatus: How could the universe possibly be infinite?
Respondit: How could it possibly be finite?
Interrogatus: But can you demonstrate this infinitude?
Respondit: Can you demonstrate this finitude?
Interrogatus: Isn't this an expansive view?
Respondit: Isn't this a limited view?

T

"I will try again," my Prince's star was sinking. "Why did you leave Germany?"

The Protestants excommunicated me; the Emperor wept all day, Mordente dared me to conjure devils, Kelley saw tigers in the crystal sphere, and the angel Michael was cold — and still he asks me why I left!

T

Fabrizio Mordente was in Prague. And Edward Kelley, having been chased out of Poland for his crystal gazing. There too was Francesco Pucci....

Poor Francesco! I dreamed of him after the Cardinal's visit. He said nothing in the dream but was smiling when they came for him with the axe. It fell, and thus in a fraction was Francesco divided. Blood foamed from the neck and head, the body grasping its hands and drawing up its knees, as if it dared call back the soul across that red divide and be made whole again — reunited before the soul itself fled eternally forth.

The eyes glittered and would not stop their dead smile. And then, as it is rumoured so often happens with a beheaded man, the lips puckered and whispered a word — one little word.

"Mercy."

I watched, smiling myself. It was myself I had seen die. . . .

Why should I fear death? In death, I am unalterably, ir-remediably *myself*. There are times when such perfection inspires an inevitable terror. And yet, at other moments, I laugh at the thought — I laugh as one who knows that he has dreamed and must sleep to wake.

This mordant state of affairs I ascribe to the simple question: *why*. Why me; why not me? Why now; why not now?

Naturally, other questions follow. . . . .

T

"What's left, Eminence? What bones make the best ashes?"

"You will burn, Giordano."

"Under duress, Cardinal?"

T

From his court in the Hradschin castle, the Emperor Rudolf II, acolyte of the Holy Grail and seeker of the philosopher's stone, surveys the spires of crenellated Prague. So many pestilential sects have set their mark on heaven. Faction breeds faction and like these soaring pinnacles would leave the world behind but cannot. High in his lonely keep, the Emperor listens. Some crazed Calixtine's cry is borne up through the air: "We are the people! The chalice is ours!"

The melancholy Hapsburg, madness in his blood also, stares blindly at the driven sky. His fist is clenching, unclenching. He breathes on glass, and beyond the pane sees what no one else can. In melting ice, a moving finger traces the Cross, then a circle and a pentagram. His head is filled with rustling, the whispering of leaves in the winter wind, dead things, the bickerings of dry old doctors in dispute. At noon, the bells ring out Angelus. The Emperor starts and with satisfaction notes that a thousand windows have fallen to the ground.

"Begone, demons! Vultures, begone!"

Thus Rudolf, in the thirty-sixth year of his age, loping down the long corridors of his domain.

T

"Giordano, our good friend," the Emperor was saying, "your fame travels in advance of you. Welcome, Giordano; welcome, thrice welcome."

"Thrice unwelcome," Fabrizio whispered. We had quarrelled in Paris — a trivial thing. Now he had gone up in the world and operated on an astral plane. Since his appointment as Imperial Astronomer, Fabrizio affected a purple costume embellished with the devices of his calling — the sun, moon and stars. He was not the only star-gazer His Majesty had raised from the dust.

"Let us be friends, Fabrizio," I said, "and I'll tell you about the angel I saw in England."

"Non Angli sed Angeli," Rudolf muttered, catching my words. "They are not Angels but angels. Ah, the English. But I think you refer to the angel Michael. For you must know that the angel has appeared to our presence and that Doctor Kelley

practises here in Prague. He is to help in our search for the philosopher's stone.''

The Emperor loved ingenuity. Scryers, necromancers, alchemists, sooner or later they all made their way to Prague.

Rudolf had made Kelley a Baron. The magician's temperament was choleric; his complexion the ashen pink colour of a crab's shell — after boiling. Otherwise, he reminded most people of a roach. He dressed always in black and wore a skull cap with pendulous flaps, sensitive about his lack of ears, the Herr Baron.

A compatriot of his, Philip Gawdy, said that Kelley could produce gold as readily as another would crack nuts, but I did not believe it.

''The operation is much advanced, Your Highness,'' said Edward Kelley, bowing very low.

I asked His Imperial Majesty how the angel Michael had seemed to him.

''Oh, Giordano,'' the Emperor had a ready answer. ''A million saffron hairs covered the angel's wings; a million faces and tongues implored as many pardons from God....''

T

Cardinal Robert Bellarmine, S.J, with book and candle, needs only a bell and censer. I think he would sooner have me exorcised than burnt.

''This book against mathematicians that you wrote in Prague and dedicated to the Emperor, contains a figure, the *Figurae Amoris*, in which the word 'Magic' is clearly visible. What has magic to do with love; and what was it that you wanted from the Emperor?''

Circles within circles, Cardinal....

''To answer your second question first, Eminence. A place at court. Money. A living. That's all I wanted and all I received.''

"And the first question?"

T

Rudolf, with his secret cabinet, ministers of grace, furthers his quest for the philosopher's stone, to which is now added an unquenchable desire to drink the elixir of immortality. For, as the Emperor says, there can be no point to unlimited gold without unlimited life....

It was after sundown one Friday in the month of February 1588 (I recollect the month and day because certain things are to be held in mind and remembered ever after, even as they occur) that Fabrizio, Francesco and I, in the company of His skipping Majesty, descended into the bowels of the Hradschin castle where Baron Kelley had his sepulchral dwelling place. Kelley was drunk on wine, hemp and opium, a ritual drunkenness, it being the fifth day of the fifth week of the fifth month of the fifth year of his ...*project.*

The Baron was so drunk he could scarcely speak. Nevertheless, he gave us to understand the potency that the figure five had for him, Austria also being the fifth country of his operations. "Not all monarchs," he said. "are as sympathetic and as learned as His Majesty...."

In his hands, the doctor was holding a human skull. It once had been, he explained, a parricide's head, difficult to come by but essential to his quest, as were the other articles of his equipment: a murderer's coffin, goat horns, a bat drowned in blood, and a black cat that dined on human flesh. These things were necessary for the magician to speak with the dead, who, because they were older and more experienced than he, could presumably give him some useful hints.

"Bohemian shades," he declared mournfully, "are too modest."

He had conversed easily with the spirits in England, and I thought of asking if he had lost the art or if the change of climate made his task harder. But then he was not so well known in Prague, and I did not want to spoil his chances of success.

Of the angel Michael, there was not a trace. . . .

It was Rudolf who began our conversation. Showing some slight signs of irritability, he asked if the philosopher's stone could not occur naturally, like those stones to which Agricola has given the name of fossils.

"Because they are found in ditches," said the Emperor.

"Or," said Fabrizio, "like the dragons' teeth that are used in China as an aphrodisiac."

"And," said Kelley, who had shaken his own head so violently at the Emperor's question that the parricide's skull almost fell from his grasp, "the horn of a unicorn. Ground and mortarized, it makes an excellently erotic cordial. Powerful," he added, perhaps thinking of the angel, "very powerful."

"These fossils," said Francesco, "are heavenly in origin, creations of the *vis plastica*, the shaping spirit of the universe. That is why Gesner calls them thunder stones, for many resemble moons and stars and other planetary bodies."

"On a clear night," said Fabrizio, "I have seen a snail in Andromeda."

"These stones," said Kelley, "like the philosopher's stone itself, are blessed with great power. And this power is conferred upon them by virtue of their origin, which is earthly and not — as dunces maintain — heavenly. They are the children of copulation amongst the rocks. In the fullness of the moon, as Cardanus says, they are conceived and born a term later. At such times, the rocks are heard to cry out, in their birth pangs or the joys of love. I myself have heard them, and know that this is certainly the case. Therefore, the stones are of great use to pregnant women and all of that sex who would become so."

The drunken doctor belched eloquently, as though he were most familiar with the travails of women. "*Hic et ubique*," he said. "But I have forgotten the rest. . . ."

"The miners say," Fabrizio observed tactfully, "that God put these stones in the rocks to remind them of His presence — His ubiquitous presence."

"True!" The Herr Baron exclaimed. "Absolutely!"

"And I have heard it said," the Emperor listened closely, "that God placed them in the rocks to confuse and deceive men into thinking the world is far older than it actually is."

"Even truer! God placed them in the rocks *after* He made the world. His Majesty is of the correct opinion, the most learned opinion, the definitive opinion. It is well known that God commanded the stones to wax and multiply...."

"But not," said the Emperor, "the philosopher's stone."

"No, no, no," Baron Kelley agreed further, "not in a ditch or anywhere that I know of. For generations, men have looked high and low. The search must, will, shall go on. It is art, Your Majesty, art and human ingenuity that will furnish the answer...."

"And are you close?" Rudolf enquired.

"As close," said this black beetle of a man cleverly, "as I am to Your Majesty himself. Which is to say, as close as silver is to gold, the baser metal being inferior in degree not kind, close enough to be familiar yet still in awe of my princely master."

"Your wit would move the stones to tears," said Francesco. "What does the Nolan think?"

I was tired of them all and said only that I was of Leonardo's opinion.

"Which is?" Kelley asked.

"That the stones are the remains of creatures long since dead, that Italy, France, Germany — all Europe — was once a great sea and will become one again."

"And to think how I have laboured, how I have suffered," the Baron lamented, "to hear this, this ..." a restorative draught gave him the word: "This *pulp*!"

Stones, snails, worms, bats, cardinals, divinities and sons of divinities, planets, plagues and parricides, damn! damn! damn! Goddamn them all!

Two thousand years before Leonardo, Anaximander had expressed the idea that the fossil stones were perfectly natural. In our own day, Bernard Palissy had argued the case before the Parisian Inquisition.

News of his arrest came when I was in Prague. He was thrown in the Bastille and died the same year as the King was murdered.

That was in 1589. Before he died, they say he repented. Bernard Palissy, in his eightieth year, was starved to death.

T

She was called Margaret and though she had no Latin she was eloquent. The Baron, Sir Edward, she said with many an alluring glance, *il dottore diaboli*, kept her against her will. Alas, but she loved him—oh! This drunken, foul, black-capped, earless crab of a man. She loved *him*? But why, if …? He had saved her from a fate that was worse than conventional. She had known him first as a father, than as a lover — with or without ears, it made no difference. Until she knew me, *il dottore* was the only man she had known, that is — *civetta!* — the only man she had ever loved. Then she did love me? She supposed … A prisoner myself (though not as I am now), I would have rescued her. But she would have none of it, nor me. When I found her again, I took her in my arms, but no! please no! *He* could not live without her. For though she knew he loved only gold and that all the world hated him, where would he be without her, his angel. And so she was cold and she laughed — an angel.

Binding this power, stronger than all the fossil stones that had captured her affections, unwillingly — willingly. But he was repulsive! — attractive! Cruel! — kind! Then he did not love her, she had said so! — she loved him all the more for it!

God was not so fortunate in all his celestial host than this Baron Doctor in his one angel. Yet she had fallen once, might she not again?

And I, as if awoken by mad viols, love's heroic frenzy, I did descant a tune or two. Such as: "If this is not love I feel, then what can it be?" *and:* "How can I live enough of life without your love?" *further:* "Gather the rose while it is still in bloom."

And she, still no, persistently no, stubbornly no, heretically no. She feared the Baron's revenge, he who was *such* a jealous and passionate man! Once in Mortlake was once enough, once by the Thames and all the flowers that in May do grow. And could I have told her my love was infinite, I would; and could I have told her it was eternal, I would. For whosoever is blinded by love that is blind does see most clearly; and here all contrarieties are resolved, in these two natures one virtue resides, into this ocean all rivers run.

"Let us love, my love, that the stars might come home...."

Words, words, shadows in the sun!

And so I contented myself with pretty things; the colour of her eyes and hair, the way she had talked of love. We embraced again, two knowing, wordless, pitying creatures, exchanging long looks of wonder and some half of pain.

Sad it is but true: great ardour is seldom achieved without great suffering. Lovers, who have once loved, learn to lie, and between their looks the death of love is lain down. Sometimes I have thought that love is the incarnation of the Masque, death himself — but sweet, as love is sweet —, beckoning thus: 'You can never know another, know me!'

Love can have no mask, or else the dance is grim....

"*Caro*, do not be afraid."

And still — *God* — still it was no, damnably no, infinitely no!

She was to be an angel at midnight and had not the time....

Then later perhaps?

"Maybe...."

I asked her then if she had heard the celestial stones sing each to each. Oh yes, she had. And did they, *perhaps*, sing to her?

Oh yes, they did....

We kissed and she wept a little, though not overmuch. And then, then we loved. She would be late! late! (this angel who was so difficult to conjure and who brought the gift of patience) no, neither late nor early but now, *now!*

There was a certain strangeness in her; the cold and the hot contrarily mixed, as befits, I suppose, a spirit of the air. And yet she was mortal.

Magnum miraculum!...

It was long past midnight when we kissed and finally parted.

What has become of her? Sometimes I see her, Margaret, my angel. How distant she seems, turning away, smiling.

T

"I do invoke, conjure and command thee, O thou spirit, Michael, to appear and show thyself visibly unto me before this Circle in fair and comely shape, without any deformity or tortuosity, by the name of and in the name of ..."

"What does this mean?" The Emperor, his head full of breaking glass, stared blankly at an empty stage. "We are deserted; the angel has abandoned us."

For the fiftieth time, Baron Kelley beseeched the Prince of Light.

"... Iah and Vau, which Adam heard and spoke; Agla, Ioth, Anaphaxeton, Zabaoth, Asher Ehyeh Oriston, Elion, Adonai ..."

The moving finger began to write....

T

"We are the people; the chalice is ours!"

The cry is borne up and lost among Prague's windy spires. Utraquist, Lutheran, Calvinist, Hutterite, brothers in God — Austria's ruin.

Alone in his solitary keep, the Emperor claps his hands and draws out a map, his finger moving on the progress of silent armies. The legions are marching, but none can see them except the Emperor. Here is Prague, eaten away; Bohemia crumbling, the Empire dissolving.

In the great hall, a crowd of fearful supplicants waits admission to the Imperial presence. They hear laughter and passing voices, cries and fitful mutterings.

Rudolf alone hears other voices.

"On a clear night, I have seen a snail in Andromeda...."

"Majesty," this unctuous murmuring, "from one and one half ounces of mercury I have refined fully one whole ounce of gold...."

"The stones are heavenly in origin...."

"Earthly."

"Heavenly...."

"Powers, all Highness, and infinite wealth...."

"Creations of the *vis plastica*...."

"Majesty, the operation is almost terminal. See, here is the *caput mortuum*, the death's head and *terra damnata* of my distillations, mere residue and ashes. More gold is required; more gold for my experimentations, to see the mercury, Majesty...."

Liar! Liar! Worse than the doctors of divinity, worse than all the soul-keepers!

Like and yet unlike the others, now there comes another voice, talking of time and philosophy, of Hipparchus and Callippus, of the Roman Menelaus and Arcanesis, of Ptolemy and Copernicus: "The teaching of Exodus could not have matured like that of Callippus, who lived fifty years after Alexander the Great...."

Alexander! Who was the Nolan to speak of Alexander, master of the world, living in memory for two thousand years, yet dead three years before he had reached the Emperor's present age; and who would remember Rudolf's name two thousand years hence?

"But the Nolan does not see through the eyes of Ptolemy nor even of Copernicus...."

And what does he promise and what does he ask?

"I cannot give you God, only knowledge...."

In return for what? Gold, gold like all the rest!

And what is God, the voices ask; what is knowledge, what is man?

Things of dust, dry whispers answer.

The Emperor's hand moves again on the march of silent hordes. The map takes fire and burns to emptiness. The voices are babbling, the bells ringing, the glass breaking....

"Who will rid me of these demons?"

Hushed, the supplicants hear the Emperor's cry.

The doors burst open and Rudolf is running, hurling his subjects aside, loping earthbound down the long corridors of his domain, turning, spiralling down, down, down, raging among the flasks and alembics of Sir Edward's subterranean apartments, the glass scattering like stars in the firmament before the wrath of God.

Meeow! Meeeoww! A black cat, Satan expelled from paradise, plummets earthwards.

And then the Emperor is kneeling. A vision of surpassing beauty is his: the Angel of the Lord, suffused in radiancy divine.

A limpid tear forms in Rudolf's eye. Pure as molten frost, it falls to broken ice.

T

The Cardinal would like to know what I mean by magic, but I have been thinking how to create the universe, and, like a poet, have constructed a fantastic conceit after the great God Aristotle. *Omne quod movetur ab alio movetur:* whatever is moved must be moved by another. In my world's centre is the world itself, peopled by Adam's sinful race. Being mad, I say the moon is perfect, and all beyond the moon mounting in perfection unto God. For the wandering planets I have devised extrinsic motors that move colossal orbs as if nailed to cobwebs, each driving each, centric cranking eccentric, fifty-five crystal spheres and forty epicycles — is it not marvellous? Here is the city of man; here of God. But I must leave room for purgatory, subdivide the levels with angels tripping up and down, and have the whole circumscribed with the *primum mobile*, the ultimate sphere that moveless moves the rest.

Could Hercules grasp this insubstantial load, he would find it heavy.

There is something, something lacking.... My universe is set in motion; the appearances look well, the stars, coruscations in the web like drops of rain, and yet I do not like it. A little music to lubricate the spheres — a little heavenly harmony perhaps? Still, there are vast blemishes in the design. Here's a comet to shed plague or famine; unpredictable blasts, though supportable by nudging this strand or that, so, so, so. Ah, how the web is sagging at its centre. Then I must leave my little world and travel to its furthermost bounds. And what do I find there, to what is my conceit fixed. Why, nothing.... Then nothing can come of nothing! My mind, the spider, is slipping on the walls of that crystalline sphere. Eight legs, and even so he can gain no purchase!

Now there comes a footfall in the corridor, a cry of command, the grating of steel on steel, the turnkey, the Cardinal and his candle — the answer to my cosmologizing.

Fiat lux!

"And have you thought of an answer?" asks Cardinal Robert Bellarmine, S.J.

"Myself, yes."

"Speak straightly!"

"The love and knowledge of nature, Eminence; that is all I mean by magic."

"And if such knowledge is forbidden?"

"Would you forbid a man self-knowledge?"

"If it leads a man to write and say that Christ's miracles were performed by magic, then I would call it self-deception. But you did not answer my question, Giordano. What if such knowledge is forbidden and condemned by the Church?"

"I do not see how it is possible, Cardinal, for the Church to condemn and forbid in one man that which itself practises as a body. Nor do I see how it is possible for the Church to forbid the existence of something already in existence. Magic, be it that of Moses or magic in the Gospels, is nothing but a knowledge of the secrets of nature joined to the ability to imitate the working of nature and to perform things that appear miraculous in the eyes of the people. As far as mathematical or superstitious magic is concerned, if that is what you refer to, I am of the opinion that Christ and Moses as well as other honourable minds were strangers to it."

The Cardinal subjects this opinion to his careful consideration, which is: "Giordano, I cannot believe that you are telling the truth. Here," — more books! — "you liken Christ to the Centaur Chiron, and seem to mock the idea of Our Lord's divinity."

"I was speaking only of his double nature...."

"Well, here again, if you do not like that example, in this book on the statues, I read —" and he does, too: what could be more ridiculous? — "of Apollo, standing naked in a chariot...."

"Eminence, I know that you cannot abide nakedness...."

"I am not talking about that!" The Cardinal trembles — a delicate hurt, evidently. "Here is Chaos, Orcus and Nox, which you have titled the supernal triad. What blasphemy is this? Some monstrous parody on the Trinity, no doubt. Why," blustering, "these are black images, infernal designs. This is witchcraft, Giordano, sorcery!"

"Ask, and ye shall be answered...."

"I say these are magical images, Giordano."

And it used to be: 'I have read your works, lingered here, puzzled over this, found much to admire — more that is good than can be called bad....'

"You do not believe that, Robert."

"I do not know what to believe, only that you are very stubborn and impenitent."

"And you, Eminence?" An easy question, an easy victory.

"What are you if not afraid?"

"I am not here to answer your questions, but most solemnly and urgently require to look to your salvation. Remember who you are, Giordano; remember *where* you are...." Rising, three knocks for gargoyle face.

"Here I am, excellency. No sooner called than present, your grace."

"I...."

"Yes?" says Cardinal Robert Bellarmine, S.J, his figure framed in the cell door, his shadow cast by wavering torchlight — a hopeful 'yes.'

"Forget ..."

"Then may God help you," he says, and is gone.

Witchcraft! I have made some study of it, have heard that Satan is a Christian Prince, as meek, as gentle, as like a child as my Cardinal brother.

In this outer darkness, the flame burns yet. See where I have conjured the Cardinal's red soul forth. How it burns in my mind, and how it speaks with a perfect understanding, so unlike the man himself.

'Afraid, Giordano; do you think *I* am afraid? No, *you* are, brother. I — I am strong in Christ. Confess, brother, *confess!*'

'To hell with you, Robert!'

Confess now and I am dead like Francesco. Persist and — still dead!

So often have I thought that the human reason would cry out at its lowly condition and would break the bonds of its vile servitude. But now I see that the reason would sooner break itself than be free. Break! Break! Madness is easy.

A man is born between two darknesses, two deaths. Neither the manner of his living nor the manner of his going amount to much, yet that much is all and nothing. Alive, I grow weary and sick to death. My life is less than life and it is more than death — why should I care for it? The season of all natures waits me. I could sleep forever — and shall. But what use is life if a man cannot die easily in himself? A dog, understanding nothing, at least knows itself, knows how to die. Only a man, this lord of creation in whom the sun, moon and stars are born, this wise and witty Magus, only he fears death. For yes, *I* am afraid, sick with fear, sick with pity, *I, I, I* — Inquisitor of myself.

What will Bellarmine do? Necessity, fate, counsel, should, in things justly and impeccably ordered, all concur in my acquittal. 'The prisoner is guiltless, Holiness. He has done nothing evil....' *Holiness!* Black is white and nature's a whore to this Holiness — another friend of learning. God, I'd like to see this stuffed Pope walk on water. 'Magic! Witchcraft! Oh, help! I´ drown!' A fish in air, a flying whale. Oh, bloated Beatitude! Gross Amplitude! What God thought of a Pope?

Yet His Turpitude is amphibious enough to float with the current — wherever it might take him.

And Bellarmine? Pliable, pliable. It is the profoundest magic to draw the opposite from a thing or a man. Were he cruel, it would be simple to make him kind. Any sign of nature in him could be turned to my advantage, but there's none. He's the Church's true servant, a fox among foxes, a sheep bleating with the fold, another Paul — all things to all men. And what is he to himself: a cardinal nothing, zero, perfection rounding off perfection? Why then it's a perfect match. He's as magical as myself and without me would not exist, a man equal to himself, equal to myself. Since all men are created free and equal, I *am* the Cardinal, my robes in tatters, my flesh not so fat, yet the same, the same. My soul, the prisoner, gives me more trouble than I care tell, but I'll reason with him; amicable and without force, shall give him the benefit of my experience that he may come to know the truth and the light:

Interrogatus: How many natures has man?

Respondit: The nature of an angel and the nature of a demon — none.

Interrogatus: Then who am I?

Respondit: Who asks?

A man should know his own mind, Giordano. And I do, Cardinal, I do. For I am you; and Fra Giovanni, the French King and the Holy Roman Emperor; friend Zuan and my lord

Archbishop Priuli; I am Michel de Castelnau and Francis Walsingham, Pope Clement and the angel Michael (even she!), the
one and the many, a unity and a diversity — myself!

But guiltless, Cardinal? I do not think so; *you* do not think
so.... Or do you?

He is a Jesuit. Then I can but hope he is like Ignatius: an
honest fanatic.

Hope? Lord and master, I am rebel to these thoughts.

T

Self-knowledge! When has he ever known himself? The dogma
he expounds is liable to prove fatal. He will not see that I am his
friend, but calls me afraid — as he should be. His insolence
grows daily worse, as if the spirit that moved him were fired with
controversy and would consume the man without any further
help. He denies what he has said and written. When I show him
his own words, in plainest black and white, he pretends that I
have misconstrued them. If God made this world imperfect,
then He was guilty of malice and envy. How can that be
misconstrued? Love is magic and magic is love. Or that? That
Fates make no distinction between the body of a man and the
body of a donkey — ? — and cause the *soul* of a man to be no
different from the soul of a donkey. Who could misconstrue
that but a donkey? No, a donkey, being the same as a man,
would know flattery when he saw it. And Christ, being more
than a donkey, more than a man, is a Centaur! These are the
Nolan's words. Is he the only one who can fathom them? Then
language is meaningless, and God, men, monkeys and worms
are all alike. We should worship cabbages, except that it would
prejudice the rights of butterflies like Brother Giordano. What
would he say to that? I know, I know. 'Well, Cardinal, if I am a
butterfly, you are a caterpillar. You crawl where I fly.'

Too close to the flame, brother; too close to the flame.

Now the Pope, a stranger to me recently, adds his scorn to

the Nolan's. "You are a theologian," he says, "dispense some theology...."

If only it were that simple! Clement keeps himself high and mighty and is far above my petty concerns. This nephew, that fledgling Cardinal, is in constant attendance; also the French and Spanish ambassadors. Young Aldobrandini has had some trouble with his Captain of the Guard (a runaway wife, it seems) and pesters his uncle for restitution of the piece (restitution or retribution), sweating and moping poetically on the Captain's behalf like Pandarus himself. And Clement listens — why I do not know. Only yesterday, I was made to wait all afternoon while he was closeted with this Cardinal nephew, and when finally he consented to see me, he was ill-at-ease and restless, impossible to talk to. Before that, il Capitano's Prince gave me such a look as would have charmed Medusa. "Robert, Robert," he said, going in while I still waited. "You worry too much." And then, hours later, smiling: "Don't worry so. Your troubles will soon be over." I wish to God they were now! But what a state Rome is in when the Pope's nephew has turned mercenary wife-catcher, and what a soldier this Captain must be that his master is moved to such extremes!

"The examination is very slow, Robert," the Pope said, meaning that he has no desire to celebrate Christmas with the case still unresolved. "The people do not like to see these things, especially at this season."

How true! A burning would be — inappropriate.

"You must forget your own feelings, Robert. We cannot ignore the reality of this world. Remember that the Church is like a red rose, growing from dark and cruel spines."

Bleeding spines, Clement: the crown of thorns on the lacerated brow of Christ....

"I know what you are thinking, Robert. But we cannot always act as the Apostles did. Try a little — persuasion. You have your special assistant. Use him, Robert."

I do not like to do it. Yet sometimes it is necessary to be cruel in order to be kind. Christ among the money-changers did not use reason....

And yet I do not like it. I have been thinking of the martyrs who have died for the sake of conscience. It is thirty years since Paleario was hanged and burned, and there are many who would call him a good Catholic; a hundred years have gone since Savonarola went to the stake, nearly two hundred since d'Ascoli suffered for his astrologizing on the birth of Christ. What a history this is; how many tortures and imprisonments in the name of Christian grace; De Monti; Galeotta, Carnesecchi, in my time gone to the gallows or the stake; de Carranza, imprisoned for seventeen years, Pucci dead, Patrizio condemned and dying in silence — and for what? They were men, and I would have disagreed with them as men. Is the Church so weak that it must be founded on their ashes? Then it is a sham Church, depraved and merciless, worse than the Church I have forseen.

I'll not be a party to torture or murder. Let Clement find someone else.

'Oh, and what is this,' he will say, 'that you find the prisoner innocent now?'

Neither innocent nor guilty, Clement. . . .

'But this is abdication, Robert. Cowardice.'

Where's the answer to that? Resign, and another is easily found, willing to act where I am loathe.

Although I do not believe in it, I could argue the Nolan's innocence, qualified, of course, with some historical reservations. What he says is not so new. His philosophy, this religion of the mind, it is a patched up thing, a crazy quilt, more superstition than science. The Cusan said as much as Giordano and was not condemned. So with Saint John of Damascus, who declared that God is a sea of infinite substance. Likewise, Gregory of Nazianzus in his *Orations*. True, the times were different — what time isn't? But infinity's a fashion, a mental habit. I could present the case that these infinite orbs are in Giordano's brain. And his other doctrines? The answer is that he's moonstruck, harmless. Let him go and the people will laugh at him for a natural. Spots on the sun? Before his eyes!

'The people have no stomach for philosophy,' Clement would say. It goes straight to their heads — and then to their bellies. . . .'

What now? It comes to this: Giordano will not abjure and will not quit. Like mummers in the pantomime, we must both play this through to the end. Darkly have we chosen and darkly shall proceed. . . .

And yet I am determined to save him, if not from himself at least from the flames. A degree of force may have to be used, not the torture but something else, something unprecedented — I am not sure what. But first I will see him again and consult the records of the old trial. Giordano is human; there must be some weakness in him, some means of bringing him back to the way of everlasting life.

The Holy Father is right. We cannot ignore the world's reality. Even at this season when God was made man, even at this time of peace and hope of peace, the reality of the world intrudes. The enemies of the Faith press on from every side; the people abandon the adoration of mystery, and not content with the body and blood of Christ, expect Him to rise again. False prophets announce the end of days, and treason sows secret seeds that no man can detect. Therefore we shall not be lulled by the celebration of Christ's Nativity, nor be too complacent in the work of God.

But, O gentle Jesus, when shall Your Kingdom come to pass; when will the lion lie down with the lamb?

T

The lights burn late in the Holy Office. It is Christmas, season of the Word Incarnate, but Christ's apostles must attend to more mundane affairs. Nothing is well in heaven, worse below, and few dare tell if the stars move men or men the stars, so changeable are human affairs. The ambassador of His twice Catholic Majesty, Henri of Navarre, sues for clemency on Giordano's behalf, projects schemes of a grand alliance between all Christian states, and the Pope, having recognized the econverted King, fears to offend him. Ippolito Aldobrandini, Clement VIII, weighs France against Spain, and passes the season in Rome, seeking to secure a kingdom which is of this earth and more. The Pope summons the Congregation of the Holy Inquisition and calls for a decision, believing that between one moment and the next there is choice and the freedom of choice, necessary illusions: "Say if he be heretic or no, we shall be the final judge, ours alone the final verdict."

In the city of the wolf, Ippolito Aldobrandini declares the forthcoming year a year of Jubilee. Plenary indulgence, the full remittance of temporal punishments, shall be made available to all sinners — with the exception of heretics and apostates.

One case occupies the Lord Cardinal Inquisitors-General; one case seemingly without solution. Arguments are taken up and arguments cast down; judgement is postponed and sentence deferred. One case, and still the lords of the Congregation wait Bellarmine's report. Will it be death or a papal pardon? Irresolution snares the Cardinal and his master, France pressing one way and Spain hard the other; irresolution, doubt, despair, until a second Aldobrandini, Cardinal nephew to the Pope, comes forward with his most Catholic, Holy and Apostolic answer.

VI

Love wol nat be constreyned by maistrye;
When maistrye cometh, the god of love anon
Beteth his winges and farwel he is gon.

— Chaucer

Cuckoo, Cuckoo, O word of fear
Unpleasing to the married ear.

— Shakespeare

Rome, June 1600

On Corpus Christi Day of June 1600, two men could be seen sitting at the table of a roadside *osteria* in the populous Banchi district of Rome, not far from brown Tiber's effluent course. One of these figures was Kaspar Schopp, idly watching the carnival that wound its redolent way past, a jostling, sweating ruck of human and animal life, celebrating the mysteries of the Eucharist to the thunder of drums and distant cannonades. Eros shooting paper darts cantered by, clad incongruously in black. A streamer, thrown from one of the floats, curved across the narrow street and fell languidly on Kaspar's shoulders.

Pagans, he thought, a look of cynical amusement enlivening his youthful features.

The other figure, oblivious to the celebrants' unchristian joys, wore an expression of wine-sodden misery. Remembering, in spite of himself, that brief time of childhood when he had accepted things as they were, remembering indeed his own youth

hen he had been a great frequenter of carnivals, Captain
ionighi surveyed the entire history of his life and concluded
at he was one of the most unhappy men who had ever lived.
What a story," he muttered disconsolately, turning to examine
is young companion and, in a mingled access of self-pity and
esentment, downing yet another glass of muscatel. "What a
rrible story...."

Kaspar was but vaguely aware that the other had spoken,
or his head was filled with the dulcet tones of the *Pange Lingua*
hich arose from the float depicting the Last Supper. There
as, he noted, something very wrong with the order of the pro-
ession, and quite probably the actors were drunk. *Pange,
ngua, gloriosi Corporis mysterium....* The Last Supper was
receded at a galloping pace by Death Triumphant (Death in
his case being a skeleton, fully twelve feet in height, cradling an
normous scythe and mounted atop a catafalque which
eposited a trail of steaming dung), and the Disciples themselves
vere followed by the nymph Amalthaea, she astride a gigantic
ornucopia that showered the people with fountains of red and
vhite wine. *Sanguinisque pretiosi....*

It occurred to Kaspar that such anomalies were not only
candalous but were possibly deliberate. *Quem in mundi
retium....* The mixture of the sacred and the profane, he
ecided, lowered the whole tone of the festival.

Fructus ventris generosi....

This line of thought was interrupted by a small boy, who,
not liking what he saw, cast a firecracker at Death Triumphant.
Pange, pange, lingua! A rendering cry came deep from within
Death's catafalque and the horses underneath bolted. The entire
ableau now reared on end, and Death Triumphant toppled into
he Last Supper like an unwelcome thirteenth guest, his scythe
nearly decapitating several of the Disciples at a blow. *Sanguinisque pretiosi ... Rex effudit gentium ...* There, in the nature
of things, Death was rapidly joined by Amalthaea. Catapulted
forward by the sudden arrest of her cornucopia, she landed — to
the great delight of her Saviour and the populace — in the arms
of Jesus, just as he was on the point of kissing Judas for the

133

thousandth time....

Pange, lingua, gloriosi Corporis mysterium!

"Ah," il Capitano Dionighi savoured the sweetness of hi glass, "it was horrible, horrible — beyond human compreher sion."

His jaw dropped as he meditated on this last statement. A roar from the crowd distracted him, and his bulging eyes swivel led from Kaspar's face, took in the fractured allegory of th Last Supper, and swivelled back again. "And I've seen a lot o life," he said, leaning over to give Kaspar the full blast of thi confidence: "Sometimes I think I've seen too much of it. Bu not enough, mind, to kill myself...."

"Ah, yes," said Kaspar, studying the Captain's face. A choleric character, he thought. The influence of Mars in Arie was predominant; the nose hooked; the general cast pugnacious the bloodshot eyes threatening sincerities to which Kaspar wa unaccustomed. "Of course, of course. A terrible sin," saic Kaspar, and asked, very politely, if he too might share in a glas of wine.

"All you can drink, all you can drink," said the Captain ex pansively, immediately recognizing a comrade-in-arms, a fellov campaigner in the battle of life. The Captain's nostrils flared and hope burned again in his eyes. Here at last he had founc sympathy and the milk of human kindness. Why should he begrudge this fellow a drink? No reason at all, none....

"But I never saw anything like that," he continued, speak ing half to Kaspar and half to the character he imagined Kaspai to be. "Nothing that concerned me so — so *personally*. If you see what I mean...."

"Ah, yes, *yes*," said Kaspar, who sensed that he wa: regarded with some ambiguity by the owner of that protruberant gaze and that his safest tactic was one of conciliation. "A per sonal matter," he added, licking his lips and falling into a ner vous silence.

"Where did I go wrong?" Captain Dionighi enquired as the Last Supper finally got under way again. "What had I done to her, eh? That's the question," said the Captain, taking Kaspar's silence as an excuse to supply his own answer: "Nothing. Nothing at all. That's right, you're damned right. Absolutely sweet *niente*, me that never harmed a mouse." The Captain lied appallingly, then recollected himself. "A drink, a drink, that's what we both need...."

Kaspar was surprised to see the Captain empty a shining heap of florins onto the table. "Never seen so much money, eh?" the Captain asked and, before Kaspar could answer, gave a corrosive sob. "Judas money!" he cried, a vein throbbing alarmingly in his forehead. "Judas money!"

Fortuna drifted past, bewinged and griffin-tailed, blindfolded on a golden orb.

Kaspar stared at the money, a small fortune to his eyes, and heard the Captain enquiring whether or not it was true that Judas had hanged himself.

"Go on, go on," he said in a voice distilled of expectancy and despair, "you're a scholar."

"In the Acts of the Apostles," said Kaspar, menaced by the Captain's enunciation of the word 'scholar', "we read that he purchased a field with the reward of his iniquity, and falling headlong, he burst asunder in his midst, his bowels gushing forth. But according to Saint Matthew, yes, he committed suicide by hanging himself from a tree."

"Just as I thought!" The Captain was unaccountably pleased with Kaspar's reply. " 'he burst asunder in his midst' — what a phrase! 'His bowels gushing forth' — a learned description! But self-murder I say it was not. It was a rupture of fate that killed him. He had the right idea, Judas did. Listen to me, Sir Scholar, make money, make all the money you can while you can. And if you're to be damned, be damned richly. But what a story! What a story! I can see that you're a man of fine understanding, sir. They hanged her too, you know; Portia was hanged and the other fellow, Roberto, was hanged, but this Coppoli, they let him go — a murderer. Who'd have believed it? A nobleman, you see, this Coppoli was a nobleman and they *let him go*. What a story!"

The Captain halted and passed a hand over his forehead.

"Who'd have believed it?" he said again, and then asked, almost meekly Kaspar thought, if this scholar, this man of fine understanding, this paragon of human virtues whom it had been the Captain's great good fortune to encounter, would listen to him. "For pity's sake, sir, will you hear me out?" the Captain begged, adding that his was the saddest story ever told, of no use to him, for his life was done, but instructive nevertheless, to one who valued both life and learning.

And Kaspar, in whom the Captain's pleas stirred only a certain weariness, said that, yes, he was listening.

"Coppoli," said Kaspar Schopp, reflecting briefly (all too briefly) on the discrepancy between language and thought, "Coppoli — I don't seem to know the name."

The Captain spat. "Two years ago," he said, beginning his story as Caesar rode in pursuit of Fortuna, "two years ago this summer...."

T

Two years ago, the dust of multitudinous cavalry campaigns behind him, Dion Dionighi, in the middle years of his life, began to contemplate the prospect of marriage. His promotion to the rank of Captain in Cardinal Aldobrandini's guard had drastically reduced the plunder of amorous brigandage on the open road. This thought troubled Dion Dionighi, who was naturally uncelibate. Was it possible that he had become a show-soldier, a creature of ceremony to ride in plumes before the Cardinal's equipage? Of course, there were material advantages to be gained from serving in the papal household, well, almost in the papal household. And there were other compensations too. The bordellos of the Banchi — Dionighi flattered his young listener with worldly confidences — offered satisfaction to a man's every whim. But the purchase of womanflesh, the Captain avowed, was in no way comparable to its free acquisition. Since he could not marry a whore, he must find himself a virgin — oh es, there were such things still to be had. And the more he thought about it, the more the uxorious urge grew upon him. What better companion for a man than a faithful helpmate to comfort his declining years; what greater solace than the joys of family, the bliss and ease of contentment in the evening of his life? A wife, a wife was the only answer.

To this end Dion Dionighi, who was not a man to stay any device in the execution, had approached his master, the Pope's nephew, and had asked for leave to visit his native Perugia, where, the Captain knew, his suit could not be other than honourably received. To this end also Cardinal Aldobrandini had graciously assented, adding — all smiles — that a man so ill-prepared for matrimony as Dion Dionighi should first confess his sins and lay open his heart before God, in furtherance of which holy prerequisite the Cardinal made a free offer of his own Father Confessor, a wise and tolerant priest, accommodating the sins of the servants as he did those of their master.

So, trembling, Dion Dionighi went to pour out his soul into the ear of God, and (as on Judgement Day) awaited the hidden reply. And had he sinned, this son of the Church; and what were his sins, how many had he committed and how often? Well — he had killed ... But how many men, my son? ... Some ... In anger? No, in the service of his Prince. That was no sin. Had he lusted after the flesh? Oh, yes he had.... Had carnal knowledge? Oh, yes. Of a woman or a man? A woman, of course. But *not*, was he sure, of a man? No, no. How many women?.... Some.... Then that was a sin, if natural. And now he longed for the Holy Estate of Matrimony, was that correct? ... Correct.... Praise be to God! It was well that this was so. And what other sins troubled his conscience. Sloth? Gluttony? Or were there otherwise any thoughts he could call his own, secret thoughts, imparted to no man or woman, doubts not in accordance with Holy Writ? No, no, there were none. Would he swear to it? He swore to it. Then he should think, *as a fornicator*, on the words of Saint Paul the Apostle who had preached on carnality in Corinth. For was it not written that every man should have his own wife, and every woman her own

husband to avoid the sin of fornication? ... Father, it was ...
And was it not shown that in marriage the Church was corporeal
as well as spiritual? ... Father, it was ... Yes. And so it was
also written that for this cause shall a man leave his mother and
father and be joined unto his wife, and they two shall be made as
one flesh. A great mystery. God had moved this erring son of
the Church to marry, and that was enough. He had fornicated in
the past, but that was forgotten and forgiven. Therefore, in the
name of the Father, he was absolved; in the name of the Son,
absolved; in the name of the Holy Ghost, absolved.

"A great mystery," Captain Dionighi remarked bitterly to
Kaspar Schopp. "I'll say it was."

But then, two years ago, the Captain (as he admitted
himself) did not have his present understanding of the great
mystery that was in store for him....

The father had come out with a fine phrase, a phrase to
stick in a man's head. What was it? Ah, yes, he remembered:
"May the helmet of salvation and the sword of the spirit be
yours, my son."

And so, donning the helmet of salvation and girded with
the sword of the spirit, Captain Dionighi rode in triumph to
Perugia, silks and gold in his train.

In Perugia, the Captain continued, the world had thrown
itself at his feet....

He went out into society, feather-capped and wearing his
slashed doublet of green and gold with the peascod belly, ve-
netians to match; with his purple sash and scarlet cloak, flashing
an eye and curling his beard, cut to a perfect pickdevant — he
went out, did this gallant Captain, beruffed and pantouffled, a
bachelor and walking rainbow of colour and wit.

Dion Dionighi had come from Rome to take a wife. Who
would it be? The town bucks made forward with their sisters,
gossiped, wagered and fought over the match. La donna
Isabella, perhaps, was she not suitable? Too old. Angelina, then
— Angelina Manfredi? Intractable, a shrew. Maria — Maria de'
Bardi, now there was the wife for il Capitano! Handsome, but

nad. Mad? It was well known — common knowledge. Portia, then — Portia Corradi? Possibly.... A little young, no? Fifteen, nearly sixteen — a fine age for a man like the Captain.

"I saw her in the Church," said Dion Dionighi. "She smiled at me. Portia, Portia...."

The Captain was unable to continue.

"And was she — pretty?" asked Kaspar Schopp, immediately aware that he had said the wrong thing.

"God, man," the Captain burst out, "don't you understand? She was hanged. Portia, my wife, hanged by the neck, her and this Roberto — *hanged!*"

Now he remembered! The executions had taken place in February, a few days after the heretic Bruno had gone to the stake. A curious coincidence. His friend the Cardinal, had mentioned the case. How could he have forgotten? And here was the husband.... Another coincidence, meeting him like this. Well, adultery was common, and executions more so. Yet the law had descended heavily on the lovers. Ah yes, murder had been involved, an accidental killing but murder nonetheless. A comedy of errors. Amusing really, but not, if you thought about it, not so amusing for the Captain here.

"That's not all," said Captain Dionighi, referring to the murder no doubt.

"Not — all?" Kasper coaxed.

"No," a tear glistened in the Captain's eye. "God, no!"

T

Rage, rage and tears! Just like a woman, even a dead one, to make him weep. Yet how he loved her, had loved her, still loved her. And how she had deceived him; how she made him weep now as she had when she was alive. Wouldn't go to Rome! What did she mean 'wouldn't go to Rome'? Now was the time to use poetry. What was it the poet had said? If only he could remember — if only, the story of his life. Change is the nursery of music, that was it. Waters stink if in one place they bide. The same with love. Apply the poetry to his present situation. Why wouldn't she go to Rome? Why did she want to stay in Perugia? Why? His job was waiting. The poetry failed. Direct tactics were necessary. Force. It was a wife's duty to obey the husband. He would tame her. No more poetry! Oh, but how he had wept to beat her. Would she ever forgive him? It was too late, too late! A fool, what a fool he had been to suspect nothing! Blind! The enemy had been devious and cunning. Surprise, she had gained the advantage of surprise. How could she do this to him? If only! What did she want? Hadn't he given her enough? Everything. Did she expect him to return without her? How did she think that would look? And the Cardinal, what would the Cardinal say if he returned married and wifeless. The expense, the trouble he'd gone to. And for what? A laughing stock, that's what she'd made of him. A laughing stock and worse — widower. No sooner married than widowered! It wasn't his fault; he couldn't help it because he had to return, leaving her there, leaving her to ... The bitch! Not yet seventeen and hanged! Fornicatrix! His own wife and her lover hanged in public! The disgrace!

T

"I am a haunted man," said Captain Dionighi — and meant it. Alone, married but wifeless, the Captain had made his sad and sorry way back to Rome, his train emptied of silks and gold. Unknown to him, his wife had a lover, the cavalier Roberto, an admirer since childhood. But worse than a lover, according to the Captain, she had a brother, and it was at her brother's house that she had remained while the Captain returned to Rome and the Cardinal's service.

There he had stayed for a year, the object of his master's sympathy. And then, last November, there occurred an extraordinary event, a catastrophe (it was no less) that would eventually

140

make the cuckolded Captain a widower.

Roberto and Portia were in the habit of using her brother's house as a place of assignment — with or without his connivance was never discovered. Now the cavalier Roberto had a friend, the nobleman, Astorre Coppoli, whose function it was to stand watch outside the house in case the Captain should return to claim those rights that by custom and law were undoubtedly his. One night, Astorre was so far neglectful of his duties as to fall asleep on watch. Slumbering, he was discovered by an elder of the town out taking the night air after wine and supper. Thinking to have some amusement, this dignified citizen dug Cappoli in the ribs, whereupon he awoke, drawing his sword and raising a hue and cry, for surely this was the Captain returned. The citizen, believing himself the victim of a crazed assault, replied in kind and drew. The pair fenced, and one of them fell — mortally wounded.

Hearing the noise of the scuffle and the cries of the dying man, Roberto and Portia hastened to join their friend, for they also thought he had fallen foul of the Captain. Both cried out in horror when they discovered the truth. The gentleman whom Coppoli had attacked lay in his last extremity. It was past the curfew hour and the watch was patrolling the streets. What was to be done? Coppoli, so it was later told, resolved on immediate flight. A friend, he had a friend on the west gate. He would let them pass. Now a voice called out in the dark: "Who's there?" Footsteps, then silence. Again the voice: "Who is it?" Quick, quick! Into the house, corpse and all! Light the lights! Laugh, make merry! *Il cadavere?* The closet in the bedroom. Hurry, hurry! The servants would soon be back.... What, leave him here? *Orrore!* Take him along? Impossible! Horses, they needed horses. The friend, Astorre's friend, would he — ? The blood! *Il cadavere* was still bleeding!

In the street below, the watchman heard laughter and the tinkle of glasses, saw Portia silhouetted in the casement frame and thought to call. But no, love should have his play.

Eleven o'clock and all was well!

But *il cadavere?* The piazza. Strip him. A robbery, they'll think it was a robbery. And his clothes? Burn them.

The Captain paused and for the first time in his narrative the shadow of a smile crossed his face. "That was Portia' idea," he said proudly. "It came out at the trial. She had a hea on her shoulders, that wife of mine. In the morning, the bird had flown. Eloped, you might say. Which is why no on suspected them — at first. No one connected their flight with th body found in the square. Clever, eh? It gave them a start, you see."

All this the Captain narrated soberly enough. He was not he told Kaspar, not one of your Frenchified soldiers, but he had loved Portia, yes, had loved her with a passion of which he alone was capable. Exactly how this love could have matured, when a distance of a hundred miles separated it from its object, remain ed unclear to Kaspar, inexperienced as he was in the affairs of the heart. Yet the heart, Kaspar realized dimly, was a great fabricator of lies, and it was important for the correct historian to maintain the distinction between fact and fiction — *zwischer Tatsache und Erdichtung, ja.* Even so, he was prepared to believe the Captain when he spoke of his love for his wife. His sincerity, in a world that placed no value on sincerity, was more precious than all the silks and spices of the orient. A rare quality, sincerity. It was plain to see that the man had suffered miserably and needed consoling. He was quite beside himself with grief. A question, therefore, was in order, a question that would bring him back to himself. Perhaps, Kaspar ventured cautiously, perhaps the Captain was in some — small — degree responsible for the fate that had befallen his wife; perhaps he should never have left Perugia to begin with, or having left, should have returned in time to prevent *la tragedia.*

"*Una tragedia terribila,*" said the Captain, agreeing with Kaspar's description of the event. "But then I wouldn't be sitting here, my friend," he added artfully. "They would have done away with me too. Imagine that!"

A man had his pride. It was not fear that had kept him away, he who laughed at fear. The very thing that had argued most in favour of his return, his love for Portia, had done most

142

to prevent it. What concessions she would have wrung from him! He was not a stone to be so unfeeling, but then he was not a rich man either — not then, at least. Of course, the news of his wife's abduction (for that was what it had amounted to) had entirely altered his predicament. He wasn't to have known, couldn't possibly have known, that she was the abductress. She had seized on the murder as the chance in a lifetime. There was no longer any excuse for the lovers to stay in Perugia. Not that the Captain bore any grudges. The cavalier Roberto, Kaspar could rest assured, was a man of no particular feeling — a coward and a fop. She had bent him to her will; twisted him around her little finger. And he called himself a cavalier! He was spineless. Such a man was not worth hating. A waste of time! As for Coppoli, there was a different animal, though of the same stripe. To kill a harmless old gentleman, a stranger, moreover, whom he had mistaken for the Captain himself! This Coppoli was obviously the real villain. But what was the Captain to do? He, who had waited long enough as it was, was not prepared to wait until the law took its course. No indeed. Yet as a servant of the Cardinal, he could do nothing that might be judged criminal. The best thing for him was to act as an agent of the law, to hasten the course of justice by rounding up the runaways. He was a man wasn't he? A man entitled to satisfaction. And a wife. That, really, was all he had ever wanted. She was rightfully his, rightfully he would have her.

Yes, it was a fine phrase; that priest had come up with a fine phrase....

Hence Captain Dionighi had found it within himself to don once more the helmet of salvation and gird himself again with the sword of the spirit. Only this time his train consisted of a troop of armed horse.

T

A bevy of cupids cantered by, clad in martial armour. A wasp settled on the table and investigated the dregs of muscatel.

Armourless Mars pursued the laughing boys....

T

The Captain began to hiccough absently. It occured to Kaspar, who had an eye for such things, that Dion Dionighi was dressed rather beyond his station in life. He was wearing a brown velvet doublet embroidered with dogwoods and marigolds. Expensive work. A fine feathered cap sat jauntily on the Captain's head, the feather registering each hiccough with a nodding motion of its veins. As if aware of the absurd impression this created, the Captain removed his hat, dusted it, and then replaced it. Dion Dionighi stared mutely at Kaspar, shrugged, grinned and hiccoughed again.

Kaspar stared at the wasp on the table, which had finished reconnoitring the muscatel. The creature had become trapped in the sticky residue of the wine and was frantically struggling to free itself. He could see that its finely jointed legs were beaded with drops of the adhesive, and no sooner did it free one of them than another became stuck fast. Its wings were beating in an invisible blur, its antennae quivering delicately, and for a moment Kaspar imagined that it was looking at him.

Dionighi cursed, leaned across the table and flailed his hat at the wasp, which, freed by the force of the blow, escaped sideways, hovered angrily above the Captain's bald head, and then was gone.

Kaspar wondered how the world appeared to this creature, liberated by the blow that was meant to kill it. Slowly, as if by a process of accretion, a doubt began to form in his mind. The image of a fisherman, blood red pearl in hand, came to him. The image dissolved, old blood mingling with old wine — a coagulation of sorts.

Adrift in the bark of nausea, Kaspar Schopp struggled to

144

master his rising fear.

"The Cardinal," he heard himself saying distantly, "the Cardinal Aldobrandini — what did he have to do with this?"

T

But Dionighi was riding in cavalcade, his train casting shadows over blind gods; north by Tiber's course to Etruscan Civata Castellana, thence inland to Terni and Foligno, Assisi and Perugia, riding across snow-scattered scrubland, tawny foothills of the Appenines, riding with confessorial blessing and a jury of steel, the din of iron-shod hooves hammering in his brain, waking and sleeping, his eye fixed on the unattainable, ever receding horizon of his dreams and desires. A free man, il Capitano. As free as the wind, as free as the sparrows (God is a good sparrow watcher), under God's heaven, a free and laughing man.

At Assisi: "These horses are broken," the hosteler said. A man of straw!

"Broken?" And Dionighi was laughing wildly. "Winded, sir. They are winded."

At Perugia: Ten thousand welcomes from his brother-in-law.

"Portia? You know the story? Yes, I thought so. They say she's gone to Chiusi. I could not tell you for certain. A terrible thing, Captain. But there are twelve of you and only three of them...."

Then on you must ride, Captain, on into December's driven snow, through ice-crusted marshes, the wind in your face, the horizon receding, unattainable, a winter dream turned nightmare. Dear God, the wind is cruel. But free, Captain, free as the sparrows and the beasts of the fields; a free and laughing man.

South, skirting by Lake Trasimeno: "Now there was a man, Captain!"

"Who, Sergeant?"

"Hannibal, Captain."

At Chiusi: nothing. A few days lost, if whoring is lost.

Ridolfo, the Spanish whoremaster, speaking impeccable Tuscan, ventures a proposition, lucrative to him, gainful to the Captain — the way of the world.

"You have something I want; I have something you want. Your wife, Captain, and her — friends."

Break his neck! Crush his windpipe!

"No violence! ...Between friends ... I was joking ... Truly ... She, they ... Roberto and Portia, Astorre as, well ... they are at Orbetello. Two days since. They are waiting for a ship, Captain ... to one of the islands, Pianosa maybe, or Spain itself. It's the truth and I'll swear to it. By my neck, Captain."

Orbetello he reached by way of Orvieto and Manciano, in two days scarcely stopping. There, at his journey's end — how the memory galled him! — he had looked down on the Tyrrhenian Sea, a Spanish galley anchored in the port. A thousand curses on Tuscany! Menelaus would not have stood for this. But the Greek was a king, had ships, an army and engines of war. The Captain's spirit was less than Spartan. How could he start a siege with only twelve men? Therefore diplomacy was in order, not force. He would have to parley, bargain with words. Did he not have warrants and depositions, evidence sworn under the Cardinal's seal? Pieces of paper! Useful, however, at times. For negotiations, invaluable. He would see the Governor, or else be damned if the fugitives escaped him now.

Name: Dionighi. Occupation: soldier and husband. In the service of: Cardinal Aldobrandini. With warrants for the arrest of: one wife, one lover, one murderer.

The Captain preened himself before the Governor. He had every reason to suppose — a whoremaster's word — that the fugitives were present in town.

In the fortress, the Governor assured him. Under lock and key.

His Excellency would, of course, surrender them?

His Excellency would, of course, not.

Not?

The Governor spread wide his hands and smiled the smile of the bland. There were — reasons.

Reasons?

"Official reasons, Captain. Reasons of state. Your warrants are useless here. So much," a smile and a shrug: "paper."

Later, the Captain would imagine that things had turned out otherwise. On the road back to Rome, he saw himself dragging his man from his desk by the gubernatorial beard. "By all the demons in hell!" he fancied himself roaring. "They are mine and I shall have them!"

But Dionighi remembered only too well what had actually happened. He had blinked, swallowed, advanced a step and faltered. His hands had started to tremble, and he noted that the Governor's desk was cluttered with paper — everywhere pieces of paper! To the right of the desk, there was a door. Who was behind that door? Portia, yes, he felt sure she was there, listening and laughing. How she had laughed at him! How she had laughed when he had recited the lines of poetry that he had learnt. Poetry! The uselessness of paper! He looked at his hands and again at the Governor. How he would like to get his hands on that throat, on both their throats! What fine strong hands, she had said, laughing. Like joints of meat. The Captain made fists of the meat. Punishment would have to be applied. Why? She was safe, wasn't she? Under lock and key. For reasons of state. You didn't argue with that. What a dance she had led him. What a dance! And why to him — of all people! Why?

His hands were shaking violently now; everything was shaking — the floor, the walls, the desk, the pieces of paper, the Governor's face, the door — the door was opening!

Portia?

"*Si?*" The Governor turned to his secretary, who stood in front of the door.

Whispering, they were whispering....

"My dear Captain," the Governor shuffled his papers, "you are tired. Rest. Go back to Rome. Go back to Rome, Captain."

147

By all the demons in hell! But he had said no such thing. For a week he lingered outside Orbetello and watched the Spanish galley. Then he took the Governor's advice.

On New Year's Day of 1600, Dion Dionighi rode into Rome, a sadder but not a wiser man.

The bells rang out the old year, rang in the new.

T

"And the Cardinal," this from the sedulous Kaspar, "the Cardinal Aldobrandini?"

T

The Cardinal, with his flaxen hair and translucent sheen, bloodless like a Bernini, the Cardinal, distressed to hear of the Captain's misfortune, flexed his fingers and said: "Women are like horses. Whoever wishes to live in a stable must eat straw."

T

The Captain called for more wine. Sweetest muscatel! Surpassing anodyne — which, however, refreshed il Capitano's memory. "I loved her," he told Kaspar, eyes brimful with tears. "I loved her more than my horse."

The Captain drank deeply. "They hanged them together," he said. "Roberto and Portia, but not this Coppoli — a nobleman. That was last February the twenty-first — Wednesdays are hanging days in Perugia. In the square outside the Palazzo Communale, they hanged them. I was there," the Captain said, "for a hundred of my lord's *scudi*, I testified at

148

the trial.''

T

The crowd packed tightly under the gallows tree, the murderous Perugini silent for once — a savage silence. What feuds had culminated in this square, what carnage the Palazzo had seen, its steps running thick with blood. But this was a hanging day, dangerous for him, Dionighi knew, for the Corradi might try and cut him down as he left the square. Well let them try! He could take care of himself, should he want to, but that would be later, after the hanging. First things first. Would he be able to stomach the sight when the end came. He knew how it was done, had seen a hanging or two in his time. The prisoners would enter the square, under guard from the citadel, then mount the scaffold where *il boia*, the hangman, would be waiting with his arms folded. And then there were the priests, he shouldn't go forgetting the priests. What next? Since this was a double hanging they would swing back to back, the prisoners climbing the ladder after the priestly business was over, up there to that platform that looked like a stork's nest over the square, where they would be blindfolded, the noose set around their necks. And then, why they would jump, for there was no machinery in a Perugian hanging, no trapdoor, *il boia* helping if they proved unwilling, taking the hazard of going with them....

A murmur ran through the death watchers, the crowd parting as wheat before the reaper, the hangman, hooded in black, climbing the scaffold steps, followed by two cowled figures. Now the clatter of hooves and the trundle of the tumbril, not from the citadel but from the Palazzo itself, the route having been changed in anticipation of trouble from the Corradi, the Captain observing armed men on every side of him now. Were their daggers meant for him? And what was this? Dear God, he could see them, the prisoners. Portia — Portia was wearing her wedding gown!

149

One by one the death watchers began to kneel. The tumbril had reached the base of the scaffold, and soon it would be the turn of the lovers to climb first the steps and then that ladder after *il boia*, who, even now was making his slow ascent, hand over hand, to the topmost platform, climbing even as the crowd knelt. The Captain was damned if he would get on his knees. *He* would be *her* last vision on earth, Dion Dionighi standing alone in the middle of the kneeling crowd.

He heard the mutter of distant prayer, then silence, an audible silence; the priestly business was over, Roberto and Portia climbing after the hangman, she addressing the crowd from the platform, forbidding her kinsmen to take vengeance on him, her husband. As for herself, she was innocent of all wrong-doing, and hoped to love her husband in death as she had in life. Here she turned to Roberto and embraced him. Dionighi, seeing the noose placed around her neck, was seized by the thought that this was the last time he would see her alive, the last time he would hear her voice, this image of her, clad in her white bridal gown with the rope around her neck, this image engraved forever on his mind. Ah, Jesus! The Captain closed his eyes, opened them and quickly shut them again, his gaze filled with the crazy vision of a white gown falling and floating from the gallows, blossoming as it fell, like a parasol in the sun.

Long after the crowd had dispersed, the Captain remained, opening and shutting his eyes and repeatedly observing the vision of the blossoming white gown, only to compare that with the figure which had replaced it, somehow draped from the end of the rope, hanging and twisting next to the equally inert corpse of the cavalier Roberto. Il Capitano Dion Dionighi was particularly entranced by the phenomenon of the corpses' arms, which had bowed out in a kind of butterfly position, and which seemed altogether too puffy and far apart from the bodies themselves. Yes, he had often seen that before in a hanged man, but he had no idea of the cause.

Portia! Portia! Portia la bella! The Captain heard a distant, childish chanting. He turned around, his head going instinctively to the pommel of his sword, eyes searching the corners of the square. There was no one to be seen; the shutters of the houses were all barred. So, il Capitano smiled, it was to be a pistol shot.

And then he heard a familiar noise, not a pistol shot but a whinny. His horse, his horse had escaped the stables and had sought him out in the middle of the deserted town. The animal had been saddled. Suspecting some trick, Dionighi checked the stirrups and bridle. "Hooves," he said, the mare obliging while he examined her front and rear shoes, checking in the frogs of her feet for stones. Nothing, and still no bullet in the back. Across the square, at the foot of the steps leading up to the Palazzo Communale, the Captain saw a child, one child, alone, and heard again that childish chant: *Portia! Portia! Portia la bella!*

The Captain mounted his horse. He turned her round and led her at a slow walk through the empty streets. The child followed him; the doors along his route were opening, the streets filling with children, holding hands and dancing, the children forming a circle around il Capitano Dionighi, a noose of little children, dancing and singing:

> *Portia! Portia! Portia la bella!*
> *Portia la bella in mano al boia!*

T

"Two hundred *scudi!* Judas money!" the Captain cried.

T

It was dusk when Kaspar bade il Capitano goodbye. At the first turning of the street he was momentarily startled by a papier-mâché clown's head abandoned in his path. The head grinned at him vacantly, reminding him of the Captain. The Gods are obvious tonight, thought Kaspar, a flight of swallows, winging over Rome, sinking down to darkness.

VII

*We ought to get to know things in order to know
ourselves. And we ought to know ourselves in
order to know God.*

Marsilio Ficino

*If natures are to preserve themselves, it is not
only necessary that they should possess a strong
desire for self-preservation and a powerful hatred
of self-destruction but also the ability to
recognize the things that are similar and adequate
and the things that are dissimilar and inadequate.
For they would be striving in vain to preserve
themselves and they would be striving in vain to
resist destruction if they could not recognize
those things that preserve them and those things
that ruin them.*

Bernadino Telesio

Rome, January 1600

A new century. The constellations fade, the lone wolf of night
slinking off to the suburbs. The day dawns like any other, hoar-
frost on the cypresses, the layered sky washed in outworn
purples. Human scavengers are stirring in the Colosseum, in the
Forum wake amid the company of ruined statuary. Inheritors of
the earth, there is no benediction for them, the wretched who
must wait on Christ their servant. And glorious is His Church,

founded on Peter's bones; glorious the sepulchre at this marginal hour, the end of night, when the cock crows, shattering the illusion of peace.

The day dawns like any other. A thousand years to Him is as this one day to His people. And triumphant is His Church, though the millenium is a long time dawning; and glorious is His Church, founded on Peter's bones. Glory be to God on High; and glory to His Church.

Gloria, gloria, gloria in Excelsis Deo!

Clement, Pontifex Maximus, building bridges in his sleep, dreams of Constantine and his warring priests, Arius and Athanasius; dreams of a God who is and is not human, the creator and destroyer of worlds on worlds.

Gloria in Excelsis Deo!

A new day and a new century. At the Sant' Ufficio, the Holy Congregation of the Roman Inquisition meets in session. Already the marketplaces of Rome are filled with talk of a burning. When, when is it to be? Tomorrow, always tomorrow — *domani, sempre domani.* A very great heretic is to die. All are resolved it must be so. But the exact manner of his death, the time and the place — how is the will of God best served in such things, and how are His servants to acquit themselves?

In the garden of the Collegio Romano, Cardinal Robert Bellarmine, S.J, breaks a thorn from the leafless stem.

In the dungeons of the Castello Sant' Angelo, Giordano Bruno calls for light....

Gloria, gloria, gloria in Excelsis Deo!

T

And pen and paper from old gargoyle face. The period of grace is almost done. And so today I wrote to the man in Peter's chair: Ippolito Aldobrandini. *The thing that has been, it is that which shall be; and that which is done, is that which shall be done: and there is no new thing under the sun.*

His Clemency, the eighth of that name, will not, I think, prove twice himself. And Robert, my little lamb, how will he bleat?

T

The time has come round when I must make my own decision and report to the Congregation. I have the documents of the first trial to hand and, reading them, they seem to foreshadow my own presence in the case. An accident, if anything is accidental. The issue is still in the balance; myself the fulcrum of Giordano's life.

Eight years' confinement has not changed the man, unless to expand his conceit. Here is the same word play, the finite infinitely conceived. Here, a reference to the tyranny of a vile priesthood — the Church. Here, I read that in Wittenberg, which he called the German Athens, he praised Luther as one greater than Hercules, come to banish that most pernicious and horrible monster, the Cerberus crowned with the triple tiara — the Pope or else the papacy, man or institution, his meaning could not be plainer. Here in this record I read how Fra Giovanni sought clarification, hoping as I have hoped that the spoken word might qualify the written, or that some outward show of contrition would moderate these dangerous words — anything, no matter how superficial, to open up his soul gradually and gain access to the inner man. Fond hope!

It is not the first time I have read these documents. But I prefer the living word to the transcription, would sooner hear from myself the speech that others have copied. Yet now, as I read on, I hear myself asking these very questions put by Fra Giovanni, and know that the responses Giordano gave to him are the same as those he gives to me:

Interrogatus: The triple tiara. What do you mean by that?
Respondit: It is enough that you know.
Interrogatus: And if I do not?

Respondit: I have praised Luther for attacking error. But his club was the pen.

Sententious response!

Interrogatus: So the Lutherans do not use force?

Respondit: The Church cast out Luther because he attempted to combat the abuses of religion. Draw your own conclusions.

So he did, this venerable Inquisitor, who was himself forced to use force, not liking it, fearing, as I do now, that torture to Giordano was as fuel to the fire. The law became harsh — to what effect? Like our own Valdesians, called Nicodemites after the lawyer who visited Jesus under cloak of night, Giordano confessed, saying he has always acknowledged the Church's supremacy and had in no way deviated from our Roman rites. It is the antinomy of law to use the law against itself — his favourite device.

"Cuius regio eius religio," he pleads — whoever controls the region controls the religion.

He shall find that necessity is a harsher law. Today I saw my assistant and gave him a free hand should I fail.

His original confession is worthless. Yet Clement, changing like the weather, has put some store by the document. "Go to him again, Robert," he says. "Remind him of his retraction," forgetting that I already have. "He has signed once and may again." This advice comes straight from Clement's smiling nephew, who, although he is unfamiliar with the case, still keeps counsel with the Pope like one of the *nipoti* of old. I am afraid the Cardinal is concocting some poison. Or do I grant him too much? More likely it is something purgative, aye, the flux. Thank God he is not Clement's son, no Cesare or Juan to murder and be murdered, but a patron of the arts, they say, and his Captain's pimp. No wonder he smiles so, oblivious of the wrongs on every side of this case — a comic player to enliven a scene or two, this little Cardinal. But I should not malign him. Though his smile rankles, he's a Prince as well as I; and will one day sit with his Lord in heaven as he does presently with his Uncle in the Vatican. And yet I like him no more than my task. All motives are inextricably mixed — my own included. Yours too, Clement; yours too. "Go to him again, Robert." Yes, Clement, yes. I'll go, obedient as ever. I'll put these records out of my mind and begin again where I had thought to end. Where's that? Wittenberg, fountainhead of heresy or of light — depending on the point of view, heaven or hell.

T

"If you liked it so much there, why did you leave?"

"I had no choice, Eminence. When the Elector Augustus died — that was in the year, 1586, I think — the Calvinists got the upper hand. And we all know what mean and narrow men they are."

"But you did not actually leave Wittenberg until some time after the Elector's death. Why was that?"

"I left in January or February of 1588. You see, Robert, I waited to see who would win. . . ."

"Who would win, Giordano?"

"Whether the Lutherans would beat the Calvinists or the Calvinists the Lutherans, or whether they would simply beat each other — as had happened in France between the Huguenots and the Catholics. When the Calvinists won, I went to Prague."

"But later you went to Switzerland?"

"That was much later. In 1591, I think. And this time I went to Zurich not to Geneva. . . ."

To the newly created Lord of Elgg's house. Johannes Henricius Haincelius was his formula. Mad John Henry Hainzell, the alchemist.

"And after you left Prague, having failed to gain a position at court, you went to Helmstedt?"

"Yes, Duke Julius of Brunswick had founded the new University there."

"A Protestant?"

"His religion was no concern of mine, Cardinal. But yes,

since you mentioned it, he was a member of the Reformed Faith. It was after he died that I went to Frankfort — that was in the summer of 1590 — and then to Switzerland to see Hainzell.''

"You left after his death because his son was a Catholic and had no liking for you and your kind...."

"Not so. The Superintendent in Helmstedt — I've forgotten his name — excommunicated me. He was a Lutheran. You can tell His Holiness that. Quite a distinction, don't you think? To be cut off, cast out, anathematized by heretics as well as true believers. You see, I refused to accept their teaching on predestination. Free will, Eminence; free will! You and I should be in agreement on that point...."

Boethius, that was his name! Some consolation. But now I find myself in a Catholic prison, I need no consolation.

"I am not interested in our points of agreement," says the Cardinal rudely, "only in our points of disagreement. Now, you were in fact living in Frankfort when you went to Zurich. I mean you did not take up residence there. It was just a visit?"

"I am pleased, Eminence, that there is no disagreement over my whereabouts. Actually, I was living in the Carmelite monastery outside Frankfort."

The council refused to let me live in the town. A man twice excommunicated is doubly damned, and I supposed they feared blasts from any one of several gods. Considering his calling, the Prior was more of a Christian than I would have supposed....

"Do you know why I am asking you these questions, Giordano?"

One of our games, this. He asks questions to which he has the answer, to which *he* knows *I* know he has the answer, then — *Ecce diabolus!* — draws some squib of a demon from his bag, struggling and screaming to accuse me to my face.

"Your Eminence, there has never been a quarrel over my position in the universe. I have not been to China, nor to hell, whatever your informants tell you...."

"Then, you will sign this paper, attesting to the fact that you lived with the Carmelite Brothers at Frankfort from the middle of 1590 until August of 1591?"

"Have I not signed it before?"

"No," hesistantly. "Let me see," shuffle, shuffle. "The light in here is not ... Ah! Here is one in which you affirmed that you visited Hainzell in Elgg in the winter of that year but which makes no mention of the Brothers. If I can amend the second paper so," scribble, scribble, "incorporating the substance of the two in the one — *there*. You are safely domiciled in Frankfort *while* you visit Zurich — just to prevent you from being in two places at one," the Cardinal smiles at his own joke. 'Sign, if you will."

I sign. And wait for the sequel.

Which is: "Now, the Prior there, a good Christian man, praises your learning in the arts and sciences — " my expectations ... "but says that you made use of his hospitality to introduce certain heretical doctors to the art of Raymond Lull ----" are never disappointed ... "and, furthermore, that you were utterly devoid of any signs of religion ----" He meant his own ... "*Whereas* in Venice you told the Tribunal that you meant to be received back into the Church, it now transpires that you were using that Church for purposes contrary to the stated end. Oh, Giordano, Giordano!"

Imposture! Fraud! Guile!

"And I thought the Carmelites were under a vow of silence, Cardinal."

"There are — exceptions. Now, if I could amend this paper again. Thus: 'During the year 1590-91, I was resident in the Carmelite monastery at Frankfort, at which time I visited Johannes Hainzell, Lord of Elgg in the Canton Zurich, *and* used the Brothers' Christian charity to instruct certain doctors' — I have left out the word 'heretical' — 'certain doctors in the art of Raymond Lull.' How does that read?"

I sign, waiting for the sequel to this as well. Soon, if I know Bellarmine, there will come the *non sequitur,* the little squib from the bag.

What was I doing in Elgg? It will follow from that.

"Now in Elgg, Giordano —" The prophet vindicated ... "you were very busy writing the *De Imaginum Signorum et*

Idearum Compositione, wherein you expound this memor
system that some have called magical — I do not pretend t
know why ----" He is sweet reason itself today! ... "thoug
perhaps you could explain?"

"Explain, Cardinal?"

"Yes, Giordano. Explain why this book and so man
others — *incidentally* — have resulted in the charge of magic be
ing brought against you."

"No such charge has been brought against me, Eminence
Nor do I know with what I am charged...."

"That is what I am here for, Giordano."

"In that book, Cardinal, I listed twelve principles, som
would call them gods or powers. The first of these is Jupiter,
who, being prime amongst the gods, is surrounded by such at-
tributes as Fatherhood, Power and Rule, and is preceded by
Cause, Principle and Beginning. According to my philosophy,
this is a figurative means of describing the reality of things in the
world. A system, Cardinal, to pick out the colours of the
mind...."

"According to your philosophy," the Cardinal gives a
practised frown. Like an orator casting for his lines, he wanders
up and down — a rhetorical fisherman. Here it is, the bait:
"You dedicated this book to Hainzell and another like it long
ago to King Henri. This same King you served until he was
murdered, served *no doubt* according to your philosophy. I say
it was with the black arts...."

"No, no, Robert." A familar accusation, pivotal to the
rest.

"Then why did the King send you to England? That is a
question you did not answer in Venice. Was it to improve your
craft or was it for something else, Giordano, something that was
indeed — as you say — natural, only too natural?"

"Meaning?" I ask, for this is a new Bellarmine. And I
thought I knew him: rough and ready, childlike in his way, a
large child fond of large simplicities....

The old mask tautens. Beneath it, there is only the greyness
of fear. His own — and mine.

"Meaning," says Cardinal Robert Bellarmine, S.J, speaking in the levelest of tones, "that in return for certain reforms of religion the King wanted an English alliance, an alliance against Guise and Spain, against the Church herself. His mother Catherine's wish, a woman as confounded by wizardry as the son himself. But let's forget these charges, Giordano. You will not find another Lorenzo Priuli in me. As reasonable men, you and I do not believe in sorcery. So much idle superstition, though you may call it science or philosophy," right hand raised, "— as you wish. Only I must have a token of your good faith; if I am to convince my lords of the Congregation that this talk of powers and influences, these images of Nox, Orcus and Chaos, are not the accursed images they are thought to be, pagan, unchristian and damnable, but images — as you say — to pick out the colours of the mind, then I *must have* a concession." The old windbag sighs. "Believe me, Giordano, I am your friend."

Was the serpent so obvious?

"Here's another paper. Take it. Go on, go on. It can be amended too. Read it, Giordano. Not now! I meant later. I'll give instructions for you to be left with light. And pen and paper, if you wish. Since you've already acquired these things, you may as well have them with my permission. And then, Giordano, then you can read this at your leisure, without any prompting from me. For you must know, Giordano —" *that it is* ... "that it is----" *a sincere* ... "a sincere----" *confession we want* ... "confession we want-------"

From the heart, Giordano; from the heart ... "From the heart, Giordano; from the heart." Rising. Three knocks. "Oh, and another thing. I shall not be here tomorrow. You and I, we are wearing each other down, Giordano. My assistant will conduct the session instead. You do not know him. Goodbye, Giordano...."

For the first time, he gave me his ring to kiss. Strange. And now I have pen and paper and light as well. And God smiles on me as He always did.

T

161

Item: I do freely and openly admit that the King's Majesty, Henri III of France, being traitorously seduced by accursed and heretical advisers, did send me into England, there with the aim of cementing an alliance between France and that Country, to make common cause against the Person and the Dominions of that Most Christian Prince, His Majesty Philip II of Spain, and through the use of murder, treason, war, piracy, and other arts, to greatly perplex His Majesty and all his loyal subjects; and that such policies as I was instrumental in furthering were inimical to the interests of the Holy Catholic and Apostolic Church.

Item: And I do further freely and openly admit that while I lived under the protection of the Queen of England, I did renounce my own Religion; and in particular, I did praise and magnify the aforesaid Queen, calling her 'divine' and attributing to her other such epithets and virtues not becoming from a subject born under the Spanish King nor to a faithful son of the Church. And that, whereas I have previously stated that whatsoever praise I gave to the English Queen was given under the principle of *cuius regio eius religio*, and that she herself was a heretic only from necessity of rule, these arguments I do now deny and call false.

Item: And I do further freely and openly admit that on the murder of His Majesty King Henri III of France, I, being then safely in Germany, did transfer my allegiance to the Prince of Navarre who at that time adhered to the Reformed Religion, and did praise him as I had the English Queen, saying that he would come to Rome and work great reforms of religion. Furthermore, in so far as I have said that the Prince of Navarre was a heretic because of his desire to rule (for if he did not profess heresy he would not have followers), this argument I do now deny and call false. And, more generally, I do also freely and openly admit that I have knowingly praised, encouraged and magnified many heretical Princes, such as the elder Duke Julius of Brunswick-Wolfenbuttel and the late Elector Augustus of Saxony, hoping thereby to gain favours from them to the greater antagonism and persecution of the Holy Catholic and Apostolic Church; and that, moreover, while living in both the heretical and Catholic lands of Europe, I did utter, instruct, and falsely preach all manner of false and abominable doctrines which I will herein later itemize and abrogate, specifically or in sum as the case may be.

Witnessed by my hand:
Die: Ianuarius Anno Domini 1600

T

As the case may be. They said King Henri was mad, and pointed to his mother, whose brain, when the physicians opened her head, was black. Or else they remembered his father who was never seen to smile — his mind, they said, had been turned when he was a hostage in Spain. But the King, his son, was not mad. Sickly perhaps, and weak-headed at times, a difficult and complicated man, though in one thing quite direct: he hated his mother.

"I do not believe in magic," he told me once, "but I fear it, Giordano. I fear it as I fear my mother."

He had every reason — both to fear and to hate.

In the winter of 1581, when the King first brought me up to Paris, he required me to interpret a dream concerning himself. My way in the world was then uncertain (more uncertain than I think it is now) and I gladly complied. A dwarf, one of Queen Catherine's creatures, had dreamed of Henri encamped in the field of Mars outside some great city — the dwarf claimed that he knew not where. An angel of the Lord descended into the camp demanding to see the King, and it was at this point that the dwarf's recollection became imprecise. Asked why he thought the angel had appeared, the dwarf would only say that the dream, which was manifestly intended for the King, had been misdirected. Yet all would be revealed in due time, of that the dwarf was certain.

Because Henri was the least warlike of sovereigns (though it was his lot always to be fighting wars), I concluded that the Lord's help in any feat of arms would not be amiss and that this angelic visitation presaged some great future good.

"It does not fit," said the King, "that one so shrunken in form should be the bearer of such portents."

As the case may be.

It was his death that the dream foretold. . . .

Henri lived in perpetual terror of dreams and prophecies ever since his father had died, struck down in the lists by the Comte de Montgomery. Nostradamus, the Royal Physician and Astrologer, had prophesied the old king's death:

> *The young lion will overcome the old:*
> *In single combat at the lists,*
> *His eyes will be put out in a golden casque.*

Michel de Castelnau told me the story at Fulke Greville's house in the Strand, many years after he had himself witnessed that fatal passage of arms.

It was a good after-dinner story. . . .

"The tournament was held to celebrate the marriage of Henri's daughter, Elizabeth, to Philip of Spain. He, unfortunately, could not be present, being too busy with God. But Nostradamus was there with his medicines, convinced that he would have a dying man on his hands before the day was out. I'd say the doctor's position was a difficult one, gentlemen. Having foretold the King's death with crystal gazing he had to prevent it with medicines — very hard. And Catherine herself was there, looking paler than usual. Perhaps the medicines were for her. Of course, everybody knew of the prophecy — and none more so than King Henri, who had been told to stay away from dangerous toys like swords and lances, especially between his fortieth and forty-first years.

"A pretty day it was, gentlemen; the field hung with the arms of England after the pretensions of my countrymen; July weather — a day more suited to dreaming than jousting.

"Thrice, the present King's father had entered the lists against Montgomery. At the fourth passage, Monsieur de Vielleville was supposed to take His Majesty's place and he came fully armed into the field, prepared to have at Montgomery. But the King told him to step aside and demanded the fourth trial for himself. Queen Catherine sent a tearful message, begging him to forbear — Montgomery pleading likewise. I suppose you could say that the Queen's fear was contagious. It certainly worked in a peculiar way. 'My lords,' said the King, 'if you are thinking of the Queen, you can tell her that it is precisely for the love of her that I wish to break this final lance.' Up to this point, his mood had been quite gay, but now he became very serious. If you ask me, the fear of the prophecy had impelled him to rashness. It was even said that the Queen had known that this would happen and had taken special care to put the word around. But that's as maybe. The King was adamant and commanded Montgomery to make ready. . . .

"Montgomery charged, driven by God knows what force. I'm not a superstitious man, but that's the way it seemed to me. The two met mid-field. There was an awful clash as of a splintering lance. When the dust cleared, Henri was reeling, though still in his saddle. Montgomery's lance had shattered his casque, entering the King's right eye and coming out at the ear, the blood and brains bubbling through his vizor. . . ."

"And the King was still alive?" said Greville.

"He still lived," said Michel. "The prophecy did not mention that he would spend the next eleven days dying."

"Nevertheless," said Greville, "the prophecy was accurate."

"That would be the poetic view," said Michel. "The King was tired of life and sick of his Queen. . . ."

As the case may be. It was not his father's death that troubled the King that year. "My mother intends something," he said. "Be careful of her, Giordano."

At the time of Bartholomew's Eve, another Italian had rendered her a great favour by drawing up the horoscopes of her intended victims. She had waited until her second daughter was married to the Prince of Navarre, and then she struck. The first attempt against Coligny had failed, but this was merely a temporary reprieve.

"A year ten months later," Henri told me, "when Charles my brother lay choking in his own blood, shouting and screaming: 'The head! The head!' — everyone thought he meant Coligny's head, the same that Guise and the mob had played football with in the streets of Paris. But it was not so, Giordano; it was not Coligny's head...."

I asked him what he meant, but he would not say.

Again, it was Michel who told me. "It is called the Oracle of the Bleeding Head. Perhaps you've heard of it. The Queen Mother's Chaplain took a young boy from the streets and prepared him for his first Communion. On the night of the Oracle, the boy was presented at a Black Mass in the dying King's bedchamber. Two hosts were consecrated — if that's the word — before an inverted Crucifix. One was black and the other white. The Queen and her party were administered the white Sacraments, the boy given the black. Then he was beheaded and the devil entered his head. Or so they say."

"You were not present?" I asked him.

"Not I, Giordano. I value my own head too much." It was true. He had a remarkable talent for survival. "And if you value yours, which you probably don't, you will not mention this to anyone.... The head with the devil in it was next presented to King Charles (it must have been very bloody in there) and several questions were put to it concerning His Majesty's health and prospects. Would he live, and so forth. If so, for how long — that kind of thing. But the poor little fellow's head would say nothing more than that it suffered violence, which was certainly the case. It spoke in Latin by the way, as the devil usually does.

Vim patior,' it said, and no more. But that was enough to start the King roaring and screaming, 'Away with the head! Away with the head!' — and I can't say that I blame him. He kept up his noise until he died a few hours later. As Henri said to you, we all thought it was remorse on Coligny's account and granted Charles his due as a man of conscience.''

As the case may be.

"The witch," Henri said. "Have a care with her, Giordano. She wants to see you.''

T

The King said that she should never have lived and it was a miracle that she had. Her entry into the world, like her passage through it, was attended by death. Her mother survived the birth by fifteen days; her father, the Duke of Urbino, his mind and face gone with the French gout, by twenty-one. Catherine herself had been married when she was fourteen years old to a child groom of the same age. For seven years, no doubt as a consequence of that disease in her veins, there were no children. Then, over the next fourteen years, there came ten, three of whom became Kings of France and all of whom bore her tainted blood. The Queen survived the tireless insults of her husband, the regency of her two youngest sons, and the conspiracy of Condé. This great and powerful lord had been spared, but only because she thought he might prove useful. When she finally tired of expediency, she resorted to horror — the persuasion of all Princes. Possibly, however, she was incapable of malice. The evil in her was moved by practical considerations, and she had learnt, through experimenting with murder, to control her feelings.

She was inordinately fond of festivals and loved animals, especially dogs, parrots and — monkeys.

She was sixty-two years of age and looked at least ten years older. I suppose I should have feared her, but I did not.

She was reading a volume of Agrippa's, the *De Occulta*

Philosophia, and asked me to expound the sentence, '*Nos veti docere, haeresium semina iacere; piis auribus offendicul praecularis ingeniis scandalo esse,*' in which the philosopher sa that the ban on his teaching has sown the seed of heresy, an that to the ears of the pious and the ingenuous, whatsoever bright and clear seems offensive and scandalous.

"And he adds, Your Majesty," I said, for she had given kind of smile at this, "that no appeal, neither to Apollo, nor t the Muses, nor to all the angels in heaven, will vindicate hir before the hearts of the Consultors, meaning the Inquisitior But there is no book, he says, however intelligent or memorable that our courts have not judged as execrable and now regard a sacred. This, he says, consoles him."

My little speech pleased the Queen. "And do you believ him?" she asked.

"As myself, Madam," said I.

"That will not do, sir," the Queen gave a low chuckle. "I is best not to believe oneself — as one does not believe others.'

She was lying in bed, from where she customarily con ducted the affairs of state, for she had expressed the wish (it wa to be granted her) that she would die in bed — peacefully. Now she beckoned me closer. "My eyes," she said, "have never see too well."

She was not, nor had she ever been, a woman of any beau ty. Her hands, much bejewelled, lay like chickens' feet on th coverlets and were in a state of constant agitation. Her face which was large and round, was crusted in rice powder, thus enhancing the natural immobility of her expression and render ing her eyebrows all but invisible. Only the eyes themselves bulging prominently on either side of a great fang of a nose only the eyes that had never seen too well betrayed her in telligence. They were very dark and liquid, and when they moved it was as if they would speak.

"You must stay in Paris," she said, "with me...."

When I answered that I was deeply honoured, her eyes clouded and her lips curled. In her, it was an expression that passed for a pout.

"But not for long," she said tonelessly. "You are young." Then, as if she had suddenly decided to make a friend of me, she took my hand in hers. "I will speak to the King," she said, "and see that he looks kindly on you. Henri is not a man," she whispered, "but you have nothing to fear from him. I will tell you a secret, Giordano. My other boy, Francis, is going to marry Elizabeth. I'll make him King of England. One day, one day...."

It was, of course, no secret. The negotiations to marry Francis, Duke of Alençon, to Queen Elizabeth had ended in floods of tears, but Catherine seemed to think this a trivial detail.

Her eyes brightened and still my hand was fixed in hers.

I was conscious of a slightly vegetable odour that clung to her person: the smell of moss.

"I have plans for you, Giordano," she said. "I see that you know how to charm old ladies.... Well, let me tell you something else. There are wicked people in England who do not want Francis to marry the Queen. You will go there, Giordano; you will go there soon. And you will speak with Elizabeth."

Francis, Duke of Alençon, died three years later of a fever contracted in the Netherlands. Since Elizabeth would not marry a living man, there was little point in trying to match her with a dead one. But that was still in the future....

"And now, Giordano," said Queen Catherine, "they say you are skilled in the curious arts."

The Prince of the Powers of the Air was at my command then — or could have been. For had I claimed to be Ahriman himself, she would have believed me.

This sweet old lady looked up and smiled. We were no longer alone.

A company of dwarves, dressed in virginal white, had crept in from the outer room. Now there came the smallest and chief of them.

"Bat," she said, "my spirit."

Thus Queen Catherine, and thus the world in which I made my way.

At Blois, the King went dancing. Six thousand yards of lace he wore.

"My mother smiles, Giordano. Like one enchanted."

The King turned his painted face and primped his flowing locks. "Do you like my ruff, Giordano?"

"Do you believe in the devil, Giordano?" said Queen Catherine.

As the case may be.

Т

Dawn broke like an old wound, inflamed and streaked with pus. The assistant caught a brief glimpse of the sky, and then the radial walls of the outer keep enclosed him. It seemed that winter had no end,

He had come in with an escort on the road to St. Peter's, across the Campo de' Fiori and the bridge of Sant' Angelo, the hanging ground. At the entrance to the fortress, there had been a slight delay while the castle guard turned out to receive him and his own escort departed. Now, as they sat around warming their hands in the guardhouse, the sergeant-at-arms gave him a knowing look and observed that he was early.

"You know what's to be done," said the assistant. He was disinclined to conversation and resented this familiarity.

For some reason, the sergeant chose this morning to assert his authority. "I suppose you have a warrant?" he asked. The assistant nodded. "Not signed, of course," the sergeant grumbled. "They never are. Nobody leaves here unless that warrant's signed."

"Nobody is going to leave." The assistant fought his rising anger. It was absurd to play games at this hour.

"That's all right then," said the sergeant. "I'll get you your men."

"Armed," said the assistant.

"Oh, of course. Head to toe. I suppose you'll want them

170

awake as well," the sergeant said, grinning.

It was not a good start to the day, the assistant reflected. Yet, when the squad was finally assembled and at his heels, he felt reassured. There was an element of theatricality to his nature, which served him well on such occasions. What was more, the prisoner did not know him — although he knew the prisoner. That doubled his advantage. Perhaps it was a cruel part he had to play, but you could not do the work of Christ with kid gloves. How would it be this time? The prisoner was supposed to be very stubborn. Well, he would see about that. If the worst came to the worst, and the prisoner broke down, then he could always reassure himself that this was merely a form of play. In any case, wasn't that what he wanted: to break the prisoner and succeed where His Eminence had so far failed?

Alberto Tragagliolo, special assistant to Cardinal Bellarmine, was not a vindictive man. He had even acquired a certain reputation for devotion and piety, and had prepared himself for this encounter with prayer and meditation. Throughout the measured passing of the canonical hours, he had sought divine counsel; in the Mass and its responses, God had secretly answered him. But now, as the descent took him down a vertiginous flight of stairs, which opened into an ill-lit labyrinth of hidden recesses, he was momentarily afraid that he would be left to find his own way out of the catacombs. A torch under the archway threw long yellow shadows, the rock walls dripping with moisture. He became aware that the guard had stopped behind him and were waiting for directions. Then the sergeant wrenched the torch from its bracket. "This way," he said, and the assistant wondered if he had heard or imagined the contempt in his voice.

The squad was marching in regular order now, their tread echoing down the passage-way. In the distance, Tragagliolo made out a figure hurrying towards them, more like a scarecrow than a man, a grease-stained bundle of rags that muttered "Visitors, visitors" as it made its fitful approach.

"Here I am," the figure announced breathlessly. "Here I am, masters...."

171

"*Semplicione*," the sergeant growled, "the keys."

Again, the assistant caught the tone of contempt in the sergeant's voice, edged now with anger, and with something else the assistant could not readily identify — fatigue perhaps, or recognition of futility.

Muttering, the turnkey shrank into the walls, his face as yellow as the stone. Tragagliolo glimpsed his eyes, the quick eyes of a ferret watching for the kill, and then the cell door was opened and he came face to face with the prisoner.

"Brother Jordanus," he began, but was unable to continue.

The prisoner was squatting on his haunches and looked up and smiled. The assistant was prepared for everything else except that smile. The cell, as he had anticipated, stank. The prisoner's clothing was filthy; his teeth were mostly gone, and those that remained were broken and black. Giordano's head, Tragagliolo noticed, seemed far too large for his wasted body; the skin, stretched tautly over the facial bones, had an unnatural sheen, bruised and discoloured, as if the skull beneath would break through its covering of flesh. But it was the prisoner's eyes, large and deeply set, and his smile which troubled the assistant and left him unable to complete his sentence.

The guard had gotten past him now, and Giordano began to laugh, a high-pitched whining laugh that unnerved Tragagliolo even more than the prisoner's slack smile.

"Gag him!" someone cried. "Strip him!"

"Giordano Bruno," the assistant summoned up the nerve to speak, "I have a warrant for your execution...."

Tragagliolo watched as the prisoner, naked and struggling, was dragged from his cell. At the entrance, he cast a wild look back over his shoulder. And still it seemed that he laughed, laughed in such a kind as if he mocked not his tormentors but himself.

T

Sign this! Sign! Certain heretical doctors, you instructed certain heretical doctors! Now this! Sign this! I do freely and openly admit ... Now this! Sign this! And I do further freely and openly admit ...

You do not know him, Giordano....

We have your letter to the Pope. No new thing under the sun! They brought me up to the courtyard. There was a garden and a tree. They had the rope slung over a branch, the noose around my neck....

Sign this! Sign, brother, sign!

You will burn, Giordano....

Under duress, Cardinal?

God knows, I'm not so witty now. I signed. And now it is dark in here. There is no sound, no colour, no taste. I am still breathing, still alive after a fashion. I was thinking of Michel again. How he would smile to see me now. Impossible, of course. He is dead. *I should have known they were not going to kill me!* The soldiers stood around, incurious. Men do not look that way when they are about to kill. I should have known....

And God. What was He doing? God must have foreseen this day; before the universe was made, God had thought of me, had foreseen that I would now deny Him, now accept. Then the Lord smiles on me, smiles as He always did. So many, many things He must have foreseen. Before His only Son was begotten, God had made His Church; before the Crucifixion, the smiling Architect took His plans in hand: an imperial leper's cure and a Bishop's forgery. Christophorous, not Constantine, wrote the title to these Roman lands, a deed backdated even as the Lord had decreed. What, in His wisdom, has He not foreseen? All things, as Augustine well knew, are written in reverse. The same God who smiled at a miracle and a lie, raised Lazarus before his death and struck Ananias down before he was born. Before the first stone was laid in place, this fortress was in His mind; before another Emperor had died, God had ordained his resting place, knew that men could call it Hadrian's tomb, knew what purposes it would serve. How many, heretics or martyrs, have died here. Pope Celestine, of the Brotherhood called

Spiritual, he who made the Great Refusal, there was one, even a Pope murdered with a driven nail. They have the skull, nail and hole to match. Or are they forgeries too? No matter, if God decreed them likewise Celestine He poped, unpoped.

So many, many things He foresaw: the clouds on such and such a day; the footsteps of this or that man's life, all humanity's forgotten minutes, cause before cause and world without end. And in the beginning, before time was, before God was, wreathed in fire and light did the Lord foresee Himself?

T

It is not the way of Christ. I did not like to do it to him, but I had no choice. "You must teach our good brother a lesson," said Clement, stung by the report of this letter. "Teach his soul a lesson, Robert, or else it goes straight to hell...."

What is hell? Last night I dreamed I was there, an immortal soul, prisoner of fire and ice. It was a dream, but I felt these robes and they were the same, pinched my arm and felt the hurt. So it is true then, I thought, what Aquinas says, the body is the form of the soul and I must be dead. There was the papal throne, atop a long flight of stairs. I began to climb; now saw Clement sitting in state, and all the lords of the Congregation gathered round. All stared down at me, stared down through the flames. A voice called my name and Clement raised three fingers as if to bless. And then I saw that he was pointing, pointing to something behind me, something nameless....

I awoke. Hell is no dream. I have this man on my conscience. Tragagliolo has disposed of the political aspects of the case; the doctrinal aspects remain. When I saw him today, I apologized — as best I could — for what we had done, and told him again that I was his friend. For once, I think he believed me.

"We are in earnest, Giordano," I said. "The fire next time."

I left him then, giving instructions that he should have food and light. His needs are well attended. Why should I think of him? I should try and concentrate. . . .

I have been pondering my address to the Congregation. These points of doctrine do need resolving. His opinions are heterodox, I would say, rather than exactly heretical, yet when I look at them in another way, they appear quite damnable. If only I could find a way of gliding round them.

T

I am a child in my father's house again. I see, though not as a child again, the hill Cicala, and Vesuvius on the horizon. I am a student at Naples again, turning the images of the saints to the wall: *il fastidio* — the troublemaker. I am a child in my father's house again. I see, though not as a child again, the white court-yard and its gnarled elm, sunlight scattered through tangled leaves, a southern chiaroscuro, kindlier than here. A fugitive, I am at the court of King Henri again, poor, soul-sick Henri, dreaming of Adocentyn, the city of the sun. The King is playing dice, his hand trembling at each cast. "My soul is like a river," he is saying; "a river of broken mirrors." A child in my father's house again, I stand before the Venetian Tribunal — judged but not condemned.

"I speak only as a philosopher, my lords. . . ."

Taking the way back, the way of dreams, a man must meet himself many times, often as a stranger. The vines are blooming, so it must have been early summer when I first climbed Vesuvius with my father. I was surprised to see how small Cicala looked in the distance. "I will be a philosopher," I told him, "like Empedocles." Later, in the evening of the same day, I asked him why the moon was coloured red. It had risen low over the mountain and looked much closer than usual. I was very young and began to count the stars until there were too many.

I am a child in my father's house again. I see, though not as a child again, the dead waters of Lake Avernus, Aeneas seeking old Anchises' shade. The Trojan's way is long prepared; the lure set in a death by drowning. Now the caverns of hell enfold him, ceaseless time offering its vision of futurity....

It was a typical day in that country, the air filled with soundless reverberations, somnolent and oppressive, yet promising great change. The sun burned fiercely, a white disc suspended above the parched land. There were no birds to be seen, and even the lizards had gone to ground. Around noon there came a slight tremor, as if the earth had cried out in exasperation, and the sun, darkening, had answered. Now there was the faintest suggestion of a breeze, dry and hot, salt-laden, bringing no relief. The earth trembled again, the sky hazing over, a few milky clouds drifting across the sun and turning, slowly at first, then with ever increasing rapidity, a vortex of pale furies. A line storm was brewing out to sea and would break over the Bay, the dog-toothed sky bearing lightning and summer hail and forcing us to take so strange a shelter. "Men go armed into hell; quick and fearful," my father said, smiling. In the sullen halls of the Cumaean Sybil we listened to the thunder of earth and sky, listened in awe as the sky shook and the earth responded, until it seemed that the world would crack and be rent asunder. "Do not be afraid," my father said, "it is perfectly natural."

I am a child in my father's house again. I see, though not as a child again, my first teacher, Fra Teofilo, in whom the grace of God's understanding shone more brightly than in all the saints, a grave gray old man; remember him now speaking to the boys, gentle yet reproving, a Christian and a scholar, not like these Romans; listen to him now, now that the years are no more than hours, and the hours measured in minutes. "Between time and time, place and place, part and part, there is only the diffusion of a single act. One and the same chaotic confusion assigns the same destinies to all: the high and magnificent change that makes the inferior waters equal with the superior, that turns night into day and day into night." So this old man, whose words like those of a prophet in the wilderness fell among stones. "God is one and indivisible, my children. Yet in this infinity of natural forms which is world and time, the infinite God reveals himself to his finite creatures. To the Platonists He does so as if nature were a trace or a shadow; to the Peripatetics, as if nature were an effect traceable to the first cause; to the Talmudists, as if it were on His shoulders or His back; and to those who are given to apocalyptic thinking, He unveils himself as if nature were a mirror, a maze, or a riddle. Yet nature is always one and everywhere the same, and it is through the study of nature, and the study of those who have studied nature, that we learn to know ourselves; and it is through knowing ourselves, that we learn to know God...."

Nature! That nature which is in me longs for life....

"There is no death, Giordano. Nothing is lost. Every single moment contains all other moments. You will understand, Giordano; one day, you will understand...."

One day! How many times have I heard that 'one day'!

"This terror of death is madness, Giordano. What natural creature fears death?"

None. Yet it has always been with me, ever since I can remember, the fear and the terror, the power and the glory, forever and forever, God and death — the same.

I would like to ask him, Fra Teofilo, I would like to ask him now if man is a natural creature....

I am a child in my father's house again. I see, though not as a child again, the face of Fra Vito, stern, uncomprehending, murmuring of eternity revealed, of the immovable sphere, the concave and convex superfices, of the firmament *celeste ed elementare, fisse e quiete.* "The sky is fixed and quiet, Giordano. According to the Bible, it is circular and perfect. Question not the Word, Giordano. Remember, the firmament is celestial and elemental. Crystalline and spiritual." Aqueous, vitreous, humorous. I see, though not as a child again, my fellow students, Serafino, Hortensio and Bonifacio, the thin, the miserable and the fat, visionary, hysteric and sycophant, my good brothers all, three-in-one, One Order, One Church, One God. Bonifacio, Serafino and Hortensio, whose heads did grow beneath their shoulders. "And he said, father, that the Blessed Virgin was not immaculate." Thus Serafino. "And he said, father that the Immaculate Mary was not a virgin." —Hortensio.

"And he said, father, that she was neither immaculate nor virginal nor blessed, for if she was then so was her mother and her mother's mother and her mother's mother's mother and her ..." — Bonifacio. Thus all three in triple-headed complaint to Fra Vito. And he, transparent, spherical, transfixed: "Are you certain?" And they, certainly certain: certain one, certain all! And he: "Thrice certainly is more than certainty. He is a heretic." To him, for whom eternity was revealed — no doubt. What miracle could have persuaded him otherwise? None, lest he had read it first in Holy Writ. "Authority absolute, Giordano. Question not the Word."

Question not the Word, Giordano; question not the Word. Not I — I'll throw it back at them. *Si fueris Romae, Romano vivito more.* When in Rome.... And elsewhere? *Vivito sicut ibi:* do as they do there. Ambrosial defence! Alibi of a saint! And it was, for Augustine, following holy memory, hallowed precept and sanctified tradition. Question not the Word? I invoke it. Did not the angel command Peter to eat all manner of four-footed beasts and creeping things and the fowl of the air; and was not this food unclean and contrary to the Law? What the Lord cleansed let no man call unclean or common. Add to this the time honoured usage of state: where the Prince rules, his subjects are commanded to obey. So will all foreigners in his land. How should I deny, how call false, when all men at all times have recognized the necessity of rule, and none more so than the Pope himself? Render unto Caesar that which is Caesar's. Therefore, I reject this confession which they obtained under threat of death. And if they say, 'But you have lived long in heretical lands,' if they carp on that point, I'll say, 'Then so did Peter, Paul and Barnabas — and among heathen too.' Never did I renounce my religion, formally or otherwise. Should I confess everything I am accused of, specifically or in sum *as the case may be*? 'But your actions,' they will say, 'how are they to be construed?' My answer: how construe those of the Apostles? And Christ Himself? He that gave the new law first broke the Old; He alone moved men to go among the uncircumcised; His spirit moved them to recognize no difference of custom, degree, religion or race — His spirit, Christ's! Let them anathematize Christ; let the man who judges me, judge God. In Rome, where Christ rules, in Rome, in Rome. . . .

Where Christ rules? No, the Pope, His Vicar. And what is he? A man like myself — or not like myself. Still, he's human, bound by the law that binds all nature. Call him mortal, whatever his soul may be. Where was Clement before his elevation? A Paduan artist, so-called; a rebel's son and d'Este's creature, God's manciple, a money grubber. The man must have some feelings. Even the devil can feel miserable, so they say; even he has some natural feelings. More than this Pope ... Appeal to him? The devil sooner! Clement, Clement, how many men have you lured to Rome with promises of honour and security, how many like poor Francesco? They came, they left — and not by the way they came.

The Cardinal then? He's my friend — more his own.

Bellarmine has made his point, and made it well. When in Rome, do as Rome does. I'll humble myself, tack a little, bide my time. Instead of taking the confession back, I'll ask the princely Robert if I can add to it. They cannot burn me for what I said in France or England, nor in any of the German lands. They cannot — but will they not? I must learn to split logic and play the game. Michel would be proud of me. Bellarmine invokes the record, then so shall I, reminding the Cardinal again how I was used in the Protestant lands, anathematized even by those that the Church has cast out. In England and Germany, I argued against those who said that God's grace was irresistibly bestowed and that all was predetermined. In all countries, I attended Mass, even where it was dangerous so to do. And now that I am home again, I'll play the penitent and prodigal son. I'll sign some more, but not the rest, not all the articles he has prepared for me. 'Robert' — ah, no — 'My lord, in these points I am contrite and humbly beg forgiveness. These other articles, Eminence, they seem as yet — unclear. My soul is deeply troubled, and in much confusion and doubt. Show me the light, my lord. Show this wretched sinner the way you have found!'

He is my friend. I'll make him believe it, even if he does not himself. There's no better example: Bellarmine, Prince, Cardinal and Jesuit — my spiritual adviser!

The vines were blooming, and later the flowers would die. "From their ripeness comes the grape," my father said. "And from these grapes, the monks made the wine they call the blood of God. They are simple men — and very holy."

Vesuvius, earth-shaker, destroyer of men and cities! The lava burns in the crater, reeking and boiling like all the fires of hell. Nature is one and everywhere the same, and the blood of Christ in the fruit of the vine is the fire of the earth in the crater of the volcano.

T

Matching wits with this man has put my bowels clean out of order. I have not the stamina I used to have, nor the virtues of conviction in the procedures of the Society. I was eighteen when I joined Ignatius, and to my mind I was old then. That was forty years ago. God will never grant me another forty years like them, half as much maybe — more than the allotted span, I hope.... Live on! Live on!

I shall. But we have put Giordano closer to death than I have ever been, and what is he now but penitential!

Is it possible? He has done it before, why should he not again? Penitential! I cannot believe him. He goes too far, and would presume even on my credence. And I had my speech half-composed too: "MOST ILLUSTRIOUS AND REVEREND LORDS, a *difficult* case ..." It was a masterpiece, though I say it myself, of equivocation. Refusing to pass judgement, I passed judgement on. Zig-zag and see-saw, I kept the balance, neither pro nor contra. And yet it was a speech that could have saved him, an articulate, jointed sort of speech, its own march and counter-march, defying direction.

"Show me the light...." I cannot think he is sincere, yet it is my duty to listen to what he says. I pity Giordano for this latest expedient. It has worked against itself. For his sake, I was prepared to overlook some contentious points. This, I can no longer do. Should I change my speech and come down on his side, there could be the ruin of both our lives. Therefore, I've drawn up a list of cardinal errors, eight final propositions. I'll give him these, but first I'll argue some questions not germane to the articles. And then I'll see whether this contrition is genuine or not. If it is, his soul is God's to use as God sees fit. If not, then may God help him — as God will.

I've done all I can, the record will show.

The record, what's that? Posterity, that makes sinners of wise men and saints out of fools. We pay our clerks to write it, pay them according to the need. Ours is spiritual, theirs material. This German now, Scioppius, he's in Rome. We're watching him, expect some promise there. Campanella's friend. Indiscreet. They say he gave evidence at the trial, though it was not needed. Well, he's young and learning.

T

The Cardinal and I have increased our mutual understanding. We have as much in common as a snake and a scorpion, though it would be difficult to say which of us is which. His Eminence was here yesterday with the articles. I'm to hold that God made the world, that the universe if finite and divisible, the human soul immortal, the earth the centre of all things, the sun our satellite, the stars part of the immoveable sphere, and all that I have written on these subjects is in conflict with ecclesiastical authority and all the wisdom, teaching and understanding of the Holy Catholic and Apostolic Church.

Bellarmine is here again today, in high good humour. "The fourth proposition," I tell him, "must be amended. I have never said or written that the sun is the centre of all things."

"You haven't?"

"Rather that there is no centre, no north nor south nor east nor west nor up nor down...."

"Details, details. Our business now is to reconcile your life's work with the teachings of Holy Church. I have brought with me a codicil to the articles."

So he had.

T

In addition to these Articles witnessed by me this day of January —, 1600, I, Giordano Bruno, son of the late Giovanni Bruno, Nolan, in the fifty-second year of my life, having before my eyes and touching the Holy Gospels, and swearing in the name of Our Lord Jesus Christ and of his most glorious mother, ever Virgin Mary, as well as renouncing all my opinions itemized in the aforesaid Articles, also declare them to be false, abominable and heretical; and that suchlike writings and utterings as I have made in the past are utterly abhorrent to me. Furthermore, it is with a sincere heart and unfeigned faith that I abjure, curse and detest all those heresies of which I am guilty and more generally every other error, sect and heresy whatsoever inimical to Holy Church; and that, whereas I have been a despised and detestable sinner, cut off and living without the Blessings of the Holy Catholic and Apostolic Church, I now declare that I am prepared, of my own free will and conscience, to appear in person before you, Most Eminent and Reverend Lord Cardinals-Inquisitors General, at such a time and place as shall be appointed, in order to answer for these vehement suspicions of heresy you have so justly conceived against me, and that I am further prepared to renounce verbally what I have here signified by my hand, and, at such a time and place as may be, I will rest content with, and abide by, whatever judgement, penalty or sentence Your Lordships see fit to impose. So help me God and these Holy Gospels which I touch with my hands.

T

"Sign this, Cardinal? It is a death warrant!"

And he: solemn, insistent, pontifical. "In the name of God, I command you to sign. Sign, Giordano; sign and swear...."

"Robert, this is betrayal!"

"Betrayal, Giordano?"

"Robert!"

"I am a Cardinal, Giordano. And you are what is described in this codicil as a despised and detestable sinner. You will sign this, Giordano, as you have signed everything else. You will obey me, as you have obeyed me in everything else. Otherwise, I shall have no choice other than to report that you are uncontrite and impenitent."

"I need time, my lord. Time to think...."

Cardinal Robert Bellarmine, S.J, smiles. "There is no time, Giordano. I must report to the Congregation tomorrow."

"Tomorrow can wait."

"No, Giordano. Tomorrow must answer today.... You have a few hours, that is all. You will make your decision, and my own will be dependent on yours. It has always been that way, Giordano. I must leave you now, leave you with this — and the Gospels."

"Is that all you have to say?"

"Ah, no. I had almost forgotten. If you do not sign this, the Congregation will add another proposition — to the effect that you have taught that magic is a good and licit thing."

The Cardinal rises to leave. "Why did you ever return?" he asks, but the question is not directed to me.

He waits for a moment in the doorway of the cell. "By the way," he adds, "there will be some others to see you — apart from myself. You need not be afraid. We have ceased to deal in fear. Think about it, Giordano; think about it...."

And so I have, so I will. But who are these others, and what did he mean: tomorrow must answer today?

The screaming has started again. They're killing a man, piece by piece. It does not matter if he lives or dies, they'll murder his soul first.

Question not the Word, Giordano; question not the Word.

January is a two-faced month.

VIII

There are three classes of intellects: one which comprehends by itself; another which appreciates what others comprehend; and a third which neither comprehends by itself nor by the showing of others. The first is the most excellent; the second is good; the third is useless.

Machiavelli

Rome, June 1600

Il Capitano Dion Dionighi had expressed a fervent wish that Kaspar Schopp burn a candle for him. It was with the aim of fulfilling this request that, the day after the Carnival, Kaspar found himself staring up at the galleried interior of Michelangelo's great dome. He had come to St. Peter's because he felt a special need to be close to God; and, despite this longing for divine immanence, Kaspar also wanted to be alone. For there were thoughts on his mind that would tolerate no priestly mediation, no confessorial outpouring of his heart. What better place, he had said to himself, than St. Peter's? A man can lose himself here, either among the crowds or in abstract contemplation of tangible mysteries. And if he has no mind for transcendence or the marvels of engineering, he can simply sit — sit and think.

A procession of priests and candle-bearers entered the nave accompanied by the chant of some vague litany, and Kaspar saw that a funeral service was getting under way. The wax from the melting candles solidified as soon as it touched the cool marble floor; the cortege followed by a ragged assembly of children who were collecting the wax, no doubt for resale to the appropriate authorities at some future date. It was a commerce that simultaneously pleased and annoyed Kaspar, a transaction that in some unintentional way imitated one of the basic procedures of the universe: conservation — frugality in the midst of plenty. Thoughts like this had preyed on him obsessively ever since he had become involved in the case of the heretic Bruno, and in order to track the beast to its lair he had actually started to read some of the philosopher's works. In more senses than one, this was by no means an easy thing to do. The Nolan's works were largely unobtainable, and were only to be had from such establishments as the Collegio Romano. Fortunately, Kaspar's good standing with the Inquisition had prevented his being tainted with the odium of heresy. For when he had asked after the books, which were on the Index newly-drawn up for Clement by Bellarmine himself, it was understood that his interests were historical and impartial.

The coffin was set down before the high altar. Kaspar was about to ask whose funeral this was when his attention was diverted by the shrill wail of an infant. In another part of the church, the ritual of baptism was being performed. Meanwhile, Kaspar observed that the service and prayers for the dead were conducted with astonishing brevity, and it seemed altogether improper that the Church should thus shuffle off the passing of one of its communicants while celebrating the admission of another. Unable to detect the workings of another universal principle in the two separate services, Kaspar rose hastily from his pew.

A crew of beggars assailed him on the cathedral steps. *Signor! Pieta! Pieta!* But Kaspar hardly noticed them. Nor did he notice that the square and the streets were still littered with the debris of the Carnival, a stinking mess of animal and vegetable refuse that would ordinarily have turned his stomach. For Kaspar had just been visited by a revelation, the force of which impelled him through the streets. Half running, half skipping, he hastened down to the Banchi where his lodgings were situated. He did not stop as he crossed the bridge over the river, and although Dion Dionighi was foremost in his thoughts, it did not occur to him that he had forgotten to light a candle for il Capitano. It was another kind of flame that burned in his mind, and when, out of breath and suffering from the heat of the day, Kaspar climbed the stairs of the tenement and reached his room, he shut and barred the door, collapsing on his bed. *Ach, Gott!* he cried. *Mein lieb Christ!* Heroically, he roused himself for the task ahead. He went over to his desk and began to write, to write with mounting fury and invective. It was a labour that would occupy the rest of the day and keep him busy far into the night.

T

At once, he said; come at once. Return with Bastiano here, my closest servant. Written in the Cardinal's own hand too. He would trust no scribe with this but wrote directly, sealing it himself and sending his secretary to urge my compliance. Kaspar, you're right, and God how this proves it! Let them think me mad, I don't care. Like Khufu's omniscient pyramid, I've calculated all the angles. I have the key, the pattern fits. I know what's been done and how. An awful crime: murder, conspiracy and worse, a trade in lives and souls, committed right here in Rome! Who'd have believed it? Not I! A month ago, I would have thought myself mad. A month ago! And now I'm kept waiting and soliloquize on a marble bench in my lord's palatial corridor. It is not to God I speak, nor yet to man. But soon, soon I'll speak out. Let them do their worst. They'll not frighten me. I'm not a timid man, not Schopp! But, oh, the crime is foul and monstrous.

The drift. It was something the Captain said that made me think. A Spanish galley, that was it, riding at anchor in Orbetello where he'd gone to claim his wife. And then the Governor: 'There are reasons, reasons of state.' A simple soldier, who'd expect him to think? None, least of all his master, the subtle Cardinal. The Captain could not see it, but I could — and did. How can I be wrong? Fate's cunning that way: a chance meeting, a tale told and the connection's made.

Come at once, his note said; come at once. What goes on in there? All morning, they've been flowing in and out, and still I'm kept waiting. Here looms one, some high Dominican trailing glory behind him. The General himself, by the look of his train. Perhaps he'll condescend to see me now where he wouldn't before. Well, that will change. And to think this is all on my account! But I must be careful, yes, not to seem overbold. I wonder what they'll offer me? A Bishopric, I wouldn't be surprised. That or else the rack. But I'll not be silenced or bought off. Let them try!

Where was I? Since last February when I saw Bruno roasted on the coals, my head's been full of turmoil. Yesterday, no, the day before — after Matins, it was — the idea began to dawn. Then yesterday in St. Peter's, it came to me. A brilliant flash, brighter than the one that blinded Saul on the Damascan road, blinded him and made me see. This tangled skein that the Fates had woven, I unravelled, made sense rule where incoherence had before, saw everything — everything! I'll not mince words. Judicial murder! The Captain's wife illegally murdered, hers no crime except on her judges' hands. Murderers! I saw it then and I see it now; for these last two days and nights have seen nothing else but. A deal was made — *quid pro quo*, a life for a life, or rather lives: the Perugini surrendered in return for Bruno's pyre. Oh, I see it, how I see it! There's not a detail wanting or out of place, the parts connected to the whole, a vast diabolical plot. But wait, wait, Kaspar; have a care. What proof do you have? I'll write to my friend, said I, the Cardinal de S-- S-------, he'll know what's best. What proof? None then, but now I have this, his letter, corroboration in the manner and speed of its delivery that I'd exposed the plot, too late of course for the Captain's wife, too late for all. But how was it done, by whom and why? There's one I could name, but have not. *Il nipote*, the Pope's Cardinal kin, or — God forbid — the Pope himself! I name no names. The plot in essence, that's the thing. The substance, *concedo*, is still lacking some, such as the go-betweens, their ranks and stations in life, whether civil or ecclesiastical, details — as weighty as maybe — but details nonetheless. I'll soon sniff them out, or else they'll crawl from the woodwork themselves, reeking of their own accord. And by the way things are moving here, it will not be long.

Patience, Kaspar; patience! What you've uncovered will keep them scurrying for a while. Here's the General again; I think it's him. How his attendants bow and scrape. Has he come for my opinion? 'Oh, Master Schopp, this is wickedness itself. The devil's work!' He says nothing but knows who I am. I can tell that. Ah, here's another, lesser than the first yet still a personage of degree. The two meet, hands on shoulders, exchange whispers and move close to the side, conversing under Aretino's bust, Castor and Pollux in sin. A pity his ears are of stone. If I just lean my head around the corner here.... What's this? They laugh — some pasquinade. One looks at me and seems deep in thought. Now they separate and sweep on their way, their attendants following, small fry in the wake of their admiral's flag. It was a Spanish galley that started this. And these brethren, men of peace not war, what will they do? Here comes my answer, the Cardinal's secretary.

— *Signor Bastiano, a word with you, sir.*

Why, he blew right past, too breezily busy. No offence intended, I'm sure. What's he but a clerk?

How I've been racking my brains to see the policy in this! So, Spain or Tuscany — the same difference, for they are allies — offers the lovers' extradition with this stipulation: *Burn Bruno, then we'll comply with your laws.* Nothing could be more simple, or damnable. It has the advantage of legality. Perugia falls under Roman sway; its law is our law, universal, Christian, true. But wait, I said (acting the part of a co-conspirator). The people. It is one thing to burn a heretic, another to string up lovebirds. And in the woman's case, there are reasons for clemency. She's young and foolish, and her husband's a terrible man. Let's light the fire, get them back and impose some lighter penance — a popular move. Certainly, said I to my fellow; but dangerous and unwise. How's that? he asked me. If they live (I remind him), they'll talk. Besides, they're murderers — whether by fault or design. Adulterers too. Then quash clemency, I replied for the other; silence them. Their flight proves their guilt. Let's hang them in the market place as an example to all that our Roman laws are meant to be obeyed even in murderous Perugia. Easier said than done (I spoke for the first again): a hanging in Perugia on the heels of a fire in Rome. It is possible that someone may make the connection. Possible (the second) but scarcely probable. Nevertheless (the first), we cannot be too sure. Some sleight of hand is called for. Policy, policy must rule. . . . I have it! What's that? Your phrase (the second again), sleight of hand. It is this. We'll burn Bruno and make certain Spain knows. King Philip is appeased and surrenders his captives for our Roman justice, Roman rope. We hang them according to the agreement — allow a chaste delay for this —; meanwhile the word is out that Bruno still lives. Though everyone has seen him burn, we set all Rome buzzing with the rumour that another was burned in place of him. By this device, our trade is covered. For no one will now think twice of Perugia and the connection's left unmade.

Not now it's not! The connection's made, and I'm the one that's made it. Too fantastic? So I thought until I considered the effect of those rumours. The *truth* is fantastic. And if my head was addled by those rumours, what of lesser heads? The brother in Naples; why even the Cardinal himself! Whoever hatched this plot knew these southern minds, how credulous they are, how willing to believe the wildest talk. The conspirators showed an excellent understanding of the Latin type — and of each other. A familial understanding, I would say. But they did not gamble on an outsider like myself getting wind of this. And now I've set the cat among the pigeons. See how they run, like the flunkey Bastiano here! But I dare say he knows nothing of this. His master will not have told him. That leaves the Cardinal and myself, no doubt these Dominicans as well — we're the only ones who know. And the conspirators, of course, although the evidence must be destroyed by now — the principals certainly are. Documents there must have been; notes exchanged, diplomatic records — too incriminating to keep! There's still the Captain's story, if he'll repeat it. A man once bought can be bought again. But that's not the point. I stand for what's right.

They must think I am mad or a fool to keep me waiting so long. Where's your proof? I know that's what they'll say, and know I've none to offer. Where's your proof; what letters, documents, witnesses or other testimony do you have? I need none. These things are circumstantial. The absence of proof, I make so forward, proves my case. A word of this, a hint so much as dropped in the right ear will set all Rome ablaze, and with a greater fire than any heretic ever suffered. One word and *chiacchiera!* Their own tactics are turned against them. The truth will out. I'm no coward, nor the fool they seem to think me. But precautions are necessary, I know. Therefore I have sent a packet of letters to Germany, letters to be opened in case of mishap to myself. It is a wise man that thinks ahead, and knowing I've done this (and I will not fear to tell them should the need arise), they will offer to buy my silence. And then, ah then we'll see.

Self-interest is no sin, and some advantage will come my way, of that I'm sure. Yet I was blind even where I thought to see, until the second, greater vision came, the truth alloyed. My vision pained me and I thought I was mad. I saw everything and remembered everything, the whole nexus stripped bare, the anatomy of man and destiny, all revealed in one cosmic moment. If I was mad, I was God mad — chosen. My soul was parched, and this vision came as the rain after drought, divinity in every drop, every corpuscle sweet and clear. Nothing is chance. How could it be? Like one in a dream, I revisited the past. From the beginning, I knew that my way was secure. With the assured certainty of a sleep-walker, I knew what was to be done. . . .

In after vision, I can see that scene again: last February, four months ago almost to this very day, when they brought Bruno out to meet his fate, a despised and detestable sinner.

191

How easy it was to justify the ways of God to man, and see, in this wretch's end, the triumph of Holy Church over heretical depravity! I heard the sentence read, the points all listed; heard how he had taught the stars were peopled, the universe infinite, Christ a magician and magic itself a good and licit thing. But worse, he had abjured, then disabjured, was delinquent to those oaths he had previously sworn; had — most terrible of all! — renounced God and denied his existence, blaspheming so foully against the Lord that his judges had stopped their ears.

An officer of the Fisc read the sentence. There was a phrase he used (I thought nothing of it then), condemning the prisoner in the name of both our Laws, canon and civil. When the flames were lit, I pressed forward with the mob and watched him writhe. He bore his death steadfastly — I never denied that. And now, now it seems that I inhaled much more than the flames. *Both our laws!* In Rome, they are the same. Who instructed his judges: God or man? What was it they feared? And what are these Laws, human and divine, what are they worth? The same Laws that sent Bruno to the stake sent Portia to the gallows. *Laws?* They are nothing absolute, nothing divine. I say these laws have been used for the advantage of the few to the disadvantage of the many; that God is wilfully ignored in this; that our Laws, divorced from divinity, are nothing of the kind, no Laws but manifest absurdities. Nor do I fear to say this, for God has given me strength. In the name of the Lord, I shall proclaim the truth; in His name, shall reveal these iniquities and corruptions even as He has revealed them to me. Oh, how hasty I was to judgement, to condemn and vilify the man I saw burned: What faith, I ask, gave him courage; what faith and what God? O death, where is thy sting? *Tod, wo ist dein Stachel?* O grave, where is thy victory? *Hölle, wo ist dein Sieg?* Death is swallowed up in victory! *Der Tod ist verschlungen in den Sieg!*

Unregenerate soul! It was my own malignity that made me see evil in another. But He who rights all wrongs has rectified this too. I have been reading the Nolan's works. Here I have read of men in the moon, how they look down to this earth, which is their moon shining in the opposite regions of the sky, he light of the radiant sun diffused by the surface of the oceans; have read and seen with the Nolan's eyes how the whole vast machine is contracted into one small mass; how Britain seems so tiny and insignificant and Italy like a thin and short hair. 'Seize the road,' he writes, 'rolling through the threshold of the great sun; mother nature discloses the route.' So I have read, and so, God willing, I will come to understand. *De Immenso, Innumerabilibus et Infigurabilibus*, the book is called, but nine years old and hardly a copy to be found! I have brought mine here and have marked a passage for the Cardinal's eyes: how the laws and customs of Egypt fell into disrepute. That much is clear. It is our own time he means, our own customs fallen low. Here also is talk of minims and monads, atoms and particles, figures and seals, which are the archetypes of all things; of a God infinite, immense and everywhere present; of man, *magnum miraculum*, the knower of demons and of gods, whose own nature is a microcosm of the larger world. It is the truth that the Lord has shown me as He showed me the rest: the tissue of lies and deceits that I accepted for the truth, the depravity of man that once I called the Law.

I am calm and doubt not that this peace is God given. Yet some indignation burns within me. The guilty must be punished; and though I've yet named no names, I see where the guilt lies. A man's integrity is most readily preserved in silence, as Meister Eckhart says — and to a point he is correct. But there comes a time when it is right and necessary to speak. My price for silence? The case must be reopened or else I'll talk. And this time the whole world will listen, will listen to me as they would not before. . . .

But how they keep me waiting! A dog is better used. Patience, Kaspar; *patience!* You must explain what you have in mind, and that will not be easy. Peace now. Here is Bastiano again. Will the flunkey speak?

— *Master Schopp, His Eminence will see you now.*

Music to my ears!

T

Kaspar was dismayed to see the Cardinal's back turned. He had not expected this and thought it a deliberate insult, as if the Cardinal had slighted not only him but history as well. For at this moment, Kaspar firmly believed that he was imbued with the *Zeitgeist* of ages past, ages yet to come.

In fact, the Cardinal was looking down on a statue in the garden of his palace and was unaware that history personified had entered the room. The statue was a fashionable piece, a Cerberus with the heads of a wolf, a lion and a dog (such a beast as Kaspar might have seen in the Carnival), and the Cardinal had commissioned it from his love of the occasional and the pagan. It was modelled after one that had stood long ago in the temple of the god Serapis at Alexandria. Attended by hierodules, the original had itself served the god as a slave, just as its copy, similarly attended, served the Cardinal — in the case of both god and man, but one slave among many. The statue's meaning could not have been better suited to San Severina's present situation, its three heads, according to a learned iconographer, signifying past, present and future. But through another, and to the Cardinal, more satisfactory association of ideas, the statue had come to represent good judgement. To contemplate those heads, as the Cardinal was doing, was to be reminded of the necessity of anticipating the future by remembering the past, an action which enabled one to assess the present accurately. As a mnemonic device, the Cardinal reflected ruefully, the statue had often been invoked by the lately deceased Nolan, in whom *buon consiglio* had been conspicuously absent, and in whose posthumous affairs, young Schopp, it appeared, had become inextricably entangled. Ah, not quite *inextricably* perhaps. For the Cardinal did not think the situation serious enough to warrant that description. Inexplicable maybe, but that was another matter. As for the statue, it had never failed him in the affairs of past, present or future, though he had frequently wondered what arcane power had moved the Alexandrians to represent the future with the head of a dog, when the present, more often than not, seemed better served that way.

A noise from Kaspar returned him to the matters of the

moment. It was a strangely gutteral sound, resembling the bark of a *small* dog — a terrier perhaps.

"Kaspar?" the Cardinal turned and was dismayed to see a distinctly fanatical gleam in the eye of Schopp.

"Well, Kaspar," he said, at last seating himself and re-examining the note that lay on his desk, "your quest for the truth has taken you far afield."

"I have never been afraid of the truth," said Kaspar, in whom the Lord was at work.

"Most commendable." The Cardinal digested this statement.

"Like Luther," said Kaspar, taking the devil by the horns,

"My dear Master Schopp," the Cardinal hoped he did not show his anger, "it ill becomes you to speak of that man here. But since you have, let me remind you that he was a pawn who served two masters: the Emperor against the Pope and the Pope against the Emperor. Had it not been for that peculiar chance, he would have perished like Huss."

"And Brother Jordanus," rejoined Kaspar, undaunted.

"Possibly, possibly. God in His wisdom saw fit to destroy one and not the other," said the Cardinal. "Though if you want my opinion, He would have done the world a greater service by ridding it of that meddlesome priest — a man of mean and narrow opinions! But I take it you are not here to speak of Martin Luther," he added, deciding that he did not like the look in Kaspar's eye.

"Nor am I here to question God's will," allowed Kaspar. "I'll come straight to the point. You have my letter. What are you going to do?"

The Cardinal felt an irresistible need to return to the window. Instead, he forced himself to read Kaspar's letter again. Really, the thing was quite hysterical, though its meaning was clear enough: 'I spoke with Cardinal Aldobrandini's Captain ... Trade in lives ... I name no names ... Undeniable perversion of both our Laws ...'

A serious charge, the Cardinal thought; precisely the kind that could do most to damage his own position. For though he took pains to make things appear otherwise, the Cardinal had been, and still was, one of the Nolan's covert supporters. He had not spoken flippantly when he referred to Luther's escaping the fire. Because that man had lived, others had died. The extraordinary fact of his survival, interpreted by his followers as a sure sign of his election, coupled with the measures that the Church had taken to repress this belief, had irreparably damaged the case for freedom of conscience. And now here was Kaspar talking of Martin Luther as if he were some kind of hero!

Yet the Cardinal felt responsible for this young scholar, who was showing unmistakable symptoms of frenzy (it was not too strong a word), felt responsible because he had warned him to be careful with his enquiries — in the full knowledge that such a warning would encourage him all the more. The Cardinal had put his faith in Kaspar, had hoped that he would learn the use and value of discretion, a quality in which Giordano himself had been all too sadly lacking. There was no denying that at the last the Nolan had proved himself stubbornly, even wantonly, heretical; had contrived to put himself far beyond the reach of his friends. But Kaspar here? Not for one moment had the Cardinal dreamed that his modest stratagem could have had such an amazing effect. Yes, he thought, looking at the letter and again at its author, this thing is more than a little crazy.

"Sit down, Kaspar," said the Cardinal, aware for the first time that his visitor was still standing. "Sit down and let me try and explain something."

"*Explain?*" Kaspar sat down.

"Yes, Kaspar. *Explain*. Shortly before your visit to Naples, you will recall, Kaspar, that I told you there were some in the Church who were interested in keeping the spirit of Brother Jordanus alive. And also, if you remember, as I am sure you do, I advised you to be careful lest it appeared that you were one of them. Well, Kaspar, I am going to take you into my confidences. I have a confession to make. I am one of those I warned you against...."

The Cardinal paused to let his statement take effect. It was quite possible, he realized, that Kaspar, in his troubled state, would think that he was lying. Indeed, he sometimes wondered himself ...

Kaspar sifted this information silently.

"I can see you're surprised," the Cardinal added drily.

The book, Kaspar was thinking; show him the book!

"Yes, I mean no...." Kaspar faltered. "See, I've brought this. One of the Nolan's books. Oh, Your Eminence, I've been thinking. If only you knew how I've been thinking!"

And the Cardinal, who had some idea, regarded both the book and Kaspar with considerable circumspection.

"Where did you get it?" he asked, trusting that he did not betray his very genuine alarm.

"From the Jesuits," Kaspar replied blandly.

"Ah, Kaspar, Kaspar...." The Cardinal was temporarily at a loss for words.

"It's all right," Kaspar was smiling serenely. "They know me."

"Know you?" The Cardinal echoed as Kaspar began to talk of the sun and sunflowers, the moon and moon-dwellers, the earth and its inhabitants....

He is mad, the Cardinal thought. Yet there was still one expedient open to him, a last resort that would mean losing this young recruit here — at least until such a time as he returned to his right mind. Sincerity and conviction, the Cardinal reflected, were double-edged weapons. He had seen the look in Fra Ippolita's eyes when he had spoken of Kaspar, mentioning casually and with an air of magisterial indifference, that he would welcome the General's help in setting his protégé to rights, adding, of course, that he did not think it would be necessary, that he could probably manage things himself. It was a narrow look, a shrewd look. In any case, the Cardinal did not want to overexcite Fra Ippolita's curiosity. Therefore, it was best to reason with Kaspar, to show him that there was not *nor had there ever been* a conspiracy; to convince him of the need for precision, delicacy and finesse.

"You and I are in agreement," the Cardinal began. "But

we must not throw caution to the wind. Now, even if you have any proof of these things you have written down — but I trust not spoken, you have not spoken of them, have you?'' The Cardinal raised an enquiring glance and was immeasurably relieved when Kaspar remained silent, a silence he took for assent. ''Good, good,'' he continued. ''Now, as I was saying, even if you have proof, do you think it would be believed? No,'' the Cardinal spread his arms expansively, ''such proof would be dismissed as fraudulent and you yourself would be pilloried as an impious and mischievous meddler. Mind you,'' the Cardinal hastened to correct himself, ''I am not saying you are, no more than I am saying there is nothing in what you claim. But you have erred, Kaspar. Believe me, you are wrong, for the right reasons of course, but wrong nevertheless.''

''*Wrong*, Cardinal? *Proof*, Cardinal?''

''Wrong to act without proof, I mean....''

''Judicial murder has been committed,'' said Kaspar Schopp, whom the Lord had moved mightily, ''and you talk like a lawyer of proof! What *proof* do I need? Do you ask for proof of the ground under your feet?''

''Compose yourself,'' said the Cardinal, with more assurance than he felt. ''It is precisely because I do not need proof of that, of the ground under my feet, that I do not go looking for it.''

''And what is that supposed to mean?'' cried Kaspar.

''This,'' said the Cardinal, who could recognize a deteriorating situation, ''I mean this, this *obscene* plot that you have uncovered. What is to be done? That is the question. It is a question you have asked yourself, and it is the question you have asked me. But you must also ask yourself: what do I hope to accomplish? Now, Kaspar, when I say that you are wrong, I mean that your method of going about things is wrong. If you persist in this course, you will accomplish nothing. You will become a laughing-stock, the butt of those people you seek to expose — *our* enemies, Kaspar. Nor do I speak lightly when I say *our*, for your enemies are my enemies, Kaspar, remember that. But you must think,'' here the Cardinal lowered his voice, ''you must hink how you have erred in bringing this book here, how you have erred even in writing this letter. What if I were not your friend, Kaspar? Why, if I did not know you, I would think you were a madman, a maniac. What an impression you would have created! For you see, Kaspar, you *must* see that there is no doubt in the Church's eyes that Brother Jordanus always was and will always be a convicted heretic. Can you bring him back to life? Of course not. You would succeed only in heaping universal odium on yourself and the cause you represent. That is what you would accomplish. I am glad you are listening to me, Kaspar — you are listening, aren't you? —; yes, I am glad because there is also something else I must tell you. Since I received your letter, I have not been exactly idle myself. Your information alarmed me, and so I have been conducting my own researches, with resources infinitely superior to yours, Kaspar; and I have found that while there is much that is cogent and convincing in what you say, there is not a shred of evidence to support your allegations. Do you honestly think, Kaspar, that the — ah — party you refuse to name (a wise move, very wise) would commit the crime of which he stands accused? And having done so, *if* he had done so, do you think he would fail to destroy the evidence, including this Captain? No, Kaspar, he would not. He would not have the slightest hesitation. He would destroy everything, Kaspar...." The Cardinal could see that Kaspar was listening respectfully and attentively, his head tilted to one side. "As for these suppositions of yours," he continued, "they are based on chance, the mere proximity of events and personalities. Let me give you some advice, Kaspar, some good advice," the Cardinal adopted an avuncular tone. "If you press forward with these charges, you will become a danger to me, and you will become even more dangerous to yourself. Ah, I realize you hadn't thought of that. But it is true, Kaspar. The man who gambles recklessly on a chance can be no friend of mine. You will remember this advice, Kaspar; in the years ahead you will remember it and you will be grateful to me."

The Cardinal concluded his speech and celebrated the triumph of *buon consiglio*. A glass of wine was called for. Yes, a glass of wine, or rather two glasses, the Cardinal thought, failing to take note of Kaspar's expression. And that was a mistake, as he would soon discover. But then there was nothing in the long cloisters of his memory and experience that could possibly have prepared him for what happened next.

The Cardinal was mentally consuming his wine and looking forward to sharing a toast and more of his wisdom with Kaspar when he heard himself called a pious hypocrite by the object of his fantasy.

"Wretch! Dissembler! I come to show you the truth and you spout wind!"

Could he have misheard?

"Fraud! Oh, infamy! A laughing-stock indeed! Not a shred of evidence!"

"Master Schopp," the Cardinal comandeered his most imperious manner: "*silence!*"

His worst fears confirmed, he leant over and rang the bell on his desk. "Bastiano," he said as the secretary appeared, "tell the *Magister Generalis* to come in. And you, Master Schopp, you will say nothing of our conversation, do you hear, nothing!"

Kaspar stood up.

"Old man, you cannot threaten me. I fear no evil. I have means to ..."

The Cardinal reached in his desk and dropped a packet of letters on its surface. Kaspar had time to recognize his own handwriting, then just as swiftly the letters were returned to the drawer and he found himself the subject of a majestic gaze, half contemptuous and half amused, a gaze that cut him to the quick.

Kaspar sat down.

"Be silent," said the Cardinal of San Severina.

T

Fra Ippolita Maria, who was a man of cultivated simplicity and precise judgement, made an impressive entrance, master of all he surveyed.

Kaspar Schopp, however, was in no mood to appreciate the nuances of character. The tentacles of fear embraced him and gave a preparatory squeeze.

"Do be seated," said the Cardinal.

The scene before him, the *Magister Generalis* thought, had been composed and prearranged. It was too well-ordered to be accidental. A troubled yet benign expression reigned on the Cardinal's face, such an expression as he had worn when he had first raised the matter of Schopp. And this other, with the mournful look of a spaniel dog, this must be Schopp himself.

He had seen him earlier in the corridor and noted that his appearance had changed for the worse.

"Master Schopp, I think?" he enquired, and observed that while Kaspar shook his head, the Cardinal nodded.

"Yes," His Eminence said. "That is Kaspar Schopp."

Very strange, the General thought. Was the man dumb?

Mystified though he was, Ippolita Maria saw no point in wasting words. "Yes," he said. "I have heard a great deal about you from His Eminence. You have been entertaining some doubts, I believe, concerning the legality of Giordano's trial and execution?"

The General looked first to Kaspar and then to the Cardinal, who nodded and smiled. Kaspar followed his eyes, perplexed by this nodding and smiling.

"Well?" Fra Ippolita returned his gaze to Kaspar and waited for an answer.

An answer. . . .

Panic was uncoiling in Kaspar. His letters, they had his letters! What would they do to him now?

"You may speak openly before this Reverend gentleman," said the Cardinal.

Kaspar nodded mechanically. He was afraid, had always been afraid he realized, gripping the palm of one hand in the nails of the other. Keep thy tongue from evil and thy lips from speaking guile! The God of righteousness was also the God of vengeance. Was it possible that he had been mistaken in the Lord? The Lord had spoken and the Lord had betrayed him!

Or else it was the Lord God that had erred. Kaspar moistened his lips and felt the pain in his hand. How could God make an error? If only he could stop thinking these things!

"Doubt," said the General mildly, "is always legitimate."

"There," the Cardinal murmured. "I told him, father. But he was not to be consoled."

"Providing, of course," the General continued, "it can be answered. To be perfectly honest, I have had my own doubts."

"We appreciate your frankness, father," the Cardinal made sympathetic noises. "You see how very distressed he is," he added, taking Kasper's misery unto himself.

"He need not be. It is sometimes very difficult to work within the established principles of the Church," said the General, directing a long, narrow look at the Cardinal, who acknowledged the accuracy of this remark with lowered eyes and relegated himself to silence.

"He is not alone," Fra Ippolita refocussed his attention on Kaspar. "Personally, I experienced very grave doubts concerning the legality of Giordano's execution. It was — and to some extent it still is — my opinion that our Brother was mentally incompetent, if not at the time of his trial, then certainly thereafter. I will explain what I mean presently. For the moment, should you think my point of view too liberal, I assure you it is not. To continue: it is my belief that Giordano's sufferings, most of which he brought on his own head, had combined with a natural instability of temperament to unhinge him. He was not, therefore, in a position to judge his own situation objectively."

The General interrupted this cogent analysis to consider the young man before him. Master Schopp, who had not said a solitary word since the General had made his entry, evidently was not listening; and Ippolita Maria, who disliked the needless expenditure of words, asked Kaspar if he had attended the execution.

Kaspar nodded again. He was listening; there was a part of

him that could not help listening, although he did not like what he heard. Mentally incompetent? God was mentally incompetent. Otherwise He would have not allowed the Cardinal to intercept his letters. It was God who was not listening; and it was God and the rest of creation that was mad.

Fra Ippolita turned questioningly to the Cardinal, who had replaced his earlier expression with a look of devout concentration.

The Cardinal raised an eyebrow, which Fra Ippolita understood as a signal to continue. Whatever had taken place between the two, the General decided, was no concern of his. Of course, that would not prevent him from making enquiries....

"Well, then," the General resumed his argument, "you must have noticed his bearing; the seeming indifference, the aloofness almost to the point of arrogance. You will recall how, when he was brought out and shown the stake, he behaved *as if no one was there*." The General paused weightily. "He behaved, gentlemen, as if his fate was happening to someone else...."

Kaspar considered this. In spite of himself, he was interested in what the General said. And he was thankful that the Cardinal had apparently not mentioned his letters to Ippolita Maria.

"He behaved, gentlemen, as if he were already dead...."

Kaspar conjugated the verb 'to die'. It was possible to say, he reflected, 'I will die' or 'I am dying' but not 'I am dead' or 'I have been dead'. Only the Nazarene had said such things.

"You see," Fra Ippolita confided, "I am also of the opinion that there may have been much more to the case than simple dementia. I think our brother was possessed."

The three men crossed themselves.

"Possessed!" Kaspar cried. The smell of burning pitch was in his nostrils: pitch and human flesh.

No more of this! He wanted to hear no more! And yet ...

"Not only that," Fra Ippolita capitalized on the point, "but he had a remarkable ability to confound those who came into contact with him. Of course, I am not speaking of literal possession," Fra Ippolita mused. "Yet it was a remarkable ability he had, one that I can confirm from personal experience. Shortly before his death, I went to see him, to reason with him, to show him the way," Fra Ippolita smiled, "although it is impossible to reason with a madman, you know."

The present, the present was being used up! History was nothing remembered; madness was everything remembered. His mind, his mind was losing its grip!

"Quite." The Cardinal broke his vow of silence and looked at Kaspar. He had been thinking that it was possible to have too much of a good thing. However, Schopp would learn his lesson — would learn and would not forget. "Perhaps you would mind telling Master Schopp here what happened when you went to see Giordano?" he asked Fra Ippolita and leaned back to observe the result, watching Kaspar closely.

Kaspar returned a blank stare. He did not want to hear, had already heard enough. If he applied his mind sufficiently, he would hear nothing: from himself and the others. Since the present existed only by reason of his being here, he should experience little difficulty. He had only to be patient and the words would go away. A question of will, that was all: the will unvanquished that would ride roughshod over the fear and the dread of nothingness. Yes, it was a question of will. Everything would pass soon, very soon, and he would feel like a new man.

Fra Ippolita hesitated. "I was coming to that. It's really very simple," he said in his best conversational manner. "You see, he took me for the devil...."

"Ach!" Kaspar swayed in his chair. Beads of sweat stood out on his forehead and he conceded to himself that he was feeling rather sick, yes, as if he would vomit. But that too was a question of the will.

"Thank you, father, thank you." The Cardinal, Fra Ippolita noted, sounded damnably pleased with himself. "I think you have said enough. Yes, quite enough."

T

"Let me give you some more advice, Kaspar," the Cardinal was saying after Fra Ippolita had said his brief farewell. "Leave Rome, for a while at least. It will only get hotter here and the heat can be unbearable. Go to the north. You need a rest. And relaxation. I have a villa near Trento."

"My lord . . ."

"Say nothing, Kaspar. Remember, be silent." The Cardinal extended his ring. "Ah, one moment. The book, give it here, Kaspar; give the book to me. Go now, Kaspar. Make your peace with man, if not with God. Go now, my son."

The Cardinal observed Kaspar's humble retreat. A man to be reckoned with, Schopp. Crazy, of course. *Furioso,* but still . . . Enthusiasm and a certain amount of rage was to be expected in the young.

He opened his book and began to read: *'Miraculum magnum a Trismegisto appellabitur homo . . .'*

The words reminded him of something and he rang for his secretary. "Bastiano," he said, "bring me some wine, some Orvieto. And, Bastiano, I do not want to be disturbed. Wait, Bastiano, wait!" He remembered there was one final task to be performed and reached into his desk for Kaspar's letters.

"Burn these," he said. "Burn them, Bastiano."

And this worthy Christian Prince again took up his book. Now, where was he? Ah, yes: *'. . . infinitus est deus, immensus ubique totus.'*

T

Kaspar's route took him back across the Campo de' Fiori. Another man would have chosen another way. Not Schopp.

In the middle of the square, he noticed a statue. It beckoned to him, then vanished.

With the simplicity of one who has found the truth, he knew that he was insane. I am mad, he thought; I am mad and will go to the north.

IX

*Although the Pope is the Vicar of Christ, he is
not Caesar.*

— Lorenzo Valla

*We are educated not by the inactive and barren
philosopher, but by Scipio in arms; not by the
schools of Athens, but in the Spanish camps. We
are educated not by speeches but by deeds and
examples.... The true judge of the world is he
who makes history. He is the sole, pious and
inscrutable judge.*

— Gianmichele Bruto

The Vatican, January 1600

Saint Agnes' Eve! A broken day of half-glimpsed cor-
respondences, the eternal intruding with its cold intimations of
mortality: Giordano's, the Perugians', my own. Aquaviva, the
Jesuit General, a man as spiritual as his name, was here; also the
French and Spanish ambassadors, Cardinal Bellarmine, and —
my nephew. I am nervous and out of sorts. My physicians
prescribe rest, and last night I was kept awake with a raging
toothache. An abscess on the root of a lower right molar, I am
told, though I fear the trouble may be deeper. The jaw is inflamed, and the tooth will have to come out. It is the only
cure....

Eight years have passed since God chose me, eight years and not a day but I am reminded of the disclaimer all Popes make: 'I am unworthy but shall not contradict the divine will.' Some men grow in this office and when they come to die can say, 'At last, God has made me worthy.' Others grow but not the way God intended, their souls and coffers running to fat, grow bloated and die as they lived, foully. Still others spend a lifetime hoping, are elected, crowned and, all the same, they die. So with my predecessors: Urban, dying as he was installed, a two-weeks' Pope; Gregory, who survived some months; Innocent, eight weeks — these three, an interregnum during which the conclave feared to meet, then myself, a mortal man like the rest. Nor am I the first to bear this style. There was another Clement VIII, the Spaniard, Muñoz, at the time of the Schism, antipope and pretender with Benedict XIV (so-called) to the great Colonna's crown. Three Popes to parcel up Christendom, three Popes and one parish — the world! Those times are buried, my title their epitaph chosen deliberately so that men will not forget. Yet there are still those who scorn and say, 'We know what's dead and buried can live again. These antipopes, for example. Or take your predecessors: today a Pope, tomorrow a corpse. *Unam sanctam*, what's that but your divine pretence? You're human, how can you rule for God?'

The Pope, whose government brings God to the world, rules absolutely or not at all. Therefore, his rule must be secure; if not, then it is a pretence and a sham. But I do not condescend to answer the cry of faction, preferring instead to let my achievements speak for themselves. I have made peace between France and Spain; have seen Henri crowned King and restore himself and France to the True Faith. I have clarified the *Index*, making much that was obscure and uncertain, clear and certain. I have annexed lost territories back to Rome; increased the revenues and restored the spirit of confidence, vigilance and the law. These things I have done in God's name and with His help, and I hope to do more yet, hope that when my time comes I can say, without pride or fear of contradiction, 'At last, God has made me worthy.'

And now, God willing, I have to rule on a man's life, invoking those privileges which have accrued to me as Pope, the right to define and clearly imprint doctrine, declaring the Church's extraordinary magisterium, the sum of revealed and interpreted truths, as my ultimate justification. There can be no weakness against heresy, no room for debate. My ruling must be final, as irrevocable to the Church as to the object of its intent.

In this book, a chronicle of old Popes, I have searched out precedents and have discovered that history affords many an inglorious example of a Pope who has ruled infallibly only to have his ruling overthrown in a generation or less, bull and counter-bull cancelling all direction and making a mockery of our claims to divine authority. Here's a famous case, cited by those who would ignore our dispensation. Pope Nicholas III, the Orsini, having rid Rome of the foreign yoke and giving her a new constitution, desired to strike a blow for Christ. Men are corrupt, he noticed. "Behold the fowls of the air," this Nicholas declared, "for they sow not, neither do they reap." Then thinking of the rich man, the camel and the needle's eye, this Pope saw the straight and narrow way and declared himself on the poverty of Christ. His opinion is written in the bull, *Exiit qui seminat*: whoever denies the doctrine of Christ's poverty and lives like a Pope is himself heretical. Yet it is not so easy to follow this Christ who first taught the rule of self-denial. Two, three decades later, all this is overthrown. Comes a new Pope. John XXII, the Frenchman, Jacques d'Euse, called the Banker of Avignon for leaving the Church some four million florins richer than he found it, and this during the Babylonian Captivity, a time of profligacy and waste. What does this Pope say and think of Our Lord's poverty? He sees the little brotherhood of the Spiritual Franciscans, though poor, have grown enormously righteous in their poverty; he sees other Orders, likewise denying the fruits of this world, outrageously swollen with their wealth, sees as only a calculating man can, smugness, hypocrisy and vice — corruptions identical with those his predecessor had attempted to combat. His answer? The bull, *Cum inter nonnullos*, in which it is infallibly written that whoever accepts the rule of

Christ's poverty and lives like a saint is heretical.

Who rules — which is the heretic, Pope Nicholas or Pope John?

Neither, I say, Though contradictory, both were right as the need required. God gave these men no finished statement, and when they spoke infallibly their words were still human. However the spirit took hold of them, so they were moved: in part according to their natures and in part according to God's. No wonder, then, that they should conflict. The wonder is that the Church has survived, and continues to survive, the worst and the best of men. Here is my answer to those who would scornfully deny the Pope's infallibility. The truth is revealed, but never completely, never all at once. For the fullness of truth in the fullness of time, God alone can understand.

Now I must judge this particular man, should I forget eternity? Scripture, tradition, the Church's magisterium, these shall be my guides: the eternal revealed in the temporal, the infinite in the finite — just as Giordano has taught. All time coheres in eternity, every turning point on the road to heaven or hell. Giordano and I must each make our own separate choices. I have heard him called an atheist. The same charge was rumoured against Patrizi when he said he did not fear God, only man. Because he was my friend, I spared him the torture; I knew Francesco's fears and was certain he would keep silent. And so he has, as silent as the grave to which he's gone. Poor Francesco! Plato was his God, subtler than Aristotle as heresy is subtler than paganism, more refined, closer to the truth. "Insidious subtleties," Bellarmine's opinion.

Giordano's an atheist? Would to God he were! But I can see no evidence of it, and neither can the Cardinal. It is three years since I summoned Robert from Naples as papal theologian, and during that time his opinions have grown more meticulous by the hour. The Cardinal breathes in with one lung and out with the other. He is a musician, his own antiphonary. When I ask him for counsel, it is like this with him: "You must proceed, Holiness, by means of counsel, decrees and solemn decisions. You must decide what is the faith and what can be reasonably debated. I can advise you, Holiness; I cannot tell you what to do."

"Then advise me," I said this afternoon, even while the pain was raging in my jaw. "Is he innocent, or is he guilty?"

The Cardinal could not say. Yet he is right, and knows that he is right. I alone must be the final judge. My decision has been too long in abeyance — *ad beneplacitum papae* for almost the whole of my reign. An honest man, Bellarmine, if that is not a contradiction in terms, an honest and a careful man to whom I owe more than I care to tell. When this year is out, he will have his reward. I will give him — something. An archdiocese perhaps. In return for which, he can defend our rights in matters directly related to this world. Between heaven and hell, there is no other!

When this year is out.... In Rome, a year of Jubilee. No door is kept barred during this year. I have but to pick up this bell and order the Congregation to terminate its session. A miserable sinner spared for the sake of Jubilee. Hosannas will be sung, and the people will rejoice. Praise to the all highest merciful! A miserable sinner? An impenitent. Because I am Pope, it cannot be done. Because I am a man, it cannot be done. To legitimatize Christ's poverty is one thing, to sanctify heresy another. And if I were not Pope, I dare not risk my soul by defying the man who would rule instead of me. Unlike my Cardinal theologian, the Law does not equivocate. For so it is written: 'Now the spirit speaketh expressly that in the latter times some shall depart from the faith, giving heed to seducing spirits and the doctrines of devils.' The faith indwelling, righteousness, Scripture, Christ's example and precept, all insist that false teachers and their works be condemned, and that no man should fear to condemn them. As Holy Father, I am commanded to see that this is carried out. The Law clearly instructs me to press toward the mark for the prize of the high calling of God in Christ Jesus, and to search out an even higher prize, that I may one day sit in heaven at my Father's table. All doors are open in this year of Jubilee; to one man they remain closed, even eternally closed, as they would be to me if I were to pardon him.

'There is nothing new under the sun' — Giordano's words, insolently flung in my face. 'The thing that has been, it is that which shall be. . . .' Oh, pithy Giordano! Why were you not like Francesco; why were you not afraid of the weather?

Yet how pertinent, how unintentially apt is the Nolan's letter. "His errors are not so new," says Bellarmine. "They have occurred before and will again." Solomon and Pythagoras would have relished the irony, both casuistical men like the Nolan himself. If nothing is new, then my task is not exactly novel. I will defend the traditions of the Faith against this other tradition which Giordano represents. O altitudino! What heights he would ascend, daring the summits of the mountains before he has learned to walk. Perfection is a circle, he says: an infinite sphere whose centre is nowhere and whose circumference is everywhere. I have seen the image before, the serpent consuming itself or the phoenix rising from its own ashes. That kind of perfection soars too high for my liking. Therefore we shall beat him down, shall bring him crashing back to earth even as Peter blasted Simon Magus from the air with a curse when the wizard floated in the Forum before Nero and the *equites*. His volatile spirits we shall match with the most volatile of elements, and as is our right, shall fight fire with fire.

He is a man drunk with God, a man who has arrogated the Divinity to himself. By virtue of some special revelation, granted to no one else, he would *become* God. There is little the Church can do to help him. Neither holy terror nor Christian grace can sway him from his sense of messianic purpose. Such a man must necessarily take all the contradictions of the world unto himself. He loves what he hates, and hates what he loves. Such a man is more than lost; ultimately, he is self-condemned. For in Giordano and in all those like him, there exists a shadow. That shadow is man's old eternal enemy. And that shadow he has recreated exactly as he would have done the world. As with every man, Giordano's world is a microcosm of the greater world, *with this exception*: being perfect, he cannot conceive of imperfection. Inhuman, his pride mirrors and multiplies Adam's fall. . . .

So the man and so his works. Yet here again, I do not think that they will be condemned for the right reason. There is much here that smacks of Manichaeanism. Christ was human, a magician. Or if he was divine, he was not the Messiah but merely the precursor of one greater than Himself. Mankind, writes Giordano, can attain to higher states than Christ. From this, it is not far to seek the means. The true Christ is the Aeon Jesus, the Messiah who was neither born nor suffered death, for how could God be incarnated in such a poor world as ours? This doctrine is contagious. Like a plague, it lies dormant in some ages and is rampant in others. It is an error as old as man, as old as the religion of the mind, so called after the fashion of the Gnostic heresiarchs. It is the teaching of the Carpocratians, condemned in the second century; the Messalians in the fifth, the Paulicians in the seventh, and the Bogomiles and the Albigensians in the eleventh and fourteenth centuries. All these sects and ages find their culmination in this one man, whose teaching is leavened with Zoroastrianism and the return to the fallen gods. There is no evil but that it is good, nor any good but that it is evil. God and the devil are one both in nature, and nature in both. I stand in the shadow and call it light. A child is born; I say it is death. Life, what's that but a dream? Man's no more than a bundle of atoms. Substance, all is substance. Nothing is real. The generations of man go stumbling into the night like some processional of the blind. And now comes our visionary brother to proclaim the reality of endless cycles, the unceasing flow and rhythm of life. And what is the true and only end of this eternal flux? It is the human mind that, having invented an idea of itself and its origins, must pry ever more deeply into the mire. From so much mental slime, our Magus plots the ascent of cosmic man; in the name of paradox, must abolish all paradox. Scripture, call that the Word of the Lord? Nature's our book. There we shall read, there learn mastery and power. The mystery of mysteries is ours, the Holiest of Holies. There is nothing we cannot do. Where should we begin? With something obvious, with something under our noses. The universe, of course! Whoever says it is finite, says God must be too. And we are called heretics! It is the Church that is false, and the Pope who is the devil.

I know their arguments and would sooner have an honest Lutheran than any of these mystical seers. Aldonistae, Humiliati, Patarini, adepts of the Rosy Cross or Giordanisti, call them by any name, they're worse than all the reforming sects! I'll put their doctrines to the test of death and transubstantiation, I'll administer the sacraments they respect, and I do not mean as in the Viaticum! There are ample precedents in my book and in Saint Epiphanius. *Stirpitus amputari*, that is the only way to exterminate heresy.

But it is true, what Robert says. I must proceed by means of council, decrees and solemn decisions. God would not like me to rail. The Faith is best asserted in measured phrasing; not too haughty but precise, exact. I am father of the Christian people, master in Christ's house. I am Peter, supreme and perpetual judge. Ambrose is my guide: where I am, there the Church must also be. I am the rock unshakeable. The keys of the Kingdom of earth were given to me to hold on this earth — where else but here? Master of myself, I must judge this man as I would judge myself — judge and condemn. Why not? If I were Giordano, I would expect to be condemned.

Aquaviva mentioned the case in audience today. A casual reference, for he'd come on other business. "Holy Father," said he, "such men are best kept alive to frustrate their expectancy of martyrdom." Why must Jesuits always proceed by indirection? Bellarmine — he's the same. Yet the point is valid, most certainly it is. But how to do it? If I keep him alive and imprisoned, another eight years could pass, or ten or twenty. I could die; the matter would be left unresolved, and I would still be accountable before the Throne of God. Alive or dead, he is our rival, arch-antinomian and enemy of the Faith. Like those Manichees who would be free of the tyranny of matter, Giordano would violate the sanctity of God's absolute commands. He is a law unto himself and therefore must deny our rights to interpret Scripture and dispose of souls — prerogatives we cannot surrender. How could I keep him alive?

"You've done so for eight years," Aquaviva said. "Another few can't hurt. His present lodging is not the best of places. In God's own time, he might die."

"So might we all," I answered him. "Then what?"

"God's will be done," said he.

"And God's will is done through men," said I. "We shall decide in our own time. Your business, Claudio?"

That drew him up and returned him to his business. "I've heard the Savelli are bankrupt. The Castel Gandalfo will be for sale...."

Day by day, these little affairs come to occupy our attention. Our coinage and postage; communications and supply, administration, *Buon Governo*, the business of the Apostolic Chamber, buying and selling, provisioning for a hundred thousand souls: these are the muscles of Rome, and the Pope is the head that directs them.

Investment in property, like that in souls, helps secure the future. Giordano's soul, now, what value does that have for the Church? He has said he would purify Rome, return it to the time of the Fathers or even before. I say it is not the God of the Fathers he worships. The living God to him is the merest residue of God's creative act, nature indeed yet nature sundered from the divine. God is not *in* nature like the juice of an orange. He is beyond nature, beyond our understanding. If the Lord has chosen to appear and reveal Himself, it is none of our doing. But Giordano has made his God a natural thing, a force or an essence like the power that moves the tides or drives the planets. The death of the God I know (and of the God who knows me) is everywhere written in his works. Such a force as he worships does not need man. It is blind, implacable, unloving. Out of the ruined transcendent, Giordano celebrates the return of the little gods: Osiris, Anubis, Thoth, Tat, Hamon — oh, they are infinite, these demiurges, idols of delusion and despair. Through their invocation, our Magus would conquer the universe, like Faustus would probe the darkest secrets of nature and command the powers of the air to do his bidding. Accursed superstition! For this alone the fire would be too noble a fate, though if it is

214

purification he wants, the fire will suffice. Even so, it is not in these heretical and abominable practices, the rites of magic, that his worst error lies. He has held up the mirror of his soul, and, forgetting the fatal obeisance of Narcissus, it is his own image, self-reflected, that he calls divine. Of that God whom I approach in all humility, who moves me to ask in wonder and mystery: *Lord, who are you?* — of the living God, there is not a trace. For it is humanity he worships, humanity that he has made omnipotent. Delusive and fatal error! How long can mankind afford to gaze in self-adulation; how long before the image shatters? The mirror of memory and magical act that Giordano calls science must surely break, and then — farewell, little gods; farewell mankind. . . .

We who are of the earth were nevertheless created spiritual beings, and cannot live without mystery or the intercession of the divine. But Giordano would tear down all forms of mystery, believing it is possible to strike beyond the veil of appearances. Great are the faults of his nature: arrogance, inconstancy and intolerance — these mixed with his prodigious appetite for knowledge and power. That a man so learned could be so unwise! Not only does he take it upon himself to interpret the Word but he would deflect each and every honest enquiry into his speculations, and always in that spirit of hideous contempt, overbearing, insolent, neglectful of all conventional discourse. I know the voice; though I have never heard it, I know who speaks. It is a hellish parody of a Saint I love, Augustine, who in his own youth turned aside from God: 'You say it is written that in the beginning God created heaven and earth. I ask: *what was He doing before?* My answer: I do not know; I do not want to know, it is not proper that I should know.' But like Augustine, I do know that voice. Inhuman, vile, it is the voice of man's eternal traducer, Satan, who first brought death into the world.

The *man*, not the devil, is the harbinger of our spiritual death. Then burn him, the still small voice whispers. The people will understand it is for the good of Rome. The people? They understand nothing — least of all our hesitation. Somewhere, we have failed Brother Jordanus. He's a man who might have served our interests; for all his faults, he could have proven worthy. But the people! They would destroy the wisdom of the wise as Paul says. When my predecessor was dead and lay in state, I saw them, the people, ogling at what they supposed was his papal incorruptibility. The brain, viscera and lights of the dead Pope had been removed and placed in sealed amphora; the vacant head and spiritless body scoured, then painted with unguent preservatives; his carcass, thus embalmed and salted, placed on view for the people to admire. There he lay in all his hollow majesty, as changeless as paradise itself. A miracle! A great miracle! Can you not smell it, the odour of sanctity? Distinctly! A holy man, a very holy man.... And he was, he was — when alive. But then I looked on the varnished corpse and wondered what use it had. Where are your works now, Giovanni Fachinnetti, where your hopes, Giovanni, but eight weeks styled Innocent and now uncrowned by death? Will you speak to the people, lay down the law? Will you rise from the dead, Giovanni? 'No need,' you seemed to say. 'They are convinced God has kept me fresh.' The people! Sometimes, I think their minds are as swaddled in doctrine as this body was wrapped in its cerements — mummified. Yet even in this state, the corpse had its uses. The people looked, they saw, they believed, Does it matter how or why?

There's a lesson here. The common people have an uncommon belief. 'Christ belongs to all those who have a humble attitude and not to those who set themselves up above the flock.' Saint Clement's words. Neither Innocent in his miraculous incorruptibility, nor Giordano with his pride, nor myself, all powerful, can alter the people. I have learnt to live with them and their imperfections — some would say I have learnt to live a lie. But the truth is supple and alone makes history possible. Without truth, there is only the opinion of the marketplace, the unending babble of secular debate. Shepherd of my flock, the sheep as well as the lambs, I must lead, as Cyprian said, with actions not words. When I invoke the Law, it is to purchase a moment of eternity, not for myself but for all my people. It is in time that I speak for the eternal, speak to the lowest and the highest of men. I ask the common people to forget the sorrows of their meagre living, their neighbours' sins, the merchant's guile, the Law's seeming indifference; to the poets I say, leave off this play of intelligent foolishness; to the philosophers, abandon your quest for universals in particulars; to our Roman knights, drop your petty feuds; to the Princes and Captains of this Church and State, remember your Lord and Master, desist for once from your perpetual money grubbing, your accumulations of rents and estates; to Kings and Lords of whatever lands, be not dismayed that earthly kingdoms should pass away; to every several man, I proclaim the truth eternal in the name of the Church universal. And this I do by the grace of her countless saints, martyrs and virgins; in the sacraments with which she begets and raises her children; in the faith which she preserves ever inviolate; in the holy laws which she imposes on all; and in the name of the evangelical counsels through which she admonishes sinners and commands the faithful to obedience; this for all time, past, present and future, for the Church militant, visible and triumphant.

There is no power on earth that can stop me. Eight years have come and gone since God chose me? It is sixteen hundred since Christ made Peter a fisher of men and the Apostle learned that the truth is to be lived, suffered and endured. For the truth is not to be encountered passively. The truth is pitiless. And now, my God, if this were some other world and Giordano were in my place, I would expect him to condemn me.

Yet I do not hate him. That's one luxury I can ill afford. My cause is not personal, and nor is Giordano's, I hope. We have never met, and therein I detect the workings of providence, for no vicious man in after-time can claim that this Pope acted from malice or vengeance. I find it very strange that we should be woven like two strands in the one design, thus not to cross. Nor will we ever. It is too late now to play the lord with Giordano or appeal to his Christian conscience. Either course, he would take as a sign of our weakness. 'What, the Pope deigns to treat with me! My victory is already half won without his beatific presence....'

It is an awesome power: to expunge (or preserve) a life I have never known. Does he understand his danger? Some men are as immune from fear as they are from pain. Yet there are others who quake if I so much as raise my little finger in their direction. Why not this man? I can only wonder, as I wonder at my own disquiet. My mind is frangible today: the toothache. I have dosed the abscess with oil of cloves, but I can no more resist probing the hurt than I can stop thinking of Giordano. What, should the Pope be reduced to this condition by a little *mal di dente*? It is *maldicenza* that hurts me worse: the backbiting of the people. They will say I am afraid; this supreme and perpetual judge, afraid to act....

If it does not cease, I will call my physicians. I have no doubt of their remedy. They will come with their pincers and knives: cut, grind and rip. The mitred fang will crumble, and his tortured beatitude will spit bone and blood into the medicinal bowl. The cure is worse than the pain — yet efficient. If only heresy were that simple to rip out!

What is it that frightens me? There was that time when I looked on Innocent, looked and recoiled, not at the corpse but at the shadow of my own death. I saw the ruin of all our days, the Church herself embalmed, saw and was afraid. Yet something else in that shell of a man still had the power to startle me. I thought I stood in his presence again, as if (according to certain tenets) his soul lingered a while in his body, there to ascertain its own state and the state of other souls too. *Petrus, quo vadis*? I thought, words that have taken on another meaning for me now. Who can say where his soul is going, if not the Pope? Of all men he is closest to God; and there is none more alone.

I dreamed of him once as he lay in state surrounded by the College of Cardinals in their mourning vestments. "Ippolito," he said, for so I was then, "this burden weighs me down. I am choking, Ippolito — suffocating." None of the others heard this, the mark of my election. I awoke then and thought of the Blessed Saint Catherine's words: "O men who are not men but rather devils incarnate, how you are blinded by your disordered love for the rottenness of the body, the delights and bedazzle-ments of this world.'' This pomp for a corpse was a travesty of the ritual, and when the time comes for me, I'll choose some simpler ceremony and insist that my last earthly wish be obeyed....

I should forget Innocent, he's dead. Yet I cannot forget him, cannot forget the past. *What is left in the Church that is not contaminated or corrupted?* The day is shot through with coincidence. My book falls open at this passage I've marked: the monk of Leyden to Clement VII, last to bear that style, Giulio de' Medici, who brought war, plague, famine and Spanish op-pression to Rome — the sum of Christ's judgement brought down on his own unworthy head. *What is there left of integrity among the clergy, of honour among the nobility, of sincerity among the people?* Thus a lowly monk called Peter, the Pope's better self, dared speak in such a voice to such a Pope. And he was a Carthusian, this Peter, a member of that Order founded by the second Saint Bruno. God forbid that my actions should make a third out of Giordano! *All is put to confusion, wound-ed, ruined, mutilated. From the soles of the feet to the crown of the head, there is nothing healthy left....* I shall read no more!

That was seventy years ago, a Biblical span against my sixty-four. Seventy years on, and what has been done to combat these manifest abuses? I have implemented the Tridentine Decrees, have everywhere pressed the need for inner reform — of men as much as institutions. Yet vice and heresy still flourish; the Church is as divided as it ever was, neither Spain nor God could crush the English schism, and I think we have been rather too hasty in cleansing the stables, have given too much en-couragement to those who expect the imminent coming of the Kingdom of God. The Kingdom? No, it is a republic they seek, not realizing that the people love to see some show of ceremony. Such men are fired by envy and would divide our office and powers among themselves. Francesco Pucci, there was one: like Giordano, another of our magical Christians, a Florentine aristocrat and a democrat as well, worse than any Calabrian bandit. I shortened his life by his head's length, and this I did without compunction. The noble Pucci longed to make himself leader of a general council of reform, a council of all spiritual persons and lovers of the truth. Spiritual persons? Oh, very! Lovers of the truth? Of Satan! If they had succeeded, Francesco and his kind would in reality have been created Popes, or Caesars, captains of all souls except their own.

Pucci I squashed as I would have a flea, not because of his beliefs but because he dared submit his cause to providence — a flea grown spiritual! The Jews say every flea's entitled to his bite, and so, at the last, Francesco had his fill of blood. He died as he had lived — in expectation of a miracle. There's the danger of all reformers. They cannot see when they are beaten, nor will they accept any compromise short of death or victory. Move against them, and they will shed blood. Do not move, and their cause becomes rebellious. I say reform must come from above, otherwise it is not reform but revolution. And even then, let the reforms be gradual: no sudden shift in heaven or earth. The Kingdom of Naples is my example: ours by feudal right, Spain's by possession — an ill-governed and turbulent state whose people must murder to assert their rights. This latest rebellion goes straight to the heart of the matter. "We have some Dominican Brothers claiming Roman exemption from our laws," King Philip writes. Campanella's brethren! After daring to ally themselves with the Turk, they throw themselves at Rome! The least of our troubles, and also the greatest: an example of what will occur when authority is usurped....

I do not mourn lost opportunities nor past errors. It is the future that frightens me, the thought that all action comes too late. I fear what we have created in Rome. Something is going out from the centre: the light of too many fires illuminates all Europe. A new kind of man has come into existence here. I see him darkly in the shadow of the flames. He is a man without faith and honour, but intelligent enough to see where his own best interests lie. He is neither a heretic nor a true believer, for this man believes in nothing other than expediency. He is essentially a man without soul, a human machine. And because he regards the mass of mankind in the same light, he is a man without compassion. The future belongs to him and his kind, and I fear them more than any heretic. Church or state are equally well served by such men. Chameleons, they are as changeable as the coats they wear. I have lived to see the incarnate dawn of this particular species. Tomorrow, the twilight.

I am an old man gone in the teeth! I grow old and garrulous, moralizing in the face of death. Actions are needed, not words. When you have done what you must, Clement, then you will feel better. Now *that* is not the voice of the Spirit....

What am I to do? Giordano's intransigence has destroyed all hope of compromise. Yet there was a time when I thought of letting him go, of making his cause ours. There need have been no vast overthrow of mind, no revolution in Church or state. With a man like this, it is often better to proceed obliquely. Subtlety, as Bellarmine well knows, is its own reward. Therefore, we should match subtlety with subtlety and not use force. Giordano is no ordinary heretic. Make him ours, and his faults are neutralized. The future is averted; the tomorrow of tomorrows that I fear will not come to pass. But events have moved too quickly for both of us, and it now seems that there is no longer any point in securing his confession — even if that could have been done. What freedom have I left? I cannot alter the past, and I am powerless to change the future. I am as much a prisoner as Giordano. Deadly equivalence! Giordano has taken one way, and I the other. But what choice have we exercised? None, I say. It is as if the way could exist without the taker, the choice without the chooser, and all is predetermined and ineluctable. Yet I am Pope and must defend the freedom of the will. What freedom? Spain presses me hard — Spain and my nephew. Then free will is an illusion, and it is an illusion that I must defend. How can there be freedom in a 'must'? Words! Because I am Pope, I shall choose, and choose deliberately, to defend the illusion of choice. It is the supreme paradox, one that I would defend with my life, and one that will cost Giordano his.

Spain is displeased with our rebellious brethren in the south, and Philip has threatened to hang Campanella's friends out of hand. So he could for all I care, were it not a trespass on our rights. But how uncommon is the destiny that shapes these events! Hardly a month has passed since the rebellion and since my nephew first came to me with this story of his Captain's wife. "Listen to me, uncle," he said; "listen to me." I listened, though I did not like what I heard, did not like it then as I do not like it now. "Cuckoldry is common, uncle; murder less so — even in Perugia. Roberto and Portia are fugitives from our laws. Spain has them hostage, our subjects. We have Giordano, and he is Spain's — a Neapolitan by birth. If we carry out the law and burn him, we'll get the runaways back. Justice is done, and seen to be done. Who can blame us? The situation is none of our making, and France can find no fault in this."

"I will forgive you your cynicism," said I, "but you have forgotten one thing. What guarantees do we have from Philip? We must have the fugitives back before I will treat with Spain."

"Either way," he said, "we cannot refuse this opportunity. God will not give us another...."

I agreed (although I found it distasteful) and made him my plenipotentiary. The negotiations have been — delicate. Spain was unwilling to surrender the fugitives without our most solemn and abiding oaths; and for our part we did not like to trade in lives....

Why did I agree? It was a free act, freely made. In such a choice, the Pope cannot afford a case of conscience. There's something I should remember to tell Bellarmine the next time he lectures me on freedom of the will, except, of course, the Cardinal shall not learn of this. Discretion and knowledge to the young; and to the old, wisdom and — sadness.

It has taken a month. And now my nephew informs me that the business is closed — or almost. Roberto and Portia will be taken under escort to Orvieto tomorrow. From there to Perugia where they will stand trial. Coppoli has agreed to help us. He will be pardoned, as much a victim of circumstance as the man he killed. God's will be done indeed! The others will be dealt with according to the law.

It was a fault of Giordano's to anger Spain. Because of that, these two lovers must hang. It is Portia I feel the most pity for. How terrible to die so young; worse not to know the reason why. At least she will not go unshriven to her grave....

The main chance! Two ideas unite and the matrix is formed: for Portia death in all ignorance, and for Giordano — what remains for him?

I found the answer here in my book. It is so — simple. Pope Nicholas, who ruled that men should follow the example of Christ's poverty, ruled for the truth; and so did Pope John, who ruled to the contrary. Giordano would smile at this, the coincidence of opposites. Truth and falsehood are what men believe them to be, neither more nor less, and the quality of their faith depends on the firmness of their belief. A circular argument, or it would be if we could live to see the closing of the circle, all fate revealed in the fullness of time. Giordano believes that he will die for the truth. It is this belief that gives him the courage to defy me and to commit his cause to posterity. Poor man! All that is left now is to disillusion him, to show him why he must die. Someone will have to tell him the whole sordid story, the truth as it is, stripped of its historical possibilities. *Because of a foolish girl, Giordano. That, and an arrangement with Spain. You see, there's nothing very noble to such a death....*

Ippolita Maria, there's my man! It is best that he should do it — as Giordano's spiritual superior.

I've polled the Cardinals. Madruzzi is for condemnation. The rest will follow his Christian example. How the pieces fit! Saint Agnes' Eve: does Portia dream of her lover now? Stupid girl! It is all so — wasteful.

Today's meditation returns me to mystery and the contemplation of mystery. How little we know of life and death; how imperfect is our understanding, yet how it is exalted and called the measure of all things! The wisest man that has ever lived cannot tell me why the sun should shine on one day and not on the next; he cannot say what force it is that drives the green shoot from the seed, nor why the flower must bear fruit, wither and die. He does not himself know why he is alive at this moment, instead of yesterday or tomorrow. He has read something of ages past, and pretends that he is a learned historian; of ages yet to come he is entirely ignorant, and yet he dares to prophesy. He is sad and he calls that a mood. He is happy, and what is that but another mood? He can never understand his own mind, yet he claims to read those of other people. He knows that all life passes into death, but when he comes to die the reason for his own life escapes him. The truth is evanescent, the guttering of a candle flame before shadow and act are forever eclipsed. Sometimes I think existence is no more than that play of illusion, and the world, nature, the passing seasons of our time, the vainest of vain appearances. The universe is a dream, and the sun of our imagined heaven could just as well be a pastel wafer painted on a paper sky. Who then is the Pope; who the heretic? My book does not answer, but asks some questions of a different order....

Between Theophylact, who sold his heavenly crown for 1500 pounds of gold, and Benedict Gaetani, who caused the imprisonment and murder of his predecessor, Pietro di Morone, what is there to choose? One-and-a-half millenia have passed since these lands came under priestly sway and during all that time theirs has been a history of simony, usury, fraud and falsehood. I say the dominium temporale is based on violence and the rule of violence. What Pope has been known to act as a true and faithful follower of Christ? Who is it that can claim to serve God and Mammon at the same time? Such a man is the Roman Pontiff, standing with one foot in heaven and the other on earth, straddling two kingdoms like a mighty colossus of corruption and depravity.

A moral man, our chronicler, but not a Pope. Rome has spoken. The case is finished.

Roma locuta est; causa finita est.

X

Vayne loves avaunt! infamous is your pleasure,
   Your joye deceite;
Your jewells, jestes, and worthless trash your treasure,
   Fooles common baite.
Your pallace is a prison that allureth
To sweete mishap, and rest that payne procureth.
                              — Robert Southwell

Morte induce ad amar l'alme canute.
Amor tragge a morir la gioventute.
[Death leads hoary souls to love.
Love leads the youth to die.]
                              — Giovan Battista Marino

Perugia, February 1600

I have been thinking how to stop time. Soon enough, it will stop
for me. And for Portia too, I must think of her. Soon enough,
soon enough.... I'm a Perugian, not afraid to die. But to hang
like a dog in the civic square! And for what? Summer dreams,
winter madness. It is a leaden age, and I should be glad to leave
it, through my way: the sword. At the time of the Baglioni, who
quartered their troops in the cathedral, their rivals, the Oddi,
knew how to die. A hundred and thirty of them were butchered
here and strung up in the square, their corpses decorating this

225

very building, the Palazzo Communale. In time, they would have their vengeance. But first the square was cleansed, thirty five altars consecrated and a Mass sung for the dead, the holy barracks meanwhile washed all over in wine. Four years passed before the Oddi returned in their hundreds to fall on a handful of their enemy, again in the square, a public place for dying. The child Raphael saw the fight, watched while Simonetto Baglione, eighteen years old and already a warrior, was cut to the bone, wounded more than twenty times, and, falling down the little pyramid of steps that I must soon take, bruised and gored, was taken up by a rescuing kinsman. Astorre his name was, the same as Coppoli but as different as the lion to the lamb, this Astorre, who came in golden armour, Mars on a white charger, its hooves slipping in the blood. Simonetto lived to fight again, until he was murdered at Astorre's wedding. There also died the groom himself, his throat cut while he lay asleep after the feast. Their bodies in turn were displayed in the square, and later, that of their cousin, Grifone, the murderer himself, whose mother begged him to forgive and be forgiven even as he bled and died. Simonetto's brother, summoned to Rome to explain the feud, bungled an attempt to kill the Pope, and was himself beheaded. So the Oddi were revenged, the Baglioni destroyed, their houses levelled, and all trace of the original crime obliterated.

They were men of marble and iron, and it was no shame in those days to fight and die. Yet I must hang, a civic prisoner defencelessly despatched. How shall it be? I will not go mewling of my innocence but will show them some contempt. I must descend into the square, face the citizenry, climb the last flight to the gallows. They're building the scaffold now, I can hear them hammering the nails into my coffin. Well then, so be it. I'll climb the scaffold in silence, look down on the square and this building, my second home, observe the fountain round which I played as a child, and, the lovers' knot securely fixed about my neck — jump....

Eternity's at the end of the drop, an end to all suffering. It is not death I fear, but the manner of my going — that sickens me. How long does a man have in that final fall, that fraction of infinity as his life and the rope are played out? They say that all the events of his life unfold before him, faces long forgotten and unfamiliar are instantly recaptured, cradle songs heard again, death's lullaby. Then the rope tautens, its pitch tuned to the harmonics of oblivion; the noose is tight, choking, and the body, not yet a body nor yet alive, kicks in the air. Still, how long is it before death intervenes and all life is extinguished from the hanging man? Who can tell, who has *lived* to tell?

Who dies first: Portia or myself? We die as we lived — together. Yet Coppoli — he goes free! Astorre's a nobleman and is therefore pardoned! And I — I hang! I should have taken my father's advice. "Wear purple stockings, my son. Become a priest. You're immune from most things then except the clap." What was it the Procurator said? "That a nobleman should kill in the service of a commoner does not suit the laws of our state." It is Astorre's fault, his the murderous deed for which I stand condemned. He played us false at the trial, claiming a plot to kill Dionighi — as if, that course being decided, I would have needed any such help! Yet all sympathy was with him, the people and the judges loving him for his loving crime. It was my office to kill Portia's husband, not Astorre's — they said this! But since I had killed no one, and since Dionighi was still alive and another man dead, my crime was against the state for having Astorre kill on my behalf — *my* crime! And if I had killed instead of Coppoli, would I then go free and would he hang in my place? *Corpo di mei!* A crime against the state! That is not why I am to hang. I have no name in the world, no family to speak of, no gold to suborn testimony — that is the reason. Is it not fitting and honourable to die for another's crime, is it not reasonable and just? A friend, he was my friend! And am I now to play the part of the noble gentleman and say all, all is forgiven? To be hanged, dissected, and grin in a glass case, is that not a worthy fate? Now by all the gods at once, what kind of justice is this?

"You must make your peace with Christ, my son," so my confessor, yesterday. Pious, mincing prig!

"You were a good student in school, Roberto. What has happened to you?"

Jesus! What school could have prepared me for this? My teachers were shallow grammarians all, Latinists of the Punic Wars.

"What has happened to me, father? Why, I'm to be hanged. You're a Christian. Get me a dagger...."

My guards at least are human. They treat me well. Pity, I suppose. I've asked them too: a sword, a dagger, anything. Not one of them will oblige me.

I blame Dionighi, that wine-barrel of a bully whose sense was in his guts. An old man, a piss-proud lecher! A wife, a wife, he had to have a wife! He plucked the prettiest of the crop all right. If only he'd known what she was like, he would not have been so hasty to tup the ewe. Is it not amazing that he should show such eagerness to exchange the goat's jig for the ram's horns? They were no sooner out of Church than the bleating began, the laughter of sheep and gossips.

Marriage did not curtail her romping. She was forced to marry him, she said, for the sake of a fat dowry and a place in Rome, her parents' profit and wish. We continued to meet, though I thought it unwise — and told her. She laughed, and I knew then that no good would come of it. "You should go with him," I said. "His master, the Cardinal. He's young...." She loved me, she said, and refused to exchange a horse for a prince, the honourable title of a Perugian wife for the lesser one of a Roman whore. She would stay to warm Dionighi's bed and enjoy mine. We were safe, she said, perfectly safe. But surely I loved her? I — God knows what I felt. But her husband, him I could not understand. "My master loves to love," he should have said — something of the sort. Who cares if it's true? Instead, he must rage and storm, threatening violence in pursuit of his rights. Once or twice he beat her, though not severely. Perhaps he'd heard the talk and knew what we took him for, the Cardinal's show soldier, feather-capped and feather-brained. He agonized about the town; drank and made no secret of his "troubles" — that's what he called them. "She's my wife," he said, emphatic on that score. "A wife's first duty is to her husband." She saw otherwise. "Go to Rome? Never!" This laughing and crying, stamping her feet — a child. She ran to her mamma, found no sympathy there, and was told to obey her parents as she should her husband. And then, then she came to me! More tears now, floods of them:

"You hate me," she said, "for marrying *him!*"

Nothing of the sort, I assured her.

"Everyone knows," she said, "that I love *you!*"

Everyone, including her spouse. Disgraced, il Capitano horsed off Romewards. What was I to do?

"It's not the end of the world," Coppoli said. "She'll to her brother's house, if her parents won't have her."

To her brother's house she went. Last November, a cruel month for love.

She was playing a small lute, a mandora, the kind favoured by Lauras who lament their Petrarchs, and she picked out a melancholy little madrigal, probably by the Archpoet himself — I do not know. We had arranged to meet where we usually did, in the music room, in a tower above the west wing of the house, commanding a view of the gardens and the street below. The house was not old, in fact was fairly recent, a Byzantine edifice richly appointed in the latest and most lavish of Venetian styles. And it was quite empty, for she had dismissed the servants, as was her habit when she wanted to entertain a friend. Her brother's affairs frequently took him out of town, and I knew that we would not be disturbed. Yet I had been feeling apprehensive all day. It was the house, I tried to tell myself, something about the villa Corradi I did not like; the house, its lacquered gloss of novelty, its golden tapestries depicting glorious feats of arms, the eyeless statuary occupying every niche — lifeless, cold.

I went over to where she was sitting and placed a light in the window.

"Are you alone?" she said.

"Astorre is outside," I answered, turning to look at her.

She smiled. "That is not necessary. It is a cold night...."

I was suddenly angry. Did she want me to ask him in? "He

enjoys it," I said. "It keeps him occupied." I turned again and gazed out into the darkness of the night. "In any case," I added, aware of the absurdity of what I was saying, "your husband..."

She was not herself that night. "I've been thinking," she said, "I would like to be far away from here."

At first, I thought she meant she wanted to join her husband in Rome. But then she shed a tear or two, and I saw it was some romantic adventure she had in mind. I took her in my arms, but she was not so easily consoled.

"I hate this place," she said. "Why don't we leave?"

"Why not indeed?" I said — words to that effect, or to no effect.

Tears suited her, she knew that. A child she was, so young — and dangerous. I loved her then, though her beauty was contrived: an essay by one of our academic masters, pale Flora weeping at the onset of winter.

I heard a noise outside. It was nothing, she said; the sound of the wind in the trees, the wind tugging the bell rope. And then I heard it again: the clash of swords cutting deep into our little play of love.

We did not see the body at first. Coppoli was leaning against the gatehouse wall and supporting himself with one hand, the other gesuring vaguely at the night. "*Assassino*," his breath came quickly; "I was asleep, Roberto, and he fell on me. *Assassino, assassino....*"

I asked if he was hurt. "No," he replied, "I don't think so. But he is," and again he pointed, this time in the direction of the pavement. Portia knelt down and held the lantern over the form of Coppoli's assailant. The light disclosed a grey-bearded, grinning face. Its eyes were open and a trickle of blood formed at the corner of the mouth. "He is dead," she murmured. It had started to rain.

"Dead?" Astorre sprang from the gatehouse. "Let me see." He now leaned over the body. "Yes," he said, his inspection complete, "yes..."

Our thoughts are seldom adequate to the occasion. A fine night's work this is, I can remember thinking; for you, Astorre Coppoli, and for all of us.

One thought, however, was more than adequate, and impressed itself forcibly on my mind. Death is irreversible, I said to myself, repeating the words over and over again. No matter how you looked at the situation, there was no denying the validity of that observation. Yes, one really had to agree. All points of view being equal, the man before us was dead. And there was nothing we could do to bring him back to life.

I do not know how long we stood in the rain looking at the corpse. It was Astorre who broke our silence. "These things will happen," he declared, almost lightly. "He attacked me, don't you see, and I — I defended myself."

"They will say you killed him." This came from Portia. "Look at him. He's an old man. They will ask what you were doing here and they will say you killed him, that you murdered him."

I should have spoken up and defended Astorre, for it was obvious that he spoke the truth. Yet the very way in which he had protested his innocence had introduced an element of doubt. Already, I could see the stern, uncompromising face of justice, and could hear the dreaded indictment, the mocking tones of the prosecution. *How does a sleeping man kill?*

"No," he said. "I swear to you it was an accident. I didn't mean to kill him."

"*Il cadavere*," she said, "we can't leave it here."

I looked from the pair of them to the lifeless form on the pavement. As if it were not enough for Coppoli to go and kill the man, here we were falling out like thieves! That sensation of imminent disaster, which had never been very far from my mind all day, rushed upon me with renewed and prolonged intensity. *Death is irreversible*; and again I repeated the ludicrous formula, and this time found it sadly lacking in assurance. A series of outlandish thoughts had taken hold of me. The killing was not simply the result of chance. I was as much to blame as Coppoli. I had committed murder. Here was no accident but a token of

231

fate itself, blind omnipotence, and that grotesque greybeard prefigured all our destinies. It was my mood that had prepared the ground for death, my hand that had struck, my body that had fallen. I smiled now, for I knew that I was afraid. "These things will happen," Astorre had said, but he had neglected to say why.

"We cannot leave him here," Portia insisted.

"She is right," I said. "We'll have to move him."

"Jesus!" Astorre cursed and retrieved his sword from where it had fallen by the body. He waved it aimlessly at the night, a futile gesture, and then returned it to its sheath, slapping his thigh as he did so.

The rain was falling heavily now, cutting across the beam of the lantern. Its light seemed to isolate us from the surrounding darkness, as if it were a beacon of invisibility instead of alarm. This can go on for ever, I thought; for eternity. Then I remembered that the watch would soon be making its rounds. "The light!" I cried. "For God's sake, the light!"

It was almost too late. . . .

I recall reading somewhere that the dead do not bleed. *Il cadavere* contradicted this law of nature, but no other.

We dragged the body through the garden, and it was only when we were safely in the house that Coppoli, exhausted and bloody, allowed himself the luxury of speech.

"Well," he said with a fantastic kind of logic that expressed all our thoughts, "what do we do now?"

What do we do now? I remember stripping the body and seeing its wounds, grinning like the old man's mouth. To the square with him, Portia said; they'll think it was a robbery. Astorre told them at the trial that it was her idea. He's well cut up, I said. Cold meat for the carrion hunter, he said. We laughed then, and could almost have been friends. Why did he betray us; *why?* He would not touch the corpse, I remember. *Eleven o'clock and all's well!* We glanced at each other and smiled again. There was some money on the body. Take it, Portia said; it's no use to him. And hurry, or he'll soon be the richer if you

don't. So will we all, Astorre said. His clothes, what am I to do
with them? Burn them! But hurry, the servants... And our
escape? I wanted to know. It was only reasonable to ask. Were
we supposed to fly? The conduit, Astorre said; he knew a way.
He'd done it before. Swim? It was possible to walk. On water?
No, no, in it, *through* it! With a woman! And then what?
Horses, we needed horses! You can find those, Portia said, *in
the stable!* So, we take *il cadavere* to the square — just like that!
— return here, steal the horses (thus adding theft to murder, a
double theft); the servants meanwhile have returned and we
escape unnoticed? Impossible! A friend, Astorre had a friend on
the west gate. He would let us pass and get the horses — at a
price. Everything had its price. Hurry! Hurry! Lug out the guts.
You carry him, Astorre said; I killed him. Let us divide the
labour of his disposal. Share and share alike. The corpse was
cold and slippery in the rain. Twice I dropped him, and that
made Portia laugh. Here, she said, grabbing an arm, like this!
An old bag of bones; we'll carry him together. My lungs burned
and I was sweating. *Death is irreversible; the dead do not bleed,
neither do they sweat.* Ah God, what a burden that was! Who'd
have thought an old man could weigh so much? I damned the
corpse; damned the day and the night, damned the rain to all
hell. You should rather thank Christ for it, Astorre said. It
washes the blood away. And all the time I was expecting we
would be discovered; all the time I was thinking, you will not
forget this night as long as you live.... Leave him on the steps
of the Palazzo, Astorre said. He's a ward of the public now.

On the steps of the Palazzo! Today is the twentieth of
February; tomorrow, I hang. Lord, let it be some other month
in some other year; let it have already happened or still to happen. I was not born to die like this! Bring a halt to time, Lord;
remit the passing of the hours. A little miracle is all I ask; a
reprieve for tomorrow or tomorrow's dissolution. *God!* That
will come without my snivelling! Soon enough, soon enough....
Why did we run? I realize the fault was Portia's, but why did I
listen? We should have summoned the constable and explained
the accident for what it was: brute chance. I said as much at the

time.... Or did I? I *thought* it, that's for sure, and the thought's as good as the deed. They'll laugh at us, Portia said; they will laugh, and then, my love, we are discovered. Well, there was some sense in that. Il Capitano could have overlooked the murder in favour of our natural crime; the supreme penalty would have been invoked all the same, and we would have been twice hanged! Dionighi — or her brother. Vengeance was his right as well as the Captain's. There's an old case, often cited as precedent. One of the Oddi found his sister gallantly spliced, and forced the man to rip out her eyes with his nails before driving him from the house. But he was only a cordwainer.... And what am I? The cordwainer lived; I will hang — perhaps with his rope. Portia too. A pair of eyes to cheat the noose, that's quittance! Anything is preferable to that death. Why did we ever meet and love, or come into the world at this time and place? Why were we not born a thousand years apart? "It is your destiny," the priest says, "to love and die." By the rope? What destiny took us to Orbetello? You will have to stay in the citadel, the Governor said. For your own safety, you understand. And as my guest, my personal guest. Yours will be the most comfortable rooms.... In hell! We shall soon be free, my love, Portia said. *Free!* It was an illusion of freedom. There was no escape. I could not forget that night, could not forget the dead man's face.... *Make your peace with God, my son.* What God? There are so many questions, and God does not answer. And still I can see that drawn face, its mouth laced with blood, strands of blood; were I blind I'd see it, the eyes squinting at me, dead, dead, the gaze of a basilisk mortifying even to the blind. From here to the Tuscan border I could not rid myself of that vision, the mask of death....

We rode by night, fearing the daytime; and did not take the public way but travelled overland. The second night, between Perugia and Citta della Pieve, we were forced to shelter from the worst of storms. Venus, star of my nativity, fell in the cusp of the horned moon and plunged behind the clouds; inconstant Arcturus flared in the north, the arc of the firmament was seared in flame and all the constellations were eclipsed, an empty sky moving over the vacant land. We would have turned back then, but for Portia. What is the matter with you? she cried, and laughed at the storm. The lightning forked again. Over there! Coppoli cried. Did you not see it? A peasant's hut was silhouetted against the flame and died into darkness. Several times the hut appeared and was gone. Nothing is real, I was thinking while Astorre kicked in the door; nothing. An old man and his wife cowered in the corner, their faces hardly visible in the light of a smoky fire. But I saw his face, I knew it.... What is it? Portia said. What's wrong? Nothing, a — *What has happened to me?* I am the same man as I was then. Yet then it seemed as if I had some memory of future things: this night — my last!

I am innocent!...

And my soul? Not one word have I spoken concerning that. Nor did I at the trial....

— *Innocent? We choose not to recognize that plea. We find you guilty, not of murder but of luring another man to the crime you feared to commit. Our jurisdiction is temporal. This Court has no concern with your soul, and it is as well for you that this is the case. Your real crime is against the state and the laws of society. You are condemned for adultery and theft and sentenced to hang by the neck until such time as you are dead. We have too long tolerated the existence of you and your kind, lying, fornicating, murderous. By acting as we do, we hope and trust to prevent the commission of further crimes. You have no defence. You no longer exist. You are nothing to this Court.*

Nothing? Why then — so I am. It is a natural offence to love, an unthinking crime. I have been careless, that is all. And careless I will hang. I should be happy to walk on air and cushion my fall with eternity. And Coppoli, what force has preserved him? Malice, cowardice, the vain desire to live. But I will not malign him. I am content to be the better man, rejoice that I did not worm my way out of the grave. Tomorrow, I will show him that I know how to die. I am quite composed now and ready for death. My life — what's that worth? It's as good as finished. What value would it have without Portia? Less than nothing! And Portia? I know I have not thought of her as much as I should, and that is a fault. But I will make amends to her. Tomorrow, when we bow down before the altar of death, I will give her my hand to kiss. It is a harsh death, but quick. Unbruised, the soul is borne starwards from the strangled body, quits this useless accretion of clay, and breaks through to the ultimate sphere. In eternity, I will at last come to know myself — in eternity or oblivion. *No!* It is heaven we ascend to. Beyond the night and the constellations of our dreams — peace.

Tomorrow becomes today. The stars go down. Already I can see where the dawn is stained over the world's rim, the white leakage of morning flooding against darkness. The end of night; how this grayness blends with the black! Yet it is tomorrow that I must die, the twenty-first of the month, not today. *Tomorrow!*

Who are these? I hear their tread and murmured psalms.

Astorre! — Portia! — Christ! What have I done?

T

Portia! Portia! Portia la bella in mano al boia! Portia's falling, falling before the fall should be; an angel, a swan. O white bird of Apollo, sing to me of the gods and the stars. I am happy. Is that a sin? Sometimes ... *The Day of the White Angel ... When I was a child, my mother asked what it meant. Do not wear white twice, the Gypsy said. Or ...* Sometimes, I am afraid. A dying fall. *Father, do not let them bind my arms. I want to be free.* Look at all the people! They're kneeling. *Roberto, look at them! Don't you like my dress. I've worn it before.* White is for pretended innocence. And black? How courteous is the hangman; how gentle and mild! There's Dion. I can see him! I can see him! Portia's an angel; a swan. *Poor Roberto, you're shivering. Drink this.* There's laughter in the wine. *Laugh, Roberto. Smile?* Last night, I wrote some letters. Last night ... Standing there alone. Does he mourn for me? *La bella! La bella!* Dionighi, the peacock. Warbling: *Waters stink if in one place they abide* — oh, piss! — *and are soon putrefied,*

236

if . . . if . . . But I can't remember the rest. I've forgotten it, Portia. I — if . . . Standing there in black. *I do. I will. I won't. I shan't! He's an old man. A turkeycock! I shouldn't be surprised if he's forgotten what to do with his —. you talk like a slut sometimes, my mother said. . . . Well, it's true. I shan't!* I did. I'm sorry for you, Dion. *Come to Rome, my chick.* The poem, it *says:* 'The Son of man must be delivered into the hands of sinful men, and be crucified, and the third day shall rise again. My child? —'

'— Yes, father?'

But when they kiss one bank and, leaving this . . . That's the Tiber here in Perugia. And the other bank is in Rome. — It's the same river, silly! — But different in Rome. I made it up for you. — Liar! — I learned it for you. — Liar! No, I swear to God. It's by an Englishman and must be a real poem. . . . 'It was Mary Magdalene, and Mary Mother of James, and other women that were with them, which told these things to the Apostles. My child, will you take the chalice?' *Drink, Roberto. Give me your hand. See, I'm wearing the ring you gave me. Have you forgotten? The stone is purest chalcedony, milk white. Do you remember what you said? 'There are some chalcedonians so large that entire drinking cups are made from them.'* There were swans on the river that day. Every year they return at the same time. Swansong! *Look, Roberto. The stone has changed colour.* It darkened to a flint-blue, the colour of thin milk. I have seen it flash fire and light as if it had a life of its own. That day, we walked by the river and then to the Priory. Spring showers came in from the hills, hazing the far-off places. I had a music lesson in the morning: exercises in the Aeolian mode. *It's no use. The note . . . Like this, my teacher said. Gently. . . . It's worse than spinning. Get some more wool, my mother said.* 'Portia, my child. Are you listening?'

'— Yes, father.'

'And as they were eating, Jesus took bread, and blessed it, and broke it, and gave it to the disciples, and said, Take, eat; this is my body.' *The night we left Perugia, father, the night of the storm, I felt free. Is that such a terrible thing? — No, but*

Astorre had killed a man, and you said to leave the body in the square. Is it true? Why did you say that? — *For the first time in my life, I felt free. That's all. I don't know* ... 'And he took the cup, and gave thanks, and gave it to them, saying, Drink ye all of it.' *And were you not conscious of any wrong-doing?* — *No, I* ... *But Astorre said you wanted to hide the evidence of the crime; that you had planned to murder your husband.* 'For this is my blood of the new testament, which is shed for many for the remission of sins.' *No, father; that is not true.* What makes him stand there? *Never look back* ... *I remember! Never look back but the next bank do kiss, then they are purest. Come to Rome, my chick. Please. How can I leave you here? I would be* ... *How many times do I have to tell you? my mother said. Be reasonable. I shall speak to your father.... Now then, Portia.* — *La bella! La bella!* We rode through the night and the rain. The moon had gone down. There were no stars. *His face, Roberto said. I know that face. It is the same.* Why are men so — ? The rain lifted from the river. The banks were green and moist; the river in full flood, the air fresh with the scent of the time after rain. *Portia, I'm sorry. I didn't mean it to happen like this. Not this way....* 'Let us pray, my children ... Portia, Roberto, it is almost time.' *Will God forgive me, father?* — *His mercy is infinite.* As the grass and the daisies. He loves me, he loves me not. As the clouds. *But there are some things beyond human understanding, which we therefore call mysteries.* As the sparrows and the beasts of the field. *Do you believe, my child, in God the Father Almighty, Maker of Heaven and earth?* Oh, *that!* Sometimes I think I could go and live with the animals, with the beasts of the field. Sometimes I *think* I could. They are so peaceful. *And in Jesus Christ, his only Son, Our Lord, who was* — I know, I know: who was conceived by the Holy Ghost, born of the Virgin Mary, suffered under Pontius Pilate, was crucified, dead and buried.... What do they think of us, the animals? *Nonsense, Roberto said. A horse does not think. It just is.* Perhaps. They recognize people, though. *He descended into hell. The third day he rose again from the dead. He ascended into heaven* ... *Hell-heaven, heaven-hell. Now what beast* would think of that! They are free.... *And sitteth on the right hand of God the Father Almighty. From thence he shall come to judge the quick and the dead. Do you believe in this and in the Holy Ghost; the holy Catholic Church, the Communion of Saints, the Forgiveness of sins, the Resurrection of the body, and the Life Everlasting?* What beast dreams of paradise or begs forgiveness? And what is heaven, a place of fragrant balm and changeless spirits, a mausoleum of the living dead? And do the dead grieve in heaven; are there tears there as well? Do they laugh? Or is there no pity and joy in heaven, no change of mood or season? It must be very dull, if it's as deathless as they say. Gold does not tarnish, nor is there any respite from the soul's eternal tedium. *And do you believe, my child, in the Lord Jesus Christ ... Kiss me, Roberto said.* I refused, and he was angry. *For the ring; not just one little kiss?* Not here, I said. The grass is wet ... who was begotten of the Father, before all worlds ... And in the summer, I would be married: the Captain's wife ... *begotten, not made, who came down from heaven for our salvation ... Where then? he said. Where? ... incarnate by the Holy Ghost of the Virgin Mary? ... My brother's house, I said.* False Portia; and foolish ... *For our salvation, Portia?* I know! I *know!* — Father, I ... When? he said. Tonight, I said. — I believe, father. — And will you confess your sins, my child? Mea culpa, mea culpa, mea maxima culpa. O felix culpa!

'Portia will you follow Roberto?'

I did not think it would be so far or take so long, the ascent and the descent. Such a long time it has taken, yet no time at all!

— *I hate this place! Why don't we leave?*

— *Why not indeed?*

You must believe me, father. There was never any plan to kill Dion. Why should we do that? It was something Astorre made up for the judges.

— *These things will happen....*

May God have mercy on your soul. He will, He will. *And Astorre's, father?* — *I ... do not know. It is a mystery, a very great mystery. I have brought you something, Portia; for tomorrow. It will ... Yes, father? A restorative. Take this, my child,*

239

and drink it: tomorrow. Today. I feel — what is it I feel? Life's a dream of death, a dream within a dream. I am calm. And Dion, what does he think? Still he stands there, his face turned to the sky. *Never look back* ... So calm I no longer feel anything much, only the indifference of the time between waking and sleeping. I remember the old graves we saw in Tuscany, and black Eros, his torch turned to the earth, love in death mourning the death of love; and the dancers in the marble frieze celebrating the end of this dancing world. How long has it been since the beginning; how long? Roberto was; Portia was. The hangman takes my hand. 'Forgive me,' he says, kneeling. 'Forgive me for what I have to do.' What ceremony death requires! Here's a purse for *il boia*, gold for the man in black. *To die is to be loved by a god, Astorre said. To die with a kiss like Endymion* ... How long has it been? Portia's dying; dark swan of night sinking down to darkness, falling falling. *Zeus and Ganymede, Roberto said; but we should not think of death....* *Love is death, Astorre said. Leda and the swan; Jupiter. The gods kill. Have you not seen Amor crowning the skull? I do not believe in immortality. Il putto, old fat lips, the baby kissing the white bone. It is the kiss of death. They say death resembles a mask,* mors larvae similis, *but I do not think so. Life is the mask.... You should not talk like that, Roberto said. The gods* ... *We shall soon be free, I said.* Poor Roberto, he's no god. All the same — we die.

What gods? Astorre said. Poets and painters have made the gods. They do not ... 'Portia —' There is something I have to say, cadenza mia: *I swear that I am innocent of those crimes for which I must die, and that I shall love my husband in heaven as I did on earth.* Why did I say that? I meant no irony. *And I ask my kinsman to forgive those wrongs he has committed....* A suspended cadence, words lost on the air. *Deus Dei, Lux Lucis* ... 'Portia, it is time.'

'— *I know, father* ...'

Luce carentes sumus, we are the dead, endlessly falling; we are the dead without light. Lord, pity us ... *Portia, the chord is played:* allegro. *How important it is to fix the angle of the light and catch the colours exactly. Do not think of it as sound. Look on it as you would a painting, the Dulce Amarum, for example. Think, and then forget. Think, and play. Lightly, Portia! Lighter than air!* I can see the tower of the Palazzo, the roof and the square beneath; the people kneeling, and my husband. *Dion!* I can see the Priory and the river, and the bridge we crossed that day. *Father, will you take these?* Someone gave me flowers: dried poppies ... How quiet it is! So peaceful. *Here, Robert said; I found this for you. — Found? — Well* ... It was Easter-time. *The stone will change colour in the light, Roberto said. Like the water in the fountain.* Chalcedony, all colours ... *Agnus Dei!* ... Milk white in the shade, and in the sun it will never stay the same ... *The wool, my mother said* ... I can see the fountain and the fire dancing on the water, all the colours! *Agnus Dei, qui tollis peccata mundi* ... Chalcedony: what does it mean? *It is a Greek word, Roberto said. Pliny derives it from Carthage, and Baeda says it is from the third foundation of the New Jerusalem, or so I was told. I don't know. There are others who place it in the land of Cockaigne. Albertus Magnus, but he is an astrologer and Greek to me....* I remember! I remember! Jasper, sapphire, then chalcedony; the fourth was an emerald, then sardonyx, sardius, chrysolite and beryl; the walls of the city were made of gold as clear as glass, and the ninth foundation was topaz, then chrysoprasus, jacinth and amethyst — all the stones found in the fire of the light breaking from the fountain and falling, endlessly falling. *Luce carentes ... Lux, Lucis,* the light! *I don't care, Astorre said. Gods or no gods, it's all the same to me. Do you expect me to believe that people are changed into almond trees or* ...

— *Agnus Dei, miserere nobis!*
— *Portia, do not forget me!*
— *Roberto* ...
— *Misericordia! Misericordia! Misericordia!*

Forever an angel a swan forever a cloud a tree, Portia's falling falling. *La bella! La bella!* How many suns there are! The horizon is closed round with fire, golden flames streaming from the western hills. On the edge of the precipice, the sky is dropping, an endless chasm, sides of sheer fall from the summit to —

— *or clouds? Astorre said.*

— *There is Castor and Pollux, Roberto said. Leda's* ...

— *Change, Dion said, is the nursery of music, joy, life and eternity.*

— *I am the resurrection and the life, Jesus said.*

— *There's no more wool for the spindle, my mother said. A drop spindle* ...

XI

It is possible to justify any experience by natural causes. There is no reason that could ever compel us to make any perception depend on demonic powers. There is no point in introducing supernatural agents. It is ridiculous as well as frivolous to abandon the evidence of natural reason and to search for things that are neither probable nor rational.
— Pietro Pomponazzi

And will it be my fault if things are so?
— Machiavelli

Rome, January 1600

It is always the same dream. I am alone at the entrance of a great cathedral. Stone people gathered under the arch are pointing the way, and it seems that I must go in. It is gloomy inside and I have some difficulty at first in seeing. I am here to meet some-one, but I cannot remember whom. I sit down and contemplate the ceiling. Liernes and tiercerons fan out in a display of transdimensional vaulting, a fragile geometry sketched in stone armatures. I am reminded of the score of a vast oratorio. It is the work of no earthly artist, this interplay of chord on chord. It is silence. . . .

My friend is waiting for me in the crypt. How stupid of me!

How could I have forgotten? I am on my feet now. The floor is chequered and recedes toward the distant altar, and I can see myself walking past the columns, past the rows of vacant pews, past the side chapels — somewhere there is a turning that will take me down to the crypt.

The fabric around me dissolves imperceptibly into the night. I am still walking, but find myself on a desolate and derelict plain. Yet something was once here, something far older than the place I have just left. I pass the ruined choirs of Avernus and the dark caves of the Cumaean Sybil. Other structures, less well defined, loom under the starlight. I see myself wandering through the colonnade of the Temple of Karnak, studying its blurred inscriptions. I am in the valley of the dead, lost among the tombs of kings and priests. There is no hope now that I will find the stairs, and my friend will be getting impatient.

It is only a dream, I tell myself; it is only a dream and you know what is going to happen.

I have almost reached the altar when I see him, the other, who approaches from the other side of night, his arms raised in greeting and supplication.

"Giordano," he is whispering. "I will tell you our secret. We shall become one, you and I...."

The Inquisitor smiles. I can see his teeth, clenched in the bite of a skull grin.

I can hear his laughter. *Filoteo, Teofilo; Magus* ...

The Inquisitor's robes are burning. His hands pluck at the flames and he writhes in the dance of death, the flesh melting from his face and baring the screaming bone beneath.

Tonight, when I awoke as I always do after this dream, I had half expected to see Fra Giovanni. Instead, another stood in my cell, his cloak wrapped about his head, though when he spoke I knew that voice.

It was Giovanni Mocenigo, come from hell or Venice.

"Did I startle you?" he said. "I didn't mean to. You were asleep, and so was the jailer. I just took the key and opened the door. Simple, wasn't it? I must say, Hadrian built himself a

244

labyrinth for a tomb."

He was facing the door. It was closed, and I knew that he was lying.

"Zuan," I said, "can it really be you?"

"None other," he said. "Though I think you will find that I've changed. *You* certainly have."

He turned round, the cloak falling from his face as he did so. The memory of the dream was still in my mind and I was thankful that his appearance was normal. Only his manner was altered. He seemed calmer than I remembered, and there was even a certain drollness in him that I had not seen before.

"Do you mind if I sit down?" he said. "I hope you'll forgive me for dropping in like this. I was studying you just now. You were dreaming. I know because your eyes were moving. Was it a nice dream, Giordano?" He smiled knowingly. "But I'm not here to talk of dreams. I suppose you're wondering why I am here. Let's call it official business. It's no trick, if that's what you're thinking. You've probably no idea how difficult things were to arrange."

"For you, Zuan?" I said. "Don't make me laugh."

"Oh, that," he said. "Do you hate me so much? I wouldn't blame you if you did. What you must have thought of me! I can understand your feelings. How the years have gone by, Giordano. It seems like yesterday since we were on the Giudecca — to me at least. No doubt things are different with you." He considered the point and lapsed into a silence.

"I presume you're not here to talk about the past," I said. "What do you want, Zuan?"

"One thing at a time. I'm coming to that. You were always too impatient, Giordano."

I began to wonder whether he had changed as much as he said. He was still a petulant boy.

"And now we're both older," Giovanni Mocenigo resumed, "are we any the wiser? You know, I saw right through you. I'm sorry, but I did. I am sure I can speak frankly. You're a lover of plain speech after all, and other things too — but let's forget about that. You wanted to go to Rome, and in fact you were running away. It didn't take much intelligence to realize that, did it? And you despised me. Of course, I was the coward — never the Nolan. Well, now you're in Rome, there's no running away. You must admit, I surprised you once. Do you think I've lost that ability? There are all kinds of things I know about you, Giordano, things you don't even know yourself.''

"Go ahead, Zuan," I said: "surprise me."

"I'll do more than that," he said, preening himself. "Do you remember that morning on the canal when we were going to my warehouse? You saw someone you thought you knew. Shall I tell you who it was, Giordano? It was yourself, the Nolan — your own pursuer and accuser."

"And executioner, Zuan; is that what you mean? Every man is his own judge and jury — every man except Zuan Mocenigo? I thought you'd be more original than that. Is that all you have to say, Zuan?" I asked. "Is this what's been troubling you for the last eight years? It must have been very hard for you."

"I thought I owed you an explanation." He sounded disappointed, like a child who has found the world to be full of broken promises. "But you're right, Giordano. I'm not here to speak of the past. I have to leave Rome tomorrow, so I'll come to the point. The past is finished. There could have been some friendship between us, but that's over now. As for the blame, history can be the judge of that. It wasn't my fault, really it wasn't. . . ."

"No, no, princeling. You were frightened."

"As frightened as you are now, Giordano. You see, I told you there's not much I don't know. You can't have forgotten that I worked for the Inquisition. That was my function, and I performed it well, even though I do say so myself. But you'd be mistaken, Giordano, if you thought I was proud of what I did . . . sadly mistaken. I'm here as your friend, Giordano; to help you."

"My friend!" I laughed. "You were coming to the point," I reminded him.

"I was prepared for that," he said. "Your taunts can't hurt

246

me. You've every right to call me a liar."

He was very abject. It was intolerable, I thought, the meanest kind of act. I had seen him like this before the Tribunal. *'My lords . . . '*

"What is this, Zuan? Remorse?" He was such a terrible actor, and that was why people believed him. It was quite a talent. "But a liar, Zuan? God forbid! You're an honest man. A liar knows what he is doing."

"I said I was prepared for this," he sulked. "But since you've mentioned the subject, it is not remorse that I feel."

"And what is it that you feel?"

"Pity," he said, his face and his voice empty of all expression. "You have no friends, Giordano."

"Tell me what you want and leave, Zuan."

"You are wrong, Giordano," he said in the same expressionless tones. "You will listen to me, as I once listened to you. You will listen to me because you have to listen. You have no choice. You will listen because you know that I am speaking the truth."

"I'm listening," I said, intrigued at this turn of events.

I was aware of the change in him now. He was sharper than I remembered; childish, of course, but even a child can have its prescient moments. And adult children are the most dangerous of all. It occurred to me then that this quality had always existed in him, and I had merely failed to see it. Or were my own faculties less acute than I had supposed; had I allowed him to gain the upper hand because I did indeed despise him?

Both thoughts disturbed me. And now there came another: the feeling that it is impossible to know another person except in the most nominal sense. Reduced to its essentials, the question of identity is no more than the skin which covers and holds together this or that assembly of atoms. We take too much for granted. Our expectation of other people depends so little on this point of view and entirely on ourselves. In those rare moments of understanding, when people are said to come into their own, it is then that we feel betrayed. We realize that they inhabit a different universe behind this soul-covering of the flesh. They are no longer a part of us, no longer something we can call our own. And in such moments, we realize that they are probably thinking the same of us.

The soul is supposed to continue unchanged after death, but I do not think it does so even in life. Behind this frangible layer of the self, this mortal envelope, we lead the existence of phantoms.

How could I be sure that this was Zuan, for what was he but an extension of myself?

"None other," he had said, and I wondered if he was aware of what this meant.

But sound is material, and he was speaking in the least ghostly of voices. "It is the future that concerns me," he said. "You see, I happen to know that you've been thinking of confessing. In fact, you've already gone some way. Sign one of Bellarmine's documents, and there's no end to what you'll sign. But that's not the point, Giordano. How can you trust them? Surely that's the point."

"How can I trust you, Zuan?" I said. Surely that was the point.

"Trust me as you did before. Trust me as you would yourself. You know I'm right," he said, and I knew that he was. "You can only die once, Giordano. They say the fire's not so bad, if you remember to breathe deeply. You've said yourself that life is no more than the vainest of appearances. What's death, then? As common as birth, and less painful. And think of the future, Giordano. Forget the past. The one thing you cannot afford is self-betrayal."

"You are the vainest of appearances," I said. "Whatever I do, it will not be because of your advice."

"The same old Giordano!" he cried. "You think you know me, but I assure you it is the other way round. For once. You are weak, Giordano, but so is the Church. The Pope and the Cardinals, they are all weak and timid men. You'd be crazy to abjure. They'll kill you anyway. You *know* that, Giordano. Why," he was smiling again, "if I thought it would work, I'd gladly change places with you. Except that I'm a coward, of

248

course. There was never any doubt of that."

"Now there we are in agreement," I said. "For once."

"Are we?" he said, and stood up. "Then there is nothing more to say. You will sign no more of the papers. You will take back everything you have confessed."

This last statement was uttered with an air of complete conviction. I thought of Venice, of that last morning on the canal, of my arrest and trial. I remembered his letters; his promise of hospitality, and those high hopes which had been mine. Giovanni Mocenigo had planned everything. I was looking at him for the first time, and I saw that, like all our memories, he was only a shadow of a shadow. And yet I would have talked with him.

"Wait, Zuan," I said. "Why should they kill me now? Why, after all these years?"

"That is something you will have to find out for yourself," he said. "Think over what I've told you, Giordano. And forgive me, if you can. Remember that things need not have been this way. Forgive yourself. Forgive God."

"He does not exist," I said.

No more did Zuan. He was gone as he came, an illusion and a dream. And like God, he did not trouble me with so much as a farewell.

T

I said that I had eternity on my hands. Nothing is ever what it seems to be. Giordano thought I was a vision, yet I could not have been more present. And although it is occasionally necessary to use deception, there are no ends and means in eternity, only the permutation of the infinitely possible against which all our lives are played out. Every man must attempt to escape the fate that is his. I helped Giordano a little way down the path that had already been taken. It was my last service: I, who had betrayed him, helped to confirm his resolve. He owed me everything. What else is there to say?

T

I was expecting my second visitor, though he surprised me in a way I would have thought scarcely possible. "Dreaming again!" he exclaimed as I sought to make him out. "Always the dreamer!"

It was cold even for the time of year, something which my visitor evidently felt, for he performed a creaky little jig and clapped his hands together. "Word painter!" he cried, radiating a charm that was entirely of this world. "Poet! Philosopher! And a dancer too, you were certainly that. Remember me, Giordano? The crossing from Dover when we were boarded by the English pirate? Remember the journey to Oxford with Laski? How rude you were to the learned doctors, the life and soul of bombast! And the angel you found that afternoon at Mortlake. Did you find her again, Giordano? We must talk about that some time. Remember the Ash Wednesday supper with Greville and Sidney; and the Queen, Giordano, how she smiled on her Italian admirer! You were a courtier, one of the finest. The future was yours. And look at you now! Whatever happened? I wrote from Paris, you know, asking for your return. Why didn't you reply? The new King was most anxious to meet you. And he still is, Giordano, he still is — especially since His Celestitude welcomed him back to the fold. Unlike you, eh?" My visitor sighed eloquently. "The black sheep. But I see that I have interrupted your reveries. God does not exist? I wonder, Giordano, I wonder. If He does not exist, then how can we poor mortals? Or anything in this wide world? But surely you cannot have forgotten your friend?"

"And protector," I said. "Michel de Castelnau."

"The same," my visitor executed an eloquent bow, "yet not the same."

I understood. Michel de Castelnau, Sieur de Mauvissière,

had been dead for the last eight years.

"But still your friend and protector," he continued in much the same vein, "though Mauvissière has suffered a sea-change and serves another Prince, one mightier than the Bourbon or Valois, mightier even than the Pope himself. You know what I mean. Circumstances change. One must adjust, tack before the wind."

He was in high good humour — for a corpse. "And what wind blows you here?" I asked. "You should be asleep in the grave, Michel."

"An unquiet grave, Giordano, just as it is a fair breeze, a sweet, mellifluous, zephyr-like breeze, warm, so warm."

The Lord of Mauvissière sighed again. "How I love this world," he said. "I found the prospect of my return irresistible — some unfinished business, a trivial matter which nonetheless demands my attention. Life's a dream. But doubt me not, Giordano. Rub the stardust from your eyes. I am here," he paused, "substantially. You see, I know what you're thinking."

"So did Zuan," I said.

"Ah well," he shrugged, "that's possible."

"What isn't with your new master?" I said.

"Close, Giordano," he smiled, "very close."

The cold made me shiver, an involuntary spasm which he must have noticed. Alive or dead, there was little that escaped Michel's attention.

"You feel it too?" he said. "Everyone does, even myself, even from beyond the grave. You have nothing to fear from me. No tricks," he drew his hands up around his mouth and grinned, "with the screaming bone. Forgive me, I was merely trying to establish my credentials. It is hard to shake the habit of a lifetime — but that is something you know already."

"Meaning that there is something I do not know?" I said.

"*Festina lente*, Giordano. Hasten slowly. You will pardon me, I'm sure, but I overheard your last conversation. It was not very edifying. You have many friends, Giordano. Myself for one. The King of France for another."

"Those times are dead," I said. "Like yourself, Michel."

"The soul is immortal, Giordano, although you do not believe it, provisionally immortal. However, theology is best left to the priests. I'll be frank with you. A man can change his mind. I had intended to change yours, to talk over old times and tempt you with memories of your former estate. But this is no place for sentiment. We are men of the world, you and I, and we must be realistic. The past is irrecoverable. No gain lies that way. To the point then. Yes, Giordano, there is something that you are not aware of, something my lords ecclesiastical fear to tell you because it would give you hope, and with hope — resolution. Wait, hear me out. My lord and I would have you temporize with the Pope. It is not a confession we want. God knows — and so do we — that you've done nothing to deserve the stake. No, it is action of another kind that we're after: action and policy."

"Meaning?" I asked.

"Your freedom," he replied.

"And what's that worth to you, Michel?"

"No, to you, Giordano?" He gave a shrewd glance, then hurried on. "But you're mistaken. Your soul does not interest me. This world is enough. Do you think the devil barters with souls, Giordano?" The Lord of Mauvissière laughed. "Do you think he is some cheap skatemonger? No, Giordano. There is nothing here that is not already in your mind."

"That is not what you said before, Michel."

Could the devil make such an error? I wondered. But he was a dream, or something less than a dream.

"It needs a dead man to dream of the dead," I said.

"Then we're both on the same footing." This time he did not laugh, but altering his expression to one of the deepest misery he announced that he envied me. "It's true, Giordano," he said. "You were once free, and can be free again. Things do not stand in exactly the same case with me," he reflected sorrowfully. "There, you see you have the advantage after all," he said, smiling again. "Phrase maker! But let us have no more talk of the devil, Giordano. I think you will find that he is very ordinary and natural. Like ourselves. He would disappoint you, really he would. You are much more interesting. But perhaps I disappoint you?"

"The grave has robbed you of none of your diplomatic skills," I said. "What do you want from me?"

"Nothing more than what you would have for yourself," he replied. "I shall be brief, Giordano. My lord and I both know that you have abandoned the folly of hope. Even so, listen to me. Campanella is in rebellion against Spain. Already, there has been some fighting in Naples, nothing serious — so far. But soon, all Calabria and the south will join him. The Turkish fleet is ready to sail. The English too, if they can see their advantage. From this there may spring a general war...."

"So this is your fair breeze?"

"You're not the only one to speak in figures, Giordano. A courtier's habit: clothe the sense to confound the foolish and speak to the wise. You know it well enough. This Roman barque is rotten. Temporize with its captain, Giordano. Delay."

"And why should I do that, Michel?"

"King Henri will come to Rome. He sees himself as a peacemaker, the divinely appointed arbitrator of a united Christian Europe. How does that sound? High flown, I agree. The King is a wise man, but he does like large phrases. Nevertheless he sees his place in history, and he will come to Rome, Giordano. Would you be his archbishop? It is done. His ambassador, perhaps? All you have to do is to ask. Whatever you want, spiritual or temporal, we can grant. Why should I lie?"

"The devil cannot lie, Michel."

"The devil he can't!" Michel grinned. "There you go again. I keep telling you, there's nothing here that has not already occurred to you. Why don't you believe me? But you are correct, Giordano; your understanding is precise. The devil's an honest soul. Then you should know, Giordano, you should know."

"I do know," I said. "Nor does he tell the entire truth. This is not the first rebellion against Spain. It will fail like the rest."

"The entire truth, Giordano?" He had a scintillating smile. It was a timeless expression, half of triumph and half of spite.

"Isn't that rather presumptuous of you?" he said. "The *entire* truth, surely that must wait on events. How do you know what is going to happen or what has happened? There is such an infinity of possible futures, Giordano. I was merely trying to select one from the many. You've already embarked some way on the course I've described. You are very proud, but not too proud to humble yourself before the Cardinal. I'll tell you something else. Without the King's help, there can be no point to this shilly-shallying. Bellarmine knows what you're doing, and so do I. You're crawling, Giordano. Wait, I *will* be honest with you, if only you would listen! Campanella has been captured and tortured. He was allowed to live, and for a time he was here — in this prison. Rome has surrendered him to Naples as Venice surrendered you to Rome. You see, it is not half-truths that I deal in but practical realities. So far, you have been lucky to escape the Spanish Inquisition. So far. You owe this to your friends. Believe me, Giordano, they are determined to save you, even though you are not prepared to help them. . . ."

"And am I to thank them for this eight years' grace?" I said. "You would talk the hind leg off the devil, Michel. Or would you prefer it if I called you by another name?"

His eloquence failed him. "I am," he said, and he was muttering, "the Lord of Mauvissière. I have lands and a title to maintain. Appearances, Giordano . . ."

"Forneus, I know what you are!"

"Oh, no," he said, "not that one, not Forneus." The shadow lifted and he was himself again. "I am sorry you do not know me for what I am," he smiled engagingly. "I am no demon who can make your enemies love you. Even I do not have that power. I am not what you think. I have no infernal legions at my command, Giordano. I am your friend who has your best interests at heart. And now you turn against me and call me by the name of a devil. It is not worth denying, Giordano. I am what I am. . . ."

"Samael!" I cried. "Only God can say that!"

"And He does not exist, Giordano, whereas the Lord of Mauvissière most certainly does."

Michel de Castelnau had been in his sixty-fourth year when I first met him. Had he lived, he would now have been in his eighty-first. It was by no means impossible that the report of his death had been fraudulent. A man like Michel, I thought, may have had many reasons for wanting the world to think him dead. Such would have been the logical, if paradoxical, act of one of nature's born survivors.

He was very downcast, and I could almost have pitied him. For a moment, I wondered if I had been mistaken. I looked at him then and tried to detect the changes that age must have wrought in him. His head was slightly bowed, and he was staring up at me. His eyes were filled with an inexpressible longing, a hope that seemed to come from an eternity of despair, as if it were within my power to save his soul.

Michel de Castelnau, Sieur de Mauvissière, was ageless. Whoever — or whatever — stood before me, it was not Michel.

"But you flatter me, Giordano," he was saying. "I thought you did not believe in a literal hell. Or do you need reminding?"

"Of what?" I said.

"Of yourself," he replied. "Seize the road, rolling through the threshold of the great sun; mother nature discloses the route. How can you have forgotten, Giordano?"

He paused, and in a sentence had aged wickedly. He was grinning again, a dotard's grin, and when he spoke, it was in my own voice: "So as there is a sun within the world, like the soul of a man which gives him light and warmth, I think our heavenly sun must be at the centre of our system and believe that there are certainly other suns and worlds on which this lake would likewise exist as a natural formation, on the moon, or Mars, or any of the planets...."

I closed my eyes. "What is it? What is it?" he was crying in his ancient voice, crying and laughing. "This lake, Giordano, this *lake*? Hell is a perfectly natural place," he said, again reverting to my own voice. "What can you be afraid of? There is nothing to frighten you here. Nothing ..."

I looked at him again and saw that he had adopted his former guise, pleasant, jovial, a quizzical expression arched on his face. This *had been* the Michel I had known. He moved closer, as if he wanted me to see him more clearly. It was the Michel I remembered from the quayside at Dover, a man still undefeated at the age of sixty-four. His hair was salt and peppery, and there were wrinkles on that face — difficult to tell whether they were caused by grief or joy. "We shall have to find a new master," I had said to him then, something of the sort, and he had regarded me in much the same way. It was almost a smile, a frozen kind of smile. I studied his expression and wondered how I could have mistaken him for something else. The corners of his mouth were upturned, the lines of his face were if anything more deeply engraved, and those under his eyes etched in a reticular formation. Now he tweaked the ends of his moustache, which were pointed and emphasized his habitually sardonic expression. 'You see,' he seemed to be saying, 'I told you so.'

Only his eyes gave him away. They were filled with an unearthly glitter. It was the gaze of a man I had seen once before during that plague year in Savona, the gaze of a man who died even as I spoke to him.

"Who are you?" I asked.

"One who knows you," he replied casually, "but one you do not know. You have looked on me many times, you have looked and failed to see. My eternal regrets, Giordano." He gave another mocking bow. "I did not think you would listen to me. When did you ever? I came to offer you a compromise, but it was too late. My apologies. As you can see, this conversation has tired me. I am not as young as I was. I must leave now and give way to another. For you must know that my lord does not give up so easily as his poor servant. I am sorry that you did not know me for what I am. Farewell, Giordano. And pity me, your friend, Michel de Castelnau, Sieur de Mauvissière. Pity me . . ."

He was gone and I saw that he had been a vision like his predecessor. Yet he had spoken to me as I would have done to myself. For every man is a vision of himself: neither more nor less, it is enough.

T

Wherever I am, there you will find me. I have flattered all Highness this, gone on bended knee to all Pontifical that, Pope and Cardinal, Emperor and King — the fools of chance. My life was a pursuit of the golden rule, unobtainable harmony. Our dreams die hard, and I have found immortality to be a qualified sort of business. Between heaven and hell there is only a slight difference of policy, the eternal ends justifying the terrestrial means. A phantom in this world (hence the source of my earthly success), I was ideally suited for the role of Mercurius to Giordano's craven spirit. I do not regret to say that I used falsehood. To state the opposite of one's true intent and from ostensible meaning draw out the reverse effect, this is the essence of my craft. I think you will find the servant worthy of his hire. I think you will find my last bow was spent in a noble cause. That is all I have to say.

T

Fra Giovanni Gabrielle da Saluzzo, Father Inquisitor of the Venetian Holy Office, inclined his birdlike head and smiled.

"*Dominus vobiscum*," he murmured piously.

He had taken care to age cosmetically. His complexion was liverish; his eyes dull, and his voice feeble. A white crucifix hung from his scrawny neck, and when his hands groped for the cross, I saw that he was blind. Even better, I thought: a natural touch. It was a passable imitation.

"I shall sit down," he said.

"Please do," I said. "I was expecting you."

"Then what is expected," he remarked serenely, "is not to be feared."

I said that I was no more afraid of him than I had been of the others, and his eyes swivelled round in the direction of my voice. Perhaps it was the light, but I imagined that he could see me. I thought of the blind beggars in Naples....

"You were right not to fear me," he said. "As for the others, that was not so wise of you. Mocenigo you should have feared from the start. Castelnau you should have recognized for what he was, and that recognition, Giordano, should have struck terror into your heart."

I asked if a man should fear himself, but my attention was not on the question.

"I *can* see you, Giordano," he whispered, staring at me, "though with difficulty. Perhaps," he mused, "I have never seen you as clearly as I do now."

"Riddles, father?"

"You have a suspicious nature," he said, and waited for my reaction.

"Why are you here, father?" I said, emphasizing the 'father'. I would let him know, I thought, that I understood his little game.

"That is not really the question you wanted to ask, is it?" He paused again. "Not so talkative, Giordano?" he enquired, cocking his head on one side and putting his hand to an ear. "Have you nothing to say to me?"

I enjoyed the show and asked him whether he was deaf as well as blind.

"Neither!" he cried merrily. "But that's better, that's better, Giordano. It shows spirit. I'll answer your question — when I'm ready," he added, immediately serious. "Your last visitor was lying," he continued. "But then you knew that, didn't you? There will be no war on Campanella's account, and King Henri will not come to Rome. He will not see Rome as a peacemaker, and he will not see Rome as a warrior; he will not see Rome now, and he will not see Rome later. I shall be brief, Giordano. The King, from whom you once desired so much, would rather forget that you exist."

"I was prepared for that," I said.

"However, there is something else you should prepare yourself for: the Congregation has decided on death."

"And the Pope?" I asked him.

"His Holiness also," Fra Giovanni shrugged. "As far as the manner of your death is concerned, that still depends on you."

"The fire *post mortem*," I said. "Is that what you have to offer me?"

"In more ways than one," he smiled. "If you see what I mean. But this also depends on you and on the degree of your contrition. That is why I am here, in Rome. I have answered your question, Giordano. Remember, I have never lied to you. It was always the truth between you and me, Giordano...."

"And you should also remember that I abjured everything," I said.

"It was a false confession," he replied, "and not because of the torture, not because it was wrung from you. You tried to convince your judges that you were a sincere penitent. They believed you, so you thought, and you were surprised when they did not let you go. Not once did you stop to consider the alternatives — yours and ours. It was a cynical move, and you have still to pay for it. Do not make the mistake of thinking that you are immortal. Do not think that because you have survived this long you will survive forever. Our patience is not as infinite as your universe. I am sorry to speak in this way, Giordano. But you are going to die. Do I make myself clear?"

"Perfectly," I said. "But you have forgotten one thing. If the Church kills me, she is afraid of the truth."

"The truth! When has the truth ever been your concern? You are lying, Giordano. You have always lied! Always, always! God be my witness!" His voice was raised, though it was still little more than a whisper, and his eyes roved from side to side as if in appeal to an imaginary audience. "Always, always," he muttered again. "From the time you first went on your travels, and before," he continued venomously. "For fifteen years you travelled over half Europe, singing one tune in one place and another in the next. On this pilgrimage of deceit, you cast aside your monastic habit, resuming it again in Bergamo when it suited you. In Chambéry, where the monks received you with suspicion, you resolved never again to return to Italy, but instead you would go to Geneva. There, at the insistence of Galeazzo Carracioli, that apostate nephew of Pope Paul, you fell in with the Calvinists and swore that, this time, you had finally dropped the guise of your Order, *our* Order. When the Calvinists were no longer to your liking, it was to France, where you initiated King Henri into the accursed art of Raymond Lull. In France, as in England, you played the politician, ingratiating yourself first with the French King and then with the English Queen, likening one to the solar lion and the other to a goddess. After the King's murder, you transferred your lavish attentions to his successor and to the heretic Princes of Germany. All this, you have admitted to Bellarmine, but you will not admit it to yourself. Finally, when you realized that the King of Navarre was too preoccupied with France and that even the Emperor Rudolf had no use for your arts, you announced your intention of being received *back* into the True Faith and committed the extraordinary folly of returning to Italy. The Pope, you said, loved virtuosi. Virtuosi! I say there is nothing but calculation here, calculation and contempt for the truth.''

His breath came thickly, and the sound of his wheezing filled my cell. ''Oh, Giordano,'' he gasped, rolling his eyes again, ''think of what you have done....''

The effect was undeniably comic, even grotesque. And yet....

Yet what? Chilling, I might almost have said. But there was nothing to fear.

I watched him then and, as with the others, detected some changes in him. The erratic movement of his eyes, I thought, *must have been* caused by blindness, or near blindness. Yet he would occasionally look up, his eyes glinting as if he saw only too well. At other times, his face was immobile and the eyes were expressionless blisters. He would sit as I had seen him at the trial and as he did now, very still and attentive, patient, unmoving like a lizard.

There was also something else, a faintly sweet odour to his person that reminded me of the mustiness of an old prayer-book. I thought this was my imagination, until the smell strengthened, growing earthy and damp.

I had no doubt that Fra Giovanni — or whatever this was that appeared in his form — was not very far from the grave.

"Listen to me, Giordano," he was saying, "another thing. There are more charges being prepared. It is said that you have conjured spirits and are in league with the devil. . . ." His voice was nearly inaudible, and as I leaned forward to listen I caught a glimpse of the old glitter in his eyes, those dead eyes. "It is rumoured," he said wheezily, "that you are a black magician, an operator in the laboratory of Satan. Well, Giordano," he stared vacantly in my direction, "what is your answer to that?"

"There's nothing in my book," I said, "that was not approved as honourable and worthy by Sixtus IV."

"Nor condemned," he rejoined, "by his successor Innocent VIII as rash, false and heretical."

He spat out the words and halted dramatically. "Do not cite the Law against me, Giordano," he said, working himself into another splenetic tirade. "My knowledge of precedent far outweighs yours. But that is one of your old tricks: to use the Law against itself, pleading the validity of custom where it suits you and denying it where it does not. No law on earth can help you now. Unconfessed, your soul goes straight to hell. And not just your soul!" he declared histrionically. "The body too must suffer the pangs of eternal perdition, and that is far more terrible than anything you have so far endured. Even the slow fire, which is the worst torture of man's devising, is only a prelude to the torments of hell, never ending agonies ingeniously contrived, ceaseless dismemberments, hideous mutilations. The most leprous beggar on earth is a happy man compared with him who feels the devil's claws tearing his flesh piecemeal, who must watch his own flesh being picked clean from the bone, whose only thought is to die and yet he cannot! The rack and the boards which have moved you to terror are apprentice instruments when set against these unimaginable refinements of pain. Already your immortal soul should recoil in horror and you should beg pity and forgiveness. Think, Giordano; for the love and mercy of Jesus Christ, confess your sins and abjure your heresies!"

"The devil's a Church lawyer," I said. "For a priest you seem to have an uncommon familiarity with hell. Is that what sent you here?"

"*Damnadatus es*," he murmured, "*Te exsecratio....*"

"You do not frighten me," I said. "Can the devil curse?"

"Do not mistake me for what I am not," he said sharply. "It is the love of God that brings me here, even into so foul a place as this. Mine is an errand of mercy and Christian grace. I knew this would be your response. Forewarned, I am armed with the compassion of Jesus Christ and the Blessed Virgin. I am very patient, Giordano, but my patience is not inexhaustible."

"The devil is a patient fellow," I replied. "And very earnest, as you are, *father*."

"Your words cannot wound me. I am beyond your scorn. The Church is my bride, and I am her faithful servant...."

"True enough," I said. "The Church is a bigamist and a whore."

"For pity's sake, Giordano!" he wailed, as if he now were the victim of the eternal torments he had described with such relish. "Will you not confess? Confess, Giordano, *confess....*"

He was cringing in the corner of the cell. "Remember Avernus, Giordano?" he whimpered. "Remember what you said to your poor brother, the oyster soul: '*Beydelus, Demeynes, Adulex, Metucgayn, Atine, Uquizuz, Gadix, Sol, Veni, cito cum tuis spiritibus.*' Will you call on them again, Giordano? They have ears, Giordano. They are listening for you, waiting for you, listening and waiting, Giordano, with their crackly claws. Demon husks! The shards of things! *Filoteo! Teofilo!....*"

"Abaddon!" I cried. "Return to the pit!"

"Abaddon is it now?" He gave a brittle laugh. "In good time, Giordano; in good time...."

"Hence, infernal mimic! Backbiter! Listener at keyholes!"

A rasping noise came from his palate. "Friend," he

whined, "why must you insult me?"

"You insult yourself! Begone! You have no claim on me!"

"Not even as a Christian?" His eyes flickered: a reptilian gaze. "Confess, Giordano. Confess, *or else....*"

"Or else what, pinchturd?" I was laughing now. "Would you have me call on Christ? Is that it, *father*?"

"Christ's love is blessed, *brother*," his tongue was quivering. "You have seen only the surface of hell: *superficies inferi*," he hissed. "Would you see more? *Dominus diaboli sum. Disciplus meus es.* Can you hear it, Giordano? Listen! The wind in the cypresses ... Listen! The creatures of night are gathering, waiting for the master, listening for the downdraft of saurian wings. Listen! See, Giordano! *Ecce angelus mortis!*"

Fra Giovanni Gabrielle de Saluzzo grinned. A sickly stench rose from his body. "*Qui foetor!*" he cried. "The devil farts!"

Then it seemed that the angel of death, whose messenger he was, had stricken his servant with all the palpable effects of his own tidings. The flesh sloughed from his face, exposing the glutinate colours of the grave, verdigris and cinnabar, the grey worm of corruption, and the blood-savaged skull beneath....

The vision passed, and I saw only a half-blind old man before me, nodding and smiling like one who is at peace with himself and the world.

"So be it," he sighed. "I am sorry, Giordano, that I have had to speak to you in this way. I am sorry that I have had to exert undue pressure. Commit yourself and your cause to the future, brother. I think that is what you have always wanted. It is useless to argue. I am old and weak. The journey has been hard and the winter is a tiring time for me. It will soon be sunrise. I must leave you then to your last visitor...."

"And who will that be?" I asked wearily.

"My superior," the Inquisitor yawned. "It is time to stretch these old bones of mine," he said, peering through his cloudy eyes and smiling like a saint. "I hope there are no bad feelings between us, Giordano. I must go now. Farewell, Giordano. And pity me, your friend...."

So saying, he vanished like the others.

And the good Lord, it is very plain, still smiles on me, smiles as He always did, smiles as only He can.

T

I have a somewhat longer statement to make than the others. I trust you will appreciate my reasons. As I have said, I am well aware that we have inspired a certain historical terror. However, the Venetian Holy Office did not see eye to eye with the Curia on the question of this man's death. Personally, I think his confession should have been enough to save him, and I am sure that all fair-minded men would agree. The methods which the Tribunal brought to bear on him during the time he was under my supervision, I found distasteful but necessary. Having succeeded in their aim, which was to make him confess, they should have been set aside. You will understand, of course, that I refer to the psychological hardships which Giordano perforce endured. The physical torture, though protracted, was (in my opinion) of a minimal effect in securing his confession. My point, therefore, is simply this: Venice erred in surrendering him to Rome. It would have been far wiser to have returned him to Switzerland or to Germany, whence he came. In the unlikely event of any future visit to the Republic, the mere fact of his confession would have rendered him harmless, perhaps even slightly ridiculous. For there can be few examples more instructive than that of a man who professes all kinds of opinions contrary to the Church, when he has solemnly sworn to alter those opinions and to amend his life in the sight of all men. Unfortunately, none of this came to pass, and as soon as it became evident that Rome was determined to make an example of him, it became necessary to proceed with the utmost circumspection.

That word again — necessary. I should say immediately that I am no advocate of necessitarianism. On the other hand, I do not exactly believe in free will. The dilemma in which Giordano found himself summed up the situation precisely: whatever he had done or said, he would burn; whatever he had not done or said, he would also burn. It is my deepest belief that if Rome had secured a further and more detailed confession from him, as they seemed on the point of doing, then his subsequent execution would have been illegal. Added to the dubious legality of his trial and the existence of an antecedent confession, this further confession, if secured, would have made his execution doubly illegal, a procedural monstrosity in point of fact. Knowing the man as I did, my duty was quite clear. In order to prevent a crime, I had to prevent Giordano from confessing again. That he died unconfessed, in the eyes of the Curia at least, had the extra, if incidental, historical advantage of rallying liberal opinion to his cause.

Finally, there was nothing supernatural or devious in my actions. His fear on that account was the product of a disordered mind, itself the result of his undoubted sufferings. The forces of universal reason, like those of universal evil, have long since abandoned such paranormal tactics as spectral visitations, which were effective only during the infancy of the human race. That is all I have to say.

T

It is not Zuan's God I worship, the God of a Venetian dilettante. Nor is it Michel's, the God of practical realities, nor Fra Giovanni's lawyer Lord, the God of precedent and decree. The God I worship does not write incomprehensible books to man, nor confound him with the ceaseless babble of a divine idiot. He does not play at hide-and-seek with miracles. He is not some unseen puppeteer, pulling the strings of men's souls to keep the angels entertained. He did not confect man from clay, nor did He make this world with a word. The God I worship is infigurable and has no name. He is invisible and multiform, all things and nothing, forever elusive and forever inescapable.

In the cathedral of my mind, I have long sought him out.

Once, in the garden of the monastery of Saint Bartholomew in Campagna, I thought I was in His presence. I was young and in love with the world. It was late autumn; the second roses were in bloom and the air was already tainted with the fragrance of their dying. The interminable talk, talk, talk of all human calculation had ceased, and my mind was filled with a perfect silence. Love ruled the rosebush and the garden; one God, supremely equivocal, held sway.

It was an illusion of the senses, the old trickery of the garden, returning from time to time to tempt me with the sweetness of death.

These three, dilettante, courtier and Inquisitor, all portrayed an arc of the truth. Each had the same intention; each intended to deceive. It is no longer possible to temporize with that which is outside time. No hope of posthumous fame, no remembrance of king's love nor fear of hell fire and damnation can play any part in my decision. If I die so then I die, and do not for that reason refuse the last administration of Christian grace. Dilettante, courtier and priest, are each in turn no more than a segment of myself. It is another I expect, a fourth apart from these, apart from myself. With him the circle is closed and my destiny is complete. And then I shall have found my God, the nameless One, master of eternal silence.

T

He came bearing the gift of the Virgin to Saint Dominic — a rosary. "Will you pray, Brother Jordanus?" he said, and kneeling, he prayed.

"Who are you?" I asked when he had finished his angelic salutation.

"One you might have been," he replied. "Ippolita Maria is my name."

There was a natural ease of bearing to him, a sense of power and reality that is found in those who are on familiar terms with themselves and the world. He had appeared in the company of gargoyle face, who had retreated, showering a thousand 'Excellencies' in his wake. No vision this, but a creature of flesh and blood. He was a type, this noble eccelesiastic, in the fat and pink of health, youthful despite his greying hair. His face was smooth and unlined, and he smiled readily. He affected a certain blunt good humour, which he wore like his habit. It was a disguise that lent him an air of invulnerability, both physical and spiritual, as if nothing could touch this man or disturb his outward calm.

"I am impressed, my lord," I said, "although I was expecting another."

"Oh," my spiritual superior remarked, "and who might that have been?"

"Nothing, my lord," I said. "A dream."

"Your whole life has been spent dreaming," he said, not unkindly. "It is time to wake up, Giordano; time to face the last reality."

"As it is also the first," I said, "if you mean death."

"Philip," he said, and it was many years since anyone had used my baptismal name, "the time is long past for theatricality. You have not always pretended such indifference to death. It is dishonest of you," he declared simply.

Fra Ippolita Maria bowed his head. He looked up then and smiled. 'I know what you're thinking,' that smile seemed to say. 'We understand each other perfectly; we are both actors on the same stage.'

We would skirmish for a little while, I decided, each trying out his respective strengths and enjoying the ritual of attack and response. We would reach an agreement and decide who was the stronger. And if we did not altogether despise each other by this time, and if language had not entirely lost its meaning, it was just possible, remotely possible, that there might be some truth spoken between us.

When he spoke again, there was a warmth, even a merriness, in his voice. "Do you remember the time immediately before you ran away from Naples, Giordano; do you remember what you did then?"

The question made no sense. Indifferently, I wondered if I was supposed to remember everything: the angle of the sun on this or that day, the phases of the moon, the configurations of the planets themselves.

"Your memory is selective," Fra Ippolita said. "I'm quite sure that you cannot have forgotten. There's an old saying: better destroy the devil than have the devil destroy you. The books, Giordano; the *books*...."

"*Certain books*," Fra Giovanni was saying, "*annotated by Erasmus, works of Jerome and Chrysostom* ..."

"*Byzantine pursuits,*" the Patriarch warbled ...

I remembered. It was not an action I was particularly proud of. The books were harmless; my notes would have convicted a saint. I had intended to destroy these scribblings before I left the monastery, but at the last minute I had been distracted by the other arrangements for my departure. Since I had borrowed the books illegally and was already in enough trouble, the last thing I wanted was to be caught returning them.

I imagined the reaction of my peers:

"He stole the books!" — Serafino.

"He read them!" — Hortensio.

"He read stolen books!" — Bonifacio.

The books would have to be destroyed....

It was in the privy that another friar discovered me in this incontinent act of destruction. He fled, of course, with a look of horror on his face as if he had seen the devil himself, fled and left me to my work. The pages of the saints and my own manuscripts went down the cistern, the wisdom of the ages and the folly of youth commingling with the pious ordure of the Brotherhood.

Should I say that I have something to expiate, a sense of disgust perhaps, a bitterness? It would not be entirely true. For I thought of Socrates then, and not for the first time in my life. Like some haruspex of the privy, I decided that there was a singular appositeness to what I had done, or rather to the reflection following the action. What better place was there to philosophize than the privy, unless it was the marketplace? And now that men's opinions were openly for sale, the one at least had the advantage of privacy over the other. Even so, I thought as I gazed down at the cloacal soup and the scraps of paper, even so — it comes to this.

Cowardice is the one quality with which I have been endowed in truly heroic proportions.

"Your behaviour then," Fra Ippolita was reminding me, "did not seem like that of a man courting martyrdom."

"No, my lord," I conceded, "and nor will it seem that way to future ages, if that is what you are trying to say. But surely you are not here to remind me of the past?"

"There is a great deal I would like to remind you of," he said, "including that forgiveness which it is within our power to grant and which it is still within yours to obtain."

"And what have I done," I asked, "that I should be forgiven?"

"You have revoked your vows, surrendering yourself to worldliness," intuned Fra Ippolita Maria; "you are a blasphemer and a heretic, you have lived long in heretical lands ..."

"Spare me the litany, my lord," I said. "Those things are past."

"But not forgotten," he snapped. "Forgive me," he recovered immediately. "I did not mean to lose my temper. But you do invite such responses, Giordano. It's a trick of yours, and you may as well assume that I am familiar with your tricks. I've been studying you, Giordano, at a distance, it's true — but not superficially. In a way, you're my responsibility. You caught me off balance just now, but that was my fault. I was thinking ahead, thinking of what I was going to say next. But you can see that I'm not at all angry now. You know, Giordano, one of the most interesting things in life is a sense of expectancy. It is so frequently disappointed. You claim that you were expecting another, and no doubt I have failed to meet your expectation. And I — I planned our conversation in rather a different way. It does not seem to be taking the turn I expected. One should cultivate a sense of stoicism, don't you think?"

He was walking up and down, stooping slightly as if he felt under some constraint. "It is hard to appreciate another's point of view," he said, halting in mid-stride to resume his argument. "I can understand that you feel some resentment against the Church. Because of that, you should not make the mistake of thinking that she is unsympathetic. I raised the — incident — at Naples, that trivial affair of the books, to show that we still have an awareness of humanity. Your actions at that time show you in a very human light, which explains why you would prefer to forget what you did. It was an insignificant episode, yet it revealed a very ordinary human weakness — fear. You would like to present yourself to posterity as a man who was beyond fear. You are one of those people whose existence is almost entirely subjective. You have never been any good at sharing things, Giordano. Perhaps you are inhuman, in the sense that saints and martyrs are always inhuman. Ordinary human emotions in them are often heightened or suppressed. It is quite a gift, to be able to ignore the past, to ignore one's own actions. Already you have begun the conscious falsification of your life in the hope that others will take up where you leave off. In death, as in life, your greatest ambition has been to impress people with your heroism. You would like them to think that you have not lived as they have, enduring the petty failures and celebrating the small successes, worrying from day to day whether they can make ends meet, shoring up their crumbling lives with little stores of hope, until, at the last, they become slightly mad, for everyone is slightly mad, until they come to die, Giordano, and must ask themselves why on earth they were ever born to live and suffer in the first place. How the Church understands the people, Giordano! She knows how impressive your life will seem to them — you who never burdened yourself with the ordinary cares of existence, who disdained to ask the questions ordinary people ask. How they will marvel at you and long to emulate that spirit which dared to test the beyond! And how the Church understands your ambition, Giordano. For it is nothing less than her own.

"You see, Giordano," he said archly, "I told you I'd been

studying you. If only you could see yourself now!" he cried suddenly. "Would you like me to be your mirror, Giordano? You are an old man, not at all what you imagine yourself to be. You are a broken, pitiful, old man, Giordano...."

"But not as old as the Church, my lord," I said.

"You cannot provoke me, Giordano," he murmured sweetly. "Your life is open like a book to me. You have confused the attempt to seem heroic with true heroism, which is always spontaneous and effortless. You have deceived many people, but you have deceived yourself most of all. That is really what I wanted to show you. There is something else, however. I was going to say — before you interrupted me — that nothing is wholly lost or forgotten. You have written as much yourself. No event in this universe of ours can ever be wasted, no particle of matter is entirely annihilated. The mind of God contains all possibilities, all permutations of matter and spirit. But I think you will find, Giordano, that when it comes to the squaring of accounts, the Lord is somewhat frugal. Yes, I think it could be said that He exercises an economy of sorts, a certain kind of symmetry in the balancing of accounts. Do you follow me, Giordano?"

"Oh, yes," I said. "No doubt the Lord had you in mind when He was balancing the books."

"I do not think you understand me," he said. "It was a figure of speech, that is all, Giordano. But I am not here to argue, I am not here to engage in dialectical niceties...."

I studied him closely, this advocate of the divine parsimony in whom the sense of power was only too well confirmed. There was no longer any need for pretence. Fra Ippolita Maria, *Magister Generalis* of the Inquisitorial Order, threw aside his mask of brotherly piety.

"You will die as you lived," he said, "a proven heretic. Yet you must understand, Giordano, you must be made to understand, that the evil you have done is inconsequential and cannot harm Holy Church. The evil you have done will die with you, but it is not for that reason that you are going to die. You have forgotten God, Giordano. Do not think that He has forgotten you."

I said nothing.

"You are still pleading for your life, aren't you?" Fra Ippolita enquired smoothly. "Do not trouble to deny it, Giordano. Forgive me for speaking simply. I am a simple man — and humble, Giordano." The General contemplated his simple humility. "The Church understands you," he continued, "because you are one of her own. She knows your ambitions, if realized, would present her with a dangerous threat. She knows, also, that you are acquainted with her own thinking on the subject of your death. Heresy has always presented the Church with a dilemma which she is perhaps incapable of solving as she would wish — with the meekness of heart and gentleness of hand that befits the disciples and followers of Christ. If the Church sends you to the stake, she is seen to act cruelly. On the other hand, history has shown that she cannot afford to let heresy flourish. The Church would have preferred conciliation, or failing that, to have wished you away, to have swept you under the carpet so to speak. This natural and reasonable wish to avoid confrontation you have exploited to the full — with some dexterity, if you will allow me the liberty of a compliment. Are you listening to me, Giordano?"

I assured him that I was....

"Good. Because there is one thing I would like to make perfectly clear. Brother Jordanus, let me tell you *why* you are going to die."

I listened to him, I listened and could not believe. Yet here was no illusion, no reflection of myself. Here was a man come to offer me a Christian leavetaking of this world: the quietus of the damned.

"Two years ago," he began, "the Captain of Cardinal Aldobrandini's guard married...."

T

I told him Portia's story, an inglorious fugue of deceit, sin, murder and flight. Or was it more a madrigal? Some strange tune by the murderous Gesualdo? No matter: one thing leads to another; all notes harmonize in the general scheme. My coda, the diplomatic exchange: Captain to Cardinal to Pope, and its variation: Pope to Ambassador to King — and back again. He listened to me, I made sure of that. I left out no details but told him plainly why Portia must die, her lover as well. Murder and petty treason! "That's it," I said. "It's finished now. The agony's over. You will die, Giordano, in exchange for these two." Did I speak too bluntly? I see no point in mixing art with life. But his reaction, that was — what's the word? — *hysterical*, I would say. Some excess of feeling in him, some more than human passion inflamed his mortal self into a seething, spittlesome rage. We are all devils he said, his voice cracking in a kind of laughter I did not like to hear. Devils, and worse. Clement himself was Antichrist to contemplate such a scheme. What had Portia done to deserve her death? Was he to confess in return for her life; was that the offer I'd come to make? I implored the Blessed Virgin on his behalf, Mary Mother of Jesus who intercedes for all sinners before the Throne of God — but Brother Jordanus was demented, crazy with rage. His sufferings, I think, had unhinged him. "I know you," he cried, propping himself up on his bed of rancid straw and pointing a bony finger at me. "I know you, *Satan*!"

What else could I say?

T

There is no hope of salvation. I have seen too much of the haggling over human souls, the petty commerce in pardons and remissions. No treasure of this world can be valid in the court of conscience. And now it is a settlement of blood that is proposed, the final transaction: life for life instead of gold for spirit. I have argued the case thus: confess and perhaps she will live. But did she ever live, had she ever any life beyond these walls? Roberto as well. Who *are* they? And their love, it must be — what must it be? Adulterous, Fra Ippolita said, the pretext for a hanging. A godly man and honourable. A Christian! The fault of their deaths is mine, he said. Their love also? What has happened has happened without me; what will happen will happen without me. They do not even know of my existence. Or do they: do *they* exist?

To create a life and flesh the bone, infuse the veins and add thought, speech and feeling to the first idea — that is divine. And to murder? Most Christian and just, providing it is ordained by Holy Church.

But that is not why he came, that is not the reason....

Roberto and Portia are fictions. They do not exist. I know that is the truth. I *know* ...

I am in the nave of the cathedral again, still waiting for my friend. The light filters through a flat expanse of stained-glass lancet windows. It has a sinuous quality, curving and refracted, arcing over the delicate traceries of gables and mullions so that line and dimension no longer seem to exist. A painter's joke, I remember thinking. For such is the way of dreams that I can also see the cathedral's façade, an exoskeleton of flying buttresses and sculptured vaults, as if the structure had been turned in on itself, and linear form and perspective, time and space annihilated.

The cathedral dominates the town, which I can see, as if from the highest tower, the streets spread out in a radial pattern below. I can hear a distant chanting, and realize that a procession of townspeople is making its way up to the cathedral.

A voice calls my name from the pulpit. The ribbed arches of the ceiling crack and break; the buttresses crumble; the illuminated panels of the windows are bulging, the leaded joins flexing and splitting. The light is torn and burns through the glass. Now I can see them, my judges, the Cardinals. "Do you know this place?" Bellarmine is whispering. "Do you know it, Giordano?"

274

"Men go armed into hell," my father said; "quick and fearful."

And Bellarmine: "The Perugians are going to hang, Giordano. No one has lied to you."

I tell them it is not true, but no one is listening. How can they?

"Remember the poisoned soldier in Plutarch," the Cardinal says. "You will burn, Giordano...."

"No, my lord. *No!*"

And Bellarmine, the Inquisitor, myself, the accused and the accuser: "There is nothing. It is finished. It is all over for you, Giordano...."

The sentence must be delivered. The prisoner kneels ...

So many times have I heard it that it comes as no surprise.

"It is what you have always wanted, Giordano," Bellarmine is saying: "Listen, brother; *listen....*"

"And you shall be bound and gagged lest you utter revilings against the Church. And you shall be clad as a heretic and taken to that place which is determined by the Law. And there you shall be surrendered to the secular arm for punishment according to the Law. And you shall be dealt with as gently as may be, without unnecessary cruelty or suffering. And you shall die *non effusio sanguinis,* without the shedding of blood."

Magnum miraculum! What a great miracle is man, a being worthy of reverence and honour ...

The god of the rose garden is death. I understand. I know what is to be done ...

That summer of the plague year in Savona, the shutters of the houses blistered in the sun. Weeds were growing in the streets. *Beware the wandsman! Beware the wandsman!* But the children no longer sang; and the bells were silent.

There came a time when I had seen enough of death. One morning I rose early and set out alone for the commune of Finale Ligure, a few miles to the south. I took the coastal road, and already had some thought of continuing into France. The day was hot (it must have been July or August) and I began to think of food and shelter, when, on a headland, I came across a signpost. What luck, I thought, for a countryman of that region was at rest there, and I could ask if he knew of an inn thereabouts.

I rode up to him, dismounted and placed my hand on his shoulder. He turned, or rather I turned him, and, smiling, he died.

The smell of the rose garden came back to me then. Finale Ligure I would never see.

It was the beginning ...

Unless you make yourself equal to God, you cannot understand God: for the like is not intelligible save by the like. Make yourself grow to a greatness beyond measure, by a bound free yourself from the body; raise yourself above all time, become Eternity; then you will understand God. Believe that nothing is impossible for you, think yourself immortal and capable of understanding all, all arts, all sciences, the nature of every living being. Mount higher than the highest height; descend lower than the lowest depth. Draw into yourself all sensations of everything created, fire and water, dry and moist, imagining that you are everywhere on earth, in the sea, in the sky, that you are not yet born, in the maternal womb, adolescent, old, dead, beyond death. If you embrace in your thought all things at once, times, places, substances, qualities, quantities, you may understand God.

I have seen Him; I have looked on God. He is very changeable; infinite His names. In other times and other places, I might have looked on others gods: in Egyptian Thebes, worshipped Osiris, lord of the dead; called the same god Serapis in Pontic Sinope, or Anubis, conductor of souls, in Cappadocian Seleucia — vanished worlds. In Croton, they said it was easier to meet with a god than a man. I do not know....

I saw them tonight: horned Osiris, breathing the blood-smoke of sacrifice; Anubis, jackel-headed, sitting atop the altar of death, another, falcon-eyed, another and another, until there emerged the one, faceless god, his body convulsed with the silent laughter of the divine spectator.

I dreamed, of course. But who has dreamed me?
Another — *you*, my friend.

XII

Let him who will, think my fate cruel because it kills in hope and revives in desire. I am nourished by my high enterprise; and although the soul does not attain the desired end and is consumed by so much zeal, it is enough that it burns in so noble a fire. It is enough that I have been raised to the sky and delivered from the ignoble number.
—Giordano Bruno

Rome, February 1600

Early on the morning of Sunday, the seventeenth of February, Cardinal Robert Bellarmine, S.J., in the company of his peers, climbed the steps of the *palchetto* overlooking the Campo de' Fiori, the field of flowers. A fair-sized crowd had already gathered in the square, and from his place in the reviewing stand Cardinal Bellarmine sensed that this crowd, for all its diversity, resembled one of those simple but virulent organisms whose existence was as yet merely rumoured by the magicians. Corpuscular images floated in his mind, and the Cardinal, who disliked large gatherings, abandoned himself to thoughts of mankind in the mass. What a pity it was that it needed a burning to unite the hearts of the Roman people! Each individual was as one in the belief of his or her own personal immortality, a belief which the main event of the morning would do much to reinforce. The crowd was a parasite; its host, death. A good day,

278

Cardinal Bellarmine reflected, for beggars and cutpurses. . . .

All manner of people circulated in the square. A pardoner mortgaged eternity while a reliquarian set up stall and traded in the knuckles of holy men under the head of Saint Anthony. Purveyors of nostrums vied with each other in a good-humoured sort of way, one claiming that his was the only infallible remedy against ringworm, another peddling a cure for the croup, a third promoting the virtues of a gold and silver cordial that was indispensable (as is well known and universally attested) in cases of uticaria and erysipelas, caused by a predominance of the sanguinary humour and aggravated by the influence of Scorpio. The end of days was nigh; a new age was dawning. An old woman sold amulets to ward off *il malocchio* — she prospered. An idiot foretold the future with dice — and did not prosper. The Captain of the Guard ordered the owner of a mangy dancing bear to remove himself and his animal from the square; the proprietor of a flea circus went unhindered. Fortunes could be had, and tame lizards; the terraqueous globe itself — and heaven.

So much boundless activity depressed the Cardinal. Ugly grey and yellow clouds were piling up in the sky, and for the first time he felt the cold. The people have to keep warm, he thought. But why are there so many women in the crowd?

Some were with their husbands, the majority in groups of three or four, and a few alone. These unattached females worried the Cardinal, and then he worried because he was worried. I should have more to think about, he told himself, than the prospect of these foolish women becoming hysterical. It is going to rain. . . .

A wandering band of *pifferari* had come down from the hills and began to play on their bagpipes and *pifferi* — a kind of fife which gave them their name. And the women started to dance; slowly at first, and in couples; faster as the tempo quickened, in a ring around the stake, which was piled round with bundles of kindling, an avenue marking the path to the centre. Separate bundles lay to one side and formed the entrance to this avenue, a gateway to be dragged close by means of ropes.

There had been no recommendation for mercy. Giordano was to be burned alive and would not be garrotted at the last minute. And soon, very soon now, they would bring the prisoner out.

Sentencing had taken place nine days ago. But even before that, on the twentieth of last month, the Pope had instructed the Congregation to reach their verdict without further delay and to surrender the prisoner to the secular arm. A formality, the temporal power was one with the spiritual in Rome, and the Governor was an officer of the Pope and a Monsignor as well. Yet the Pope's ruling had pre-empted the Congregation's verdict; the sentence had been handed down before the judgement. Of course, the verdict had never been in any doubt. His Holiness had merely wished to hurry things on a little. Even so, Cardinal Bellarmine found the procedure disturbing. If the judgement was to follow the sentencing in every case, it was but a short step to execute the accused first and try him afterwards. All the Cardinals knew the meaning of that phrase: *surrender the prisoner to the secular arm.* Supposing, then, that some of them had favoured acquittal. Could it not be said that the Pope's direction had influenced them against their better feelings — in his own case, for example?

Bellarmine was distracted by a roar from the crowd. In the space of a heartbeat, it seemed to have doubled and redoubled. There will be a crush, he thought, but the guard was clearing the way. Was this the prisoner? Ah, no. Cardinal Bellarmine heard the crack of a whip and watched as a cross hove into view, dragged by a company of flagellants. They were stripped to the waist and each one bore the mark of the whip. The crowd praised God and rejoiced. Yet there were some, the Cardinal noticed, who turned aside. Why should one man invite punishment and another fear it? There was no answer. The whip cracked again and its lash made him whince. Surely, he was unafraid. Surely, the bite of the whip was so much less than that of the flames; surely, these had sinned and were justly punished. *Surely. . .*

He remembered his last meeting with Giordano. That had been on the morning of the ninth, immediately before the sentencing. He had gone to see him, knowing that it was far too late. Giordano had taken everything back; and even denied the existence of God.

"Your God, Eminence," he had said.

It had always been too late, the Cardinal reflected.

His sense of failure gave way to an apprehension of futility. After sentencing, Giordano had turned threateningly to his judges and had uttered these words: "It is with far greater fear that you pronounce, than I receive, this sentence." What pride! What impudence! And also, it had to be said, what courage. Robert Bellarmine acknowledged defeat. Giordano, condemned to a heretic's death, had triumphed.

The Cardinal detected a wave-like motion at the edge of the crowd. There came a cry of command, and the guard formed a cordon around the stake, forcing the dancers to retire. Below and immediately in front of the *palchetto* itself, a separate and smaller stand had been erected, sufficient to accommodate one man. A herald of the Fiscal Procurator's office climbed the steps of this structure, stood for a moment in an indecisive attitude, then hastily retreated. A hurried conference followed between the herald and some officials of the Inquisition, who thrust a scrolled document into his hands. The sentence, Cardinal Bellarmine thought. The entrance to the square had been cleared now, and the crowd was hushed. A few drops of rain fell like lead from the yellow and gray skies, and the Cardinal heard the distant beat of a solitary drum.

A little nervously he leaned across to his neighbour, Cardinal Madruzzi. "Can you hear it?" he said, and the Cardinal confirmed that he could. Robert Bellarmine was suddenly elated. His heart was beating furiously, his faculties were heightened, and a sensation that was curiously akin to pleasure swept through his body. Absurdly, he turned to his other neighbour and said, "They are coming."

The Cardinal of San Severina did not acknowledge this remark. He was staring fixedly ahead and his face was pale, very pale it seemed to Cardinal Bellarmine, who had always feared this man, the more so because he had been prominent among those who had argued for Giordano's condemnation from the beginning. Self-interest, of course. For the Cardinal of San Severina, it was rumoured, was one of the Nolan's secret friends. He was regarded as an unscrupulous and ambitious man, who had once declared that he found the massacre of Saint Bartholomew's Eve, the 'Bloody Wedding' of Paris, to be "a glorious day, and one exceeding agreeable to Catholics."

Was it remorse, Cardinal Bellarmine wondered, that made him look so pale; was he harbouring some last minute doubts; did he regret that he had argued the case, and argued it forcibly, for the death of his friend?

In fact the Cardinal of San Severina's keen gaze was searching the crowd for a particular object: Schopp, Kaspar, lately arrived from Germany and recently introduced to the Cardinal as a man to be watched.

The Cardinal caught sight of his secretary, Bastiano, and the Dominican friar, Brother Gryphius. And there was Schopp, wedged in between the two, his eyes straining to catch sight of the procession that was already entering the square. There was something oddly familiar about Schopp. Only now, as Cardinal Bellarmine made his pointless observation, did he realize what. It is as though I have met him before, the Cardinal of San Severina thought, in another time and place long forgotten; it is as though I am remembering the memory of a memory, like Saint Augustine.

The procession came to a ragged halt and the drummer at its head looked up as if in surprise. He gave a few desultory taps, then covered the drum with his hands, the sound dying into silence. The guard snapped to attention as a plumed officer saluted on horseback. The Brothers of Death laid down a forest of spindly crosses, and the dark heavy cross of the flagellants was also lowered to the ground, some of these unfortunates kneeling, others prostrating themselves before the *palchetto*. For the first time, the Cardinals and the crowd had a clear view of the prisoner. His emaciated frame was clad in a torn white shift that had been daubed with a red substance; his hands had already been bound and tied behind his back, and he was

282

gagged. Cardinal Bellarmine watched as the sergeant-at-arms stepped forward reluctantly to fix a placard and a halter around Giordano's neck. The conical cap came next, and the sergeant was tugging at the rope, dragging the prisoner to his place before the herald's stand.

Cardinal Bellarmine made out the word 'philosopher' on the placard. Giordano gave him a quick stare of recognition. The Cardinal swallowed and averted his gaze. Momentarily, he wondered whether he could bear such degradation. The old fear coiled tightly in his stomach. He glanced at the stake and saw that it was blurred, slightly out of focus. Yes, he was feeling really quite light-headed. I have nothing to fear, he told himself, and was startled by the abrupt blast of a trumpet, its lingering cry washing over the square. The rain was falling steadily now, a green drizzle in the uncertain light. A gust of wind swept the square and carried in its wake the echoing tones of the trumpet's clarion call.

A trifling delay ensued, an interval marked neither by sound nor the absence of sound, during which time the tableau appeared suspended, as if the participants were unsure of themselves and what they must do next. The ritual of avoidance, Cardinal Bellarmine thought; nobody *wants* to act. A profound torpor descended on the square. Everything seemed inconsequential and diffuse. He had been expecting more precision, greater alacrity, but now, as the flags snarled in the breeze and the herald resumed his position on the stand, the hiatus took on gargantuan proportions, as if the fullness of time had come into being, as if the Campo de' Fiori were a locus for infinity itself, and contained, within its four walls, a world out of time. The place of execution, he was thinking; so it has always been and always shall be, in the beginning and in the end. Even this moment is eternal and cannot die. It has happened before and must continue to happen, forever and forever in the mind of God.

But now the Brothers of Death closed round Giordano and forced him to kneel. The Cardinal watched as one of them offered him a crucifix and it was refused. The reading of the sentence was protracted, the herald droning interminably on and stumbling over the unfamiliar phrases. Words, words, the Cardinal thought, recognizing them as his own. . . .

Finish it, finish it quickly!

The Cardinal heard a child crying in the crowd. A woman shrieked. And then the guard were leading Giordano to the stake, binding him there, dragging the gate closed, advancing on every side, torches of blazing pitch in their hands, the pyre burning as the crowd roared and Giordano turned aside from the image of the cross and was engulfed by the flames.

— *What bones make the best ashes, Cardinal?*

Cardinal Robert Bellarmine, S.J, imagined serpents in the fire and smiled to himself. The victory was Giordano's now: how could it have been any other way?

I have accomplished nothing, he thought. It is as though I have never existed.

The dancing had started again, and the smoke stung his eyes.

T

It was still dark, the wind scouring the Tiber from the west as Brother Gryphius crossed the bridge of Sant'Angelo. A stone angel directed him down the gauntlet of angels, their wings poised for flight. "Who are you?" he asked, but the angel was silent, its mouth pursed in a Botticellian pout. Torches flared along the embankment and the moon sank behind the fortress, bathing its impenetrable walls in a pale nimbus. Now was the hour of quickening shadows and petty murders. Brother Gryphius heard the flurry of wings and the dying scream of some small animal. The clock above the gatehouse struck the hour, its tones drifting across the river: four o'clock. The Brother stared down into black waters. A drowned angel floated past; he did not see his own reflection.

A fragment of conversation came to him. "You will of course obey," Fra Ippolita said.

"Naturally," Vicar Paul of Mirandola added, "you understand the importance of this mission."

Naturally and of course no ...

That had been yesterday afternoon at the della Minerva monastery. Or was it the day before yesterday? Never had time seemed so indefinite and yet so arbitrary.

"You will go to him," Fra Ippolita said. "We are sure you can succeed."

Brother Gryphius looked at his superiors in disbelief and shook his head.

"But," Vicar Paul said, "we insist. We command you...."

And Brother Gryphius refused to obey.

The angel's wing was broken. "Don't you get tired of standing here?" Brother Gryphius enquired, and the angel indicated that it was a creature neither of air nor water. "Nor fire nor earth," Gryphius said, "like myself."

The angel frowned loftily. "I did not mean to upset you," Gryphius continued, "but I do not think you are very astute — for an angel. I don't suppose you could even tell me why today is today. What's that? God knows, you say. But at least He has an excuse. He does not exist."

The angel acknowledged this with a polite silence. A lone sentry outside the guardhouse coughed in his sleep. Brother Gryphius sat himself down to think.

He had risen early, left the monastery, and found his way to the Campo de' Fiori. The city was deserted at this hour, the square almost so. A company of soldiers, gathered round the light of a fire, had shouted at his approach. "Come and warm yourself!" It was, he thought, a hospitable invitation.

"Gladly, gladly," he had said, and stepped forth into the light and warmth.

Brother Gryphius found himself seized from behind, a short sword drawn at his neck.

"What have we here," one of the company cried incredulously, "a friar!"

"A man of God!" another laughed.

"Or a conspirator," said the first.

The grip relaxed experimentally; Brother Gryphius struggled and was thrown to the ground. "Bind him," his assailant commanded. "Let's see if he fits...." And Brother Gryphius was dragged to the stake and bound there.

"What do you say to that?" he asked the angel. "Nothing, as usual...."

The Brother had protested that he was an honest man. "Then you'll burn," said one who was in authority, a remark which provoked more laughter.

"Yes," Gryphius agreed, smiling nervously.

"So you think that's funny, do you?" his tormentor enquired.

"No. I ..."

Other voices joined in. Perhaps he knew the heretic? Maybe he was the heretic and had escaped? Don't be a fool! Why would the heretic come here? To be burned of course. He looked very like him. No, he was a conspirator. Likely a thief. A common criminal. Hang him!

"A drink! Some wine for the friar!" They released him then. "We mean no harm," one of them said. "It is a cold night. We are all men under God's heaven."

"I must go now," he said.

"Then go," the soldier replied, "in peace."

A voice cried after him as he left the square: "Be careful, holy man!" — a cry lost amidst the sound of laughter in the dark.

"So you see," Brother Gryphius addressed the angel, "God is not the only one who has a sense of humour."

Brother Gryphius descended into the huddled tenements of the bank. The gutters were choked with refuse and the sour scent of decay assailed his nostrils. Several times he slipped on the cobblestones; once on the body of a cat, its fur matted in death, its corpse bloated. Brother Gryphius heard the scattering of rodent feet: small red eyes watched his passage.

The street narrowed into an alley as his route took him past a frontage of peeling stucco and vacant windows, a monotonous façade capable of seemingly endless replication. Occasionally, a recessed archway, which led, he knew, to an airless courtyard, interrupted the faceless wall and beckoned to him, darker than night. Somewhere, a dog bayed at the moon. Brother Gryphius thought of the pursuer and the pursued. He halted, allowing his own footsteps to catch up with him, halted and listened to the dripping of moisture. The street was empty. In a few hours, it would be crowded.

A flight of stairs cut into a defile brought him to the embankment. The bridge was not too far away and he could see the fortress across the river.

"It is difficult, you know," Brother Gryphius remarked to his silent familar, "to prove that anything exists. For example, I always have to imagine other people. Even when they are really there; perhaps especially when they are there. . . ."

The angel smiled.

"You are nothing," Brother Gryphius said. "Unnameable and unknowable."

The angel was immune to flattery.

"God is nothing."

The pale host was unmoved. Hermes or Jehovah, Tat or Jesus, it was all the same to them: fathers and sons, copies of copies.

"Why?"

Because. . . .

Torchlight wavered on the opposite bank. A shadow was crossing Rome, a grey dawn breaking over the Alban Hills. Brother Gryphius thought of Hermes Termaximus and the two lands of the Nile. The fortress rose through the dawn, its implacable bulk dominating the eternal city.

The night is a time of wisdom, he was thinking; the morning a time of death. Minerva becomes Serapis. Why should the gods concern themselves with the fate of man?

A papal messenger rode by. The massive gate of Hadrian's Tomb opened to receive him and did not close. Brother Gryphius watched as a black pennant was unfurled. He turned to the east where the falcon Harakhte flew with the sun, the great falcon feathered in many hues. He saw a garland of dead flowers strewn on the floor of the ruined temple of Avernus.

"Someone had to be my brother," he said to the angel.

The statues indicated their indifference.

"God is death."

The angel extended its mutilated wing in a cold arrest, an Orphic embrace, as if stone would test the free and insubstantial void. Nothing. The generations were as dust.

Brother Gryphius could hear the distant chant of ritual, a threnody to forgotten gods, hymnal and dirge:

> *Khnum and Amon,*
> *Patient artist,*
> *Preserver of innumerable works,*
> *Goatherd and shepherd,*
> *Driving his flock*
> *To the shelter....*

He was holding a blood red pearl in his hand. "Take it," Giordano said. "It was my mother's." The volume of the chanting grew, solemn and penitential across the slow moving river. *Domine sancte, Pater omnipotens, aeterne Deus* ... "Look! Look!" his brother was shouting: "A miracle! A cloud! The Tabernacle of the Lord! I was speaking of distance, *buffone* — distance and perspective ... Vesuvius, it lives, it breathes, it gives life to other things....."

"Nothing."

The angel stared down, its eyes pitted and sightless, its face scarred by a myriad excrescences. Brother Gryphius read infinity in its gaze; order and chaos in the design of the small, callousness in the unyielding stone. The river mirrored the sky, a tree, a cloud; the statue reeled like a drunken man, a god, a parody of mutable flesh. Nothing. Brother Gryphius abandoned his vigil. Unnoticed, he joined the procession of the Cross, *via dolorosa* winding its way down to the Campo de' Fiori, *per dominum Iesum Christum*, the field of flowers, *Fililum tuum, qui tecum vivit, et regnat in unitate Spiritus sancti Deus*, and the place of execution for heretics, *per omnia saecula saeculorum.* "Everything is the same," his brother said. "The hill Cicala, the volcano, the house and the garden. There is no beginning and no end. There is no death. God is everywhere...."

— *I speak only as a philosopher, my lords.*

He saw Fra Giovanni in the interrogation room of the Inquisition. "We seldom have to use them," the Inquisitor said, pointing at the instruments. He could see Lorenzo Priuli. The Patriarch of all Venetia was leaning across the dais, his fox eyes glinting, his voice wheedling: "The truth now. I want the truth." And the people were approaching, hurrying, running. The pack. Hellhounds. Gates were unbarred, shutters thrown open, the people crowding onto their balconies, thronging in the narrow streets below, the tenements angled crazily against the sky, turning, turning. "Answer me, *frater*," Lorenzo was saying. "God is everywhere," Giordano said, "even in hell." And Brother Gryphius was running with the crowd, past the guard and the penitents, past the Brothers of Death and Mercy — *Misericordia!* —, hastening to catch sight of his brother, running, until the guard blocked the way, and the crowd, confused, turbulent, threatened to run riot over the square. The tide faltered and ceased, rolling back, its inertia spent. Brother Gryphius found himself at the very front of the crowd. The man next to him swayed and muttered that God's justice was about to be done.

— *Giordano!*

Their eyes met, a finite moment infinitely divisible. Brother Gryphius heard the beat of a drum, the crack of a whip, the trumpet's call and the brave flurry of Christ's golden banners. He saw the Cardinals arrayed in their crimson finery; the crosses thrown to the ground, his brother being led to the place of judgement. Hearing and not hearing, he listened as the sentence was delivered; seeing and not seeing, he watched as it was executed, *ad maiorem Dei gloriam*, the crowd shouting and roaring, one with the fire that blinds and burns. I am my brother, he thought. And the blood of Christ in the fruit of the vine is the fire of the volcano. The pack was on him now, the stench of their breath mingling with the scent of hyacinths crushed underfoot.

"Nothing."

T

Why has this happened? Robert Bellarmine asked himself. *Why?*

T

Magnum miraculum, San Severina was thinking. *Infinitus est deus, immensus ubique totus....*

T

In the city of the wolf, Kaspar Schopp had every reason to feel pleased with himself. Already, he had gained access to the inner-most circles of the Vatican; he had rendered the Inquisition valuable service in the peculiar case of his friend Campanella, and the Cardinal di S-- S-------, who, as the world well knew, was an ardent foe of heresy and error, had done him the favour of promising him an audience.

But this morning, Kaspar was subject to a rude awakening. He had been dreaming of the Inquisition. Friend Campanella was on the stand, evidently swearing out some kind of charge.

"You are accused, Kaspar," he was saying. "Do you *know* the crime you have committed?"

In and out of the dream, the waking Schopp reminded himself, with Cato's help, that dreams proceed by opposites.

The reversal of reality was a common play in the theatre of the mind. Therefore, the dream Campanella could not alarm the waking Schopp. And indeed the dream Campanella had compromised his charge when he assured the court (it was empty) of the prisoner's innocence.

The dream Schopp had protested: *Nicht doch!* And the waking Schopp considered this circumstance. I have denied my innocence, he said to himself Jesuitically, but that does not mean to say that I have affirmed my guilt.

Wunderlich!

Kaspar discarded the manifest.

The papal arms were displayed behind Campanella, and Kaspar observed them closely. The keys and the triple tiara changed into the head of a man, the Pope no doubt. But what was this? The effigy transformed itself into a coin, a coin or a — a medallion! Yes, that was it. He had seen such things in Germany: medallions depicting the head of a Pope. Inverted, they showed a demon who was also a Pope, and on the obverse side, a Cardinal who was also a jester....

"Your Eminence?" Kaspar said.

The Cardinal grinned and nodded waggishly, shaking his cap and bells.

He looked again and the medallion changed again. It became a beetle, a large death watch beetle.

"Out of bed, Schopp," it said. "I am dawn."

"You?" But the creature had vanished.

Dreams!

Kaspar stared out of his window. The winter sun streamed in, pale Aurora promising a fair day. A trifle cloudy, but ...

He remembered the date and was suddenly hungry.

In the *pescheria* of San Andrea, Kaspar Schopp breakfasted on bread and wine. Wholesome food: a simple communion.

Fish heads eyed him from the gutter. Knives flashed, and he watched the *pescivendole* cleaning their produce for the Sunday market. Solid women, the Roman fishwives; a type more German than Italian, they met with his approval. The smell, however, did not. But at this hour of the morning the senses were hardly awake. Kaspar yawned and called for more bread, more wine.

The talk of the marketplace drifted past, the talk of money and prices, the talk of ordinary folk going about their business. The sky darkened, colouring the square in half-tones. It could almost be dusk, Kaspar thought. What am I doing here, a stranger among strangers?

He was feeling ill-at-ease. The day had surrendered its promise. A drab day. No fugitive gods lurked behind its forlorn reality. He gave a weary smile. The day was perfect (or imperfectly) itself, as jaded as an old empiric who offers miracles for the price of a drink.

"...ashes," a girl's voice said. "Your wine."

Kasper looked at her. What did she mean?

"The sky. It is the colour of ashes."

"Ah," he understood. "Sit down," he said.

She turned. "And why should I," she mocked him, "'sit down'? Your bread, Signore Schopp!" — and she was gone.

A fishmonger's daughter. No Aphrodite, he thought. Still, she knew his name. But then a great many people knew that. She had mispronounced it, of course, had said *Skopp*....

"*Schioppo!*" he called after her. A mistake: he had meant to say *Schioppio*.

"Signore — *Gun?*" An explosion of laughter.

"*Si,*" he said. "Signore Gun *Cannone*."

Squeals of laughter. He surprised himself. Perhaps the day held more promise than he had supposed. He would return. Later ...

Meanwhile he had an execution to attend.

Kaspar swallowed his wine. He was not looking forward to the *auto-da-fé*.

Kaspar considered the question as the sky darkened again. The day's opacity frayed his nerves. Or was it the dream perhaps? It did not do to enquire too closely into one's motives. As often as not they were the imagined consequences of an act already committed — instead of the causes they were declared to be. Not for Schopp the error of false causality. What then?

Well, there was inquisitiveness, there was no denying that. And affirmation, the strength gained from witnessing the fatality of nature. It would be self-deception if he refused to take *that* into account. Other people's deaths concern us only in so far as they remind us of life, our own life. The moral sense could express its outrage; the intelligence bowed to reality, *das ding an sich*. Things were what they were. Actuality could not be subverted by wishful thinking. You had to go along with events. The world was full of people like Giordano, dreamers who believed they could alter the course of history. But history had no course, and it was useless to talk of reform or progress. It was useless, even, to talk of the will, especially the freedom of the will. The formula enslaved mankind. It enshrined guilt as the highest moral principle: man was free. *Ergo*, he was free to sin.

Giordano would suffer because he had broken nature's unwritten law: he had defied reality. He had met strength with weakness. He was a fool and therefore he would die. All that remained was to see how.

The day held out no extraordinary terrors. Acceptance was all. I know who I am, thought Kaspar Schopp, in whom the feeling for reality was innate. And I know what a heretic is....

A slow chime of bells from the Church of Sant' Andrea announced the *vigila matutina*.

Dissonance. Kaspar rose from the table. He looked for the girl, but she had disappeared. The sky was drained of all colour now, achromatic, leaden. A few drops of rain were falling. He left some money on the table. It was more than enough.

He decided to take a short-cut through the cemetery adjacent to the Church, a delapidated jungle of fallen eagles and mossy tombs, the detritus of Empire and death. The cemetery was shaped like the Star of David, six major pathways forming the triangles, and a host of lesser pathways, overhung with ivy and the skeletal branches of elms, traversing the centre. It was a maze, a labyrinth within a labyrinth, an incomprehensible joke surrounded by the slum dwellings of the bank. What god had confected this riddle; what relation was there between the first-created and this crowded burial ground of man? It was a world of the dead, this sublunary world, the inhabitation of lost souls and restless spirits, unattainable and undemonstrable. Yet he could feel their presence, the silent watch of generations long deceased, and it seemed to him then that the past had taken possession of the future, that the present itself bore no relation to the creator's grand design — if indeed he had a design. All things must change, thought Kaspar Schopp sententiously. The halls of heaven become the bowels of hell. Let the dead bury the dead.

A narrow gate brought him onto a dank and dingy street. Many times he had walked from the Piazza San Andrea to the embankment, yet he had never seen this street before. Surely he would have remembered it! An open sewer coursed down its centre, and the street itself terminated in a blind wall, the sewer plunging into a feculent pool that might once have been an artesian well. An amorphous white fungus colonized the slopes of the well, and its surface was coated with slime. Kaspar recoiled in horror. Here was a conduit to finality, the abyss and place of eternal night!

He retraced his steps past the cemetery gate, took a turning to the left, and found himself on familar territory. He could hear a faint chanting now, and knew that this would be the procession on its way to the Campo de' Fiori. The volume of the chanting grew, its course parallel to his own.

Kaspar hurried. At the corner of the next street, he came to an abrupt halt: a blood-curdling cry sounded in his ears, a piercing and strangely animal wail that penetrated to the bone. An interval of silence followed. It occurred to him that he was too late; that the fire had already been set, and that he had heard the death agony of a heretic. But the shrieking started again. It was prolonged, agonizing, and utterly inhuman.

Kaspar rounded the corner to see a man reeling drunkenly over the flayed body of a mule. It was difficult to tell who was the more exhausted, the beast or its owner, and both stared at each other with the ageless and perfect understanding of the tormentor and the tormented. A length of knotted rope hung loosely from the man's wrist. His entire body swayed, and his free hand shot out in an attempt to steady himself. The beast threw back its head, bared its teeth and again uttered that piercingly shrill cry, bringing a renewed onslaught from its owner who struck the animal repeatedly across the head and muzzle, the blood foaming freely into the gutter. Kaspar advanced resolutely. The man gave him a sullen stare, raised his whip as if to strike, but then thought better of it. He turned and lurched unsteadily down the street, pausing at intervals to glance back. The mule struggled to its feet, shook its head, and followed. Kaspar extended his arms despairingly. He felt that he had something to explain to the beast, but did not know what.

The sound of the procession came to him again. It was closer now, much closer.

T

Kaspar Schopp stood next to a man he was yet to meet. He looked away from the flames at the cloud-torn sky. It is finished, he thought. *Es ist alles nichts.*

T

The Cardinal of San Severina watched Kaspar Schopp. An enthusiast, but for what cause? The guard ripped open Giordano's charred body and held up his heart for the crowd's inspection. The heart glistened and was very bright. New fires were being lit, satellites to the central sun, the rain hissing on the baskets. Soon, the ashes would be scattered to the wind. *Stirpitus amputari*, the Cardinal thought, our ultimate justification. "So perish all heretics!" the pale young man shouted — yet another lie to add to the catena of lies. What a pity it was that the Curia

295

emphasized spectacle to the neglect of certain historical factors. All things being equal, the Cardinal reflected, the truth was as complicated as a lie. All things being equal, it was important to be on the side of historical rectitude.